The Catnap Ramblers

book 1

VINCENT AND THE CAT

J.B. THWAITE

Napuke Books

Ebook: ISBN 978-952-65297-2-1

Paperback: ISBN 978-952-65297-0-7

Hardcover: ISBN 978-952-65297-1-4

Book cover and illustrations: J.B. Thwaite aka Napukettu.

Publisher: Napuke, Finland (http://books.napuke.com)

CONTENT INFORMATION

Includes themes unsuitable for younger readers.
For a detailed list of potentially upsetting or triggering content, please visit
http://books.napuke.com.
There is a helpful glossary and cast of characters at the end of the book.

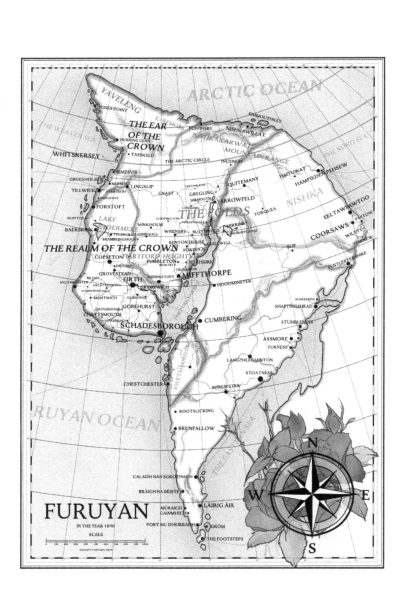

FURUYAN

IN THE YEAR 1890

SCALE

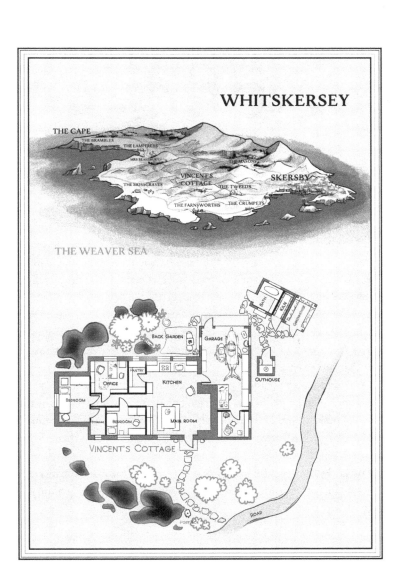

Note from the Author

This book is written in British English. Here is a bucket of z's for my American readers to take along and add where you see fit. Take the whole bucket with you, so you can collect all the extra letters (mainly u's) into it. You can return it at the end of your read, and I will take care of the recycling. I ~~apologise~~ apologize for the inconvenience!

Because this story has fairly many points of view and a couple of time jumps, I've added character-specific dinkuses (the decorative thingamabobs) at the start of every chapter and scene break (where the point of view changes) to clue you in.

I am deeply sorry for any typos, extra commas or grammatical mistakes in this book. I and my editor have been on a lengthy expedition to hunt and catch the pesky things, but we are only human, and some may have slipped through. My inbox is always open should you want to point them out to me.

And lastly, I am grateful to anyone willing to give my story a chance. It's something I've been working on for over a decade, so I sincerely hope you enjoy it!

Dedications

To Jari for arranging the time for me to write these books and putting up with me while I wrote them, and my wonderful beta readers (especially Jules and my editor Lauren), as well as countless others who've cheered me on along the way (you know who you are).

And lastly, to my dad, who introduced me to the concept of difficult choices you should not force your child to make, but who found the first draft of this book intriguing enough to read several times, and, in doing so, encouraged me to keep writing.

CHAPTER 1

On the small arctic island of Whitskersey, the slight increase in daylight had yet to lift the weariness after months of winter darkness. Most of the low-growing trees and bushes were still bare. The decayed remnants of grass formed disgusting, moist blankets across the rocky fields where packed snow had covered it only days prior.

The weathered wooden post box at the side of the road was bursting at its seams. Rushing past it, young Mr Jones knocked it down with his suitcase, the contents of both spilling across the yard with a spine-chilling crash. He stopped in his tracks and held his breath in shock.

Holy sh—!

He leapt to check on the typewriter that had fallen out of his suitcase with such awful noise. It had sustained some nasty scrapes and dents, but thank Guardian, it seemed fixable. He wiped his brow and exhaled but couldn't afford to feel relief just yet.

Worried that the owner of the house had heard the commotion, Mr Jones wasted no time gathering his clothes and packing them, the typewriter and some other belongings back into his suitcase.

Please, please, please, do not come out!

He turned his attention to the letters. Some were partially soaked, but most were dry if a little crumpled. He hastily wiped a few onto the front of his trousers. Why on earth did there have to be so many? Holding the first few in a stack in one hand, he pushed the rest into a pile with the others.

Uttering a couple of choice curses, Mr Jones pushed up the post box and rammed its pole back to where it had been mounted between some cracks in the rocky ground. It took some tries to get the damn thing to stick and stay upright. The letters gave him an equal amount of trouble, the staggering amount of them refusing to fit back in without using considerable force. He thrust them in with no mercy.

When he was satisfied that he'd covered his tracks adequately, he dusted himself off, picked up his suitcase and followed the hotchpotch row of stepping stones to the front door. A layer of loose, unswept gravel crackled and scrunched unpleasantly under his feet.

"Just jump in. It will be fine," he told himself. This wasn't quite the grand entrance he'd had in mind, but he wasn't deterred by minor hardships. He took a quick breath and gave the door a brisk knock.

The man answering the door was not outright deformed, per se, but the way his heavy knitted sweater clung to his body at places and hung loose at others made him look comical. He had large hands and even larger feet, long limbs and the sort of slouch that was emphasised by the round shape of his shoulders. Rumoured to be in his late thirties, he looked older than his years. His pasty complexion emphasised the grooves on his face and the patchy stubble and dishevelled hair did nothing to improve this image.

The haggard appearance took Mr Jones by surprise, but he recovered quickly. Nothing could detract from the joy of meeting his childhood idol, Vincent the Traveller, like this, up close and in person.

"The name is Oscar Vernon Jones. A pleasure to meet you, sir! I was sent from the mainland office." Mr Jones wiped his hand on the side of his coat and stuck it out for a handshake. His words were received with momentary confusion, but Vincent's expression soon changed as he seemed to recall what business he had with Mr Jones's office.

"You're the new editor?" A hint of disbelief weighed down his bushier than not eyebrows.

"Yes. Here are my credentials." Mr Jones handed him the envelope. The matter had been settled by Mr Jones's employer the summer before, but it seemed proper to reconfirm the contract now that they were finally face to face so he added, "I can be at your service henceforth until the end of September or as the weather permits, sir, as I believe was discussed."

"Indeed." Vincent paused to gawk at the envelope. He stayed in stasis for long enough to cause Mr Jones some considerable distress.

"Is there a problem?" Mr Jones tightened his grip on his suitcase.

As Vincent slowly thawed from his bearish slumber, his eyes brightened and he directed his gaze back at Mr Jones.

"Are the ferries running early this year?" The lanky man grabbed Mr Jones by the arm.

"I suppose so."

"And the postal service?" Vincent turned his attention to the post box at the other end of the yard.

There was no forewarning for the forceful shove that propelled Mr Jones and his suitcase some five steps backwards from where he'd stood, to his mind, steadfast. It was only then that he connected the significance of the ferries to the letter-flow and correspondence with the outside world. The post box had not accumulated its contents over time due to the negligence of its owner; it must have been filled to its capacity this very morning!

Vincent galloping through his front yard like a bull elk in rut was a testament to the budding excitement of spring.

I t took another couple of weeks for spring to stop dragging its feet and add a dash of colour to the pale landscape. By then Mr Jones had settled into Vincent's vacant guest room and made himself comfortable in the man's office, where the two of them were to work on Vincent's book.

Vincent's sizeable writing desk stood next to a small window with a view towards the only town on the island. There was no delightful bustle of people to provide him with distractions, though. The terrain and distance made sure of that. Instead, seemingly endless rocky hills stretched in every direction as far as the eye could see, with patches of fresh grass strewn here and there, swaying restlessly in the wind. It wasn't much to look at, yet Vincent seemed infinitely more interested in it rather than the book he was supposed to be writing.

From Mr Jones's much smaller desk nearby, there was even less to see: a mere corner of the window. It was mostly obscured by the massive typewriter he'd lugged here with him and Vincent's frown-wrinkled forehead as he procrastinated, either by staring out the window or responding to the piles of letters he was receiving every day. The postman no longer had trouble fitting everything into the poor, battered post box, yet Vincent still somehow managed to devote most of his day to his replies.

At first, the man had been excitable and starved for company, but his demeanour gradually toned down to a more pleasant, almost normal level of talkativeness.

Even so, he was keen to engage in idle conversation whenever Mr Jones was around. Since this meant there wasn't much for Mr Jones to edit, he tried to keep out of Vincent's way to avoid any of these unnecessary side-tracks.

B ored with watching the grass grow and frustrated by the lack of progress on the book, Mr Jones headed into town to run a few errands and 'to see the sights'. Once he'd determined there was absolutely nothing here to see, he took a seat at a café near the market square and sipped on a substantial, rugged cup of morning coffee while penning a letter to report his progress to his supervisor.

The coffee, as it happened, was delicious. He was inspired to mention it in his letter, along with a description of the prevailing weather and a detailed account of the harrowing discomforts of his journey. In hindsight, he regretted mentioning the coffee, but not enough to discard the opening.

'Regardless of the aforementioned obstacles, I have arrived and taken my post as scheduled,' Mr Jones wrote. 'Mr Vincent has been welcoming and easy to get along with, but alas, I haven't much to report.' He wrote this with much greater regret, knowing that it could very well lead to an order to return home.

'Yet,' he added. As a man of integrity, he would not resort to lies or forgery, but surely no one could fault him for having some self-confidence and optimism?

'I have found Mr Vincent's working habits as mundane as he has himself described. As far as I can tell, there has been nothing out of the ordinary in the way he has prepared for writing his book. He has a myriad of little booklets and journals he likes to refer to when such a rare occasion as a slump occurs, but I believe these are merely to refresh his memory. I have unearthed no evidence to support the claims and so being, there's nothing to suggest, at present, that the accusations are true. I will write again in a week's time.'

He ran out of space at the end of his sheet and had to squeeze his signature awkwardly between the last row and the edge of the paper. It was not ideal, but with his penmanship flawless and his coffee cup nigh empty, it would have to do.

Mr Jones packed his writing implements back into their leather satchel. He was not here to waste time. He wasn't here solely to edit Vincent's book, either. His mission was to gather information for an extensive biographical article or an exposé, and if that failed, to settle the ongoing office bets. He would prove those pessimistic old codgers wrong about Vincent, and Vincent's supposedly lacking writing prowess!

Out of Mr Jones's nineteen years of age, he had been aware of Vincent the Traveller for over a dozen. As a wee lad, he'd heard the rumours of tales being told, and later read the fascinating descriptions of foreign customs and exciting adventures from the periodicals Vincent wrote in. Despite having been barely old enough to read, Mr Jones had tried to get his hands on each one. He had even studied to become an editor solely so he might one day have a chance to work with Vincent.

Vincent sold his stories to finance his trips, then returned every summer to live on this island, which, according to hearsay, was his birthplace. That was the extent of what people knew about the man. How he'd travelled to so many exotic places and met all of those important people—even royalty—was an ample source of speculation when even his surname—the most obvious key to open those doors—remained a mystery.

Though he did not seem the mysterious type, it was surprisingly difficult to get him to shed any light on his private life. If one managed to rope him into an interview, he would openly recount the specifics of whatever project or adventure he was then working on, but deftly dodge the personal questions. This only fuelled the fire.

Mr Jones struggled with the guilt of possibly having to betray the trust of his childhood hero should he uncover a dreadful secret and share it with the world, but if Vincent had indeed lied about something, perhaps he deserved to be betrayed? With nothing such yet to report, Mr Jones was relieved. Perhaps the truth was even more magical than the stories led to believe? Whatever the case, he'd realised his dream. He'd get to spend the entire summer with Vincent and hear some of those stories first hand!

Mr Jones carefully folded the sheet of paper, tucked it into an envelope, and wrote the address on top. He slurped the last of his coffee, tipped the plump waitress picking up his cup, and headed for the post office.

Once done with this business, he decided to see what he could squeeze out of the locals regarding Vincent. However this played out, this would be the best summer of his life yet. Absolute best, no doubt about it.

CHAPTER 2

With the mornings still quite nippy this early in the spring, Mr Jones had difficulty relinquishing the warmth of his bed. He tossed his quilt aside to force himself to worm out of his protective cocoon and scrambled to get dressed in a gradually orderly fashion. By the time he had donned his breeches, shirt and striped vest, he was alert enough to turn his attention to airing the bedding and making the bed. Besides the disarray of knick-knacks collecting dust on every open space, shelves, tables and windowsills, the room seemed satisfactory when he left it.

Vincent was often up in the early hours of the morning, sitting in the study looking like he hadn't slept at all. Presumably he didn't stay up all night every night, but he did sometimes take a curious nap around noon when the rainfall and wind were often at their heaviest. Today he seemed more chipper than usual.

"Splendid, you are up. I'm heading out today. You are free to accompany me if you'd like." Vincent put on his coat and gloves, which seemed a touch too thick for the spring weather, nippy though it was.

"Where are we going?"

"To the cape. To see an old friend. Don't worry, we should be back well before dark."

Vincent's response left Mr Jones none the wiser, but before he could follow up with another question, the man had already disappeared into the garage accessible from the main room.

Oh great, thought Mr Jones, another distraction and a day away from writing the book. But if it yielded any new information about Vincent, it would not be a complete waste of time... Youthful optimism. He clung to it with all his might.

Mr Jones followed Vincent into the garage. It was his first time allowed in, and it certainly made an impression. Bits and bobs were scattered around the room, creating a delightful chaos, the kind where what's in the middle is more important than the mess it's causing.

An oblong contraption the length but only half the width of a horse carriage was parked in the middle. Attached to it was what resembled one of those modern bicycle sidecars that had recently been adapted even for steam-powered velocipedes.

Closer inspection revealed skis underneath. Surely, those could not be the only option, as the snow had already melted some time past? But he could see no wheels anywhere. At least not the kind that would fit this monstrosity.

"Take a seat in the sidecar. I'll fill her up and check the flaps. This won't take but a moment." Vincent prepared the strange vessel for launch.

Mr Jones hesitated, but his pride outweighed his sense of self-preservation, and he climbed into the sidecar. By the time he'd figured out how to fasten the seatbelt, Vincent had finished his preparations, opened the garage door with a remote lever, and sat in his saddle in the cockpit recess.

"Hold on, the lift-off's always a bit rough." Vincent turned another switch, and the engine roared into life. The words 'lift' and 'off' made Mr Jones's stomach churn in an alarming fashion, and he turned to stare at Vincent.

Vincent was busy calibrating his gauges and checking whatever readings he found appropriate to check. He did give Mr Jones the subtle warning of a thumbs-up before he pushed the throttle, but Mr Jones found himself clutching onto his seat with all of his eleven fingers burrowing through the leather and face turning as white as his knuckles.

What had seemed like a mere drizzle felt like hail against his skin as they sped high up in the open air. When Mr Jones dared a glimpse, the garage door was nothing but a speck on the side of a miniature house, until it, along with the house, disappeared behind some stunted trees.

Fortunately for Mr Jones, he hadn't yet had the chance to have his breakfast, as it would have undoubtedly resurfaced by the time his stomach caught up with him.

What the contraption lacked in style, it certainly made up for in speed. What it made up in speed, it quickly snatched away in lack of manoeuvrability.

Only narrowly dodging an embankment and a slightly steeper hillside, Vincent brought the vehicle to a stop at a short stretch of land between the sea and a field, surrounded by some long since greyed but still hale fencing. With deep grooves not suitable for any type of farming, the stretch of land was not quite as hale. Mr Jones had no trouble guessing what had landed there several times before, with varying degrees of success. He wished he had had the foresight to request a safety helmet prior to departure.

Vincent had many friends on the island, but he seemed especially close to Mr George Bramble. According to Vincent's quick briefing, Mr Bramble was a gnarled but tough and sinewy old man. A fisherman by trade, he had been tossed and thrown about by the sea and survived the lot of it, but because of his failing eyesight and aching joints, he'd recently retired to the odd fishing round or two in the summer when the sea was at its calmest.

"He had a loving, devoted wife not long ago, but she unfortunately passed..." Vincent let out a heavy sigh, took off his hat and looked into the far off distance. To show respect, Mr Jones tried to assume an equally sombre posture.

"...Inordinate amounts of gas." Vincent's voice was a mere whisper, but he dragged the first word to give it the appropriate weight. "Whereupon he finally took it upon himself to open the door for some fresh air. She took this as the gravest of insults, packed his belongings, tossed them out after him and closed the door. That's why he's living out here alone. He may joke about the unfortunate occasion and merrily describe the way both sisters share their ailment, but it's a source of discomfort for him, and as such, perhaps not worth prying further into."

Vincent's bizarre advice aside, the house they entered could have used a woman's touch. It wasn't in complete chaos, but a tattered shirt here and some scattered fishing equipment there hinted that things hadn't found their way back to their rightful places. The kitchen table was a whole hub of miscellaneous items on their way to nowhere. Despite the mess, it was a comfortable place in which to spend a day sheltered from the occasional gusts and showers.

And spend the day they did. Mr Bramble taught Mr Jones a fair number of the tricks of his trade. Even half-blind, he tied the knots and cleared and repaired the nets with the ease of decades of experience. The way those knobbly, leathery fingers moved so deftly regardless of their appearance intrigued Mr Jones. He wondered whether he could have trumped the man with a little practice and the aid of his extra digit.

Mr Jones had no intention of embarking on a fisherman's career, yet these distractions proved more than welcome while Vincent did the old man's bookkeeping, supply orders and various other tasks that required reading and writing small print. He even fixed the storm-trodden wonky front door that wouldn't close properly.

"You should ask Arthur to bring you a new door next time. This one is on its last legs. There's a crack the size of my ego next to the hinge here, and you'll freeze if you leave it like that for the winter," Vincent said as he fixed it.

Mr Bramble bequeathed to Mr Jones the details of their arrangement as they sat down for a cup of coffee.

Apparently, winter came to these regions with force. Once it did, it was virtually impossible to leave the island, and the islanders had no choice but to sit tight and wait for spring. At the beginning of last winter, when the storms had come in early, Vincent had turned up bored out of his mind, offering to help with whatever needed doing. By the sounds of it, he had visited nearly everyone on the island more than once to find someone to chat with or something to do to pass the time. Since Mr Bramble hardly minded even the frequent visits now that he was living alone, the two of them had spent more time together than most.

Mr Jones could see why Vincent was fond of the old fisherman. He himself enjoyed his time at Mr Bramble's house more than he'd expected. Of course, that could have had something to do with him not wanting to board the frightful contraption again. Had it not been a several-hour walk, he would have gladly returned on foot.

The trip back to Vincent's house went much the same way as the one preceding it. When Vincent parked the now alarmingly wheezing and hissing vehicle neatly into the garage, Mr Jones no longer wondered how he had travelled to so many far-off places in such a short time. He also swore he would decline any and all future invitations for adventures with the man. Even the smallest ones.

CHAPTER 3

Vincent refused to own a telephone. Instead, his telephone messages and contact requests were brought from his town office to his post box, along with the other correspondence. When Mr Jones asked him about it, he gave some vague explanation about valuing his privacy, but there was something decidedly off about him. The peculiar tension around the eyes, perhaps? Was there even a hint of a crease...?

When he received a particularly private message, he sent Mr Jones out on some trivial errand while he took care of it. Delivering a letter to Mrs Bramble—the fisherman's flatulent wife—was one of those occasions.

Mr Jones was blessed with an eager and active imagination. By the time he reached the door of the sisters' townhouse, he was sweating buckets filled to the brim with dread. He considered slipping the sealed envelope into the post box and making a quick escape to avoid any noxious gases, but Vincent had insisted it be delivered to Mrs Bramble in person and that Mr Jones was to wait for her response before returning. It took quite some willpower to ring the bell and remain standing until the missus answered the door.

The aroma accompanying Mrs Bramble was thankfully not of the cab-bage variety, but a warm, slightly suspicious scent of floral pot-pourri. Mr

Jones felt silly. She was perhaps not the most dazzling crown jewel, but she had aged well and was much fairer and more delicate than he had expected. She most notably did not seem the type to do much booty-tooting. Was this another one of Vincent's bizarre jokes or a downright prank? Would he do such a thing, and if so, why?

Mr Jones delivered the letter and received a reply without much delay. As he finished his errands and returned to Vincent's house, the image of Mrs Bramble's melancholy smile still lingered in his mind and left him feeling uneasy.

T hree days after the delivery of the message, Mrs Bramble's sister, Ms Buttercup, came knocking on Vincent's door. She unleashed her fury the instant she was let in, with Mr Jones too much of a coward to make any effort to stop her. In his defence, Ms Buttercup was considerably larger and sturdier than her sister, and objectively frightening as she thundered and bellowed, demanding to see Vincent.

Whatever her issue, Ms Buttercup did not bother to clarify. Instead, she pushed past into Vincent's office, and before Mr Jones could follow, shut the door in his face. He could hear her screaming through the door as a testament to her impressive volume, but to his displeasure, the door still sufficed to thwart the actual dropping of the eaves.

Annoyed to be kept in the dark but afraid to put himself in harm's way, Mr Jones could only wait and see what damage Ms Buttercup inflicted on poor Vincent, and whether he would be needing the doctor.

A fter a half an hour's tirade, Vincent escorted the now marginally less hostile Ms Buttercup out of the house. Mr Jones had never seen such a grave expression on his face before. A glimpse into Vincent's office revealed that the woman had somehow dislodged some of the heavy or well-fastened items right off their posts and relocated them across the room. She'd left such horrendous destruction in her wake, yet Vincent himself seemed miraculously unharmed.

In fact, once Ms Buttercup was out the door and out of sight, the man looked to be in a splendid mood, as if none of it had happened, and the state of his office merely amused him. What was this remarkable state of denial?

Mr Jones had a tougher time ignoring what had just happened. Something ugly was beginning to simmer somewhere deep within him. This unsettling incident, and the few frights before it, had effectively quelled whatever longing he'd had for adventure. He was also beginning to realise he'd been a teeny, tiny, wee bit naïve to think he could merely show up, be his charming self, and waltz his way into Vincent's good graces.

Contrary to his expectations, he was getting nothing but mismatched pieces of the jigsaw puzzle—small unexplained discrepancies, secretive messages, random visits, Vincent's irregular moods—and they were all the wrong size and shape to be put together to form anything grand and exciting, much less a scoop.

These useless morsels of gossip were nowhere near enough to fill his stomach. Instead, they grossed him out to the point of him losing his appetite. Any attempts to make sense of things felt futile. The awful mode of transport, the mountains of fan mail, the tacky knick-knacks around the house, the fart jokes... He'd become a laughingstock if he tried to compile an article about any of it.

If he could prove Vincent could write his damn book on time, perhaps there would still be something worthwhile to salvage from this mess? The last of Mr Jones's fleeting energy was probably best used to enforce Vincent's laughable excuse of a schedule.

Alas, even that did not seem to be on the cards, at least not today.

"Today," Vincent said, grinning happily. "I thought we should venture into town for some acquisitions." The way he savoured his words hinted that he'd been ruminating on this delicious idea for the first part of the day and was not likely to take objections kindly.

Mr Jones suppressed his sigh. Though he hadn't been short on time or effort, he was yet to find the words to object to anything Vincent said. While this did not seem the likely time to grow a spine, the thought of the monster contraption lurking in the garage certainly provided plenty of incentive.

"All right, sir. How about we make it a brisk walk?" Mr Jones suggested, clinging valiantly to the remnants of his optimism.

Vincent scratched the back of his head, looking bemused to be facing this absurd suggestion. Watching him addled for a brief moment was worth it, even if the answer was not to Mr Jones's liking.

"I fear it may take too long on foot, Jones," Vincent replied. The strange sensation of hearing Vincent address him by nothing but the surname startled Mr Jones. Had he imagined a hint of sarcasm in Vincent's voice when he'd said "mister" before, and if so, was this then a mark of acceptance or endearment? Or had he just lost the last of his esteem in Vincent's eyes? To recoup his losses, what else could he do but succumb to riding the metallic heap of junk? Anything...?

Regardless of Vincent constructing and tending to the thing with all the care it required, Mr Jones could not force himself to believe it was a safe mode of transport, even in the least meaningful sense of those words. There were no wings to speak of! While it easily reached high speeds, it did not look capable of flight unless flung into the air by a trebuchet.

With no other recourse, Mr Jones gathered the courage to request a helmet, but his relief at being able to voice such a request was short-lived.

"A helmet? What on earth for? It's just a quick trip to town," Vincent mumbled, preoccupied by his tinkering of the flaps.

By the looks of it, the flaps had something to do with steering and altitude, and they were about the only feature that appeared feasible. Since Mr Jones failed to disguise his urge to piss in his trousers, and Vincent was presumably not keen on his young companion soiling himself while sitting on the leather seat, a bone of sorts was thrown.

"Well, I suppose it can be arranged." The creases on Vincent's forehead deepened into gorges. "I shall add it to my list of acquisitions."

When it became clear that the man did not have any helmets lying around, Mr Jones bit his lip and sank into the sidecar. Vincent seemed pleased by this show of effort and promised to 'take the less hazardous route', which, according to him, would take a minute or two longer, but did not have as many frequently shifting obstacles to dodge. That the obstacles on this 'less hazardous' route were static did little to ease Mr Jones's nerves. This, however, he kept to himself so as not to cause further stir.

The upside to Vincent's contraption was that the emotional torture it provided via uncertainty was staggeringly short. Mr Jones hadn't had time to call on very many deities to urge them to spare his life before they were at the edge of town, where Vincent had a rickety parking shed to stash his supposedly precious vehicle.

The real challenge was yet to come. Vincent had long legs and could reach impressive speeds even on foot. He was also very excitable and now truly excited. With some hopping and skipping, he pranced from one specialist to another, collecting paper books, inks, gears, tools, oils, nuts and bolts, various electrical equipment and even the safety helmet that Mr Jones had requested.

Payment was never mentioned, and no money changed hands. Vincent seemed to have an account wherever he went. Mr Jones had no reason to believe he had any trouble settling these accounts, since the shopkeepers and specialists were happy to supply him with whatever he needed. It wasn't just his celebrity status, either. Everyone they met, even at random, appeared to know him personally and stopped for a brief chat. None of these tidbits made the puzzle come together any better, or whatever was on it, any more interesting.

Mr Jones cradled his newly acquired muted green helmet as they made their way back to the contraption. There was still one more stop before returning home, but he was tired and the anticipation of the ride to come was proving a distraction. Vincent and the shopkeeper were discussing something, but he had trouble following what.

Had he been paying attention, he could have had a decent chance of preparing himself for the things to come. The foreboding scene played out before him was lost on him, and none of it affected his sleep the following night. Instead, he dreamt about decorating his new helmet with pressed flowers and leaves.

CHAPTER 4

E dward Steadfast welcomed Vincent into the front room of his modest engineering and spare parts shop. Vincent was an excellent customer, as well as a dear childhood friend, and not a rare sight here when he was on the island.

A sluggish, apprehensive-looking young man trailed after Vincent, struggling under the weight of what were probably Vincent's latest purchases.

Having a servant seemed unusual for Vincent, who was undeniably sociable, but only on his own terms and in carefully curated increments. There was always a degree of separation between him and other people. He would go on frequent visits to other people's homes but rarely invited anyone over to his. That he had a stranger in such close proximity for the best part of the day was not something he would do voluntarily, even if the lad seemed useful.

"Oh, Vincent. Good to see you! Everything you ordered has arrived save for the five-millimetre tubes." Edward hastily checked his list of orders. "They should arrive next Thursday or Friday. Can you wait until then, or should I try to see if I have some old bits lying about?"

Edward's catalogue was a broad mix of things he ordered in or made himself in his shop. Vincent was often asking for parts that needed specialised machinery or expertise to make, so Edward was forced to order them in more often than not.

"No, it's all right. I'll come get them later. Unless... you wouldn't happen to be able to make a delivery? How big is the package?" Vincent fingered some of the newly arrived premium-grade copper coils. "Can you add a few of these in for me? Say, six?"

"Of course. I don't know about delivering. The tubes are fragile and my ride ain't as smooth as yours, but if you don't mind the risk..."

"I'll come pick them up. How much is the total? Do you want me to settle some of it?"

"Let me check." Edward opened his ledger. While browsing through the accounts, he asked the question still weighing on his mind. "Is this your new house guest?"

"Ah, yes, Jones. He's here for the summer, to edit the book."

"Right." Edward lowered his reading glasses to take a proper look at the lad. He seemed to be in his own little world, staring at something at the far end of the shop. The poor boy looked exhausted. Edward took Vincent a step to the side and lowered his voice. "Does he know you've been trying to write this book for years?"

"I don't think so."

"Try not to lead him on too much. It must be hard enough as it is for a young city boy like him on an island like this." Edward gave his advice in earnest but couldn't help but laugh at Vincent's reaction. First, the man looked mortified, then pleased, upset and confused, repeating each expression a time or two.

"It's not so bad. It's summer, for heaven's sake." His face finally settled into its usual relaxed smile.

Vincent was probably what most people considered reasonably charismatic, but having shared a fair chunk of childhood together, all Edward could see were these rapid-succession awkward and sheepish mannerisms that preceded the smiles.

This was why he had such a hard time taking Vincent's fame seriously. People sometimes changed when they grew up, but if he looked at Vincent, really looked at him up close like this, the man seemed to only have grown in stature and beard. Even now, he looked like a baby deer still learning to walk: excited to jump and go faster than his legs allowed, and falling on his snout trying. It was subtle, but Edward took pride in always being able to tell.

Why was Vincent so excited today, anyway? Was it the parts, or...?

"Can I show you something?" Vincent pulled out a roll of blueprints and spread them over the counter, on top of the ledger where Edward was supposed to check his account balance.

So much for that then, he thought. He pushed his glasses back up and perused the prints, intrigued.

"This seems a novel and elegant way of circumventing the problem. Can the encasing withstand the heat, or will it require more cooling still?"

"It's for operating under temperatures below zero, so I'm not worried about it overheating."

Vincent had had trouble getting the speeder engine to run in low-temperature conditions. It had something to do with the mineral he used as fuel becoming inert and not producing enough power. Edward wasn't clear on the specifics since that side of it was beyond his expertise.

"Do you have a pen?" Vincent helped himself to the first writable surface he could find and, with the pen Edward offered him, scribbled down a fairly comprehensive illustration of the things he'd taken into consideration to come to his conclusion. Edward took a brief look at it, made a few additions to aid himself with the mental calculations, and nodded.

"You don't suppose I could perchance drive it sometime?" He tried to sound as offhanded as he could. Vincent looked at him and chuckled—not a promising sign.

"I wouldn't dare to promise anything without consulting your wife first." He picked some nuts and bolts from a container on the counter. "Can I have these?"

It was kind of him to ask, though he was already dropping them into his pocket before Edward had time to respond.

"Sure, why not..." Edward sighed. He was used to it. Frankly, it was a relief Vincent was acting his usual self and doing so well, all things considered. It had been alarming to hear he'd spent the winter here. "Let me get the rest of your things." Edward headed into his storage room at the back to collect Vincent's order.

If the progress on the speeder was going to make it operable in sub-zero temperatures and give Vincent the freedom to travel regardless of the weather, Edward would toss in whatever extra that might be helpful. The harsh, dark winters were a natural part of life for the islanders, but it was easy to forget Vincent was not originally from around here. He'd never handled the winters very well.

Edward prepared a crate for Vincent's things and carried it and a few larger loose items to the front of the shop. Vincent's page boy was leaning on the counter, almost half asleep, curiously hugging a bright red helmet, unaware of the magnitude of the obstacle this crate and the parts within would present to the book Vincent had forever been meaning to write.

Edward felt sorry for the lad, but, if nothing else, this would be a valuable life experience that would teach him resilience in the face of adversity. Jones would also learn that people were rarely who they first appeared to be. The earlier he learned these things while dealing with Vincent, the better.

"Hey, do you need this?" Vincent was now coveting some of Edward's own personal tools.

"I'll send the bill to your office." Edward jotted a note of it on a separate piece of paper and tucked it into the ledger. It was no use trying to dissuade Vincent. If it wasn't something Edward needed for work before he could send for a new one, it was easier to let Vincent have it.

Though Edward often felt like he'd known Vincent forever, the truth was he'd missed the first nine years. What people assumed was quirkiness picked up during his years of travel was something he'd had at an early age, possibly even before he'd arrived on the island.

Most people had a public and a private persona, but rarely was there such a stark and easily misinterpreted difference between the two, and rarely did people put on such a convincing and deliberate show without there being more overlap between the two.

Edward had seen firsthand how the really rather socially awkward little Vincent had learned the art of giving people what they expected from him. Vincent had also learnt that once he could gain the momentum of overflowing visual excitement, it was difficult for others to turn him down or keep him from realising his wishes. Excitement was contagious. As a compelling distraction, it made people around him predictable and easy to manipulate.

While Edward had come to understand what these tactics were about, he could not resist playing along. After all, the best times of his life were somehow connected to Vincent and Vincent's excitement. His very marriage to his wife was something that likely wouldn't have happened had Vincent not been there to encourage him. It was strange how one man could make such a difference, yet so little made a difference to the man.

"All right, thank you..." When Vincent was truly excited about something, he would fall silent and become unresponsive. He sounded borderline apathetic now.

With Jones already overburdened, Vincent picked up the crate himself, although, had Jones had his hands free, he probably would not have let the lad carry it, regardless. The way he was holding the crate and gazing longingly at its contents reminded Edward of the dragons in fairy tales protecting their hoarded treasures.

While it was an honour to be asked for an opinion on the blueprints, Edward couldn't help but feel sad that this was as close as he would get to any acknowledgement of their friendship. There was no verbal goodbye, just a quick nod, and Vincent was gone again.

CHAPTER 5

The summer had passed its middle point, and as it had, Vincent had packed an emergency escape bag. At any sign or news of a change in the weather, he was ready to hop onto his contraption, speed to the harbour and board the outbound ferry.

Mr Jones had stumbled onto this bag several times, causing his nostrils to get painfully acquainted with the surface of the garage door, with the rest of his body following not far behind, confirming the structural integrity of the impact site.

The skin of Mr Jones's nostrils was wearing about as thin as his patience, and his restraint fared only a fraction better. The schedule he'd tried to enforce was in shambles. Of the three hundred pages that the mainland office had requested, only about twenty sheets lay ready on his desk. With nothing else to work on, he had polished those sheets to perfection, but twenty alone would not a full book make, no matter how many fanciful illustrations were sprinkled on those pages.

Mr Jones hadn't the courage to reprimand Vincent about the lack of progress, but even if he'd had, he wouldn't have had the words.

What was he to say? 'Please work?' Would swear words help? How about volume? How could he possibly express how frustrating it was to watch someone polish the sidecar for the fifteenth time? Was there a way to convey respectfully the urge to wrangle someone's arms backwards and give them a good, deep kick on the buttocks with a knee, because when they finally sat down to write in the office, it was to reply to letters from the Queen of North Whateverland or their distant cousin's dog? Preferably something other than actually committing said action, as the consequences probably would not be as enjoyable as his imagination led him to believe.

Mr Jones would have considered paying one or two months' salary for a manual for situations even remotely similar to this, had such existed. Not that he was doing much to earn that money right now, but with his income meagre and his savings accordingly low, this meant a substantial sacrifice.

The least Vincent could have done was to invite him along on his next trip abroad. Certainly, Mr Jones had done all in his power to try to befriend the man, gain his trust and to show how easy and convenient a companion he would make. He hadn't soiled the sidecar seat once, yet. The helmet had helped a little with the nerves. He'd used a scarf to muffle his shrieks and screams, so he barely made any noise anymore. He'd also been doing the dishes and the meals, most of the cleaning, and even some of the gardening. Laundry too, whenever Vincent permitted him. The man was particular about his white-wash and suits. The ironing he did strictly himself.

Bringing Mr Jones along on his travels would have been just the thing to prove those claims of great adventures, so why not take the opportunity? Why did the stupid contraption even have a sidecar if not for bringing someone along?

"All right," Vincent said after gobbling up the breakfast Mr Jones had again prepared for him. "I shall write today!"

The pompous announcement cheered up Mr Jones somewhat, but he was hesitant to celebrate yet. It wouldn't have been the first time something came up at the last of the last seconds, and Vincent would pack Mr Jones into the sidecar, to go swooshing off somewhere.

Sensing Mr Jones's doubt, Vincent grunted and repeated his statement with further flourish. It remained as incredible as before, but not wanting to dampen Vincent's high spirits, Mr Jones forced out a gleeful little squeal.

And so there was writing. And thankfully, he kept at it for a long while. There were even some through-the-night endeavours and chapters that required several days of continuous attention. But then, as quickly as it had arrived, the inspiration-train left the backward station that was Vincent's jumbled mind, and work again came to a halt.

It was around this time that Vincent began to vanish on his own little excursions without taking Mr Jones along. While grateful to not have to climb aboard the sidecar of death, the continuous exclusion affected Mr Jones's mood, and once he had edited the latest chapters until no improvements remained, he was outright upset to be forced to figure out what to fill his days with himself. Without his usual network of friends or his usual hobbies of stamp collecting and dirigible spotting, he was stuck at Vincent's cottage with most of what was there off-limits to him.

Vincent's cottage was an eclectic old building pieced together using lime mortar and what were probably leftover pieces of local stone of various sizes. The front yard was spacious enough for a few apple trees, but Vincent did most of his gardening at the back of the house. There was an oak tree with a swing, some large rocks with various cultivated mosses that thrived even in this harsh climate, a bench, a shed for gardening tools, and a kiln.

Whenever Vincent fired his kiln regularly during the summer, he used the radiating heat to warm up his tiny greenhouse. The exotic plants he grew in there did not appreciate cool nights, but, keeping them warm like this, he had even succeeded in pollinating and producing seeds.

Mr Jones did not understand why anyone would want or need this many hobbies. Watching Vincent keep a small hive of bees for pollination, throwing jars, cups and pots for his plants and messing with soil, fertilisers and inventive hydration systems did usually provide good entertainment amidst the frustration, though. Now that Vincent was away, and these things were scattered around unused, the house and its yards were a sad sight.

Mr Jones sat in the swing at the back of the house, eyes wandering from one destroyed tree or bush to another on the garage side. He was admiring the contrast between them and the cultivated side that was left unscathed and wiggling his eleventh finger while he waited for Vincent to return. There was no sight of the man, even though the air was cooling down as the evening drew near.

Bored as he was, it wasn't altogether too difficult to imagine what it was like being here during the winter when only the closest neighbours were accessible on foot, and everyone was growing weary of one another's faces.

Vincent had mentioned being stuck inside for consecutive weeks because of the weather, for as long as he had rations and wasn't forced to go out. The sturdy snowploughs cleared the main roads every other day, once a day, and he'd said he would sometimes hitch a ride into town on one. There were also 'the snowtrains', but their schedules were heavily dependent on the weather and thus not very reliable.

At present, Mr Jones had the freedom to go into town whenever he pleased, but contractually obligated to stay at Vincent's side, he was similarly cooped up here with nothing to do. He was almost desperate enough to want to try his hand at some of Vincent's hobbies, although with no one around to give him permission or show him the ropes, he was afraid to touch any of the tools and supplies.

The wind was picking up. Mr Jones was starting to feel cold, so he headed back inside. The window sills in the house were filled with rows of statuettes of mythical creatures Vincent had allegedly encountered somewhere on his travels. He'd made most of his kitchenware himself, and what wasn't ceramic he'd whittled or carved from wood—yet another pastime.

Vincent had never struck Mr Jones as the home-loving type, but the interior of his house appeared like a magpie's nest of decorative knick-knacks or needlessly cutesy household items, an approximate half homemade and the other half acquired somewhere along the way. It was all organised, but not in an apparent manner. There were a lot of shelves, cupboards, trunks, boxes, nooks, niches and other such spaces for storage or display. It all added up to a surprisingly cosy, homely atmosphere.

Mr Jones wandered through the house, trying to think of something to preoccupy himself with. He went through the pantry to decide what to make for supper later on. He wiped some of the kitchen surfaces, mind wandering around Vincent and what to write about if he did end up writing his article.

The man had his quirky side to be sure, but there was nothing newsworthy about Vincent's old-timey, grandma-scented cottage. There was an inglenook in the main room, for heaven's sake! Mr Jones could not recall when he had last seen an actual inglenook.

Where he was from, houses had had to be rebuilt many times over because of fires, earthquakes, floods and feuds with the neighbouring countries. Inglenooks hadn't been in style for decades, if not centuries! You rarely saw this type of *old* anymore.

In fact, the whole house reeked of old. As a passing thought, Mr Jones wondered what the current rates were for an article in the Trans-Continental Historical Journal and whether they would accept a three-page think piece on inglenooks.

Deep in his thoughts, Mr Jones was startled by Vincent finally stepping in through the garage door. Not only had the man parked his speeder without alerting Mr Jones, by the looks and smells of him, he'd lit the kiln before coming in.

The bathing and toilet facilities were in a separate little hut at the back, alongside the shed and the kiln. The kiln also warmed up the water for the bathtub, and the hut was always comfortably warm when the kiln was in use. It was likely Vincent was planning to take a bath after whatever he'd been up to the whole day. He did smell to be in dire need of it.

Mr Jones enjoyed bathing, so he welcomed the chance, even if Vincent's tub was rather crude. Next to the tub there was a smallish four-paned window, through which you could see across the moors, all the way to the sea. If it was dark, the town lights lit up the sky faintly, so there was always something to watch while enjoying a soak.

Vincent, however, was usually in and out in a matter of moments. It was one of the things that made Mr Jones wonder if the man was flawed somehow. How could you not take time to enjoy these things? It was such a shame. As soon as the water was ready, and without saying so much as a word, Vincent disappeared again to the back of the house to wash up.

"How would you like some supper?" Mr Jones offered, hunger now surpassing his interest in bathing. Vincent was drying his short, muddy-brown hair after his quick wash. There was an aroma of soap about him, so presumably he'd somehow reached a satisfactory level of cleanliness in the two minutes he'd been away.

"I would like it served on a plate, most definitely, with some wine on the side. There's some in the cellar." He pulled on some comfy bottoms and cleaned his glasses before putting them back on.

Mr Jones threw a shirt at him. Vincent caught it, set it aside, and sat down at the table. He could have shown some respect to the company he was in, but chose to remain shirtless instead.

Mr Jones stomped into the stone crevice cupboard the man so joyfully referred to as 'the cellar', picked up an unlabelled bottle that seemed like it might have been wine, poured the stuff into a glass in front of Vincent's stupid face, and returned to cooking.

"Is it done soon?" Vincent seemed completely unaware of his impending doom. He would have continued to be as unaware, even had there been cinematic orchestral background music announcing what was to come.

Right around when the imaginary horn section boomed to its fullest to outdo the percussion and the string section, Mr Jones turned around. When he did, the view of Vincent's surprised expression quieted down the orchestra to a passage less voluminous, yet ominous in its comparative subtleness. A few low and rumbling piano notes played in Mr Jones's mind as he finally spoke.

"It will be done much sooner than your book, I suppose." It wasn't much of a complaint, but at least he'd managed to open his mouth. Vincent tilted his head and frowned.

"Indeed," he responded. "Cooking does usually take less time than writing a book... but I can appreciate the poignancy of your sentiment."

Mr Jones considered replying to reiterate his point, but since Vincent had so willingly acknowledged the situation, it was difficult to berate him further.

"Look, after I've installed the new parts on the speeder, I promise I will get back to the book for as long as I remain here. Does that sound reasonable to you?" Vincent proposed.

Mr Jones gave it a brief thought so as not to appear too eager, and nodded. Vincent often seemed spontaneous, carefree, and even reckless, but he wouldn't outright break a promise.

Though relieved by the concession, Mr Jones's imaginary symphony soon crashed and fizzled with a solitary, off-beat strike of the cymbals. Even if the speeder took mere days to finish, and even taking into consideration

Vincent's writing pace when he was diligently writing, a quick calculation confirmed that the page count would fall short come September. There simply wasn't enough time to finish the book.

T wo days after Vincent's promise, a plan of sorts began to take shape in the darker recesses of Mr Jones's head. And when it did, it did so with relative haste.

CHAPTER 6

Vincent was true to his word and spent most of his time in the office, producing pages at a steady pace. The added haste had no discernible effect on the quality of his work, and the new pages were still a joy to edit. This surge of energy showed no sign of waning as they worked through the month of August. Mr Jones had little recollection of anything other than sleeping, cooking, eating, and editing. He only wished this would have been the norm from day one.

As the end of the summer drew near, Vincent grew impatient, even unpleasant, to be around. He had his emergency bags packed, but they did not seem enough of a reassurance to him. Each morning, he read the weather section from the paper, compared it to previous forecasts, and checked for changes. The people at the weather station were professionals, he'd say, but even professionals sometimes made mistakes. Predicting the weather was not an exact science.

As long as the days were sunny, or even remotely bright, Vincent stayed readily at his desk. In the early afternoon of a particular day in September, as part of his plan, Mr Jones placed several mirrors and lanterns at the window to Vincent's office. He was careful with the placement, making sure they weren't visible from the inside. The effect was subtle, but they gave out enough ambient light for the evenings to seem a tad longer and the weather a degree less murky. He also secretly fired the kiln a few times to keep the outhouse toasty.

This seemed to do the trick, if only because Vincent was working in such deep concentration throughout the day. He'd even missed a rainy day or two while writing!

Come to think of it, if he was really this thick, didn't he sort of deserve what was coming to him? This was not a particularly masterful plan. The few forged weather reports had been no problem for a newspaperman such as Mr Jones. Having them printed in town without raising suspicions had been more of a challenge, but even so, Mr Jones was the first to admit that a plan this crude and convoluted shouldn't have succeeded. Perhaps he had put Vincent on too high a pedestal in his youthful ignorance, and the man was indeed an utter clodpate?

Mr Jones's suspicions had been confirmed some days ago when he'd received a letter from the mainland office admitting that he wasn't the first editor they had assigned to edit for Vincent and that the man's appalling inability to cooperate had driven all of the other editors away after weeks of frustration. Hearing this, Mr Jones felt humiliated, but he also became more obstinate and desperate to win over the others before him.

He didn't outright hate Vincent, but the accumulated disappointments and frustrations did make executing the plan surprisingly easy. He'd had plenty of time to convince himself that this was not a big deal, and that Vincent was being melodramatic about his unreasonable phobia of the winter. If the man wasn't going to invite Mr Jones along on his next journey, there was no reason to let him go on his own. After the distress he'd put Mr Jones through, he at least owed him to write the damn book!

Mother nature was an ally in this venture. She provided a sufficient amount of warm, sunny days for Vincent to be lulled deeper into what he was doing, and, as in the previous year, the meteorologists had predicted an early winter. Vincent wasn't blind to the yellowing and falling of the leaves nor deaf to the sound of the autumn winds, but the meteorologists on his version of the paper had missed the mark more royally than usual. The subterfuge provided just enough confusion for Vincent's senses to be thrown askew.

"What day did you say it was today?" Vincent asked in the evening of the first day of October. It was largely due to Mr Jones's frequent assurances of it only being September, and that the winter was not going to arrive early this year, that Vincent was still here.

"How many pages did you write? How many words?"

"Fourteen, about five thousand. Is it still September? It was so dark out today." Vincent frowned. He had been doing it a lot lately.

"It's already getting very late." Mr Jones had been moving the clocks back and forth an hour or two to enforce the illusion of more daylight. His conscience was giving him some trouble for this level of deception, but he insisted it was a matter of professional pride and only right that he did everything in his power to get the job done. He would succeed where everyone else had failed because he was ready and brave enough to make these tough decisions and go the extra distance.

"Ah, time seems to fly by these days," Vincent said but didn't sound wholly convinced.

"Would you like a glass of wine?" Mr Jones offered, trying to appear to be routinely at his chores.

It was due tonight, it certainly was. The first snowstorm of the winter, and the culmination of Mr Jones's plan. He had seen a few flakes fluttering in the air earlier and frost in the mornings for a full week. Ice was already forming. And of all of this, Vincent still seemed gloriously unaware.

The game had been thrilling so far, but also quite sickening to the stomach. Mr Jones had never experienced such a high as when he held Vincent's future in his grasp like this. Albeit only a matter of one winter, it would influence the next seven months of the man's life. But it was just seven months, he told himself. Seven months was not a lifetime.

His hands trembled as he poured the wine. It would be less of a hassle to deal with a sleepy, befuddled Vincent than a raging, sober one.

Mr Jones had yet to see Vincent truly angry, and it was not something he was keen to see. He'd experienced the wrath of his father and his boss, but neither of them scared him as much as finding out what Vincent would look like truly furious. He told himself it was probably not going to be as bad as he envisioned. Besides, wasn't there a fair chance he wouldn't even have to find out? After all, maybe Vincent would see his side of it and compliment him on his impressive wit and determination.

V incent was enjoying his third glass of wine, having just finished his supper. He had written an especially tricky chapter that day and felt like he'd earned a celebratory evening off. He wasn't much of a drinker, but with his recent lack of sleep, the long hours of writing and his high-strung nerves, it was a welcome dessert.

Today had seemed like an exceptionally long day buried away at his desk. Probably a little colder too, since the fireplace was guzzling more firewood than usual. Vincent watched Jones, the editor, feed it with peculiar enthusiasm. Was the lad even more sensitive to the cold than Vincent himself? In that case, it would not be long until they could leave the island with good conscience. Maybe as soon as tomorrow?

"Would you hand me today's paper?" Vincent requested. He'd made an effort, for Jones's sake, to write as much as possible while there was summer left. To give it his undivided attention, he'd let the lad take care of the chores and keep track of the time, even if he couldn't resist checking the weather forecasts to ease his nerves.

Jones had assured him he was on top of everything and that everything was fine, so why could Vincent not shake the feeling that something was wrong? The storm season shouldn't be arriving until at least a week from now, yet there was something eerily familiar about today's weather.

Vincent didn't mean to cast any doubt on Jones's integrity, but he needed to confirm the date with his own eyes for his peace of mind. Jones was reluctant to hand over the paper—another sign that something was amiss. Usually, the lad was ready and eager to serve. It was the sole reason Vincent had adjusted to his presence so much better than expected.

The job description did not mention cooking or cleaning, but Jones had done those of his own accord. It was nice to have someone else take care of the chores for a change. Vincent hadn't had that since... he couldn't even remember when.

He did feel some guilt exploiting his status as the young man's idol, but as long as Jones voiced no complaints, he figured he was free to reap the benefits. That hint of guilt was why he'd written more than he'd intended.

Granted, it was never going to be a whole book.

Vincent had agreed to writing one merely because agreeing to it had been quicker than trying to weasel himself out of it. He'd figured that by the time anyone wanted anything from him, he'd have come up with an excuse or two, or been somewhere far away where complaints could not reach him. He hadn't expected the long line of nagging editors to follow him around so persistently.

"Mr Vincent?" Jones's tone was worried enough to rouse Vincent from his thoughts. He'd been staring at the date on the paper without really understanding what he was reading. Oc... tober. Was that before September?

October last year, there had been snow. Piles upon piles of snow. Ridiculous amounts of the stuff pouring down from the sky. By October, the ferry had already stopped running.

"Yes, Jones," Vincent said. He'd intended to intonate a question, but his preoccupied mind was incapable of relaying such information to his muscles. "Jones, it's October, is it not." Intonation remained too much to ask.

"Only just, Mr Vincent." Jones and his chair, on the opposite side of the table from Vincent, had taken a few steps back, as if he were preparing to brace for an explosion.

"Funny thing, Jones. It's October. It's awfully summer-like for an October. Brighter. Warmer," Vincent listed.

The way Jones was kicking back the last few logs behind him suggested he was indeed listening, though his face remained blank. Vincent shooed away the sinking feeling that he'd lost the game before he'd even realised it had begun. He emptied his glass.

"Yes, sir," Jones said, guard still up and arms ready to fend off any flying objects.

"October. Hah." Vincent's throat felt dry despite him just downing the rest of his wine. "You know what this means, Jones?" His intonation slowly returned to normal, aided by the slight intoxication taking the worst of the edge off.

Obviously, the boy had no idea. He was simple in the head. Inexperienced, thoughtless, inconsiderate, the way young people often were. Not that Vincent was all that old himself, but evidently, he was now old enough to understand how the people around him must have felt when he had been this young and stupid.

It was good that he was drunk because it framed the situation a touch more hilarious than his sober self would have seen it.

Jones just stood there, silent.

The betrayal stung, yes, but it wasn't as bad as the frustration. Vincent couldn't even begin to explain how immensely selfish and unthinking Jones's choices were. You simply did not tamper with things you did not understand!

Had he failed to make it clear how important it was for him to get off the island before the winter? No, surely not? To knowingly jeopardise that... for what, for a book? A man's mental health for the sake of some pages? Jones's efforts could have gone towards finding his own adventures, and actually *living* for himself, instead of waiting to read about someone else's miserable life.

Lord, the brain-burning, suffocatingly dense stupidity! Vincent could curse Jones to the lowest depths of hell for all eternity, but he also couldn't acquit himself entirely. He was appalled to have been so careless, to let himself end up in this situation where he hadn't a clue what the weather was like outside. It was likely too late to remedy that now. He was nevertheless compelled to go take a look.

Vincent made an effort to appear calm as he stumbled to the front door. His inner turmoil was no reason to make a fuss, and having Jones panic over his reaction would only make the situation worse.

He opened the front door to the darkness lit by the two large oil lanterns on either side of his porch. Their light reflected from a fresh, thick layer of snow and the flurries of near-to-weightless flakes dancing all around him. The snowfall was nowhere near the force of a blizzard, but based on past experience, it was heavy enough for all the roads to be closed by morning.

A quick glance at the ornately decorated wood-backed thermometer at the door indicated that it was too cold for the speeder to start. He'd improved the fuel-intake system and brought the operating temperature down to almost zero with the new parts, but at minus twelve, it no longer stood a chance.

Even had there been a ferry leaving at this hour, he would have had to get to it by foot. The thought was sobering but not sobering enough to reach his fumbling feet. The distance and conditions already deemed it an impossibility without the handicap, and by morning, there would be so much snow he would have to shovel for hours just to open the front door, which, under these circumstances, wasn't even advisable.

But the landscape sure was beautiful. He could not see the stars, but the light of the lanterns hitting the snowflakes somewhere above him made them seem like sparkling star-like dots as they fell. The snow clung to tree branches like bubbly heaps of foam, and when some of the heaps grew too big, they broke off, forming swirly veils of icy dust carried away by the wind.

Vincent's breath was visible in the cold. As he cooled down without his winter coat, the puffs became a little smaller. He stood there staring until Mr Jones pulled him back inside and guided him to the table.

He realised he had started crying, although he was confused as to when. It wasn't the kind of crying that involved sobbing or wheezing, but pain in the corners of his eyes forced the tears out. He wiped his face to his sleeve, and while leaning on his elbows and the table, hid the tears with the back of his hand until they stopped coming.

Another bloody winter stuck here. Stuck in this bloody cottage, and to top it off, stuck with Jones, having to write the bloody book. No interest in writing the damn thing, anyway.

This was unhelpful. Vincent tried to straighten himself up.

Get a grip! He slapped himself squarely on the cheeks. It gave him but a brief respite from the thoughts.

Another bloody winter... Stupid Jones and his bloody stupid book... Stupid Jones, stupid... It was no use. He could feel himself spiralling deeper. There was no escaping it now. He poured himself some more wine, and while it didn't all hit the glass precisely, there was enough for him to reach a numb state of stupor after a couple more tries.

CHAPTER 7

The following morning, at precisely six o'clock when the sun was yet to rise and the cottage was dark, Mr Jones woke up to an eerie noise.

It was difficult to describe the sound or what might have made such a sound, but Mr Jones's imagination was already hard at work trying to map out the possibilities.

Something was scratching at the render by the window of the guest room, but no tree branch on Vincent's yards could reach the windows or walls of the cottage. Mr Jones wrapped his covers tighter around himself and tried to ignore it for a while. When it persisted for many minutes, he got out of bed and crept to the side of the window to take a peek.

It was too dark to see much else but the erratic, almost horizontal movement of snow passing the window. Even when he strained to see past the noise, there didn't seem to be anything out of the ordinary out there, although at present, the best he could do was a mere half a metre from the tip of his nose.

He tiptoed to Vincent's bedroom door and checked that the man hadn't gone on an insanity-fuelled morning rampage around the house. No, thankfully not. The sound died down, and Mr Jones was left wondering if it had been his imagination playing tricks on him all along.

Since he was already up, he got dressed and headed into the kitchen for some coffee and to plan for breakfast as a peace offering for Vincent.

The man had taken yesterday's news better than expected, but he'd passed out before the situation had been resolved, so Mr Jones couldn't be sure whether he'd be beaten up or tossed out into the snow once Vincent woke up. A ready-made breakfast might soften the man a little, and a full stomach probably made for a more fruitful conversation than if Vincent was both hungry and hungover.

Mr Jones jolted and spilled his coffee. There was that blasted noise again!

This time the sun was high enough to colour the horizon light blue. The view from the kitchen window to the backyard was dim, but now clear enough to distinguish shapes.

Mr Jones dabbed the front of his shirt with a hand towel and leaned over the counter to see better. Nothing but snow out there. The nerves from the day before were probably still making him overly jumpy and anxious.

A grey shadow sped past the window.

"Oh, shi—!" He dropped the towel and scrambled back, away from the window. What the hell was that? A wild animal? It had to have been at least the size of a fox! But there were no foxes on this island to his knowledge. He was further startled by Vincent turning up right behind him. The man muttered something illegible to shoo Mr Jones out of his path and headed into his garage.

"Where are—? What are you—? There's a *thing* out there!" Mr Jones tried to locate it again by peering through the window on his tippy-toes.

He wanted to stop Vincent from going but was too afraid to grab a hold of or confront the man, who, against all reason, was heading straight for the back door. Had that creature been big enough to do significant damage to an adult human being? Had Vincent become so self-destructive he was deliberately going out there to place himself in harm's way?

After less than a minute, Vincent reappeared from the garage and headed back toward his bedroom. Confused, Mr Jones peeped into the garage to see what the hell the man had gone in there for, if not to head out.

Before he could adjust his eyes to the dark, a vicious, foul-smelling ball of fur on four legs strolled into the main room like it owned the place.

"Feed the cat," Vincent said.

The cat? That thing was a cat?! Mr Jones stared at it in disbelief. The thing jumped onto the dining table and started to groom itself. Vincent kicked open one of the lower cabinets in passing and disappeared back into his bedroom.

Feed the cat. Mr Jones wasn't sure he even dared to move with that thing on the loose in the house! It was much too big to be a cat, and it was eyeing him maliciously, as if waiting for him to make the wrong move so it could sink its teeth and claws into him. It lay down and made itself comfortable but continued to observe Mr Jones's every move.

Mr Jones inched his way toward the open cabinet, not daring to take his eyes off of the monster now in charge of the dining table. There were some cups and bowls at the bottom of the cabinet and a few of them read "Mr Swifty".

The thing had a name? And what, this was Vincent's cat? He'd had an actual pet cat all this time? Where had he stashed it, and why couldn't it have stayed there indefinitely?

"What do I even feed you?" Mr Jones filled one of the bowls with some water, but Vincent had said to *feed* the cat. He'd have to give it something to eat, too, so as not to disobey the instructions.

He set the bowl of water carefully onto the table and pushed it a little ways closer to the alleged cat. After rummaging through their provisions, which were already running low, he made an offering of some cheese and a piece of salted ham. He slid those across in another bowl.

If he was going to have to share the house with that thing, being tossed out no longer seemed as bad.

T he first few days were rough as expected, but once Vincent got back on his feet, he continued to write, much to Mr Jones's surprise.

The cat was here to stay as well, but it came around to mooch as it pleased, so it was thankfully not in the house throughout the day. When it was, it was usually lounging by the fire or sleeping at Vincent's feet.

After two weeks, Mr Jones noticed something oddly familiar about Vincent as he sank deeper into his shell. It reminded him of when they'd first met in the spring. Vincent didn't seem depressed, nor passive or glum, but he became much less talkative, and he had that look about him like he was about to withdraw into a cave and not come out before spring.

When Vincent wasn't writing, he would sit in the garage at the potting wheel and throw clay, oblivious of the world around him. The shelves he'd emptied in the summer were soon full of pots left to dry. The kiln was on almost constantly.

Trying to grow anything out of pots this time of year was a fool's errand with such scarce daylight, but Vincent still gave it a try.

His baths started to take time. He could spend an hour, sometimes even closer to two, and Mr Jones was compelled to check on him every few minutes, afraid he might try to drown himself in the tub.

Vincent also frequently told Mr Jones off if he tried to clean the house, accusing him of hogging all the good chores. This left Mr Jones with not much to do except for the daily ordeal of wading to the post box to see if the newspaper had been delivered. Usually, it hadn't. Letters were also very, very few these days. Having to return empty-handed was harrowing with Vincent always waiting inside, nose neatly pressed against the window, despite having time and time again volubly predicted the box to be empty.

Mr Jones had entertained the thought of writing a letter himself just so there would be something to distract Vincent from his obsessive rota of hobbies. The thing holding him back was not wanting to know whether Vincent was truly stupid enough to not see through a fake letter. That, and not wanting to ruffle the man's feathers now that they had successfully resumed working on the book together. They were getting so close—with less than a third to go—he could almost taste the victory.

During the breaks in writing, Mr Jones was horrified by the amount of logs Vincent converted into sculptures, only to burn them when they were finished. Vincent would take a cursory look at them, but then simply add them to the fire when it needed to be fed.

It was equally discomforting to watch him watch them burn before starting a new one, doomed to share the same fate. Several evenings were spent like this, and Vincent's hands were consequently starting to get dry and shed skin. He did not seem to care.

Whenever the weather was slightly less hostile, Vincent would venture out to make the place more habitable by shovelling snow from the garden path, making way to the post box, or clearing the fronts of the windows.

It took about a day or two for the snow to envelop everything again. He would then repeat the tasks.

By November, Mr Jones was unnerved enough to consider retrieving help for Vincent, who was by then organising the garage for the fifth time. If not a psychiatrist, then maybe a representative of the religious kind? To provide some spiritual guidance in case Vincent's mental faculties proved too impaired for therapy.

It was difficult to tell how bad things were because the man hardly spoke. Mr Jones wasn't sure whether it was because he was still angry or if it had something to do with the forced isolation. Either way, nothing seemed to improve the condition.

Because Vincent hadn't planned to stay for the winter, there was no food or decorations for the upcoming Midwinter festivities in December. Considering the lack of previous years' decorations stored anywhere in the house, Vincent probably hadn't celebrated the year before.

Missing out on his favourite holiday was a setback for Mr Jones, but frankly at this point, if he could persuade Vincent to keep the cat in the garage for the day, that would be enough to get him into a festive spirit.

A neighbour had come by to stock the storage room with meats, cheese, flour and the like, but other than basic foodstuffs, there wasn't much to work with, even had there been interest in celebrating. The closest Vincent came was making some colourful little sleigh bells from clay to give as gifts. Once those were done, he was forced to cut back on the kiln usage to ration the amount of firewood they had. There was enough to last through most of the winter, but this meant Vincent needed to turn to some of his less consuming hobbies.

The next activities he rediscovered were paper-folding and quilting. Mr Jones had also never seen a man knit, though he had read about it once in a magazine.

Knitting, crocheting, sewing, embroidery, making little yarn figurines, even baking, were on the list of things Vincent did, usually for just one day or so. The next day he would move on to something else, and once he ran out of things to do, he would start the cycle again.

Vincent was like a one-person trinket factory. Because there wasn't much room left in his house for the things he made, he either gave them away or burnt them without hesitation. Mr Jones cringed every time hours' worth of work met its end, but at least Vincent seemed to enjoy watching the things he'd made burn crackling in the fireplace.

CHAPTER 8

One November morning Vincent came out of his bedroom looking almost well rested. He even greeted Mr Jones with a nod.

"I thought we might see about getting ourselves into town today."
He did not sound as irate as he had on most days since the beginning
of October. When he proceeded to prepare a pot of coffee and poured
some for Mr Jones, Mr Jones could not curb the twitch in the corner
of his eye.

"Is it a good day for that?" Was today going to be the day he was
kicked out, or worse, taken somewhere remote to freeze to death?

"As good as it will be. If I've not miscalculated, today is a ploughing
day. Getting back in the evening may be tricky, though. I normally stay
at a friends' house until the next opportune ride back, but I can't abuse
their hospitality by bringing you along unannounced. Still, it's better
you come. I'll need the extra pair of hands." He sipped his coffee and
spoke to Mr Jones as if to a servant, but if that was the only price to
pay for the earlier misconduct, Mr Jones was willing to accept it.

"I may be able to procure a means for our return this evening, but should
things not work out in our favour, you will probably have to sort out and
pay for your stay at a guesthouse." Vincent was undoubtedly still cross with

Mr Jones, but at least he was talking again and appeared remarkably sane compared to his recent standards.

"All right. What did you have in mind, sir?"

"What do you mean?"

"I mean, what is our business in town, if I may ask?"

"Well, look at this place." Vincent gestured at the room as if it were unmistakably obvious. Mr Jones's brow distorted into an absurd shape as he checked whether extreme squinting might help him see better.

No. Everything looked normal to him.

"Food, for one, Jones! And materials. Equipment for renovations. I'll need some tools as well. Something has to be done about this. It's... well, you see how it is! How is anyone supposed to keep their sanity here? It is a dilapidated rubbish-hut filled with junk. A shack. A shack is what it is. And I need more light. Oil. Wicks. Sand. Not to mention I am running out of seasoning, am I not? The taste of your cooking has been ghastly lately." Vincent paused to look at Mr Jones. "Any questions?"

"No, sir." None that Mr Jones dared to ask at that precise moment, anyway.

"Good. The plough should be passing us any minute now. I'll go hail the man in for some coffee, and we can leave after breakfast." Vincent grabbed his coat, went out the door and left Mr Jones to his own devices to sort out the breakfast. Bacon and eggs, perhaps? It was hard to go wrong with bacon and eggs, even with limited seasoning.

A fter breakfast, Vincent, Mr Jones and Edward Steadfast, the man apparently in charge of ploughing around these parts, left the house together. Edward was a man markedly on the heavy side in both size and character. Contrary to Vincent, he seemed, as his name suggested, patient and reliable.

The plough was also enormous. Equipped with jet engines and chained tires that were approximately Vincent's height—the tallest of the three of them—a ladder was required to reach the cockpit.

It was remarkably quiet thanks to the size of its engines. Most of the noise came from the rushing air, and even then, the hum was low enough that they didn't have to raise their voices much to be heard in the cockpit.

As somewhat of a vehicle-enthusiast, Vincent seemed eager to drive the plough, and Edward permitted him for the length of the road that was solely in Vincent's use. When they reached the main road, however, Edward took over again.

With Edward at the helm, it should have been an uneventful trip. However, together with Vincent, they formed an unpredictable team. Mr Jones mused with confidence that this was solely Vincent's poor, nay, awful influence.

As they ploughed through the close-to-powdery snow, Vincent egged Edward on to test how quickly they could rush from one house to another.

The two of them roared with laughter when the occasional post box or fence got knocked down amidst the recklessness. They would meekly apologise to the owners and pay for the damages, but regardless of the compensation, Mr Jones found the mirth inside the cockpit far too coarse and distasteful to call good fun. Instead, he lowered his head and tried to avoid being seen. He wanted nothing to do with these childish shenanigans.

It was only to be expected that this was the day the snow plough decided to break down. Edward was more meticulous than most, but the root cause of this breakdown had somehow slipped his checks.

Neither of the two supposedly responsible adults admitted that their behaviour could have had anything to do with the predicament they had landed in.

The unsettling part was that it had happened right in the middle of one of the more perilous stretches, and as the daylight faded and the weather got worse, it became impossible to repair the thing.

The situation could have been worse. Fortunately, the plough cockpit had some space, and the heater system worked separately from the malfunctioning jet engines. Edward's wife had packed him lunch, and though they divided it by three, there was enough to fend off the worst of the hunger.

They made themselves as comfortable as they could, and despite it not being late yet, Mr Jones tried to get some rest. With only a few dots of light on the dashboard of the plough visible in the dark, Vincent and Edward amused themselves for quite a while by telling stories and recalling their trite childhood memories.

It had been over a month since Mr Jones had heard Vincent speak this much, and it did not take the man long to become hoarse, eventually rendering him to grunts and barely visible nods.

Mr Jones wasn't sure how long the conversation persisted since he'd dozed off midway, but presumably Edward and Vincent had slept well through the night because they were up and perky again at the crack of dawn to fix the engines. Mr Jones lay at the back of the cockpit, refusing to wake up fully, clutching to his overcoat for its precious warmth.

It took an hour and a half before everything was in order, but the two now snot-nosed and red-cheeked men climbed back into the cockpit, chatting happily, and the trip to town could continue.

V incent made his usual rounds through the shops and stores in town. By his own words, he wanted to be absolutely sure he'd thought of everything he could possibly think of, and, once he'd exhausted all the things he could think of himself, he'd turned to Mr Jones to double-check if he had missed something worth thinking of at this juncture. Mr Jones tried to think of something else worth remembering, but the best he could muster was a pharmacy visit and after that, the two of them deemed everything all thought through.

Done with the shopping, Vincent took Mr Jones to the café near the market square, where the two of them enjoyed cups of mint tea and assorted pastries. Mr Jones missed the opportunity to order his usual robust cup of coffee, and felt a bit like a little old lady sipping the tea and nibbling on the dainty little cakes and tarts that Vincent had ordered as a set.

Vincent was engaged in conversation with some of the other patrons, so Mr Jones dared not mention it. There was a sense of normalcy about this tea break that he knew now to appreciate and would not knowingly disrupt.

Having been engrossed in various conversations long after finishing his cup, Vincent stopped mid-sentence, stood up, excused the abrupt manner with which they were to leave, and pulled Mr Jones out into the cold winter air. Mr Jones barely had time to be shocked by the quick temperature change when he was hoisted aboard a snowtrain and plopped into a seat in its back-most carriage.

The snowtrains were trains only in the sense that a locomotive pulled along several carriages in a row. Instead of following a conventional set of train tracks, the locomotive lumbered over and through the snow using a recent invention called 'continuous tracks'. The carriages slid behind it on skis.

Before this particular train had been stripped of some of its bulk and modified to its current use, it had probably served for years on rails as a proper train. The interior was simple and somewhat dated, but the well-worn leather seats seemed soft enough to be comfortable even on a long and bumpy ride.

"Ah, that was lucky! I'd forgotten about these." Vincent shoved some of their acquisitions under the seats and into the netted compartment above their heads. Then he sat across from Mr Jones just as the train nudged forward. "They only go our way on Sundays, if at all in this weather. Great luck with the timing of the plough breakdown." Vincent pulled a packet out of his pocket, folded it open and popped a sugar sweet into his mouth. "Want one?"

"All right." Mr Jones wasn't keen but didn't want to turn down the offer.

The sweets were spicy and effective in clearing up the sinuses. Mr Jones's sinuses didn't really need clearing at present, so he was gifted the delightful sensation of his nose being burned off. Vincent did not seem perturbed in the slightest. What sort of monstrous nostril hair did he have that could ward off this pain?

"How long does the trip take?" Mr Jones asked, instead, still bravely sucking on the 'sweet' but praying for someone to douse the inferno spreading from his mouth and throat and into his honker. He looked across to another compartment in their carriage. There were four compartments in one and three carriages in total. Quite a few seats for a train heading to such a remote area.

"Two hours, I'd imagine. It makes a detour around the cape." Vincent sounded a little nasal.

The carriage was warm, if warm was anything above outside temperature. Sitting down without moving, Mr Jones quickly realised that the trip was going to be chilly. He tried to shake his feet a little and massaged his hands together to keep them warm, and after a while, Vincent was doing the same.

The man did not appear bothered by the cold, but his nose was running, and he had to use his handkerchief more frequently than before.

If Vincent was falling ill, maybe they should have stayed in town, near a doctor? But then Mr Jones thought about their extensive shopping tour, and came to the conclusion that surely, with all of their acquisitions, they were prepared to handle a case or two of the sniffles. He decided to worry no further and concentrated on keeping himself warm.

CHAPTER 9

After two and a half hours, the train stopped at the stop closest to Vincent's house. They got off, and Mr Jones helped Vincent with his newly amassed belongings. The distance to the door wasn't long, but there was snow to the knee and no visible path, so it took them another half an hour to clear their way through.

The house itself was cold from having stood unattended for over a day. Vincent hurried to light the fire and the small separate log burner that warmed the bedrooms. He also fired the kiln in order to heat some bath water. Only then did he have the chance to get out of his snow-soaked clothes.

He warmed up half-dressed in front of the fireplace until the bath-water was warm. Mr Jones had also changed into drier clothes, though as luck had it, he had been wearing some appropriate shoes that had kept his feet well and dry through the wade.

Since the last thing the two of them had eaten was a bit of cake and those ghastly sweets, Mr Jones decided to attempt supper. He put away the acquisitions that had been left in the middle of the floor while they'd changed their clothes and put the kettle on.

Mr Jones had never had the chance to learn how to cook anything but passable food, so pretending to know what he was doing and daring to be experimental was surprisingly much fun. Recently, he had produced some quite delicious meals amidst the usual drivel, so now that the spices and herbs had been restocked, he was determined to make a good impression.

As he was cooking, he barely noticed Vincent returning from the bath, shivering until he wrapped a robe around himself and huddled closer to the fireplace. For such a tall and gangly man, he could fit into an unexpectedly small space huddled up like this.

Mr Jones had already forgotten his presence, busy with the cooking, when he stumbled and nearly fell over on top of him, at which point he gave the man a glare. It was left rudely unreceived. Since the intended receptacle of his glaring did not respond, Mr Jones poked him in the shoulder. This produced a grunt, and Vincent looked up.

"You are in the way, you realise," Mr Jones pointed out with some impatience. Vincent wasn't really that much in the way, but having been startled, Mr Jones couldn't resist a grumble. There could have been casualties! Namely, the carrots he was carrying on a chopping block, which could have fallen across the floor before they reached the pot. It had taken him a while to cut them into uniform cubes, and he was proud of his unusually decent workmanship.

"I'm sorry," Vincent replied quietly.

This threw Mr Jones further off. The angry Vincent hadn't apologised for anything. He'd barely been polite or civil. Besides which, this apology did not seem the tiniest bit sarcastic!

"Well, no harm done." Mr Jones dropped the carrots into the pot and returned to the table to chop some onions. With occasional sideward glances, he observed the unmoving lump of robe and moist hair near the fireplace. It was disturbing him.

"Are you still cold?"

"Yes."

"Was the water cold?"

"No, it was fine."

"Are you coming down with something?"

"I'm just cold." Despite his insistence, Vincent did still sound nasal. "Does it have to be something more complicated than that?"

"I haven't seen you huddled in front of the fireplace like that before, so it made me wonder."

"You haven't been here through the winter, have you?"

"No."

"Then shut up—!" Vincent's voice made a squeak when it broke from being hoarse.

Mr Jones finished chopping the rest of the ingredients and let the pot simmer under a lid. He fetched a blanket from Vincent's bedroom closet and threw it around the man. Vincent said nothing, but he did pull it tighter around himself.

"If you're feeling ill, it's better to take something for it before it gets worse," Mr Jones reminded him carefully. He sat on a stool next to the fireplace and watched the glowing embers, trying to see what Vincent was seeing.

When he turned to actually look at the man, he noticed his eyes were closed. The moment of wasted effort bothered him only briefly, before he slammed his palm against Vincent's forehead in a rush to test if he had a fever. The forceful blow made Vincent flinch, and he eyed Mr Jones, perplexed and angry.

"What on earth are you doing?" He sounded like he was clutching on to mere shreds of his patience. "I said I'm just cold!"

"Your forehead is a bit warm." Mr Jones wasn't entirely sure whether his own hands were colder than usual, but Vincent did seem flustered, so he tried to summon all of his confidence to sound authoritative. "I think you should take something and rest."

"I'm hungry." Vincent sulked.

"It will take a while, unfortunately."

"I'm *hungry*," Vincent repeated meaningfully. He stood up and went to rummage through the pantry for something quicker.

"A half an hour, sir. Can't you wait that long?"

"I'm hungry!" Vincent declared angrily. "Andgh—" His voice gave out again as he was about to say it. He swallowed and continued with a whisper. "My throat hurts..."

"You've caught a bug of some variety. Sit down, I'll make you something." Mr Jones pulled Vincent out of the cupboard.

It had to be the fever making him this impatient and difficult. Indeed, Vincent had been easier to deal with drunk, depressed and annoyed than now, sporting what probably wasn't even much of a fever.

"Fine," Vincent croaked, and sat down at the side of the table, closer to the fireplace. He pulled the robe and blanket closer to his skin and closed his eyes again, perching on the stool like a sleeping owl.

Mr Jones prepared the herbal concoction his mother used to make for similar illnesses: meadowsweet, rosemary, sage and honey mixed into a gill of brandy and topped with hot water. It wasn't much, but he hoped it would keep Vincent preoccupied until supper, and with something in his belly, perhaps the man might be persuaded to go rest without much more ado.

No matter how quick Mr Jones was at mixing, Vincent seemed displeased to have to wait. He was also a little too happy to chuck down the mixture without knowing what it even was, though Mr Jones managed to get him to stop at the last minute to leave a little for sipping while they waited for the supper to be done.

"It isn't particularly foul-tasting, this," Vincent commended. "I actually like it, I think."

"Well, you would," Mr Jones muttered under his breath. He'd made it with two gills to be on the safe side. Vincent wasn't a drunkard per se, but he did seem to like the taste of alcoholic beverages.

"What did you say?" Vincent asked, though his heart wasn't quite in it.

"Nothing." Mr Jones stirred the pot.

The two of them spent the next twenty-five or so minutes in silence, Mr Jones with his back toward Vincent, who at least presumably eyed the fire drowsily.

Once he had finally deemed the pot ready to eat, Mr Jones served it and sat down opposite of Vincent. Despite having so loudly demanded food some minutes prior, Vincent ate with uncharacteristic reluctance.

Mr Jones tasted the food to check whether there was something wrong with it, but that didn't seem to be the case. It was a shame; he'd made an effort. This reminded him of Vincent throwing his wooden sculptures into the fire.

"You're so wasteful."

"What?" Vincent looked up from his bowl.

"You, ah... how should I put this." Mr Jones tried to put it into words that might best reach Vincent in his current state. "I think you should take more care when eating. As well as with other things. And not just... throw it away." The explanation was naught better, but at least Vincent seemed to be giving it some thought.

"I don't understand. Are you talking about the food?"

"The food. Other things. Why you don't try to make the best of a given situation," Mr Jones explained. He was uncomfortable having to be this straightforward, guessing he'd not yet seen the true depth of Vincent's anger.

"You don't mean this blasted winter?" Vincent growled, though with not much energy.

"No, not the winter. What you do. This stuff." Mr Jones gestured at the figurines that had been spared a fiery death.

"The bits of wood? You are concerned about the bits of wood?" Vincent looked genuinely baffled.

"Not merely the... the bits of wood. I mean, everything in general."

"I don't understand."

"The things you do, they should mean something, shouldn't they? Why do you throw them away so easily?"

"They were first tries or defected versions..." Vincent blinked and wiped his eyes as if this whole conversation was causing him great fatigue, and it had nothing whatsoever to do with his fever.

"They looked fine to me. And another thing," Mr Jones spoke out while he had the courage to do so. "Try to taste what you are eating. I actually did make an effort."

"Oh?" Vincent looked down at his bowl. He blew his nose and tried again but looked as much at a loss. "It doesn't taste much of anything. I'm sorry." The second apology. Well, at least he was eating. It was too soon to say whether any of this was truly cause for worry.

Mr Jones sighed, exasperated. How much he'd have given for a healthy Vincent for the duration of a bite! The pot was actually quite good. It was his best yet. That it would fall into a man's stomach untasted seemed a grave injustice. But what could he do? He couldn't even be upset.

V incent was as good as comatose. He was leaning closer and closer to the table until he was lying next to the bowl, half asleep.

"May I suggest the bed, sir?" Mr Jones collected the bowls and cups to take them to the sink. He felt oddly motherly doing this. He'd never had to take care of an ill person before, but he'd had his mother do it for him.

Food, drink, warmth and rest, he seemed to recall. The first three had been taken care of, and the fourth was imminently advisable. However, Vincent seemed far too tired to move anywhere, much less across to the other side of the house and to his bedroom.

The house wasn't all that big, but the distance was enough for Mr Jones to wonder if he could carry Vincent that far if need be. It did not seem likely. He'd probably have to drag the man.

"Let's go. I'll help you to bed."

"I don't want to," Vincent mumbled.

"Why not?"

"It feels like someone is watching me when I close my eyes."

"It's probably the damn cat. There's no one else here." I sure as hell have no interest in watching you sleep, thought Mr Jones.

"Besides, the steak... it's still dancing,"

"What?"

"The fillet steak. Rare. Dancing, right there on the fire." Vincent pointed at the fireplace. Mr Jones tested his forehead again. The fever was on the rise despite the meadowsweet.

They had bought something stronger from the pharmacy specifically for this purpose, but Mr Jones could not for the life of him remember what it was called. The parcels, bottles and packets were all too similar.

He searched through Vincent's medicine cabinet, hoping to spot a clue on one of the labels. Some of them read "take two along with a meal" or "mix into one cup of warm water" but nothing about the ailments they were meant to cure. What was it with these small town pharmacies and their lacking labelling system?

"Mr Vincent. The cold medicine. Which one is it? Is it the one in the bag, or in this bottle?" Mr Jones asked after managing to limit his selection to only two suitable candidates.

"The bag, clearly," Vincent replied, but it was difficult to tell if his judgement could be trusted. Mr Jones didn't have much choice, though.

He reasoned that, while it might be medicine for something else, if he followed the dosage, it couldn't do that much harm, could it?

He measured the correct amount of powder into a cup and poured some hot water into it. He mixed in some ice to cool it down and offered it to Vincent, who merely stared at it with no intention of drinking.

"Look." Mr Jones resorted again to treachery. "The steak will come and eat you unless you drink this."

Vincent's eyes widened. He looked at the cup of medicine and then at the fire. With surprising agility, he took the cup and threw the contents in a magnificent little arch straight into the fire, where the supposed dancing steak was making its performance and presumably now faltered due to this clever interference.

"There!" Vincent shouted victoriously, although the sound out of his mouth was much less glorious than he'd probably intended. He held his throat, and his face filled with regret from what seemed like considerable pain. First shocked, then irritated and frustrated, Mr Jones began to prepare another dose.

A fter the third time of him falling ill, it occurred to Mr Jones that Vincent must have had an abnormally weak constitution, or at least a particular weakness toward chests and colds.

He hadn't reported any animated cuts of meat since, but the fevers were a regular occurrence. His fluctuating health was affecting his already poor mood, especially when Mr Jones made the mistake of asking how he was doing.

One evening after supper, Mr Jones was minding his own business, trying his hand at whittling. He'd been stuck trying to decide his next move when Vincent's voice had interrupted his struggle.

"If you cut that side, it won't stay upright unless you attach it to something. If you clear out the bottom part and adjust the hem a bit, it can sit on the side of a window sill or the like."

Mr Jones had been facing the fireplace so that the chips were easier to throw straight in. He turned around to see if Vincent was spying on him behind his back, but no, the man slouched over the table with his cheek firmly on the tabletop. He looked bored out of his skull, making a structure out of toothpicks, and didn't even seem capable of paying attention to anything Mr Jones might be doing.

Baah, the nerve of the man! He was giving unsolicited advice without even bothering to check what he was talking about! Mr Jones bit his tongue so as not to tell Vincent off.

"I thought you asked." Vincent rolled to his left side to see better. "If you cut off the side like you said, it will definitely ruin the balance."

The side in question was the side of a long dress Mr Jones had tried to carve for his female figurine. It didn't look quite right, so he'd wondered if carving some bits off altogether might save it. He hadn't said anything, though.

"Sure you did." Vincent tested his own forehead. "Ah, is it the fever again? I could've sworn you said something… Well, never mind." He turned back to his toothpicks.

This wasn't the first time he'd said something odd as of late, but Mr Jones had assumed the fevers had taken their toll, and Vincent had developed a habit of babbling nonsensical things to himself. It wasn't surprising that they were both mulling similar topics after spending so much time together, but this was silly. How could someone be answering the questions he'd thought rather than voiced?

"Yes, that's what I thought, but Dr Poppycock assures me it's my imagination playing tricks on me," Vincent mumbled, yawned with his face against the table, and once done, slowly got up. "I think I'll turn in early. Maybe the hands won't be watching me again tonight."

Mr Jones tried to avoid staring. He was fairly sure he hadn't said anything. The tips of the fingers he'd placed over his lips had not moved.

He'd heard Vincent mention Dr Poppycock before, though reservedly. The man was apparently Vincent's therapist. This could have made for a scoop with the right sort of embellishments, but it would have to wait for some additional information and evidence.

And frankly, at present, Mr Jones was more concerned about having to share such a small cottage with someone so clearly in need of therapy. Vincent wasn't necessarily insane or dangerous, but he was seeing and hearing things and paranoid, to boot. What was there to stop him from snapping and completely losing it? But—

"I'm fine. I'm just a little under the weather and need some rest." Vincent was already moseying his way towards his bedroom.

"I didn't say anything." Mr Jones was momentarily confused, trying to remember whether any of his recent thoughts had been offensive. Maybe there was something here, in the air or in the food, that was causing him to be losing his marbles as well? Was it the almost constant darkness messing with him? Was it something contagious? And if so, and if this was real, would he be hearing Vincent's thoughts next?

He shivered. This was indeed no time to be worrying about a scoop! If this was real, then who had been watching Vincent almost every night?

"Don't be silly. There is no scientific proof that the human brain could be capable of telepathy. Mine most certainly isn't. Now, can you pipe it down a little? I'm going to see if I can catch some shut-eye, by myself tonight." Once he'd evicted the cat from his bedroom, Vincent closed the door behind him.

Mr Jones was left behind, unsettled, wondering what sort of trickery had caused this disturbing illusion, or if he himself was starting to go bat-shit crazy cooped up in this house.

Vincent regretted evicting the cat from the bedroom. It was empty and quiet inside his little fever-bubble, and he could have used the company, purring at his feet.

With the fever messing with his head, it was difficult to tell what was real and what was not. Had he fallen asleep yet? No? These moments somewhere in between were always the most confusing. Everything seemed the same. Everything seemed normal.

It can't be real, can it? Am I losing it now? Did he slip me something? But when?

Dr Poppycock had said to ignore the voices. That it was likely some sort of manifestation of his repressed, subconscious desires. But if that were so, shouldn't he have listened more carefully, so he could take care of what was bothering him? The doctor meant well, but he wasn't always particularly logical.

The cat was sitting right outside the door, licking its paw. Vincent could just about see him within the confines of his bubble. That was comforting. He was probably dreaming now, though. What he was watching was a dream and not real, he reminded himself.

How did he know about the hem without looking? Did he take a peek while I was busy? He must have. It has to be a coincidence. Several coincidences.

Mr Swifty turned around and disappeared into the void where the voices were coming from. Vincent was left alone in his bed. As long as he was alone, it was fine.

I didn't say anything.

How long would these words echo in his mind, this time? They must have been something he'd heard before and now re-heard because of the fever.

There was less noise when he was alone all day. Fewer words to echo in his head like this.

He missed Ren. She was usually soft-spoken or quiet. But he couldn't afford to mess that up with his madness, so he was glad of the current arrangements.

He's intentionally trying to freak me out. He must be doing it on purpose. He acts all nonchalant, but he's after revenge!

This part was familiar. It triggered a chorus of voices repeating similar sentiments:

"The boy is an imbecile. He is insane!"

"He's frightening us on purpose. How despicable!"

"He's acting compliant, but he's got the devil speaking through his mouth, it's filthy! It's all lies. He's making it up!"

"That child is from weak blood and of poor morals and character. He is possessed by the devil. He is beyond anybody's help."

"I wish you'd never been born!"

Vincent chuckled.

Just as when you repeated a word until it sounded like gibberish, he'd heard it all too many times for it to make sense anymore. Maybe if he could rest undisturbed for once, perhaps the fevers would relent, and he'd be rid of this memory noise. He was really quite tired of having to listen to it.

He's not who I thought he was.

A miasma of disappointment seeped into his bubble as if it were a sponge pulling it in.

So it was a nightmare, was it? Again? Vincent instinctively tried to take a deep breath, but it always left him feeling stuffy and dissatisfied. Perhaps because his body had already settled to a slower rate of breathing, it didn't supply enough air to keep up with his overactive mind?

If he had to be confined to this bubble with no escape, they could have at least made it tight enough to not let things through like that. He wished he could have drawn the curtains shut to be left alone. Speaking of which—

This is ridiculous! That conniving piece of—! He's made me all paranoid! There's nothing here but the damn cat and a whole bunch of snow for the breadth of the whole bloody island. I need to stop playing this stupid game of his and go to bed. Sheesh.

—There was definitely something watching him just on the other side where he could not see. The fever made it feel so real. If he hadn't had the benefit of speaking with Dr Poppycock, and if he hadn't become aware of his own fallacies and weaknesses, he could have sworn there was someone right there.

It could seem as real as day, but this was a dream. Ghosts did not exist. It was his jumbled mind trying to make sense of his surroundings. And who could blame it for making mistakes after all he'd been through?

He needed to try to take care of himself to survive through this winter. Next year would be better. He'd be far away from here, somewhere warm and comfortable, where his body and mind would not be breaking down all the time. He owed it to Ren to do better. He needed to shut it all out and rest.

Hopefully, the fever would be gone tomorrow, and he'd be freed from this bubble.

CHAPTER 10

Without much to compare to, Vincent had always thought he'd come from an ordinary family. He remembered a kind and caring mother and a dependable, if slightly distant, father, who had treated his wife in a warm and affectionate way. They had lived in a regular townhouse in a regular town, with two servants and a pet bird, and he'd never had any complaints, as far as his memory served.

How it had all gone so wrong, so suddenly, was a mystery to him. He strained to remember all the details his young self might have not understood, but even his adult perspective gave him no further insight.

One day his father had asked him, "Would you rather come with me or stay here?"

An innocuous-seeming question for a four-year-old, expecting to be asked things like whether he wanted to tag along to go shopping or see the marketplace together.

His father had had some luggage packed behind him, so Vincent had suspected he was heading to see a relative or going on a business trip. It hadn't occurred to him that he was being asked something of consequence.

Vincent had never been fond of the cold or the damp, and since the weather hadn't been altogether nice that day, he'd said he'd prefer to stay home with his mother. He'd noticed the disappointment and displeasure on his father's face, but his father was a surly man and often looked glum without an apparent cause, so Vincent hadn't guessed to be concerned. He'd merely offered to come to the front steps to see his father off, regardless of the rain.

A young woman who Vincent had hardly known, but who had come to the house regularly, had accompanied them to the front steps. Vincent had watched his father pack the luggage into the carriage with not a word said. He'd then watched his father help his mother into the carriage, and without either of them looking back, they had sped away and disappeared into the grey downpour.

To this day, Vincent could not wrap his head around how the two of them had abandoned him with such ease. He'd been too stunned and confused even to cry out after them.

The strange woman, who had stayed behind, had stood next to Vincent for a while in the rain.

"When are they coming back?" Vincent had asked.

"They're not," she had responded.

There had been a hint of sadness in her eyes, and an unsettling chill in her tone as she'd spoken. She had tried to guide Vincent back inside, but in shock, he'd refused.

"Fine. Be that way. See if I care." She'd left him standing there. That was all Vincent could recall about her, whoever she had been.

It hadn't mattered that he'd eventually thought to scream and cry. There hadn't been a peep from the neighbours to check on him. Just the deafening sound of the rain hitting the slates somewhere above and water sloshing down the spouts.

No one had come to get him from where they'd left him. No one would have cared had he run.

T he events after that day were hazy due to either his age or the fever he'd contracted. The next solid memories were not from a relative's house or an orphanage, but a workhouse for children. He wasn't sure how he'd ended up there, but presumed he'd fallen gravely ill, and his relatives had refused to take him in to avoid having to pay for his expenses. The workhouse would treat and raise destitute children free of charge.

Life at the workhouse hadn't been easy for a five-year-old; it hadn't been torture either. The matron of the floor had been fair and taken care of her charges, unlike some of her colleagues. She'd been said to deal harsh punishments for any attempts at mischief, but because she kept such a strict schedule, there hadn't been opportunities to test whether this was true. It had taken no time at all for Vincent to understand that things were easier if he followed her orders without question.

Not that Vincent had had any reason to question the matron. On the contrary, he'd had plenty of reasons not to. Having feared that a wrong word would send him into exile from even this stable existence, he hadn't dared to try his luck. This was why he'd learned everything there was to learn in such a short time, and why his stay at the workhouse had ended so soon.

O n his seventh birthday, the matron gave Vincent some nearly unused, striped breeches and a shirt, neatly carved wooden cufflinks, hale and freshly shined shoes, a pair of crisply white socks and brown braces with the letter B embroidered on one side. He looked like quite the solid little boy in his new outfit, and no later than he was in it, he was sent away to the new house.

Though the matron had only ever spoken two words to Vincent outside of her instructions, he recalled her looking uncharacteristically emotional while waving goodbye to him.

Perhaps she was proud of her achievement? She had never been unkind to Vincent, but as per her job, she had successfully dispelled any notion of playfulness and culled the child out of him.

V incent was lifted into the carriage and sat in his seat, back straight and hands folded neatly, almost like a small statue, as the butler of Benton House informed him of what to expect from his future. Vincent listened carefully, wondering if this next stop would be better or worse than his last.

When they arrived at Benton House and exited the carriage, next to the butler there stood a stoic little machine of a person, ready for whatever housework would be assigned to him as a hall boy, and not much capacity for anything else.

Benton House was a house of some respectable size: there were seven formal reception rooms, seventeen bedrooms, three dining rooms, a library in each of the four wings and a front room with a hall for each of the six entrances. There were studies, sunrooms, drawing rooms, bathrooms, stables, kitchens, the scullery, the bake room, the laundry, countless staircases, cellars, hidden passages, not to mention the staff quarters and other utility rooms in four different floors, spanning into four directions of wings.

Each of these rooms and each of the people living and working in them had different sets of rules. Some of these rules Vincent had to learn by heart even before he had settled in properly.

The most important rule at Benton House was not to be seen. It was the staff's duty to be available without delay, but never be in the same room with a member of the household unless explicitly summoned. Usually only the butler or the housekeeper had this privilege. The rest of the staff received their orders from either of them.

"If you come across a member of the household or one of their guests, divert your eyes at once, face the wall, stand, be quiet and wait for them to leave the room. Then exit quietly through the nearest passage," one of the hall boys, Marcus, explained to Vincent. Marcus was short and lean, but older than Vincent by three years. He spoke with surprising confidence for one his age and stature.

Unlike Vincent, Marcus had lived in this house most of his life. He knew it like the palm of his hand would come to know the shaft of his penis sometime in the not too distant future. That was not to say he was an ugly boy, but someone of his background rarely had any opportunities for social interaction, and though he wasn't yet of age to truly worry about such things, it was already looming there at the periphery of his awareness. His answer was to act as if he already had the things he'd likely never have. What did he have to lose? His dignity? What was that worth? Nothing.

Vincent hadn't the slightest of clues what Marcus's empty show of confidence was about. He listened to his senior as if to a sage old man, and had he known how to write, he probably would have taken notes. He wanted to do everything right and be a good boy like he'd been taught. Things seemed to go so much more smoothly when he was being a good boy.

The reason why Benton House had more than one hall boy was because one simply wasn't enough to clean, trim and fill all the lamps, polish all the boots, do the infamous slop duty and the other duties in the servants' hall.

The job of the second hall boy, Liam, was to take care of the servants' boots. Marcus took care of the lamps. The two of them shared the other tasks with a scullery maid, Bryony, who was in her early teens.

Despite there being the lot of them, each day started at five in the morning and ended somewhat after nine in the evening. There was always something that could be delegated down to a hall boy if one ran out of boots to shine, lamps to set and chamber pots to empty.

As for Vincent, he became known as the slop boy. He was too small to be of proper help with the slop duty because the buckets were too heavy for him to carry. Instead, his job was to sneak around the house to check which rooms needed seeing to.

He was also given the gruesome task of keeping clean what was called 'the sluice room'. Because he had to spend a considerable amount of time in there cleaning buckets, chamber pots and bedpans, he often smelled the part, despite his efforts to keep clean.

This was why he ate last—if there was something left after everyone else had eaten—and was banned from entering the kitchens or the baking room, no matter how alluring the scents that drifted into the servants' hall.

There was, of course, the theoretical chance of moving up from the unenviable position of the hall boy, but without any particular talents, there wasn't much to look forward to.

Vincent made an effort to learn to read from the various small guide-books and pamphlets that were handed to the staff. Marcus wasn't an especially bright boy, but to his credit, he was always patient and willing to help Vincent with his reading. However, reading alone did nothing to improve their chances for a promotion.

Though adequate at the things he'd been taught to do, Marcus lacked the motivation to improve himself past the mandatory requirements. It was understandable, considering his bleak upbringing. No one had bothered to encourage him to make anything of himself since, to be fair, he probably wouldn't ever amount to much even if he tried. As an inadvertent role model, his habitual pessimism started to rub off on Vincent.

Benton House was not a place for equal, nor even for remotely decent, opportunities. A girl could aim to become a senior housemaid or the housekeeper; a boy could try for a footman or the butler. One had to climb through some posts in between, but most were filled for years to come, and when the time came to pick a successor, there were always many to choose from. The customs of Benton House were such that, if the butler or housekeeper had kin to fill the spot, they would not hesitate to do so. There was no requirement to pick within the house, and it was not unheard of to be kicked out entirely, even after decades of diligent efforts. It was a ruthless environment where, if you weren't liked, you would not be staying for very long.

Vincent soon realised that simply doing as told was not going to be good enough. The members of the household may have valued his compliance, but they were not in charge of his day-to-day living conditions.

The rest of the staff prioritised loyalty, flexibility and willingness to pitch in beyond one's duties. They were more interested in a good sense of humour, in personal cleanliness or even the low volume of one's snoring.

Vincent knew he needed to be liked by the others to earn his place at the servants' hall, but since he'd never actually been taught many social skills, it was easier said than done.

CHAPTER 11

The winters at Benton House were rough on the servants. Vincent was almost eight, and though the majority of his duties hadn't changed, he no longer had to spend as much time in slop duty or the sluice room as before. After gaining some skills working in the laundry and the kitchens, and due to this newfound cleanliness, they let him sleep at the servants' quarters instead of the little cot at the end of the servants' hall, and he was also finally permitted to eat alongside the lower staff.

Alas, this blessing of a warmer bed and better meals came too late as he had been mostly malnourished for the summer and fall, and the chills and runny noses of the other servants he hadn't come into contact with much before provided ample source for peril.

Despite having been exposed to a vast amount of filth while in slop duty without catching so much as an occasional belly ache, he was not so lucky with the circulating colds. Since he'd been instructed not to appear in the kitchen with a runny nose, he sat useless in one of the less-used hidden staff staircases.

He couldn't go back to bed because no one did that when they were sick. Things needed to be done, always, and he needed to look like he was doing them. If he was in the servants' quarters before his bedtime, he was considered truant and lazy.

Although Marcus could be trusted to take on some of Vincent's work, he did so in exchange for the sneakily procured baked goods Vincent could get his hands on for being on the good side of the head housemaid, who in turn was close to the cook. Though he didn't need to repay these favours right away, the longer Vincent was ill, the longer Marcus had to wait for his treats, and he was not fond of waiting.

Thus, on the fourth day of the fourth time being ill with the sniffles, Vincent felt understandably dejected as he sat on the stairs, listening for footsteps, ready to appear as if going somewhere.

This particular set of stairs was nice because it was so seldom used. Vincent was lucky to have realised this early on, or else his wait for better health would have been even more unpleasant.

The servants' quarters tended to be cold at night, and the night before had been especially frosty. Despite this, he didn't feel too cold, though his muscles were achy, and he was very, very tired.

On the other side of the thin wall, there was a sitting room with a roaring fire. It was almost close enough for Vincent to feel its warmth, if just almost. In the quiet darkness, he could hear it popping and crackling, and imagined how pleasant it must have felt to be sitting in that room.

There were people on the other side of the wall, talking. Perhaps three voices. Vincent listened to them, dozing, shaking himself awake from time to time, and drifting off again shortly after.

He'd sat there for long enough to know that the conversations made very little sense. Sometimes they were talking to one another coherently, but one of them would say something without anyone reacting to how preposterous and out of character it sounded.

After a while, Vincent's butt began to hurt from sitting on the hard surface. Too tired to do much about it, he tried to shift his position and distract himself with whatever else was said in the other room. He'd learnt that eavesdropping was bad no matter the situation, but their talks did not sound private. They were telling such bizarre and fanciful stories about their lives, their travels and their thoughts, it sounded like they were meant to be heard. It was as if they were telling them to anyone who would listen. Anyone. Even him.

U sually, Vincent required very little caretaking. He made sure he did the things that were asked of him, was where he needed to be, and stayed away from where he wasn't supposed to go.

He complained about things, but he did it in private. He ate what was given, slept when he was told to, and drew as little attention to himself as possible. That was what he'd been taught at the workhouse.

He wasn't very good at his chores, but he was a quick learner, so the maids had patience with him. He was much less hassle than Marcus, who hardly cared if he was flogged every once in a while for slacking or stealing.

The first few months of staying at Benton House had gone smoothly, but as November came along and the corridors and staircases remained chilly, Vincent's health deteriorated further, and his diligence began to suffer.

He kept out of the way, but that was now mainly because he did not want to face the head maid, who tried to get her hands on him for the chores he'd left undone. He'd been feeling especially poorly this week, and Marcus seemed to be growing tired of making up for him.

Vincent had managed a few hours in the laundry in the morning, but the laundry room got steamy, breathing was heavy and the work was rough. He was warm when he kept moving, but the wet sleeves quickly grew cold when he escaped to take a break at his usual spot.

He was a skinny boy, so there wasn't much there to keep him warm. He shuddered, and his teeth clattered as he pulled his knees closer.

It was times like this that reminded him of the absurdity of being here instead of home. He'd had friends he'd played with. He didn't know where they were now, and he no longer remembered their names. His mother had promised him he would go to school once he turned seven, but he had been at the workhouse at the time, and no one had come to pick him up.

Instead of being home with a family, he was sitting here alone with nothing but his self-pity as company.

He'd thought about running away, but the world was a big place, and he was just a small boy. He'd learned that most people weren't very nice, and he was better off somewhere where he had a few allies and people weren't hostile on account of his mere presence.

Sitting on a creaking step in the darkness didn't seem much better than wandering somewhere out there, but at least he was sheltered from the rain. All he wanted to do was sleep until it ended.

Vincent leaned against the wall. There were probably boots to polish. Marcus would be angry to have to do it alone again. Vincent didn't feel particularly great about making his only friend do the work they were supposed to share, but he was too tired to move. When he breathed slowly against the wall, the warmth of his breath felt pleasant. He tried to focus on it and rest. Maybe if he rested another five minutes, he would feel well enough to go polish the boots.

Vincent's thoughts were getting muddled by the conversations from the room beyond the wall he was leaning on. Something about giraffes with long necks. A safari adventure.

There was a crack in the wall where, if you looked low enough, you could see a tiny glimpse of the room. Vincent lowered his head to look.

Normally, he couldn't see anyone from this angle, but there was an old man there now, standing next to the corner of the desk. His mouth wasn't moving, but he seemed to be recounting the story. He tapped his forefinger to his lips and fingered a pen in his other hand, likely taking a break from either writing or reading.

Vincent watched him no longer curious but loath to move. After a few minutes of staring listlessly through the crack, he realised the man had turned and was looking right at him. He said nothing, but his eyebrows rose in a confused upward frown.

Vincent bolted up from where he'd sat, unsure whether to make his escape up or down the stairs. He opted to go down, because it was faster and because he was too tired to climb, but this was a mistake. The passage led to a corridor that was linked to the adjacent room, and when he reached it, the old man was there waiting for him. Vincent froze.

"Don't run. Is anyone looking? No? Good. Come here, boy." The man gestured for Vincent to come closer. Vincent hesitated but knew he had no choice but to obey. He couldn't have looked presentable, his clothes dirty and tattered from work, so, horrified to be seen this way, he tried to pat them and straighten his hair in hopes it would help.

"Good, good. Come in here." The man gestured for Vincent to enter the room. Up close, Vincent recognised him as one of the Bentons—the brother of the head of the house, to be precise. He was much older in person than in the picture Vincent had been shown when he'd been told to memorise their names.

"Sit," the man ordered. Vincent looked around, but the seats were much too clean and good for him, so in order to obey, he meekly sat on his knees on the floor. Mr Benton looked at him surprised but said nothing.

"I need you to listen to this and nod if it's all right. All right?" Mr Benton held up a letter.

This seemed like a strange task, but Vincent nodded. His heart was pounding from the fright. He didn't know what to do, what was expected of him, or whether the head maid or the housekeeper would hear of this.

It was one thing to be caught slacking but quite the other to be caught in the presence of a member of the household. He had received a flogging once, and he wasn't keen to repeat the experience. He should have run up the stairs, he scolded himself.

Mr Benton read the letter. To Vincent's surprise, it did not sound like a formal letter. Then again, what sense would there be to read a formal letter to a child?

"Well?" Mr Benton asked. Vincent frowned. It hadn't contained any of the complicated words adults usually liked to use. "Well, answer me, boy. Is it good?"

Vincent quickly nodded.

"Did you understand everything?"

"I understood everything, sir," Vincent replied as promptly as he dared.

"Good, good. Then it's settled." Mr Benton folded the letter and slipped it into an envelope. Vincent watched him seal it with wax and his official seal. When Mr Benton noticed Vincent was watching him, he breathed out a huff.

"Fine, fine. I'll tell you what it is, boy." He took a moment as if to debate with himself whether he cared to know Vincent's name or not, then continued without asking. "It's going abroad where they speak a different language. That is why they speak ours very poorly. The letter needs to be simple for them to understand. I should think that it will do if a stupid little boy such as yourself can understand it."

Ah, this made some sense to Vincent, who stood up, now daring to hope for a chance to leave without further repercussions to his eavesdropping.

"Yes, go now, you. I have no further use for you." Mr Benton shooed him away gloriously negligently. Vincent hurried out of the room and into one of the staff passages before the man could change his mind.

I t was difficult to break a habit, so Vincent found himself in the same quiet staircase. He'd tried to seat himself away from the crack, but somehow Mr Benton, who spent a lot of time on the other side of the wall, had a knack for knowing when he was there.

Instead of dragging Vincent out, the man would stand closer to the wall and read a piece of text or a letter and command Vincent to knock once if it was fine and twice if there was something wrong with it. It had taken Vincent a moment or two to gather the courage to knock, but the steps were creaky, and this close to the wall, Mr Benton would have heard if he'd tried to sneak away. If he'd defied the man so blatantly, there would have been consequences.

"Is it the latter part that is unclear?" Mr Benton asked, voice strained from the annoyance. He did not seem a bad man, but he had a temper, and his patience extended only just enough to allow Vincent his brief hesitations.

Vincent knocked once. At least this way he was making himself useful. The head maid would probably not see it his way if he was ever caught, though, so as soon as Mr Benton turned to other things, Vincent slipped away to his proper chores.

The trips to the staircase were daily now. Even on the better days, Vincent needed that moment to steady himself before he could return to do as much of his work as he could, whilst avoiding the head maid.

Avoiding the head maid was especially tricky during mealtimes, but he'd managed it because the men and the women were seated at opposite ends of the room. It probably wouldn't take long until the head maid ran out of patience and enlisted the housekeeper or the butler to take care of Vincent, but perhaps by then this awful illness would have let up some. It just didn't seem to be doing that at all.

Mr Benton sat in his favourite reception room. He'd procured a desk for himself despite the objections of his brother, who preferred to keep the house in as many segregated compartments as possible and despised using one room for the purpose of another.

Causing his brother this discomfort was an added perk. Mr Benton, though the older brother, had forfeited the role of head of the house because of his insistence to travel and dab in professions the family deemed less than ideal. He wasn't particularly bitter, but he did like to make his brother's life a hair more difficult, out of principle.

What a strange house his brother ran. On the outside, it seemed a well-oiled machine, but it had its quirks.

One of them was the strange scruffy boy that loitered in the stairs behind the wall. Though Mr Benton wasn't very fond of children, knowing the sneaky little thing was there more often than not made the reception room only better. It was like having his very own spy at the back of things. He could ask the boy all sorts of things and he'd knock back 'yes' or 'no'. Sometimes, he didn't even have to ask for there to be those one or two tentative knocks.

"How about 'predisposed'?" Mr Benton suggested.

The answers had been slow to begin with, but today was a record. Either the boy had become complacent and bored, or the questions were too difficult for him. It was difficult to tell.

Had Mr Benton had the skills to judge something like that, he wouldn't have had to ask for advice from the boy in the first place. He'd learnt that what seemed obvious to him wasn't always as obvious to other people, but it wasn't easy to keep that in mind at all times, especially when he lost his temper.

"It means that he had the tendency or inclination, in advance... Are you listening to me?" There was a faint knock. "So, is it all right, or should I try something else?" Silence. "Hello?" A knock. "Well?" Silence. "What is wrong with you today? You are being absolutely useless!" Mr Benton groaned. He needed this letter sent out today and could not afford to postpone the matter yet again just because the recipient did not comprehend his words.

Humorously enough, there was a single knock to agree with the last statement. Mr Benton found himself chuckling, and his mood lifted a little.

"Fine. How about I say, 'he was already inclined'. Would that be simple enough?" A knock. "Good." He penned the sentence and continued on to the next. It was slow going when he had to coax an answer out of the boy.

When he finally got to the bottom, signed his name and read it through, it felt satisfactory. At least the effort had been worth it.

He checked the time. There was plenty of it for tea in the drawing room with Ms Florentine, the daughter of the head of the neighbouring Chillwell estate. She was a delightful girl and showed some promise playing the harpsichord.

"None of this laziness the next time, do you hear?" Mr Benton called to the other side of the wall. A knock, though with a delay. "Promptly, boy," Mr Benton added, hoping to instil some speed into the replies again. This time, the reply took even longer.

"Really, you—!" He bit his tongue in an effort to calm down. "Do I need to give you a firm beating as a reminder?"

There were two very slow knocks, far apart. Either a cheeky 'yes, yes' or a lazy 'no'.

Mr Benton stuck his eye to the crack to see. It was dark in there, but he could make out a form some way away. He raised his fist to where a sturdy knock might rattle the boy back to his senses but hadn't the time to make contact when he was interrupted by a heavy thump.

What on earth was the boy doing now? Mr Benton peeked through the crack again and pressed his ear to the wall. He spread his arms apart, palms against the wall, and strained to listen.

Silence.

He could just about see the boy leaning against the wall right where his hand was on the other side. Deeming this an opportunity to slap the wall to startle the boy, Mr Benton took a deep breath to strike.

The wall was peculiarly warm against his palm. The walls of the house weren't very thick, which was why the annoying creaking of the stairs always carried into the room if the servants weren't careful.

He hesitated and listened for one more minute. It was enough for him to calm down and determine that, instead of directing his anger at the wall, he needed to get a hold of the housekeeper. He yanked the string of the bell vigorously until the woman appeared, flustered.

"Cockroaches, in the wall. I want them taken care of right now," he ordered.

"Sir?"

"That wall there. Check it immediately. I am going to the drawing room." He rushed past the housekeeper. "I will have you sacked, if everything isn't exactly as it ought to be when I get back," he added, before he left the room.

The head maid, Mrs Sivens, was a stern and stalwart young woman in her mid-thirties. She had the hardly coveted task of keeping the hall boys and scullery maids in check and out of trouble. As the head maid, she could have easily delegated this to someone else, but she felt honoured to be trusted with the responsibility and wanted to make sure it was done right.

Lately, one of the boys had been stirring trouble by constantly going missing and shirking work. She'd initially had high hopes for him, as he'd displayed a promising mild temper and responded to orders eagerly. But alas, the duties of the hall boys weren't very pleasant, and the daily toil quickly exposed the boys' true characters. She'd known not to expect too much from a boy-child of that age, yet, when he'd begun to slip up so soon after his arrival, she couldn't help but feel disappointed.

Mrs Sivens believed that if you applied yourself and knew your place, you would be rewarded in the end. A noble man's servant was in God's graces so long as they did what God asked of them. Sometimes the younglings needed to meet the other end of a stick to see this truth. Perhaps it wasn't too late to put the boy back on the right path with the right kind of a reminder? But to do that, she needed to find the rascal first.

The housekeeper informed Mrs Sivens of Mr Benton's unusual request to deal with some cockroaches in one of the staircases. Anything coming directly from Mr Benton was an urgent priority, so she knew to investigate the matter momentarily.

She retracted her judgement of Vincent upon arrival at the scene, at least for the time being. The boy sat in the dark, bent over himself, shivering, eyes closed and red in the face. He was sweaty, clammy and feverish, all the signs of being seriously ill.

Benton House had its share of illness during the colder months, and this year was no exception. Two had already been confined to bed, something the staff were allowed only in extreme circumstances. The ill were carted to one of the outbuildings where they could rest in separation and receive whatever treatment was available. It often wasn't much, but they did receive it if they absolutely needed it.

Had Mrs Sivens caught the boy earlier, she could have dealt with the situation more swiftly. Thankfully, it had been the older of the Benton brothers making the discovery, or it could have ended much worse for the boy. She also couldn't blame Vincent for how he'd tried to handle it. She knew all too well the dangers of neglecting work, especially if the housekeeper found out. The mere sound of her keys was enough for Mrs Sivens to recoil, recount and make sure she was on top of all of her duties.

Mrs Sivens lifted Vincent up into her arms. As the head maid, she couldn't afford to be a weakling, but carrying the boy shouldn't have been this easy. She left the second head maid in charge of the servants' hall in her absence and ordered one of the scullery maids to come with her to the gardener's cottage.

Since the head gardener was not busy this time of year, he could probably be persuaded to keep an eye on Vincent. Mrs Sivens would have never dared to suggest it, had it been anyone else, but she'd known the man all her life. He was getting old, and frankly, a little senile, and no longer cared about things like rank. Most of his daily work was already done by the gardeners working under him.

"There's no need to knock. He won't be able to hear it. Be good and open the door for me, will you, Bryony?" Mrs Sivens waited for Bryony to do as told and carried Vincent into the cottage.

The boy looked ghastly. He hadn't reacted much at all to being hoisted and hauled away.

"Fetch water and some towels from the lower closet." There wasn't much they could do for a servant patient since the doctor would never agree to see him, but Mrs Sivens knew enough to try to lower Vincent's fever. She would do what she could, but if it wasn't enough, she could only make the necessary preparations.

"Will I die?" Vincent asked, as if reacting to Mrs Sivens's inner monologue.

"No, no. Nonsense. You'll be fine. You just need some rest." The poor boy was delirious. At least he looked calm, so if death did take him, it would probably do so in a peaceful manner.

"I don't want it to take me," Vincent said, eyes still closed.

"No one is going to take you," Mrs Sivens assured him and lowered Vincent into a cot that was normally used by one of the garden boys. This one had left the house for the winter and would not be back for months.

"Maybe I could become a garden boy," Vincent mumbled. The child did not seem sane. When he opened his eyes, they weren't fixed at anything. He just stared. Who knew how long the fever had ravaged his brain?

"I don't remember."

"Shush now, boy." She tried to remain calm and reassuring, but the random snippets unnerved her.

"I'm sorry."

Under normal circumstances, it would have been a mystery why he was apologising. After all, there were many things he could and should have been sorry for. Mrs Sivens, however, felt increasingly certain that he was responding to her, though she had said not a word of the things he was referring to.

She'd heard similar complaints from some of the senior servants lately. That Vincent spoke in his sleep and that he said vile things, preposterous claims that the other servants found disturbing. He'd been sent back to sleep in the cot in the servants' hall on account of it. Mrs Sivens had meant to have a talk with the boy about the sinful nature of spreading lies, but she hadn't yet had the chance.

"I know it's wrong, so I don't do it."

"Shush," she told him curtly. Get out of my head, demon child.

"I'm sorry," Vincent repeated, though he seemed weak from the mere effort of responding.

No, I'm sorry, thought Mrs Sivens. Even if the child was possessed, he was one of God's creatures. It was up to God to be the judge, not her. She needed to do her best to nurse him back to health. She would deal with the rest of it later.

CHAPTER 12

Vincent stayed at the gardener's cottage through most of the winter. This was not solely because he was ill so frequently. No, it was mainly because his unpredictable feverish spells unsettled everyone around him.

He wasn't sure why, but people kept speaking to him without moving their lips. Even when he stopped commenting on it, they looked at him with panic in their eyes, assuming that he was listening in on them when he wasn't supposed to and that he might repeat the things they were saying.

All the rumours that started circulating were automatically his fault. All the small incidents were due to him being possessed by the devil. It was better to stay at the gardener's cottage. After all, whatever Vincent said during his fevers, the head gardener couldn't hear, even had he been interested enough to listen.

"Oh, rickety sticks." The man would spout nonsense, no matter what was said to him. He didn't seem to mind not hearing, as he had no trouble substituting what was said with what he wanted to hear. "Slivers in saplings and spindles. 'Tis sheer swill, boy. Read this," he'd say and offer Vincent a book about horse manure and its many uses, or a herbarium of whatever he was growing in the garden.

While staying at the gardener's cottage could occasionally be boring, it was like being on holiday. Instead of a 16-hour workday, Vincent only had to work for five. The rest of the time, he slept or read the books the head gardener lent him.

The five hours consisted of the sort of labour that was a joke to a seasoned hall boy. All Vincent had to do was keep the cottage clean and water the plants. He'd also twist little loops out of thin willow switches.

The gardener did not specify why, but he did check that the switches were all done to an exact standard. Whatever they were for, Vincent figured they were probably important and used his utmost care when twisting them. Once there were many enough, the gardener taught him to make baskets.

I n March, Vincent was allowed back into the house, but by then, the damage was too extensive, and even Marcus looked at him with suspicion and kept well at a distance.

Vincent spent a lot of time in the staircase corridor for a new reason. He tried to do his duties as quickly as he could to slip away and avoid being under the eyes of the rest of the staff.

There were whispers and none too subtle glances exchanged. He tried to be thick-skinned, but it was difficult to ignore the kicks he received when he passed some of the footmen, and most of the maids avoided him with no pretence. He hadn't been so out of favour even as the slop boy. One could have mistaken him to be carrying the plague the way the staff were acting.

Mr Benton rarely came to Benton House these days, so no one was in the reception room. Through the crack in the wall, Vincent could make out a slice of a shiny suspended globe. It was right next to the desk, and the desk was not too far from the door, but it was still well out of Vincent's reach even had he dared to enter the room.

Vincent tried to read what was written on the surface of the globe, but all he could make out was 'te Skerries Island' above a tiny little dot with a vast spread of blue around it. He felt something akin to intrigue, but he hadn't much experience of such emotions, so he didn't know what to make of it.

There was an urge to find out more, but who could he possibly ask? The only person not avoiding or ignoring him was deaf and in another building.

The glimpse of the globe was Vincent's only link to this mysterious island somewhere far away from where he was. He tried to imagine what it must have been like out there, but the strangeness of it was too all-encompassing and there was nothing to fill in the void.

Beaches he knew of. They were where land and sea met. What was on beaches or what they consisted of, that he did not know. Did the land just end? Or was that 'a shore'? What was the difference between a beach and a shore? Which of the two did islands have?

There were books about these things in the several libraries in the house, but all of them were off limits to Vincent. He'd learnt to read from staff guidebooks and honed the skill by reading about gardening, but even had he feigned wanting to learn to read better, he knew he wouldn't be given access to actual knowledge. He would be offered the guidebooks again, or the Bible, and none of them had the appeal of a book about islands.

A servant did not need to know. A servant's place was at work, dedicated and unquestioning. A servant did not need to read well. It could be useful, but it was not required. A servant most definitely did not need to know the difference between a beach and a shore. Vincent had no basis to ask, even had he had someone to ask from. He looked at the 'Island' and wondered if or how he could ever get any closer to it.

M arch turned to April. Vincent's health was finally improving, the weather was mild and spring had the feel of summer drawing close. The musty staircase remained the same and Vincent had little to no chance of going outdoors, but his life at Benton House was undergoing small changes.

More parties were held at the house, so there were more people to avoid, with the members of the family and their guests crowding the halls. There was also bustle, albeit quiet bustle, in the passages.

Vincent became good at not only being quiet himself, but also at discerning the near silence of others from actual silence. He was caught sitting in the staircase corridor once or twice, but thankfully by servants who were too busy to think much of it. They were startled and picked up speed as they passed him, but no one reported him to the head maid or the housekeeper, so he could still return to peer through the crack to pass his scarce free time.

Normally a hall boy wouldn't have had the luxury of this much free time, but the positive to Vincent's predicament was that, as long as he kept out of the way and things got done, no one seemed to care where he was.

The downside to the bustle of April was that the reception room was used from time to time, not by Mr Benton, but the other members of the family, which meant that Vincent had to take extra care not to be seen or heard when the wall between them was so thin.

The noise from the room sometimes drowned the subtle sounds of the other servants, so Vincent had to be on his toes at all times, ready to move, if he wanted not to be caught. This made the staircase much less relaxing than it had previously been. What made it even less relaxing was the sudden announcement coming from the reception room:

"Bring the boy here. The small, scrawny one. I don't know his name, why should I know his name? He's a hall boy, probably. Usual-looking. The one that was ill this winter." Mr Benton was talking to the housekeeper. Vincent flinched.

The choice was to run up or down, and this time he chose up. Unfortunately, this too, was a mistake. The creaky stairs betrayed his whereabouts, and it did not take long until two maids and a footman had him surrounded in the narrow upstairs passage. Knowing how grave an offence it was to scream, he kept his mouth shut, but he did try to struggle a bit. It didn't make much of a difference.

Vincent was shoved into the washroom. One of the maids held him still while the other one scrubbed. His skin was red but mostly clean by the time they were done, and a clean set of clothes was hurriedly given to him to dress. The maids did not think he was quick enough dressing up, so some of this was done for him. They even combed his unruly hair before he was forcefully pulled back through the staff passage and to the reception room door.

The reason for this abrupt treatment was clear. Though Vincent was but a lowly hall boy and did not deserve such service, the guests in the room weren't used to seeing the likes of him. It would not do to subject them to such a sight, no matter how absurd Mr Benton's request. Mr Benton's brother, the more pompous and important Mr Benton, awaited just as eagerly, to see what sort of creature would emerge.

Vincent was pushed into the room. There were more people present than he had expected. He hurried to recall the advice in the guidebooks, how not to speak unless spoken to, and how to always remember to stand up straight with arms neatly at the sides. He had the impulse to turn toward the wall and wait without moving, but this was different from passing in the hallway. They were all looking at him and there was nowhere to hide.

"He's so tiny!" one of the ladies suddenly burst out to say, evidently unable to curtail her surprise any longer.

"Yes, he is, isn't he?" another one said almost admiringly. "Like a miniature, almost!"

"Shush ladies, you are shaming the lad," Mr Benton said, but clearly in jest. No one of his status would come to defend a servant unless to make a joke. Vincent stood there frozen, hoping for it to end.

"This be the cockroach crawling in the walls?" the other, less familiar Mr Benton asked.

"Yes, yes. Indeed. I may have referred to him as such once or twice. A useful cockroach, this one. Something which can't be said about most cockroaches." Polite laughter followed this statement. Both of the Misters Benton seemed pleased.

"But the time has come to fumigate, ladies and gentlemen." Mr Benton continued and patted the top of Vincent's head. He then shook his hand as if to be rid of dirt. All of this seemed unpleasant to Vincent, but he dared not move. "Mrs Sivens, take him to the drawing room. I will be there shortly," Mr Benton instructed the head maid, who stood at the door awaiting orders. As Vincent was escorted out of the room, tea was served to the guests to distract them, and shortly after, Mr Benton followed.

V incent had not expected there to be people in the drawing room. Mr Benton closed the door in front of Mrs Sivens and turned to face the man in the room. There was also a woman present, but she looked away and stood ignored.

"This is the boy," Mr Benton said. The man took Vincent's chin and lifted his face up to take a better look. It was not done roughly, but unused to being touched, Vincent flinched.

"Fidgety little thing, isn't he?" The man let go of Vincent's chin. His hands smelled starkly of fish and seaweed, but the Benton household rarely ate fish, so these smells were only barely recognisable to Vincent. "A little on the small side, but I see nothing that can't be fixed."

"Will you take him off my hands?" Mr Benton asked.

"I'm sure we can find a place for him."

"Good, then it's settled. Will you be staying for supper?"

"If it's all the same to you, we had best be going."

"All right, that is probably indeed for the best." Mr Benton turned Vincent around by the shoulders and bent down a bit to say something. He gave it a couple of starts, but couldn't come up with the right words, so he ended up merely patting Vincent's shoulders, checking that his shirt was tucked in and his collar was straight, and pushing him toward the door to leave with the sea-scented man.

The stranger took Vincent by the wrist—which was hardly pleasant—but his grip wasn't too tight, just firm, so Vincent did not struggle. He glanced back at Mr Benton, unsure what to think, baffled about what was happening, and unprepared for the sudden departure.

Mr Benton, though never very affectionate, waved briefly and watched them go. It took some years before Vincent understood the man's kindness. For now, he was too overcome by worry to form an opinion and too alarmed to act in any other way aside from obeying.

CHAPTER 13

The carriage was plain. Vincent had a faint recollection of having been on one of these kinds of horseless carriages before. It was one of the few faint memories of the time before Benton House.

The hissing and clunking steam engine moved it along at a steady pace, the pace being the only steady thing about it. Several stops had to be made to pick up more coal, and the thing negotiated bumps like it had no interest in ever reaching an agreement. Vincent felt as if his insides were being beaten into a fine paste, but they did eventually reach a town and its harbour.

A small white and red ferry sat at the end of the pier. The quiet woman took Vincent by the hand and led him across the plank and onto the gently swaying deck. Vincent was discombobulated by the carriage ride, so it took him a while to find his sea-legs. The woman seemed accustomed, despite wearing heels. She guided Vincent steadily to the seats.

Though she was attentive, she seemed preoccupied and regularly sought the sea-scented man's eyes. The man did not seem to pay any mind to her but concentrated instead on a small notebook with rows of indecipherable scribbles in it. Neither of them spoke much. Whatever questions Vincent had, he was too discouraged to ask them.

The seagulls circling around the ferry were much more talkative, but unfortunately, Vincent could not understand what they were saying. He would have wanted to know what birds they were and why they had come to see him off.

All this fresh, cool air was making him drowsy, but he was too worried to relax. He'd never been on a ferry. The couple beside him did not seem malicious, but he wished he knew where they were taking him and what sort of work they would put him to. The uncertainty kept him on edge, even as the afternoon turned into evening and all he could see were the lights of the ferry cast out to sea and flickering on the waves.

Vincent was given a blanket for warmth. Many of the other passengers were fast asleep, either sitting in their seats or huddled at the side of the deck. He didn't know it at the time, but this was one of the first ferries of the year, after weeks of unrelenting, stormy weather. Many of its passengers had waited a long time to come aboard. It was carrying more than its usual load, and that was why there weren't enough seats for everyone on board.

As a passing thought, Vincent wondered if he was supposed to give up his seat to someone else. After all, he was a hall boy and these other passengers were actual human beings. Ultimately, he was too tired to do so, but felt bad for taking up someone else's space.

V incent wasn't sure if he'd dozed off, but before he realised, they had arrived. It was just after dark and the air was foggy and grey, but the surroundings were so different from what he was used to, he couldn't help but gawk at the barely visible pale, rocky shore in front of him.

Amidst the darkness he could just about make out a series of long piers leading to boat sheds standing on stilts at either side of the lamp-lit dock and different shaped boats, some with tall masts and some with no masts at all, lining the piers.

The woman coaxed him to stand, though with patience. She took his hand again and guided him off the ferry, making sure he did not fall behind or get trampled by the other passengers.

Vincent made a point to memorise the shape and colour of her clothes and hair, in case she let go of his hand and he had to find her again. It was the first time he really took a good look at her. Her expression was sad and tense around the eyes, but she nevertheless seemed determined. She carried herself differently than what Vincent was used to seeing: more sure of herself and her worth. In fact, though she'd acted the obedient wife at Benton House, she was now in the lead and the sea-scented man followed in tow, rather than the other way around. It reminded Vincent of someone, but he couldn't quite recall who.

"Could you fetch our things, luv?" She spoke to her husband in a gentle but level tone.

The man grunted in agreement and peered to see where the ferry cargo was being unloaded. The woman pulled Vincent aside from the crowd and fixed and fiddled with his hair before she spoke.

"Welcome to Whitskersey, luv. This is your home now. My name is Aster. You'll be staying with us for a wee bit, until we find you a better place. Don't worry, luv. No harm will come to you, I promise." She smiled, and though her smile hinted melancholy, Vincent felt reassured. This felt better. It felt promising. No one had taken the time to be this kind to him for a long time.

Though not ready to trust her, Vincent's tension finally eased somewhat, and he wobbled alongside Aster as they started up the street and away from the dock.

Her husband trailed after them, hauling the luggage with both hands. He seemed quite content doing so. Something about this felt so much more natural, so much more comfortable to Vincent than life at Benton House ever had. He squeezed Aster's hand and hoped to never have to let go.

Aster didn't have children of her own yet. She'd tried with her husband, but it had ended in a miscarriage the year prior, and she was still too afraid to try again. Having Vincent as a houseguest at their little house in town was a welcome distraction, even if he was a bit of a peculiar handful.

He spent a lot of time in the cellar because, as he put it, it seemed where he ought to be. Both Aster and her sister Celandine, who lived together with them, had had to pull the boy out of there on occasion to sleep in his bed.

The bed was a little small, but a proper bed in a proper bedroom. Granted, it was their guest room and not specifically decorated to the tastes of a child, but Aster had added some toys and decorative things with Vincent in mind. It was a clean, airy and fresh room, so she couldn't understand why Vincent did not seem to like it. Sometimes she'd come by in the morning and find him rolled into a blanket, under the bed or in a corner. It took him more than a week to stay in his bed for the whole night.

The other children Vincent's age were already in school, but considering his peculiarities, Aster and Celandine agreed it would not be smart to enrol him just yet. They began to homeschool him to get to know him better and see where he was in terms of his development.

There were surprising gaps in his social skills, sense of humour and understanding of the world, though he was much further along in some areas than what either of them considered normal. He was unusually apt at reading for an eight-year-old. His vocabulary was broad. He seemed to know words even she hadn't heard and could explain their meanings precisely when prompted.

To cultivate his strengths and patch some of his weaknesses, Aster borrowed books from the library and fed Vincent one every week. They weren't thick, but he swallowed them at quite the speed. He seemed most drawn to books about the island and its flora, fauna and even geology, fishing and history. Once he'd meticulously studied those, he moved on to studying foreign countries. His thirst for knowledge about the world was astonishing.

Aster was quite pleased with Vincent's reading hobby, especially when she finally managed to get him to do it elsewhere than in the cellar, where it was much too dark for reading and too cold for a little boy to be spending so much time.

Teaching Vincent to play was much more challenging. He was timid about the very concept of having free time. He showed guilt and even became fearful if Aster did not give him enough chores during the day. She'd had to give him some to keep him from crying in abject terror, because he'd thought he was going to be discarded for being useless. Furthermore, she'd had to keep a close eye on him to tell him to stop or else he would continue to do them until late in the evening.

Aster had explained to him several times that she didn't need him to do anything around the house but that she would be happy if he used his time to do something he wanted to do. To this, he responded by staring at her, confused, and offering to polish some boots while he wasn't busy.

When he spoke, he sounded exceedingly polite and grown up. It was endearing, but knowing his background, it also broke Aster's heart. She was determined to give Vincent his childhood back, so to keep him busy, she did her best to think of tasks that were as close to play as possible. These included painting the garden shed, collecting decorative rocks for the garden, and looking for things around the house that Aster said she'd lost. The last one was a fun little game she also enjoyed herself. She knew perfectly well where all of her things were, but it always took Vincent a while to search for them if she hid them right.

Since Vincent was naturally inquisitive, Aster directed his attention to learning useful things, such as cooking and gardening. He also helped her husband George with some of the chores of his trade such as curing the fish and tending to the fishing gear, and it didn't take him long to absorb most of what there was to know about fishing, without ever having fished himself.

Once Vincent started to come out of his shell, he became a surprisingly social and bubbly boy. He made friends almost compulsively, and, as the summer drew to an end, the sisters reconvened and deemed him ready to go to school. It would do him good to be around other children his age who knew how to be children and could teach that to him.

CHAPTER 14

S omewhere at the back of his head, Vincent still felt distrust toward people and situations that seemed benign; there was no telling when a perfectly fine day could turn into a night of nightmares. Even so, he felt like he had exited a long, dark tunnel and all the fresh air and light was exciting him into overdrive.

School was every bit as wonderful as he had imagined. There were children who played with him without wanting treats in exchange. Vincent found himself becoming greedy of all the attention and fun, and it did not take long before he got into some rather unexpected trouble.

Vincent forgot himself periodically. His eyes would start shining as if he'd gone mad, or so he was told, and he'd feel a strange compulsion to ask questions from everyone around him until he was told to stop for being too nosey. He wasn't sure why he was doing this, but he couldn't help feeling like he had to.

His questions could be inquisitive, but they were also accommodating. Something along the lines of 'are you all right?', 'do you need something?' or 'do you want to play with us?' When someone gave him something, he enthusiastically gave it away, right away, because he felt so compelled to please the people around him. He pulled the more socially awkward and

quiet kids into games, gave them snacks, shared everything and became
cross at the teachers if there wasn't enough to share. This sometimes resulted in him not eating any lunch during the day because he had shared it
all away. He didn't mind because, as he pointed out very matter-of-factly,
he was 'well fed at home'.

He had the tendency to clean up the classroom by himself even when he
was told not to. They said it was supposed to be a group activity to teach
everyone the meaning of teamwork and responsibility, but it being such an
insignificant task he could easily do on his own, it made no sense to bother
the other kids with it.

Once his preoccupation with the other kids died down a little, he was
getting told off for being too engrossed in whatever he was doing. So engrossed, in fact, that he didn't pay attention to anything or anyone around
him. Celandine and the teachers at school seemed to be distressed by it,
monitoring him at all times, even when he was doing harmless, inconsequential things. Sure, he'd been hit by a stray ball in the school yard a couple
of times when he was busy with something, but that hadn't hurt nearly as
much as a footman's kick. He was also frequently toppled and run over by
the other kids, walked into a pit while looking up at the sky naming the
clouds, and stung by a bee while following a trail of ants, but these things
happened. There was no reason to get so worked up about it.

When he ran out of things to inspect in the yard, he couldn't resist
sneaking into the mechanics classroom. It was a treasure trove of supplies,
tools and machinery you could combine to make something truly fascinating. He'd almost got caught there on a number of occasions, but thanks to
his instincts, he'd ducked under a workbench or behind a crate in the nick
of time each time. Until the day came when he hadn't.

The teacher had to shake him awake before he realised he was somewhere he wasn't supposed to be. Thoroughly appalled by his own careless-
ness, he burst into tears. This time he was surely going to be thrown out,
both from the school and maybe even from the island! The thought was
so unbearable he continued to cry until they gave him permission to spend
most of his breaks in the mechanics classroom, so long as he followed a list
of rules they provided for him.

S ome of Vincent's closest new friends joined him in the mechanics classroom sometimes. Thankfully, this special treatment was let slide by the rest of the children, who were less inclined to be interested in mechanics and didn't think that being allowed into a stuffy classroom during playtime counted as favourable special treatment.

This was when Vincent made his first contraption. It was a little toy automobile that could move from one end of the classroom to the other with just one wind of the spring mechanism. It wasn't much, but it kept Vincent busy and out of trouble for a few months.

Never had Vincent been as happy and acquired as many new skills as when he was allowed into the mechanics classroom. Yes, he'd been taught to do chores and to memorise guidebooks at the workhouse, but this was different. Here he learnt to make choices for himself and to think and solve problems. For the first time, he learned how to draw and write. The other children teased him mercilessly for learning such simple things so late, but he was too happy to have learned at all to pay them any mind.

W riting was almost as fascinating as mechanics. He could jot down whatever he wanted, and it would stay on paper, exactly as he'd written it, for anyone to read. Unsure what to do with the skill, he asked Aster and discovered the fun of writing letters. Most of Vincent's pocket money from then on went to stamps and mechanical parts. He didn't get a lot, but it was more than he'd ever received, and it was enough to pay for seven letters each month.

Seven was a large number for someone like Vincent, and being Vincent, he made sure to stretch that number to as large as he could. He wrote small, and he wrote without margins. Writing this way, he could fit six full pages into an envelope, and the postman would agree to take it with just one stamp. Any more than that and he received looks and had to bribe the man with one of the sisters' biscuits.

Being a resourceful lad, Vincent did not just send letters to his friends. He sent them 'abroad'. This meant that he went to the docks, waited for the ferry, talked to the people who were heading out and asked them if they knew anyone 'abroad' who would like to receive a letter. Sometimes he could save the first stamp this way because people would take his letters out there for free. He even received a few replies and made regular pen-friends.

It pained him when the ferry stopped going and the mail flow from inland died down for the winter. Because he was building something big at the time, and most of his stamp-money went toward parts, anyway, he saved by delivering the remaining letters around town himself. He usually did this on Saturdays when there was no school and he'd finished all of his homework the day before.

One early Saturday morning before anyone was up, Vincent had already dressed up and prepared his mailbag, ready to go. He'd thought the winters were chilly before, but he soon discovered they had been mild compared to the weather on the island.

There was snow. He'd seen snow before, but it was a rare occurrence once or twice a year and it did not stay on the ground for longer than a day or two. Here, it was up to his knees by October. He had to wear special shoes and a heavy coat before heading out. They were hand-me-downs, but in such good condition, they felt as good as new.

Aster had knitted him a hat, scarf and mittens. Celandine had patched his trousers and mended a ripped seam of his coat. To Vincent, the sisters were something better than a mother, and having two taking care of him like this was like being spoiled rotten. Not only did he have Aster and Celandine, he also had Mr Bramble, who, though often away fishing, was a splendid substitute for a father.

Why these people, who were in no way related to Vincent, took such good care of him when his real parents hadn't, was unclear to him. It sometimes made Vincent suspicious, even anxious. Whenever he was not preoccupied by his excitement, he tried to make sure he was giving them something in return by being a good boy, doing chores and acting in a way the grown-ups called 'adorable'.

Vincent reached up to the door handle and peeked out. There was indeed snow. The streets were covered by a layer as thick as the distance from the toe tip of his boots to his heels. His feet were not very big, but the amount of snow was still impressive. He pushed the door closed behind him, carefully, so as not to make noise as he'd been taught.

Getting to go out was a luxury. Though he usually always gained permission by asking, he did not want to risk upsetting Aster or Celandine by waking them up. He'd left a note on the kitchen table that he was 'out on post rounds' and hoped it sufficed. If he got back before they woke up, he would destroy the note before either of them saw it and act like he hadn't been out yet.

The air smelled delicious. A neighbour was up, so Vincent could catch a whiff of a faint aroma of tea and scones, but that was not all. Snow. The snow smelled crisp and fresh and the cool air made Vincent's nostril-hair gather together for warmth. He breathed in for the fun of it. Then he exhaled a beady line of clouds like a steam engine and lunged down the few steps from the front door to the street, gaining speed.

Running with the snow crackling under his feet made it all the more exciting, and he almost missed the first turn, not paying attention. He'd planned his route in advance and accounted for some unnecessary but probable stops, such as at the handrails of the stairs near the shoemaker, where he enjoyed hanging upside down to watch the passers-by frown or chuckle at him, or by the bakery where, if he played his cards right, the nice lady offered him a freshly baked breakfast roll.

There weren't many people about, but more turned up as his rounds progressed. By the time he was at the other side of town, most of the little shops were turning their open-signs and people were leaving for work.

It wasn't a big town, so it didn't take Vincent long to learn most of the streets. It was large enough for there to be some parts he rarely visited, but small enough not to get lost in. Well, at least unless he really wasn't paying attention. Vincent had, once or twice, managed this feat when it had been dark or foggy.

Vincent had twelve letters in his bag. He usually had eleven, but this week, he'd added one after hearing about the birthday of a friend of a friend at school. He didn't know her all that well, but she wasn't very popular so she probably would not receive many birthday cards. Vincent had written her a short—only two-paged—letter with a small card attached he'd drawn himself. He hadn't spent an awful lot of time on it so as not to invite misunderstanding, but he'd drawn her a kitten with some cinnamon buns and a few nuts and bolts, which he thought were probably a safe thing to draw because they weren't flowers or hearts.

Flowers and hearts, he'd heard, meant you wanted to marry the girl someday. Vincent figured he wasn't equipped to make this big of a decision yet and decided to play it safe by picking other more neutral topics. There was a short poem in the letter about boats, fish guts and a tree house, and though some of the boys at school said that writing poems was for sissies, Vincent thought this one in particular was very manly, but also quite nice and meaningful, so the birthday girl would still probably appreciate it. The fish guts were a gamble, but she did not seem the squeamish type and they were essential for tying the different themes together.

Vincent's handwriting had improved immensely, partly due to practise but also out of necessity. It was no use writing letters if no one wanted to read them, and he'd noticed that the neater he wrote, the more likely his letters were read and replied to. He also added some embellishments and took a few artistic liberties to pique the reader's interest.

He didn't know this at the time, but some of the parents of his friends were grateful for his efforts, as his letters were possibly the only thing their children read voluntarily, and it went a long way to improve their literacy. It was not a big thing, but sometimes the smallish things grew into bigger things later on.

The name and address were especially neat on top of the envelope. Vincent inserted the first one through the slot and listened to the sound of it hitting the bottom of the mailbox. No one here was up yet. Vincent continued onwards. Around the sixth letter, he could hear the creak of someone raising the lid to retrieve the letter at once after it had fallen. To this, Vincent responded with a whispered greeting. A similar such greeting came back and was followed by the sound of socked feet running frantically up the stairs somewhere inside. Vincent smiled. They were so loud, and no one seemed to care. It was wonderful!

The sun was up, but it was still early. Vincent delivered the birthday girl's letter before taking a short break at the dock. He was warm from the running but didn't sit for long knowing his trousers would eventually lose the battle against his frosty seat, and his bottom would get cold.

He jumped up and down a few times, then inspected the underside of the nearest pier for debris he could use for his projects. He sometimes found useful nuts and bolts and bits of wood, but this time ended up with nothing.

It did give him a chance to study the mechanism with which the pier was connected to the cement slab on land. There was a slot there, up which the pier would slide as the sea froze over and ice pushed the structure inland. They had even left plenty of leeway so that nothing would break as it did so.

Vincent, as one with such interests, found this to be extraordinary ingenuity. Maybe one day he could come up with something useful like that!

Having dawdled more than he'd intended, Vincent began to worry about getting back. The last of the letters were quick to deliver because they were all addressed to the same household, but he was shaving it close. Celandine, at least, would be up by now. Although, if she was true to her routines, she would not notice Vincent gone, nor Vincent's note, until she was done with some of the washing up and started making breakfast. Vincent hurried back.

As luck had it, Celandine did catch him at the front door, but hadn't a clue as to how long he'd been out, so she merely eyed him sternly and told him to wash up for breakfast. Vincent smiled and was happy to oblige.

CHAPTER 15

When Vincent got the sniffles, he really got the sniffles. It had been worse at Benton House when his small frame had taken the full blow of whatever germs he was exposed to, but even if he was eating better and had gained size and weight, the new selection of cold bugs really gave him all they had to offer. It was unpleasant, very unpleasant, but having weathered worse in worse conditions, he was not fazed. Aster, on the other hand, seemed rattled and worried about every little thing.

"It's not that bad." Vincent tried to calm her down. It was the first proper case of cold he'd had this winter and he hadn't even a fever, just a sore throat and a runny nose. He'd made the mistake of mentioning the soreness, and Aster had become unduly alarmed. Vincent usually did not disclose these things, as in the past, it had made no difference to anyone if he felt sick or not. But Aster had specifically told him to tell, and he did not want to disobey. Why was she overreacting like this?

"It's probably best you don't go to school today." Aster offered Vincent a handkerchief.

"Bah," was all Vincent could say to convey his disappointment without being too demanding.

"We don't want all the other kids getting sick, do we, luv? So it'll be rest at home for you, all right?"

"All right," Vincent said but couldn't help sounding annoyed. He'd been looking forward to today. He was so close to being done with the thing he was working on in mechanics class. There would now not only be a day going to waste, but also a whole weekend in between him and the completion of said thing. It seemed so incredibly unfair!

And yet it was small compared to the next cold. The first had only lasted a day or two, but by the next, Vincent was reminded of a familiar pattern. He tried to play it down because of Aster's anxieties, but there wasn't much he could do to hide the runny nose and red cheeks, and he had to admit he felt a bit too poorly to want to go to school, no matter how tempted.

Vincent didn't mind the discomforts of being ill. He was more worried about the consequences. It hadn't been a year since he'd alienated the people close to him by becoming the insane, possessed demon child, so, desperate to keep himself from saying something horribly offensive, he stopped talking altogether.

It seemed to worry Aster initially, but she was already worried, so a little more made no difference. After a while, she came to the conclusion that Vincent had stopped talking because of a sore throat and, satisfied with this reason, no longer expected him to reply when spoken to.

"Would you eat something? I could peel an apple for you," Aster offered. It was the morning of the third day and Vincent felt quite ill, but not ill enough to stay in bed. He sat in the kitchen where it was warmest and watched Celandine prepare breakfast.

"How about soup?" Celandine suggested.

Vincent nodded. He had nothing against soup. His head felt stuffed today, the way it had when the trouble had started, and it made him feel highly strung. He tried to remain alert and on guard to avoid a mistake, but because he wasn't sure what he'd done wrong before, he didn't know what to keep an eye out for to prevent it from happening again.

The prospect of upsetting the sisters made Vincent weepy, but he did not want to worry them, so he tried to distract himself by concentrating on something else instead. Since his attention span wasn't great under the best of circumstances, trying to concentrate now seemed a gargantuan hurdle.

"Some bread with that?" Celandine asked again. Vincent nodded.

The straight questions were easier to recognise, especially if he could spot their lips moving. It was when they were talking more to themselves that he probably wasn't supposed to answer. Maybe. On occasion, their lips would move even when it was something that wasn't meant for him. It was often impossible for his child's mind to tell which was which, and if they said something he was supposed to reply to, they would be almost as annoyed having to repeat themselves or wait for an answer.

Sometimes people would say such vile and false things he felt compelled to defend himself. Those replies were usually the worst received, so whatever he did, he had to remember not to defend himself.

Celandine set a bowl of soup in front of Vincent, offered him a spoon and a loaf of bread, and sat down next to Aster for a moment. The two of them were chatting about things that were of no interest to Vincent, so he turned to the soup.

Celandine's cooking was always tasty compared to what he'd had to eat at Benton House. It was probably tasty, even without this stark comparison. Vincent couldn't taste much of anything for the cold, so he merely enjoyed the warmth and texture of the broth as he swallowed. His throat didn't feel too bad, but it was probably mostly because his head felt hazy from the fever rising. He tried to calm his nerves and put his mind to eating, but it was dreadful to try to do two things at once when even one was a problem.

"Is it too hot, luv?" Celandine asked. Vincent almost missed the question, as the susurrus in his ears began to grow louder.

"Huh?" he replied carelessly.

I can't believe he did that. He should have asked me.

Twenty-two and a half. Come again tomorrow. I should go pick up the flour for tomorrow. And we may need cheese.

Whoo boy, that was close! Shoo, why did the wee child have to jump across the street like that? Have a care!

I'll have a coffee and a ginger biscuit. That should be enough.

But he hates me, I can't believe he hates me.

I wish I could have seen his face when I pulled up that thing. It was enormous! Ahhahaa!

Vincent frowned. That didn't sound at all like Aster or Celandine. It sounded like a whole swarm of people, some voices cascading, others talking all at once.

"What is it, luv?" Aster leaned closer and tested Vincent's forehead. *Feels quite warm. Oh, dear.* She turned to reach for a small washcloth, dampened it with cold water and pressed it gently around Vincent's cheeks and face. It did not seem to help the voices.

Quite right. I don't care what she says, there ought to be laws for that sort of thing!

Crimson. Lavender. Crimson. Hmm. What about mauve? No, better make it crimson this time.

I have never seen such a huge head on a human being before, dear God!

It was no longer a mere susurrus; it was drowning out all else.

Vincent tried to concentrate to hear if either of the sisters said something, but the noise was too loud. There were too many voices. Male, female, children, gruff voices, smooth voices, familiar voices, strange voices, tiny voices, big voices, shouting, yelling, crying, laughing, all at the same time. Vincent covered his ears and crouched down. It was worse than before, much, *much* worse. He couldn't breathe.

Preoccupied by making it stop and trying not to scream from the frustration, Vincent wasn't sure when exactly Aster had taken him into her arms to rock him gently.

"There, there, it's the fever, isn't it?" Her voice was slightly clearer than the rest, and Vincent tried to focus on it to ease the confusion. He woke up from the noise to feel the cool washcloth on his forehead.

"I don't want to... I'm not..." Tired by his illness, Vincent struggled to find the words to explain how he felt. Maybe if he could explain it to them well enough, they would understand? Aster hushed him gently and kept cooling his forehead.

"Please don't hate me, please..." Vincent whispered, and clung to the front of Aster's ruffled shirt. "Please..." He started to cry. Why was this so much more painful and frightening than the handful of times he'd cried before? There had to be something seriously wrong with him. All he could do was try to convince them he wasn't bad, that he was good, that he wanted to stay, that he did not want to go back.

Aster hushed him gently and held him close. He needed to shut up before she got angry, but he couldn't help himself. The noise around him was loud again, roaring like the stormy sea. People were yelling at him, angry and upset, and he didn't understand why. All he knew was that he needed to shut up and not say anything.

Whatever you do, do not defend yourself.

I t took the sisters less than a week of similar fevers to decide that something had to change. To Vincent's relief, it wasn't as bad as he'd feared. He wasn't cast out completely, but moved into a cottage well outside of town, where he was cared for and homeschooled by Celandine. He was often lonely and missed Aster, George and the few friends he'd made, but when he was ill, he was glad to be where he could rest peacefully and not be surrounded by the crowds of yelling people that rendered him witless.

CHAPTER 16

M r Swifty had lived on the island all his life. He'd quite enjoyed it. There was plenty to eat, places to discover and enough friendly neighbours for a comfortable standard of living.

He frequented some of the barns, storage rooms and other out-buildings in the area during the summer months. Winters were a little rougher for strays around these parts, but there were a few kind-heart-ed locals who let him stay in their front room or attic in exchange for keeping the mice population in check. Some were even kind enough to feed him occasionally.

The Brambles' cabin at the cape was a little out of the way, but one of his personal favourites. Ever since Mrs Bramble had disappeared, however, the quality of service had dropped to such an extent, Mr Swifty made the effort to wade through the fresh blanket of snow, all the way back to Vincent's house.

There was a flap made specifically for Mr Swifty, so he could enter even when no one was at home. Sometimes the snow would cover it, and he'd have to dig a little to find it. If it was buried too deep, Mr Swifty would circle around the house to see whether Vincent would be around to open one of the doors, to avoid any unnecessary labour.

He hadn't expected Vincent to be at home since he usually only came around during the summer months. The man had spent the last winter here, though, so Mr Swifty had dared to hope this might be the case again. Vincent seemed exceptionally responsive to requests, kept his cottage toasty more often than not, and didn't skimp on the offerings. Dethroning Mrs Tweed, he was now the number one option.

As luck had it, Vincent was there, but for whatever unfathomable reason, he had replaced his previous houseguest with a most unpleasant moppet! The kid had no respect for the rightful pecking order and insisted on treating Mr Swifty like a pest. Thankfully, Vincent lent no ear to his nutty opinions, and Mr Swifty got to enjoy his usual spot in the corner of the inglenook, unpestered. He wouldn't go against Vincent as the owner of the house and the provider of the food, but the cowardly moocher was easy to keep at bay with a hearty growl and a hiss.

When the pesky sponger had gone to bed and Vincent sometimes remained in the main room, Mr Swifty would glide to his side, jump onto his lap and let out a proper purr to show appreciation. It wasn't often that he bestowed this privilege upon a chosen someone, and as a like-minded free spirit, Vincent seemed to understand its value.

The man had always been kind toward Mr Swifty, with the sole exception of that time he had stepped on Mr Swifty's tail. Mr Swifty had bitten the attacking slipper without mercy. Sadly, Vincent's toe had been in said slipper, and, with not much protection, it had been thoroughly pierced. This had caused Vincent, an otherwise docile and calm-tempered man, to raise his voice and to throw Mr Swifty out through the back door. Mr Swifty hadn't dared to crawl back in until late the following night.

Inside the house, Vincent had scattered interesting toys on the shelves, sills and tables. It had taken some empirical testing, but Mr Swifty had soon determined which of them were exclusively Vincent's property and which he could mangle without reprimand. Vincent had even made some especially for him and left them in the corner of the inglenook, along with a bowl of water and some dried meat snacks.

This year's selection was equally pleasing and more consistent than the year before, provided that the ninny of a lodger did as told and served him the right stuff when Vincent was too ill to do it himself. Mr Swifty could get all three meals without having to leave the house, though he sometimes did, regardless, to engage in the sport of finding shrews, voles and other small creatures amidst the snow.

Hunting was enjoyable, but he had reached an age where the warm inglenook had its apparent advantages.

It also gave him the opportunity to observe Vincent's day-to-day doings, and he did so with great interest.

"Ah, Mr Swifty. Hasn't it been another spectacularly boring day today?" Vincent slouched over the far side of the table from where Mr Swifty sat.

"Well, I don't know. Has it?" Mr Swifty responded to test the waters. He'd noticed that he was most likely to be heard when Vincent looked flustered and tired. He was looking positively beaming with red today, and there was no sign of that interfering freeloader, Jones.

"It certainly has so far. And even if it weren't, I don't think I'd have the strength to do anything worthwhile," Vincent mumbled. This appeared a very promising start.

"Isn't it, then, a good thing not to have anywhere to go?" Mr Swifty asked swiftly.

"Hmm, you have it good. All you ever need to think about is finding food and a warm place to sleep."

"What? You think that's easy? When you're not here, the house is cold. The neighbours never let me past the front room, and the front room is often chilly."

"They do feed you all right, don't they?"

"That they do. I almost never have to take hunting seriously. And that is good. The prey is lean this time of year. Nowhere near as tasty as some of the leftovers the Crumpet family leaves out for me."

"The Crumpets taken a shine to you, have they?" Vincent rubbed his nose and eyes tiredly.

"I tolerate their toddler. They think it's cute. And I try to keep a neat appearance. They seem to appreciate that too." Mr Swifty was reminded to start grooming himself, as he hadn't done so for a while, and the warmth from the fire was starting to get a bit uncomfortable.

"Oh yes, they had a son, did they? When was that? I don't even remember."

"Spring before last. You weren't here then. Didn't you visit them last winter? I recall you leaving the house a lot at one point when the weather was clearer."

"No, I went to see the Farnsworths and the Brambles, mostly. And then all the way into town for the appointments with Dr Poppycock."

"How is the old man? I've hardly seen him since he moved into town."

"Same as always, I reckon. Talking to him is a waste of time. He wants me to make rugs, soap and candles, as if I weren't already up to my ears with crafts."

"None of those bear any interest to me. Couldn't he have suggested fishing or hunting?"

"I don't think he has the imagination to suggest hobbies that could be in any way athletic or manly. Most of his patients are women bored by their husbands in need of something to do. I'm assuming he's dispensing exactly the same advice to me as he does to them. That's why the market is filled to the brim with crafts in the summer. The wives make them during the winter and then sell them as soon as the weather improves enough." Vincent seemed to remember something. "Ah, yes," he said, "they also hold a market for the Midwinter Festival. Perhaps I should attend this year."

Last year, Vincent had had a gloomy spell around the time of the festival when the previous lodger had left. Vincent had stayed in bed for about a week. Mr Swifty remembered having to scavenge the pantry for food items until Vincent pulled himself together enough to care to feed them both again.

"That might be nice. I'm going into town next week too. Sylvia, you see."

Sylvia was the governor's cat, a lustrous white long-hair with the sweetest round ears and the puffiest tail Mr Swifty had ever seen.

Well, besides his own. He was quite proud of the state of his lengthy grey whip of fluff. It was especially remarkable considering that he was a short-hair except for said tail and the backs of his legs.

"Everybody has got someone." Vincent sighed and let his head fall onto the table with a thud. Mr Swifty jumped onto the table and sat next to the man's ear, pushing him gently. Then he whispered into the ear in front of him.

"You would probably have someone too if you weren't so, gosh darn it, picky."

"Pffft," Vincent pffft'ed, sliding into a quiet moan.

"You don't have to be so dramatic about it. Self-pity won't get you very far. Just pick someone."

"What do you know? You have your Sylvia. She's probably perfectly cute and cuddly and not at all a treacherous, conniving, selfish little b—" Vincent's complaint fizzled into a tired whine. His face was still firmly planted against the table somewhere under his shaggy head of hair. He could have used a haircut.

Mr Swifty hissed at him, though half-heartedly, to remind him that such vulgar words should not be uttered in the same sentence as the name of his lovely Ms Sylvia. He then poked Vincent with his paw for good measure, but made sure his claws were withdrawn to avoid tangling himself on Vincent's hair and knitted sweater.

"I bet everybody has someone but me. Even Jones seems to have his eyes on some of the girls in town, or wherever the hell he went today." Vincent lifted his face up for enough time to express his discontent.

"Fools," Mr Swifty noted briskly. "He makes awful food and doesn't know how to read!" The dimbus had given poor Vincent the wrong medicine. It was no wonder Vincent was feeling poorly.

D r Poppycock's office had that distinct musty stench of old that many of the houses had around here. The doctor, too, was a fairly old man, at least compared to young Mr Jones. He wrinkled his nose in distaste of the decor while the doctor still had his back turned. These people were so backward out here, and hopelessly behind the times.

Dr Poppycock turned in his chair, massaged his greying temples and invited Mr Jones to sit on the sofa reserved for his patients. For the time being, Mr Jones played along and began by telling some of his more mundane worries. Being able to talk about them felt refreshing, but because it was not why he was here, he quickly shifted the topic to Vincent and Vincent's problems.

"I heard someone mention he hadn't left for the winter, despite my recommendation. So, it is indeed true, he is still on the island?" The doctor stroked his impressive moustache. It resembled the tail-end of a squirrel rather than anything reasonable a gentleman would wear.

"Yes." Mr Jones felt a pang of guilt but refused to let it interfere with his ambitions. "Due to some unfortunate circumstances, he was unable to leave. I'm afraid he isn't faring well."

"This does not surprise me," Dr Poppycock replied, appearing most displeased by the news.

"I'm not worried so much about my own safety, you understand." Mr Jones picked up the ink blotter on Dr Poppycock's desk to examine the silver goose on its knob. What a ridiculous choice for a motif in an office! It reminded him of the silverware used during the Midwinter festivities. "Although, I do admittedly find his episodes a little unnerving, considering how far we are out there in the middle of nowhere, should something happen."

"I'm afraid I would have to see him personally, so as not to break doctor–patient confidentiality. All I can do is urge you to persuade him to come to me."

"He hasn't expressed any willingness to do that, sir."

"Ah, yes, he can be stubborn at times." The doctor rubbed his bushy beard, mouth puckered and face twisting into a thoughtful frown. "I am not wholly unsympathetic to your predicament, but unfortunately, it is quite the unpleasant process to force someone into psychiatric care. I would recommend trying to get him to come willingly. Otherwise, it might be for the best to leave him be, so long as he poses no danger to himself or you. He doesn't, does he?" Dr Poppycock cocked an eyebrow along with his question. Mr Jones was tempted to claim Vincent did, but he wasn't sure whose word the doctor would ultimately trust, and it was too big of a risk to test.

"No, not yet at least," he said instead. "But he has been under the weather recently. I fear it is affecting him mentally. He seems to be in an increasingly fragile state."

"Oh, you need not worry about that. He was a sickly child, from what I've been told. My theory is that it's just how his body is conditioned to respond to the situations he finds unfavourable." Dr Poppycock turned around to reach for his notebook. "But that is all I can tell you for the time being. If it gets serious, you should consult a physician, not me. He's far more likely to respond to a physician right now." The man flipped through his notebook. "Ah, here's the address of Dr Jacobs. That's where he goes for his check-ups. I'm afraid we are out of time. Do tell Vincent to come and see me when he can."

"Will do," Mr Jones said, hiding his disappointment. He set the ink blotter back on its tray and the goose seemed to mock him as it rocked a few times back and forth.

To put in this much effort and gain so little, was a disgrace! He would have to be more persistent to get what he wanted. Somehow, he'd have to find a way to persuade Vincent not only to come and see Dr Poppycock, but also to allow him to stay while they had their talk. He wasn't sure Vincent trusted him to that extent, so the only alternative was to eavesdrop.

As Mr Jones left Dr Poppycock's office with Dr Jacobs' address in his hand, he wondered if the physician might be the key to solving his conundrum. Going through his options, he was in awe of the depth a person could sink to in order to get what they wanted.

He was, of course, referring to himself.

I t was frightening how easily Mr Jones was able to obtain what he needed. That Dr Jacobs was a naïve, simple man had helped a lot. The doctor had suspected nothing when Mr Jones had turned up inquiring about the side-effects of various medicines. It had taken some digging to find a suitable drug that had the appearance of cough medicine, yet produced the desired effects, but he'd found just the thing. Now all he needed to do was get Vincent to take it.

CHAPTER 17

The infuriating scrounger was acting shifty. Mr Swifty observed him come in with the suspicious, smelly packages and bags filled with curious jars of pickled vegetables, salted fish, and tarts and other confectioneries. He offered Vincent, who was lounging half on top of the table as per his custom, a selection on a plate.

As a safety measure, Mr Swifty casually peed on these offerings. It did the job, because the ungrateful mooching scoundrel tossed Vincent a rag and retreated into his room to sulk. Vincent was not pleased about this act of kindness, but that was no reason for Mr Swifty to be careless.

Jones could not be trusted. Especially after the penny bun pie that had brought with it the return appearance of Mr Steak and his meaty dancing fellows. While amusing to watch, it did not seem to improve Vincent's mood and when Vincent was in a rotten mood, the stay at his house became less of a luxury.

"Captain Birchbark, on the maiden voyage of his ship Maid Amber-Custard the third! Stormy seas! It was raining octopi by the dozen!" Mr Swifty declared, hoping to help Vincent with the closing words for the book he was writing. They were morphing into a fictional short story the further Vincent wrote.

"I will have none of that, thank you." Vincent erased a portion of what he'd written. "Captain Percival Cogboot, fierce pirate of the eight seas, feared even on various lakes and ponds. He was a man to appear out of nowhere to pillage and plunder—" Vincent stopped. "That does sound a tad overused. Would he rather poke with sticks and torment only ever so lightly, instead?"

"Captain Birchbark," Mr Swifty repeated, "It was raining octopi! With quite some force."

"How would you know? You weren't there." Vincent wrote his sentence about the poking and the light torment.

"Neither were you." Mr Swifty huffed. There was quite a lengthy pause as Vincent wrote, refusing to be interrupted. He got all the way to the bottom of the page before he stopped again.

"Blasted deities! This book was not supposed to be about pirates. Whose idea was this?" He turned to look at Mr Swifty, ready to place blame.

They looked at one another for a moment, and Mr Swifty gave him the look he always gave him when he felt he was being an idiot. Vincent frowned.

"Look at me. I'm talking to a cat. I really ought to go out more. What do you think, Mr Swifty? I hear Aster and George have finally made amends, so should we visit them this afternoon?" he suggested.

"Only if you carry me in your rucksack when we come back. The snow gets so nippy late in the evening."

"I should probably bring a bag, just in case."

"Bring some cheese for me to have on the way. It gives me gas, but Mrs Bramble serves me cream, which will do the same, and it's the Brambles, so no one will notice."

"I'd better take something to eat for the trip there. I wonder if we have cheese left."

"None of that stuff the freeloader has brought. Meat is good, too. Mmmm, do you still have that chewy meat?"

"Ah, look, there was still some heart left for you. You like that, don't you?"

"Indeed, thank you." Mr Swifty purred at Vincent's feet as he peered into the cool end of the pantry.

Vincent was a good man. Peculiar, of course, but you could always count on him to be considerate, even when he was feeling better, and the conversation was technically one-sided.

Mr Swifty watched Vincent dress in layer upon layer of clothes before wrapping himself into his winter coat. He put on a pair of blue mittens he had knitted himself, on top of which he pulled some thick leather gloves. Similarly, he had a blue knitted hat that he covered with a bigger leather one with ear flaps hanging from its brim.

After slipping into a warm pair of boots halfway up to his knees, he opened the door and let Mr Swifty hop into the cold winter air ahead of him. Mr Swifty occasionally glanced back to check that Vincent was following, even if his footsteps were audible at all times.

As a seasoned veteran of walking to the cape and back, Mr Swifty knew the way even with his eyes closed. It wasn't the easiest terrain to negotiate. On a different day, he wouldn't have bothered to leave the house at all because deeper, softer heaps of snow could easily add several hours to the journey. But today a layer of ice about the thickness of his paw had formed on top of the snow, and it was enough to support his weight.

The chain of shallow paw prints formed a remarkably straight line across the snowy landscape and all the way to the Brambles' cabin at the cape. It wasn't this straight just for the sake of Mr Swifty's pride, although he did like to think he was a clever little creature. More than that, he was in a hurry. After all, it was bloody cold outside and the sooner he got to where he was going, the sooner he could be at the warmth of a roaring fire.

He had his coat of fur, but it didn't do much to warm his paws, and there weren't many things that quickened the step better than having to walk barefoot through snow. Thanks to this and Vincent's long stride, they were at the Brambles' cabin in a couple of hours and just before dark.

M r Swifty yawned. He'd spent a comfortable night sleeping at the foot of Vincent's bed after they had returned from the Brambles' cabin late in the evening. He always slept well after a brisk walk outside. Vincent had tossed and turned a little more than on most nights, but the bed was wide and the corner he occupied was usually left undisturbed.

"Good morning," Mr Swifty said to Vincent, who was also yawning and opening his eyes slowly.

"Good morning, Mr Swifty." Vincent rolled out of bed as agilely as a sack of awkward-shaped boulders. "I guess you're wanting some breakfast. Let's see if I can find you something." He pulled the cover along with him and used it as a cape.

Mr Swifty stretched diligently before following the cape. He could not restrain himself from yawning, cued in by Vincent who repeated the process several times before he appeared even remotely awake.

The fire was out, but the fireplace retained heat well enough, so the main room was still lukewarm. The deceitful cadger was nowhere to be seen, but there was a plate of suspicious biscuits left on the kitchen counter. Vincent did not seem interested in them. Good.

"Some meat would be nice," Mr Swifty suggested at the door of the pantry, when the man merely stared into it, seemingly unable to decide.

"Indeed. How about bacon and eggs?" Vincent reached for the packet of bacon and the egg basket.

"Isn't that all you ever have?" Mr Swifty rolled his eyes.

"I can't think of anything else right now."

"Fever seems to be on the rise."

"Yes." Vincent tested his forehead. "I'm talking to you, aren't I?" He turned to look at Mr Swifty.

"Well, you always talk to me," Mr Swifty pointed out. He did the cat equivalent of a shrug.

"Yes, but you seem to be replying." Vincent did not even bother trying to stifle the next big yawn. "Maybe I'm still asleep and this is just a dream."

"No, it's the fever. Now give me some breakfast. I'd like my bacon raw and eggs without the whites, please."

"You're such a lovely source of encouragement, dear old pal."

"Just doing what I need to do to get these things done. Now move it... please." Mr Swifty pushed against Vincent's feet to get him to move.

"Fine, fine. I hear you. No time to be ill when you've got a cat to feed."

Vincent filled Mr Swifty's breakfast order before starting on his own. Mr Swifty had already eaten by the time Vincent got to frying his bacon and eggs. He seemed to be chewing on something. Mr Swifty jumped onto the counter to check what it was.

Ah, those damn biscuits! He took a tentative sniff, but the stupid things were so packed with spices, it was difficult to discern anything out of place. Vincent put down the other half of the biscuit.

"Do you have any of those round yellows? I heard Mrs Bramble say they were good for 'vitamin sea'. It will help with the cold," Mr Swifty advised, hoping it would divert Vincent away from the suspect sugary spice discs.

"Vitamin C? You mean oranges?"

"Yellow, orange, same thing. It's not as if I could tell them apart. Half the time I think you people are making things up. They all look the same to me."

"I might have some. Thanks for your concern." Vincent was about to go rummage in the pantry, so Mr Swifty stopped him post-haste.

"Finish what you're doing first! You don't want to burn down the house!"

Frying made Mr Swifty nervous even under normal circumstances, because it involved burning hot things, but more because it made those unnatural crackling and popping sounds. It did not seem smart to let Vincent leave his skillet untended while he forgot himself in the pantry. He was periodically staring into thin air as it were, and Mr Swifty had to push his calves to get him to stop.

"You're being a bit of a busybody today, aren't you?" Vincent combined his next yawn with a short neck massage.

"You should be grateful." Mr Swifty huffed and jumped up onto the countertop. "Someone needs to look out for you. You're such a scatterbrain."

Vincent was impulsive and unpredictable and often did things Mr Swifty did not understand, but he'd learnt to recognise some of the recurring patterns. Fever meant those patterns were thrown askew and nothing good was likely to come of it. And then there was that biscuit. He should have peed on that stuff as soon as he'd had the chance.

Vincent smiled.

"Thank you," he said. Then he did the unthinkable and picked Mr Swifty up to hug him.

It was one of those things Mr Swifty found deeply baffling. The scratches behind the ears and neck were nice, but the crushing intimacy of a hug made him uncomfortable. Vincent usually seemed to share this aversion, so Mr Swifty was shocked by this turn of events.

Sure, he had allowed some of the women-folk to squish him every now and then because there were treats in it for him, and he admitted to enjoying Vincent's lap for the comfort it provided, but those were the only two exceptions!

"All right, that's enough affection, thank you." Mr Swifty tried to squiggle himself loose from the grip. Vincent was amused by this but let him back down onto the countertop. "These surprise hugs have got to stop. At least give me a warning beforehand."

"But then you'd have time to run away." Vincent poured his bacon and eggs onto a plate and turned off the gas cooker. "I'd better relight the fireplace. Looks like it'll be a clear and cold day today."

"Yes, do that," Mr Swifty agreed, disgruntled that his objections hadn't been taken as seriously as he'd hoped.

It wasn't as if he didn't like the occasional pat on the back or ruffle of fur. Vincent had long fingers. They were apt at scratching and ruffling. Just that, if he absolutely had to do that whole body stuff, a little forewarning would have been nice!

"Don't you start sulking. Who's going to keep me company if you don't?" Vincent asked while loading the fireplace.

"The dust? The logs? The bacon? You look ready to include them in our conversation soon, anyway."

"Uh huh, really?" Vincent tested his forehead again. "Should I fetch the thermometer to be sure...?"

"Cheeks are red, you have the congested, stuffed-up look, and who knows what was in that biscuit you ate. Rest is what you need, and you don't need me for company then."

"You have someplace to be?" Vincent frowned. He used a gas lighter he'd constructed from whatever spare parts he'd had lying around to light the fire. He was an impatient man and having to relight the fireplace every day was not something he enjoyed doing for the time it would have otherwise taken him. The lighter expelled a large, bright-blue flame and made the sort of noise that made you want to take a few cautionary steps backwards, if not flee from the spot. It did its job though.

"I might," Mr Swifty replied.

"Like where?" Vincent put down the gas lighter and sat down on a stool. This was good because it made him sway less.

"None of your business," Mr Swifty said curtly.

"You don't have to be so snappy about it." Vincent reached over to the countertop to pick his plate of bacon and eggs. He was barely teetering on two of the legs of the stool, and the smallest error in judgement would've sent him falling sideways to the floor. With luck rather than skill, he managed to retrieve his food without mishaps. Though the plate was now in front of him, he didn't look much closer to eating it.

"No appetite?" Mr Swifty asked. If Vincent wasn't going to eat it, Mr Swifty still had room for seconds. It didn't matter that the flavour had been somewhat ruined by the cooking process. It was still bacon and eggs.

"No." Vincent sighed. "I should eat it since I made it. I should eat something, at least."

"I don't mind unloading it for you, if you'd like," Mr Swifty offered and parked his butt next to the plate. Vincent wasn't too keen on him walking on the table, but the man had long since given up on trying to shoo him away.

"No, I'll eat it. Eventually." Vincent took a piece of bacon and held it up between his fingers. After watching it for a while, he dropped it back on the plate.

"Doesn't look like it."

"I'm building up to it."

"It's getting cold." Which was when it was much easier to eat, but humans seemed to prefer scalding their mouths when they ate, the curious creatures. Vincent at least held this strange and strangely persistent notion that food should be eaten while it was still steaming or sizzling. It seemed painful, but Mr Swifty respected the man's preferences.

"I know," Vincent mumbled. He then seemed to fall asleep for long enough for Mr Swifty to relieve him of a couple of bacon strips without him noticing.

There had been a time when Mr Swifty had been more worried over Vincent's irregular behaviour, but after a while, he'd grown used to it. He could see how sleeping on a stool against a table could sometimes be refreshing, though he couldn't quite understand why Vincent had chosen to fall asleep on top of his eggs.

Mr Swifty decided to help him out a little by licking his nose until he rolled away from the plate. Vincent continued his nap for a while longer and then woke up to give the air another blank stare.

"I had a dream you were talking to me," Vincent said when Mr Swifty walked past his view.

"I talk to you all the time. What else is new? How's that fever of yours? Is it getting any better?"

"Evidently not, since you're still talking to me."

"I'm always talking to you; you just don't always understand what I'm saying."

"You're a cat. I'm not supposed to understand what you're saying, ever."

"And yet there you are, doing it perfectly fine, anyway."

"Yes, but this isn't real. It's my imagination playing tricks on me."

"Oh, really? Is that so?"

"Don't taunt me. I'm not feeling well."

"If my words are your imagination, then how come I can say that there's a juicy rat living in the Brambles' cellar? You don't know this. You haven't seen it. You can even go check if I'm telling the truth. It's there. I've been waiting for the right time to have him for lunch."

"It's my imagination putting words in your mouth. Most people have rats in their cellar. I bet there is one in the Brambles' as well."

"How about if I tell you that Ms Rose has a birthmark on her left thigh?"

"I don't want to find out if that is true or not."

"Then how do you explain all the times you've known how people feel and what they think, and you've helped them along with whatever problems they were having? Was that all just a coincidence?"

"I'm good at reading people, as well as paranoid. I've had practice."

"Yes, but—" Mr Swifty was starting to lose patience. Why was he always so stubborn about this?

"Stop trying to convince me I'm going insane. There's no such thing as telepathy. They're all just coincidences. I'm tired and stressed out, and I have a fever. It's nothing but my overactive imagination."

"Ass." Mr Swifty turned around to show said portion of his body to Vincent, then sat down facing the other way. After a moment of silence, he could feel Vincent stroking the tip of his tail with the back of his hand. He hadn't bothered to lift his cheek from the table, much less move, so that was as far as he could reach.

"Sorry. I didn't mean to hurt your feelings. I'm sure you're a very intelligent cat. I just can't afford to think we're actually having a conversation right now, with the bubble right there and someone keeping an eye on my every move." He then proceeded to blow air at Mr Swifty's long tail hairs so that they fluttered in the warm air.

"I'm telling you, you're not crazy. You're a little eccentric, but you're not crazy." Mr Swifty moved his tail back and forth to avoid the attention.

"I think I should start seeing Dr Poppycock again."

"I'm not opposed to that, but I don't think you need to. It's more likely Jones put something in those biscuits."

"I need some rest..." Vincent got up shakily. He recovered the cape of a cover he'd discarded while making breakfast, and tottered back into the bedroom, dragging it behind him.

CHAPTER 18

Dr Poppycock was astonished to see how quickly Mr Jones had managed to drag Vincent to his office. The lad had to have been incredibly persuasive!

Vincent didn't seem to have lost weight but looked as lanky and lumpy as ever in his oversized attire, and the tan he'd managed to acquire during the summer had long since faded to reveal his usual sickly pale complexion.

"Good to see you," the doctor lied. "I'm glad you came." Not so much a lie, but common courtesy devoid of substance.

"Thank you. I—, what are you still doing here?" Vincent glanced at Mr Jones, who was about to follow them into Dr Poppycock's office. "Wait outside."

Mr Jones looked highly displeased to be shown out of the room, but Dr Poppycock was sure they would have no trouble managing without the young man. The doctor asked Vincent to take a seat and sat down behind his desk.

This would be interesting. Vincent seemed to have a constant inner struggle between his excessive belief in what was scientific and his lack of understanding of phenomena of the more peculiar, spiritual nature.

Dr Poppycock wasn't an extremely spiritual man himself, but, whilst he did enjoy the scientific view, he felt there were some things about the human psyche that mankind had yet to fully understand. Taking a purely clinical view and closing one's mind from all the possibilities did not seem entirely wise. That was why Dr Poppycock was willing to give certain things the benefit of a doubt.

In Dr Poppycock's expert opinion, Vincent was—lacking a better scientific term—quite bonkers. He was a lovely mixture of traumatic neurosis, obsessive thinking, recurrent compulsions, hypochondria, paranoia and dementia praecox, to suggest but a few. Dr Poppycock was yet to pick the best suited diagnosis but considered it a welcome challenge to try. Perhaps this time he would reach a conclusion or come up with an all new diagnosis.

"How are you doing?" he asked. Vincent seemed more distraught than he'd expected. More scattered by his usual nervous disposition.

"Fine," the man replied, then withdrew and corrected himself: "No, not fine. I mean, at the risk of sounding too direct, I seem to be broken again."

"Ah, this breakage you speak of, what seems to be the problem?" The doctor used his most professional, calm therapist's voice, because it always put the patients so well at ease.

"I have— I seem— I," Vincent waffled, unable to even start. This could take a while. "I, I seem to have something wrong with me. I don't know where to start."

"Wherever you feel comfortable, take your time." Something about his condition seemed even worse than the year before, though at the time he wouldn't have thought it possible.

"I've been hearing those voices again. The ones that aren't there. Also, I swear Jones has been enabling my delusions. I'm not sure why. To tell you the truth, I am here because I wanted someone to talk to..." He lowered his voice. "...about him. I don't trust him. You wouldn't have an acquaintance who would be willing to give him a place to stay until spring? The current arrangement is not working for me. I fear it might not end well."

"Oh? What has he said or done that makes you feel uncomfortable or as if he was, as you said, enabling you?" Paranoia could be such a nasty ailment to deal with, especially for someone living such an isolated lifestyle. Vincent seemed to be firmly in its grip now.

"He confirms things. As if they were true."

"You mean the voices?"

"Yes."

"And you suspect he might be doing it for... what reason, do you think?"

"I don't know. To mess with me?"

"Does that sound like something Mr Jones would do?"

"Not as such," Vincent admitted.

"Have you considered the possibility that Mr Jones is, in fact, not speaking to you at all when you say that he is confirming what you say? Perhaps you are hearing what you want to hear, or mistaking what he is saying?"

"So you think it might just be my paranoia?"

"How does that make you feel?"

"I— I should be able to tell what's real and what is not."

"I hear you have been ill recently. You need not be so rough on yourself. Fever can temporarily cause confusion in any of us. It is not uncommon."

"Yes, but he insists on talking about it, even when I don't think I'm all that feverish. Does that mean I am finally losing my mind completely? Can you recommend a medicine for this?"

"I would not be as quick as that to medicate you, my friend. We have been through worse. I am sure we can give it some time to wait and see. Have you stayed in contact with your friends and family? Have you had anyone else to talk to besides Mr Jones?"

"Not as of late. I briefly visited Aster and George, but that was almost a week ago. Edward occasionally pops by with the plough and stays for a while if I'm fit to have a decent conversation."

"That is good. You should spend a little more time with a wider circle of people. It will keep you grounded and give perspective."

"I'm not sure... I— I don't want to alienate the few friends I have on the island. If I start hearing voices in their presence, what if I scare them off? I'd rather not become a laughingstock, nor a hermit indefinitely. Are you sure you do not have a drug for this?"

"What if we started the sessions again and looked into finding somewhere for Mr Jones to stay, since in your mental state, the situation doesn't seem healthy for either of you? How would that make you feel?"

"Honestly? Relieved. He is young. We have nothing in common, nothing to talk about. I feel like I ought to be entertaining him at all times.

I'm not a monkey that can dance to a tune on command. I just want to concentrate on my things and get this winter done with."

"That is good. You have goals and things you want to do. That's a good sign."

"I suppose," Vincent agreed.

Dr Poppycock had no trouble remembering the rough patches of depression Vincent had endured the year before. In all honesty, excluding the paranoia that had worsened somewhat, the current symptoms were promisingly mild in comparison.

"Have you thought about moving back into town? You would be closer to Edward and me as well. I do not mind being available for my patients. Especially you. I understand you are a bit of a celebrity, but I won't hold that against you. You're the decent sort, all things considered."

"That is comforting to know," Vincent said, voice laced with a layer of sarcasm. "But I'd rather not. The voices seem to get worse when I am here."

"Right now, are you hearing them?"

"No. Not right now."

"It should be fine, then. Don't worry about it so much. Stress only makes worse the little neurosis and problems of the mind that we all deal with. Have you done those breathing exercises we talked about, to reduce the stress?"

"No, I don't... I don't want to do any breathing exercises. Really. What good are they? I am perfectly calm. It's not as if they happened continuously, the voices. I think I'd rather stay where I am. It's quiet there."

"Oh well, you can't say I didn't try." Dr Poppycock chuckled. "I can prescribe sedatives for you, but I do think you can sort this out without them. Take some deep breaths and listen to your own thoughts instead of the voices."

"Ah, I'm not sure how that will help. I've not felt like myself lately. Things seem even more confusing than usual. I suspect Jones might have done something to me..." Vincent's brow furrowed. "I sound paranoid, don't I?"

"Really, ask yourself, why would Mr Jones want to do such a thing? He seems like a nice lad. He's worried about you. Isn't it more likely that you are directing your anxieties toward Mr Jones because you have this void of understanding that you so desperately seek to fill with anything that might make sense to you? I know it would be easier and more comforting if there was an obvious reason for all that we think and feel, but mostly it's figments of our psyche and who we are. That's what we have to deal with as humans." Dr Poppycock felt pleased about phrasing it so well. Vincent did not seem to share the opinion. Too bad. It must have been beyond his current capabilities.

"I still think he might be poisoning me. He cooks most of my meals. Maybe he has something against me? Maybe someone has sent him here to kill me? He was the one to trap me on this island. I swear, had it not been for his tricks, I would not be here."

"What exactly do you think he did?" Dr Poppycock asked to humour Vincent. Perhaps, if he thought the thought through on his own, he'd realise its ridiculousness.

"He— he... I don't know the exact details. He schemed so I wouldn't notice the time. And believe me, I was checking, but I still didn't. And then, before I knew it, there was snow, in bundles. Does that sound like me, to not notice at all like that? I mean, it's ridiculous. He did something sneaky. Tampered with the newspapers. And the lights. Things like that," Vincent explained.

Dr Poppycock felt sorry for the man. He must have been under a lot of stress because of that book he was writing, to pin all of this on Mr Jones. He had probably just been careless. It was so much easier to place the blame on somebody else than to face one's own weaknesses.

"And now you think Mr Jones may be giving you something that is making you hear the voices again? The same voices you heard last year, even well before that, as you said."

"Well, not the same voices exactly. His voice. I could have sworn I heard him talk to me, but then when I looked, his lips weren't moving and he was glaring at me. What am I supposed to think? There is no such thing as telepathy. We've had that discussion time and time again. So, what else can it be?"

"Indeed. You appear to be harbouring some serious resentment for him, since you have decided he's to blame for you having to stay on the island for another winter. Perhaps, if you could forgive yourself for being stressed out and making a simple, careless mistake, you could give up on that resentment?"

"Are you saying it was my own fault that I missed the ferry?"

"No, no. It's not my job to place the blame. I'm just saying, as a factor which caused you to miss the ferry, stress should not be taken lightly. For whatever reason, you are now blaming Mr Jones, which isn't healthy. Your brain is directing this anger and resentment towards the young lad with less than valid reasons. If you can forgive him and yourself, then perhaps the voices will naturally go away. Take some time to yourself and listen to what your inner self has to say to you."

Vincent did not seem pleased. Dr Poppycock sighed.

"Really, have you done any of the exercises I gave you? It's no wonder that things haven't much improved from last year. I don't mean to lecture you, please don't take this the wrong way, but I need to emphasise the importance of following my advice. I cannot stress this enough. You must learn to relax and just be, or you will wind yourself up to death."

"I would prefer not to do that."

"Have you thought of any new hobbies to try?"

"I did some needlepoint and push ups. I found neither enjoyable. It's difficult to find things to do with such limited space. I've tried all else I could think of."

"How about, instead of a book that comes laden with all sorts of pressures, you tried writing a diary? You seem in sore need of an outlet for your feelings. Could you perhaps consider giving that a go?"

"A diary?" Vincent exhaled heavily.

Dr Poppycock had seen Vincent in his less receptive moods, but this was reaching new territory. Usually, the man would accept at least an idea or two. He'd even tried crocheting to please the doctor.

"Yes, a diary. How about it?"

"For myself? For no other reason?"

"Yes."

"But it seems like such a waste of time."

"You could try cutting newspaper clippings and making a scrap-book of sorts." Dr Poppycock was getting a little desperate, but there had to be something he could offer Vincent before sending him home. Something to do to keep him busy for at least a week until they could see each other again.

He urgently needed to rearrange his schedule to squeeze Vincent in there as often as possible. The man was such a hopeless, hopeless mess.

"You mean cutting things that have no personal meaning or connection to me, out of a newspaper and into a book? And then write what? 'Dear diary, I heard voices again today.' What if that falls into the wrong hands?" Vincent was looking at him like a man facing a halfwit with a complex mathematical problem. It was just that type of inappropriate contempt and bafflement. Dr Poppycock admitted it hadn't been one of his brightest ideas, but it was sad that Vincent was so unable to improvise and think outside the box.

"There are locks. You could keep it in a locked drawer," the doctor suggested. He knew his suggestion would fall on deaf ears, but he felt obliged to try.

With this level of paranoia, perhaps it was time to consider medication after all.

"The risk seems too high. I'd rather not unless there is a motive or a reason for this activity that I haven't grasped. Take me through this again. I would be writing in it, what exactly?"

"Daily things, how you feel, what you did. Express yourself. Perhaps draw something. I think you've mentioned at some point that you like to draw."

"That was when I was nine," Vincent replied bluntly. He was being so little help today. He must have been seriously in need of some counselling.

"You could pick it up again."

"I drew pink dinosaur ruins. The bony, bloody kind. And fossils. I was fascinated by them."

"It could still prove a surprisingly good outlet if you kept an open mind!"

"Frankly, I would rather stick a pencil into my eye and twist until I hear a pop."

"There's no need to be vulgar, Vincent. I would have grasped your point with a less graphic explanation." Dr Poppycock huffed. He tried to sound mildly amused to lighten the mood. It was more of an effort than usual.

"I suppose I could try the needlepoint again," Vincent relented.

CHAPTER 19

"And how are you today?" Dr Poppycock asked in his usual manner. Vincent was the first patient of the day, and today also the last.

With the Midwinter Festival drawing near, the doctor had decided to take a few days off for the preparations. He would only see the most pressing patients, and Vincent was definitely one of them.

The man looked especially tired today. The winter was taking its toll.

"Could be better," Vincent replied, face glum. "I've been talking with the cat again."

"Mr... Swifty?" Dr Poppycock checked the name from his notes. This had happened before, but Vincent hadn't mentioned it yet this year.

"Yes."

"And has he been replying to you?"

"Yes."

"Does it happen frequently?"

"Only when I'm feeling under the weather. I think the fever brings it out."

"In that case, I don't think it's anything to worry about. So long as he doesn't talk back when you feel well." Dr Poppycock smiled gently.

"Hasn't so far."

"What sort of things does he talk to you about? Perhaps you should listen. It is probably your inner self trying to tell you something."

"He tells me to give him something to eat," Vincent replied, abashed. Dr Poppycock laughed at this, though benignly, so as to help Vincent relax.

"Anything else?"

"Well, he insists that Ms Rose has a birthmark on her left thigh. I don't know if that's true."

"Perhaps your subconscious is telling you you're in need of female company," Dr Poppycock suggested. He'd brought up the subject from time to time, though Vincent did not seem receptive.

"I guess."

"Are you sure you wouldn't want to spend the holidays in town? No offence to Mr Swifty but it might do you good to have some humans to talk to." Dr Poppycock had been glad when he'd heard Mr Jones had moved out after their last session. Vincent seemed to be doing better without the added stress. But this was a tough time of year for the man, and it did not seem wise to let him stay alone at his cottage where his depression could so easily become worse.

"I guess, but—" Vincent looked away.

"If you're unsure whether you're suitable company for your own family at present, I would be happy to lend you mine for the duration. I have most of my family gathering this year, but there's still a guest room available. We'd love to have you over."

Though Dr Poppycock believed in not taking an unhealthily keen interest in his patients, Vincent was an old acquaintance. It would be less of a worry to have him over where they could keep an eye on him.

The man was not bad company. He told interesting stories if you could get him in the mood for it, and he was a good listener. Because the majority of the doctor's family were women, it wouldn't hurt to have one more man to keep him company and help adjust the balance a little. And it would have the added benefit of Vincent perhaps agreeing to go see his own family for a short while when he knew he had a place to retreat to if he began to feel anxious.

"I don't know."

"You can bring Mr Swifty along. We won't mind at all."

"I'll think about it."

"That's all I'm asking." Dr Poppycock nodded. "I'll schedule our next appointment for Thursday. It's only a few days away, but try to decide by then. You can come to our house on the day if you choose. Just bring your suitcases and what have you."

M r Swifty wasn't particularly pleased about Vincent's holiday plans but felt charitable enough to not make a fuss about following along.

There would be more people at Dr Poppycock's house, especially of the female kind, and that translated to an increased chance of receiving food items by using his charms.

Mr Swifty had strict standards of hygiene, so people usually responded to him more favourably than other strays. He'd found that if he let them stroke and pet him, almost no one refused the honour. Bestowing some purrs and meows on the onlookers also made them appreciate him more.

"I'm really not sure about this," Vincent muttered, eyes downcast as they stepped down from the snowtrain.

He hadn't understood Mr Swifty's attempts of communication for a while now—not since the dodgy leech Jones had been removed from the premises after the dodgy biscuit incident—so Mr Swifty knew not to bother voicing a reply. Even if the man had been in a receptive state, it was probably not a good idea to risk drawing attention when they were in public. Vincent had enough of a reputation as it were. There was no need to add to it.

Dr Poppycock's wife, Petunia, was already at the door when they arrived. Vincent shook hands with her and introduced Mr Swifty, who saw no point in this mindless loitering at the entrance and entered the house to get in from the cold.

It was hardly his first visit to town. They may not have been formally introduced before, but Mr Swifty knew who each of them were—at least, to the extent he cared to.

"What a lovely cat!" he heard Petunia say, but he had no interest in her praises.

Whatever Vincent said or did with Petunia after that was of no consequence. Mr Swifty prioritised trying to win over all the women in the kitchen and started by strategically announcing his arrival at the door.

A few of the ladies turned to look. When Mr Swifty could be sure his presence would not cause any strangeness or panic, he stepped slowly across the room to make friends with each of the women in turn.

There, making pies, were the good doctor's sisters Marigold and Poppy. The two of them were a little on the loud side but gentle with their pets, and they promised to give Mr Swifty tummy rubs once they were done, as right now their hands were covered with flour.

Behind them stood little Ren. She watched the pie-making, eyes gleaming, until she noticed Mr Swifty and knelt down to greet him. Though Mr Swifty had always found these smaller humans somewhat suspicious and unpredictable, he knew this one was not inclined to pull his tail, so he let her stroke his fur for a while before moving on.

Making the roast was Petunia's sister Flora and helping her, their cousin Holly. In charge of the vegetables were the only man in the room, Briar, and his wife, Daisy. The two of them were too busy chatting with one another to notice Mr Swifty, but they didn't currently hold anything of interest anyway, so Mr Swifty directed his efforts toward Flora and Holly.

The roast smelled delicious. Surely, there had to be something here for Mr Swifty's benefit. As luck had it, Holly was fond of felines and did not spare her affections. She was generous with the leftover slices of meat, and Mr Swifty spent the rest of the evening in a contented slumber on her lap having been well fed and cared for.

M idwinter was celebrated by gathering at the market square for some snacks, dance and other entertainment. Warm drinks were served and conversations were had until late in the evening, when people returned to their homes for a glorious feast of roasts, gravy, tubers, sweet swede casserole, minced pies, baked rolls, cakes and ginger biscuits.

They had decorated their houses with dried flowers and evergreens, and knitted or paper-crafted little Midwinter mascots: goats, geese, ravens and foxes. Spruce trees had been hauled indoors and were laden with tinsel and glass ornaments, and people exchanged gifts as thanks for the kind deeds of the year passed.

Mr Swifty had seen enough winters to be well aware of these traditions, but he could still not fathom why the darkest time of the year was celebrated with such devotion. He was also surprised that Vincent had remembered to bring gifts along, although it did explain the extra luggage he'd carried.

As they opened the gifts, Vincent explained he'd merely done some winter cleaning and decluttering, and even apologised for bringing the myriads of little ornate pots and figurines he'd individually, carefully wrapped for each of the people present.

To the small human, he'd specifically knitted a red-and-white hat with earflaps and a pair of matching mittens, all adorned with delightful dangling pairs of bobbles that swung back and forth enticingly when moved. They were begging to be grabbed into a merciless paw-lock and punished with a flurry of kicks, so Mr Swifty obliged a time or two, much to Ren's dismay and mirth.

Vincent himself received a few pairs of socks, mittens, and even a long blue scarf to go with his usual mittens and hat. The women were showering him with crafted goodies and spiced wine, and the attention he received was only second to Mr Swifty, who was, without a doubt, the fluffiest and most adorable male of those present.

The evening went by slowly, but to everyone's delight. Ren reluctantly went to sleep an hour or so past her bedtime, and the adults stayed up until close to midnight, when finally, one by one, the guests and family retired into their respective rooms and the house became quiet.

Mr Swifty followed Vincent into the guest room at the top of two flights of stairs. The room was comfortable and spacious, and they had no trouble settling in. After a half an hour or so of trying to fall asleep but failing, Mr Swifty raised his head to ask a tentative question.

"Can't sleep?" He whispered in case he'd misunderstood.

"No," Vincent replied. "I think I may have had a little too much to drink."

"Ah, perhaps a glass of water might help?"

"It might," Vincent agreed.

He exhaled heavily and got up to go. Mr Swifty stretched and followed, though regretful to leave the warm nest he'd made for himself out of Vincent's clothes.

"I could go for some leftovers," he noted, hopefully. Enough time had passed since dinner for him to have made a little room in his belly for some more tasty goodness.

"Pig." Vincent chuckled and tottered down the stairs.

"I can't help it." No one should be judged for wanting to eat something so delicious. It was more of a crime to leave it uneaten.

The two of them tiptoed into the kitchen, where Vincent served Mr Swifty a thin slice from the roast and some fresh water. Mr Swifty wouldn't have minded a bit of cream to go along with his treat, but since he'd eaten such irregular food today, he suspected his tummy would disagree.

Vincent poured himself a glass of water and sat on a stool not far from where Mr Swifty was eating on the floor.

"Are you sure you're not having any? It's delicious. I wouldn't mind another slice," Mr Swifty mumbled between bites.

"No, I'm fine." Vincent yawned. He seemed sleepy but still a pinch too restless to sleep.

"Well, I'm going to go ahead and say it: I wasn't too happy to be dragged here, but contrary to my expectations, I've enjoyed this. It is a marked improvement from the company you were keeping before. Thank you for bringing me along."

"You don't have to be so formal about it. We're family, right?" Vincent leaned to a small table next to him and watched Mr Swifty eat. It would have been creepy had Mr Swifty not been so used to it.

"Don't be silly. I'm a cat and you're a human. I can tell us apart."

"I didn't mean by blood." Vincent did not appear amused or patronising, but that was probably because he was drunk. That usually made him make less sense.

"Oh, you meant family, as in very familiar with each other?" Mr Swifty asked, a little curious. He hadn't really thought about it much. Vincent was a feeder: a human who fed him and did his bidding. Granted, he did prefer the man over most of the other people he had doing things for him. Still...

"Do you not agree?" Vincent asked in return, now with that hint of sadness that he sometimes had when he'd been indoors for too long.

"Am I required to do something specific?"

"Not really. Nothing I can think of." Vincent looked uncertain. Before Mr Swifty could respond, the man continued, "I guess you might be morally obligated to keep me company and help me out if I needed help. I think friends and family do these things for one another."

"Oh, it's a deal of sorts?"

"Well, you could call it that. But the gist is you're supposed to want to do them."

"Why?"

"You like the person, so you want to be nice to them, I guess." Vincent frowned. "I haven't really thought about the concept since... I don't know, childhood."

"Hmm, I do like you Vincent. But I can't be obliged to do things for you. I have enough worries of my own," Mr Swifty said. This deal sounded altogether too demanding to partake in.

"Oh," Vincent seemed genuinely disappointed. "Well, then, can I at least be your friend?" he asked.

Mr Swifty could not quite fathom why anyone would be willing to settle for a one-sided deal like this, but he did not mind humouring Vincent.

"Sure," he replied. He thought about it for a moment and then came up with the closest thing he could relate to and knew the meaning of. "I think it's called a henchman."

"What?" Vincent's frown deepened.

"You know, a person to do your bidding. Because they like you. You're like my henchman and I'm your boss," Mr Swifty explained.

He was pleased to have reached an understanding, but just as he was about to commend himself for it, Vincent started to giggle. He was trying to hold in a bigger laugh, but was doing a poor job of it, since what leaked out was a strange—and frankly quite unbecoming—noise.

"What's so funny, if I may ask?" Mr Swifty did not find Vincent's amusement appropriate, so he gave the man the pungent side-eye.

"Yes, sure, certainly that's what it must seem to you, now that I think of it." Vincent was still struggling with his bubbly mirth.

"You are confusing me. Are you happy to be my henchman?"

"Sure…" Vincent doubled over to hold his stomach, trying his best to stifle the laugh but failing.

"Are you having a fit? Do you need assistance? You are laughing, so I assume you must be amused or happy, but you don't seem to be doing it right. Isn't there supposed to be a sort of 'ha ha'-sound involved and not just this weird wheezing?"

"Ah heh… I'm trying to be quiet so I don't wake everyone up, you silly." Vincent dried the tears from his eyes.

"Now you are crying? Does it hurt?" Mr Swifty dropped the rest of his slice of roast and stepped closer to see if Vincent was all right. "Did you break?" He nuzzled a little closer still to sniff Vincent's face as he was doubled over, then pushed himself against the man's legs. This usually calmed him down if he was having a meltdown.

"Ah haha, no, don't worry." Vincent was smiling. That was a good sign as far as humans went, but Vincent sometimes smiled when he was upset, too. This didn't seem to be it, though.

Mr Swifty felt a bit perplexed by this sudden show of illogical behaviour. He backed away slowly to resume eating his snack.

"All right, if you say so," he said before digging in again. "I mean, you'll let me know if you're about to break, right? I need to know these things."

"Ah, I'm sorry I made you worry. It's all right, really. I'm fine now." Vincent sat up straight and cleared his throat, quietly. "You sure seem to care a lot for someone reluctant to be my friend."

"Oh?" He could scarcely afford a misunderstanding, so he was quick to try to dispel any false notions Vincent might have about this relationship. He would not be roped into slaving for this blathering nincompoop! "Don't get confused now. As the boss, I have certain responsibilities, such as taking care of the well-being of my underlings, but that's as far as that goes."

For some reason this seemed to make Vincent want to laugh even more. It was getting a little irritating.

"Look, I'm trying to have a serious conversation with you," Mr Swifty said, exasperated that it was getting almost as difficult as talking to a wee kitten. Vincent was normally a bit more sensible. At least a little bit.

"I'm sorry. I just— the way you looked just now, it was just... priceless..." Vincent struggled. He'd tried to take a sip of water, but it was not working out well for him, and he was spilling some all over himself.

"Stop laughing and drink your water. Look at you, you're making a mess. What a disgrace." With Vincent in this state, Mr Swifty could only offer a reprimand. He'd have to try to make more sense of it when the man was more in his right mind. The priority, for now, was to prevent him from breaking himself any more than he evidently already had.

Unable to sleep, Dr Poppycock decided to indulge himself with a private midnight snack. When he exited the little downstairs library, he heard what seemed like a conversation in the kitchen. He cracked the door ajar and listened.

It was one-sided, but peeking in, he wasn't surprised why. What did surprise him, though, was how the conversation seemed to move back and forth so effortlessly.

"I know, I know. I'm sorry," Vincent was saying.

"Meow," the cat seemed to respond.

Dr Poppycock could've sworn Mr Swifty sounded upset over something.

"I'll give you another slice, stop sulking."

"Meow. Mwrawr." The cat paced around a little irate. "Mewr."

"Just one and that's it. Or else we'll be up all night."

"Meow meow."

"Indeed. And I could use another glass of water, I think." Vincent offered a slice of roast to Mr Swifty and poured some water into his glass, albeit somewhat shakily.

The man seemed drunk still, but it was no wonder after all the attention he'd received from the ladies. They had wanted to ensure he enjoyed himself, so they'd been generous pouring the wine.

"Meoowwrrr, meow..." Mr Swifty meowed softly and quietly. Dr Poppycock hadn't heard the cat meow much the whole time the two of them had been here.

"Yes, but I don't think she meant it quite like that."

"Meow."

"Really, that's not very nice," Vincent said.

The conversation continued like this for quite some time. At times Mr Swifty didn't actually meow in return, but they exchanged looks and it was as if the dialogue had continued seamlessly.

Dr Poppycock found it a marvellous example of the ingenuity of the human imagination. It was fascinating how Vincent's brain was filling these short breaks with full sentences as if the two of them were having a real conversation! The cat's mannerisms supported what was being said. During their sessions, there had been some hints of Vincent's extraordinary ability to read people, but evidently this expanded to animals as well.

"Thank you. I do appreciate it." Vincent seemed to be in a relatively good mood talking to his cat.

It was his cat, clearly. Mr Swifty was known as a stray, but there was no mistaking it. The animal was not this attached to any other person.

Mr Swifty meowed again, jumped onto the table and pawed Vincent's sleeve. As the conversation died down and a game of pawing and poking ensued, Dr Poppycock deemed it the best moment to enter so as to avoid walking in on something private or embarrassing.

"Ah Vincent, you're here. How like-minded we are!"

"James," Vincent replied happily, then recoiled for a moment, "or should I refer to you as the doctor?"

"No, James is fine among friends," Dr Poppycock said, amused. It would make the doctor-patient relationship a little more vague, but under the circumstances, it seemed silly to hang on to conventions.

"Ah, good. Here for a midnight snack?"

"Yes, something along those lines. And yourself?" James was a little surprised to find no plate in front of Vincent.

"Just some water." Vincent gestured at his glass. "Though Mr Swifty here was in the mood for some roast. I hope it was all right…"

"Yes, of course it is! When I said to take whatever you need, I meant it. No need to act like a stranger in our house. Especially not on a jolly occasion such as this," James reassured him, and reached to pat the cat. The rascal dodged out of the way. "I'm sure he must have liked it more than he likes me, so it didn't go to waste. And there's plenty left."

"Yes, he's a bit of a pig." Vincent appeared apologetic still. "I'm also a bit of a pig. That is to say, well-fed and kept in good spirits. Thank you so much for inviting me."

"That's quite all right. It's been wonderful having you, Ren and Mr Swifty here. To tell you the truth, I find all the women-folk insufferable sometimes, and it was a relief to have them focus their attentions on you three for most of the evening." James dove into the pantry for some ham, cheese and a sesame-seed covered roll.

"You are welcome." Vincent laughed, not too loudly. "And it's truly been a pleasure."

"Well, then the feeling is mutual." James fished out a stool from under the table and sat down to eat. "I think I may want me a slice of that pie after this. If I can manage it."

"Ah, the pie. It's not every day you get such delightfully luscious minced pie."

"Would you care for a slice? I think there are two or three pies left and with my wife's side of the family heading out tomorrow, there won't be as many of us here left to eat them."

"I might be persuaded to take a slice. In a bit." Vincent leaned back and raised the back of his hand to cool his forehead.

"How is everything?" the doctor asked in his usual manner before he had time to catch himself.

"Are you asking as my doctor, or...?" Vincent glanced at James from between some of his fingers.

"Just asking," James said, a little embarrassed about his habits. "As a friend, I suppose. Not that I am worried. I just thought... to ask, is all." He tried to make it sound light and off-handed.

"Everything is fine. I feel it went well. I've no complaints." Vincent smiled as he said it, and he looked to be in a better mood than what James had seen him in a long while. It could have been the wine, but James liked to believe it was the good company and atmosphere.

It would have been marvellous to have Vincent closer by for the winter, to keep the young man out of his depressive pits and cubby holes. It was never a nice thing to watch a person become so troubled, while feeling so unequipped to help, no matter how much he tried his best to be a good therapist and a friend.

"That's good to hear," James said. "Which reminds me. Ren seemed to really enjoy herself this evening."

"Oh?" Vincent lowered his hand, seemingly surprised.

"Yes! She was sulking when she had to go to bed before the rest of us. She's clearly missed you. You should come by more often when your health permits it."

"I wouldn't have made good company the past few months."

"You made good company for her tonight."

"She did seem to like the gift I gave her, at least." Vincent kept smiling.

The girl had absolutely adored it, almost as much as she adored him, but he seemed oblivious of it.

Vincent laughed, seeming a tad embarrassed.

"I know I said it's for the best that she stays at Ms Buttercup's, but I do think it's important you keep in touch."

"I know, I know. I did promise her and I'm not going back on my word. She'll just have to wait a while longer."

A winter was a long time for a ten-year-old. James hoped this one wouldn't cause any irreparable harm to their relationship. Before James had time to decide how to best respond, Vincent continued as if with a reply:

"I understand. It's for the best, though." He turned to look at James. There was an ever so short pause as James thought of what to say, and just as he was about to open his mouth, Vincent continued, "Indeed. Oh well, it can't be helped."

It was getting a little unnerving now. James frowned.

"Ah, what is...? What?" Vincent, who had a moment earlier appeared to be preoccupied by something and looked the other way, turned again toward the doctor. "Am I making you uncomfortable?" He didn't seem to be aware why, though. "You'll have to tell me if I am. I mean, I can be a bit dense sometimes, and I'm admittedly not at my sharpest right now."

He was still doing it. James brought his fingers to his lips to make sure they weren't moving. To test it out, he thought about pie. Pie, pie pie pie pie pie pie pie pie, piepiepiepiepiepiepiepie...!

"Pie?" Vincent said, confused. "The pie. Ah yes, didn't you mention something about having some pie?" He appeared a little more confident now.

That must have been it. He must have remembered the mentioning of pie from before. It was a coincidence. After all, it would have been embarrassing if all these years, James had been telling Vincent he was imagining things, and it actually turned out to be true. That he was in fact able to read minds.

Vincent chuckled.

"Yes," he said.

What yes? What was he replying to? thought James, now searching for blame in the few drinks he himself had had that evening.

"Yes, it would be a bit awkward." Vincent chuckled again.

"What?" James asked.

"If I were able to read your mind and you'd been telling me all these years how it's just my imagination. But that's silly. I don't know how to read minds. I'm not sure why you brought it up all of a sudden."

"Ah, I didn't..."

"Oh? Then why—? I could've sworn... Uh, forgive me, I've had a bit too much to drink." He took another swig of water. "Maybe the pie will balance it out a little bit." He tried to regain his smile in an obvious effort to diffuse the situation.

"Look, Vincent. I was thinking about pie. And what you said," James said before trying to form it into a more coherent sentence. It was a little frightening to be in the middle of something and be interrupted with an answer to what you were thinking.

"That's strange. Have you by any chance become a ventriloquist?" Vincent frowned. "I could have sworn you were talking just then, but your lips weren't moving. You seemed quite good at it!"

"I think I need a stiff drink," James said before Vincent could comment any further. There was some brandy in one of the cupboards. James fetched it along with two glasses, not to be rude. He poured into both, though a bit more into his own.

"You're not seriously thinking I can read minds, are you, old fellow?" Vincent asked, a bit alarmed. "It was probably a coincidence, as you said. I told you I read expressions well. And we're both drunk. Surely, it's a case of all three enforcing the illusion."

"Quite some coincidence." James huffed and emptied his glass. In all of his years, he hadn't been faced with this much confusion over a mere coincidence.

Although, once he got through the initial shock, it did begin to seem amusing rather than startling. His brain began to wrap itself around the possibility that it had been a joke or a clever trick or such. "It's a trick, isn't it? You almost had me fooled!"

"Haha, yes," Vincent admitted. Though he didn't seem to be as much in need of one, he too, took a fair gulp from the glass that had been offered to him.

"How did you do it?" James asked. He was keen to know the secret. Maybe it was something he could learn himself.

"I don't know. It just happens." Vincent had appeared momentarily concerned but was clearly happy and relieved now that the situation seemed to be resolving itself.

"Do you use some sort of subliminal messages to get me to think these things?"

"I might. I don't know." He shrugged. "Maybe we've known each other for such a long time, I can guess what you're about to say?"

"Yes, that must be it." James nodded, although there was slight discomfort in realising he was that predictable.

"But it's a neat trick, isn't it?"

"Indeed!"

"I wish I knew how I do it." Vincent scratched the back of his head clumsily.

"You're saying that to avoid having to tell me your secret! But that's all right. We're allowed to have secrets." James nodded knowingly.

"Yes, like the fact that you were listening there at the door before you entered." Vincent grinned.

"Oh, you saw me?" James had been sure he hadn't been spotted. He'd been so careful, too. Damn. He was probably getting old.

The men had been drinking and chatting for some time, and Mr Swifty was getting bored having to watch their stupidity. He snuck out of the kitchen and up the stairs to where Petunia was sleeping with her hot flashes. This meant that the second-floor balcony was almost always accessible via a window that was ajar in her bedroom.

The Poppycocks lived in a three-storey townhouse right next to the market square, and so the view, though not as high up as the highest buildings, was somewhat more spectacular than elsewhere in town. The weather was clear and Mr Swifty could see the stars for a change, so he took his time to enjoy the view and the fresh air.

During this time of year, with the light fixtures and ornaments twinkling and swaying back and forth in the wind, it was quite the sea of sparkle. There was a huge lantern-lit spruce tree in the middle of the square, and its glow was magical, alive, fluttering against the pale, dark landscape.

Mr Swifty spent a good while trying to see whether there was something worth stalking and hunting somewhere below, but with everyone and everything either asleep or indoors, he retreated back into the house.

M r Swifty headed downstairs to check whether the inane conversation had finally ended. By the looks of it, Vincent was having trouble following what the good doctor was trying to say, but that wasn't as much Vincent's fault as it was James's, since the man had begun to slur quite significantly. Even Mr Swifty had trouble understanding what he was trying to say.

"I believe he is talking about the sailing event," Mr Swifty tried to help when Vincent appeared at a loss. "You know, in the summer. With all the sails. That's what's like scales on a fish." Mr Swifty took pride in himself for making the connection but was growing tired of the mental gymnastics. "Maybe he shouldn't be having any more of what he's having."

"Aghreed, but he doesn't seem whillin' t' stop," Vincent whispered.

Mr Swifty jumped onto the table and took matters into his own paws. He sat promptly on top of the doctor's hand so that he was forced to pull it away from the glass and leave it unguarded. Then all that was left was to topple the glass over. There. Mission accomplished.

"Now you don't have to be the one to ruin his evening," he said and pushed on Vincent's hands as the drunken doctor stared at his spilled drink. "I think I deserve a reward. Perhaps a piece of the roast? But should you be trusted to handle a knife right now? Maybe you should give me the whole roast to gnaw on, just to be safe."

Vincent chuckled but got up to fetch something from the pantry. It wasn't the roast, but a thin slice of ham he'd managed to carve sans bloodshed. Mr Swifty accepted it without grumbling.

"Maybe it's time we go t' bed," Vincent told James, who was now doing his best to wipe the brandy off the table with a piece of cloth he'd picked up from who knows where. He was doing remarkably well despite the state he was in.

"Yes, I thinkh sshh thime to cahl it a nite," James articulated. Mr Swifty translated it for Vincent, who seemed to struggle with comprehension even more than usual. Considering that Vincent's goal coming down to the kitchen had been to sober up a little, it could safely be said that he had failed.

It was possible, however, that he was now drunk enough to pass out once he got to bed, and Mr Swifty was counting on this being the case as he coaxed the men to go to their respective bedrooms, devoid of patience for any further foolery.

CHAPTER 20

Head heavy, swaying and reeling softly from the drinks, Vincent stumbled into the guest bedroom. He needed fresh air.

"I'll... just for a bit..." he tried to explain to Mr Swifty. The cat had already curled up at the foot of his bed and eyed him with one eye cracked open. He seemed to be judging Vincent's life choices, but voiced no objections, so Vincent opened the window just enough to lean outside to clear his head.

The night air had the sharp and sobering feel of frost, with a faint undertone of the lingering scents from the day's festivities. It didn't take away the gentle rolling sensation messing with his sense of balance, but it felt wonderful against his flushed face.

Vincent realised he'd been a touch too nervous about this evening, so he'd carelessly accepted most of the drinks the ladies had offered him. Thankfully, Ren hadn't seemed to mind it. She'd seemed her usual self, let him know what she'd been up to lately and how she was doing.

Despite not being at his best, Vincent had managed to avoid saying anything upsetting to anyone. It had been so noisy by the end of the evening he hadn't dared to open his mouth much, but no one had noticed him withdrawing. They had accepted his polite smiles and vague nods as replies when a reply was expected, and as confirmation that he was paying attention when it wasn't.

If he could've trusted himself to handle these situations, James's suggestion to stay in town, and closer to Ren, would have probably made the winter go by a little faster. He'd just never been quick enough to think on his feet and continued to struggle with what to do when his head was flooded with voices that weren't supposed to be there.

He'd almost bungled it at the last minute, back there in the kitchen. Fortunately, James had been at least equally drunk, if not more, and let it go without digging deeper.

Vincent inhaled greedily but had to let the air out with a few sloppy coughs when it proved too cold.

"Better not get sick again," he told himself, and took a step back.

He was more determined than ever to keep himself fit and together until spring, so he could pack everything up and leave with Ren like he'd planned. This time, he wouldn't take any risks. He would leave as soon as he was done with the preparations. He'd leave right away if he could—

"Oh! Right!" He slapped his forehead. Why wait until then? Why not encase the whole speeder for increased comfort, use a dual fuel system and propel it forward like a plough?

To cover the distance on ice, the amount of fuel needed would have made the vehicle so heavy and the crossing so expensive, it made no practical sense. He had some money saved, but he wasn't that rich... But what if he could make such an aerodynamic speeder that it would glide across with less fuel? What if he could switch between the fuel sources on the fly, and make use of the current fuel system once the engine was already hot, and switch back when it cooled again? He just needed to solve the issue with the filters clogging up... If he could stop the hydraulics fluid from coagulating when the temperatures fluctuated—!

Vincent slammed the window shut, a little too excited. The sound immediately made him cringe, and he glanced at Mr Swifty.

The cat eyed him sternly.

"Sorry, sorry," Vincent whispered and redid the window clasp with a bit more care. "I know, my friend, my pal. I'm an idiot. I hope I didn't wake the whole house with my ruckus."

It wasn't the best time to be innovating, but he needed to jot some things down in case they'd still make sense once he'd sobered up.

"Where's my pen? Mr Swifty, have you seen it?"

"What do you need a pen for?" Mr Swifty did not look pleased but jumped down from the bed to help. He was such a good cat. Vincent smiled.

"I think there's a substance with antico-g... antigo-ah-gulant properties. I think it's used in the textiles industry. It's called ph— something. I'm not goin' to remember this in the morn'. Help, where's the pen?"

He was going to fix the speeder, pack his stuff and take Ren, if she still wanted to come, to somewhere warmer and brighter until he could feel like himself again. The book was so close to being done that he might even get paid for it soon. If he sold off everything unnecessary, he could probably avoid making debt, despite ransacking Edward's inventory for all the parts he needed for this project.

"Here." Mr Swifty nabbed a pen from the side-table and brought it over to Vincent.

"Paper?"

"I'm helping you out, but no more of this once you've written it down. You need to sleep."

"Yes, yes." Vincent took the notebook Mr Swifty located for him and decided to sit down on the bed before he fell down from the dizziness. "Ph... e, n..." Was that an e or an a? Was his handwriting even legible? He tried to concentrate. Phenabinol, possibly. It would probably be enough for him to figure it out the next day.

Once he'd jotted it down, Vincent browsed through the notebook. It was the one he'd picked from a pile to write his diary in, but he hadn't got very far. There were some pages filled prior.

"What's this?" It took him a while to recall.

"Oh, I don't think you need to be reading that right now," Mr Swifty tried to plant himself on top of the open notebook in Vincent's hands. Vincent frowned and pushed him to the side.

There were some admittedly rather disturbing sentences he'd written while depressed last year. Thank goodness he wasn't as depressed right now.

"What was I obsessin' 'bout, anyway?" He turned back a few more pages, closer to the beginning of the book.

Ah, yes. His chest felt tight. He'd brought this along back then. There were a few names and addresses, as well as reminders to check on leads.

"You shouldn't be reading that. Go to sleep." The cat was wise, but Vincent couldn't help himself. It hadn't all been bad. He was still smiling. He had family out there, and soon, he'd take Ren to see them.

"Vincent."

"Huh?"

"Sleep."

"Yes, but—" Something bothered him about it.

"This is how it started last year. You need to sleep."

"But they're watchin' me," Vincent replied without thinking.

"Let them watch. You need to sleep."

"But—"

Maybe if he looked at the correspondence again and checked the files they'd sent. Maybe it would make more sense this time.

He couldn't shake the feeling that there was something important missing from his early memories, but there had to be something somewhere to fill in the blanks. This couldn't be all of it.

Maybe he'd lost it because of the fevers or an injury of some sort? He'd been through a lot, so it would stand to reason that some of it might have affected his memory.

The cat grabbed the notebook with his teeth, pulled it out of Vincent's hands and tossed it to the floor.

"You need to sleep, you clotpole!"

Vincent didn't answer but let himself fall down to watch the slowly tilting ceiling. He felt sick. The edge of the bubble was right there and seemed to be closing in. Was he already asleep? What was he supposed to remember? It was something important. It had to have been important.

He'd spent most of November last year combing through the files obsessively, but then Aster and Celandine had intervened for Ren's sake, saying he could get back to it again when his health had improved and things were more stable.

They'd picked Ren up a few weeks later because of his worsening fevers and depression.

It must have been important because it had caused him to neglect Ren.

Something important... He was too tired to think. Must have been something, someone?

Mother?

CHAPTER 21

Vincent had barely turned fourteen when he received a postcard from a place he'd never heard of before across the continent. It read:

> Hello Vincent. I am visiting my cousins at Làirig Áir. This postcard is by a local artist, and I used a local stamp, as I know you like those. Thank you for your last letter. I always look forward to your letters. Maybe someday you could come over to meet me and my friends, and I can show you around. Làirig Áir is very beautiful. I will be here all year. Hope to hear from you soon. Rowan.

Vincent had never considered leaving the island up until then. He'd given some thought to what he wanted to do with his life, but he'd spent his time weighing professions and planning projects rather than listing places he might want to visit or experiences he'd like to have.

He started saving money. Celandine noticed this and inquired why, but Vincent wasn't yet ready to disclose. He had to plan it through first, to figure out if it was even feasible or worth committing to. There was no sense in bothering Celandine if he ended up changing his mind.

He was also a little afraid she would say no, and since he did not want to do anything Celandine did not approve of, the presentation had to be airtight to win her over. He wasn't as worried about Aster because Aster was busy taking care of her newborn son Arthur and would either let Vincent have whatever he wanted or agree with her sister's judgement.

To get to Làirig Áir, Vincent would have to take the ferry, several carriage rides, a train, a boat and possibly even a horse. He'd had to do some digging to gather this information, but since he'd always been curious about a huge variety of different topics for no reason other than knowing, no one thought twice about him asking questions and rummaging through library books.

All of these different methods of transportation sounded troublesome, precarious and expensive to arrange, so Vincent's attention turned to a mechanics project he was working on.

It was a vehicle of sorts.

The fuel he used was in abundance all around, cheap as dirt, but difficult to harness. It had a disappointing tendency to become inert in subzero temperatures and did not do well with moisture, but the latter was easy to counter with proper insulation, and the former merely ruled out some seasons and climates from his itinerary. Thankfully, Làirig Áir was located far down in the South, close to the coast, and experienced warm summers and mild, dry winters.

The equipment required to refine the fuel was expensive, but at least it was a one-time investment. The maintenance costs for the specialised engine parts, as well as the other wearing parts, would be astronomical, unless he could make sure the thing was durable enough to not break often. The daily running costs, on the other hand, were laughably low.

Vincent started to collect supplies around May and had all he needed by June. Constructing the thing took over a month, but when it was done, Vincent decided it was time to have his talk with Celandine.

"Oh, luv, are you sure your friend Rowan meant it literally?" Celandine did not seem altogether against it, but she seemed worried, and rightfully so. Làirig Áir was so far away, Vincent had had to hunt for a specific map to find it. There was no chance of him making it back before October, even if he left Whitskersey right away. That meant more than four months on the road alone, two each way, and because he wanted to see the sights, it was likely to take at least double that.

"I'll be back next spring," Vincent promised. Though he liked the idea of meeting Rowan after exchanging cards and letters for a few years now, it was not why he was going. It was an excuse to go see what was out there. It would be an adventure. A pilgrimage.

"Are you sure you're ready? Perhaps you should wait a year to be sure."

"I've got all I need. I've got it all planned out."

"Are you absolutely sure?" Celandine sighed. "I know you're responsible for your age, and have a lot of skills going for you, but it can be dangerous out there. You need to be careful and pay attention to where you are. Not everyone is going to be on your side, so if you get into trouble, I need you to promise me you won't hesitate turning back and coming home."

She wasn't too fond of the idea of Vincent riding his contraption out there unsupervised, and she was very expressive of that opinion. She'd seen the test runs, and her feedback on them had been less than stellar.

It took another two weeks of convincing before she actually agreed to let him go, but when she did, Vincent was on his way with no one to stop him. He was off to see the world as his own, a free young man.

I t was late September of Vincent's fifteenth year when he arrived in Làirig Áir. The journey hadn't been easy, but his careful planning had paid off, and nothing especially noteworthy had happened on the way. He'd seen and learnt a few new things, made a couple of new penfriends, worked a few odd jobs and established a stable routine for life on the road.

Làirig Áir was beautiful in the way that new places were when you weren't used to them. The town was popular with artists, nestled between two hills with rich nature and scenic views out to the sea, the town itself providing a vibrant street culture. Its inhabitants—a significant number of which had moved in from across the sea—seemed, for the most part, happy and relaxed. Vincent was excited by the prospect of making lots of new friends.

Strings of colourful flags criss-crossed over some of the streets with street-performers practising their crafts. The walls of the houses were decorated with wave and wind patterns of varying hues of blue on a contrasting bright white background. Decorations of this type were not common to the area and set the town apart from its neighbours. Perhaps the inhabitants were also a breed of their own?

Vincent had sent a letter in advance, so Rowan knew to expect him, but because he had no address on the road, he hadn't heard anything back. The address on the postcards led him to an apartment in the approximate middle of the town. He was nervous to announce his arrival, but his worries seemed unfounded when he was welcomed with open arms.

The thing that caught Vincent off guard was that Rowan was a girl and not a boy, like he'd hastily assumed from the name and her handwriting. She was also a few years older than him.

Neither of these details had come up in their correspondence, and when Vincent kept his mouth shut about his initial confusion, she also said nothing. Perhaps she hadn't even realised Vincent was younger than her because of his irregular appearance and unusual speech patterns. Either way, Vincent's delicate self-esteem was grateful for this small blessing.

"I'm so glad you came! I didn't think you would. Wasn't it a long trip? It was, right? Did you come alone? I could never. The bandits would have me. I'd probably get lost. It must have been a great adventure, though. I wish I could have been there. You must tell me everything about it!" She smiled at Vincent unreservedly and continued to explain that, although Làirig Áir was wonderful, it could sometimes be a smidge lonely. Most of her friends were back home and her cousins were often busy.

Because her plans had changed unexpectedly, Rowan said she would only be there until October. There were still a few weeks left, though, so she showed Vincent around town, introduced him to local food, customs and entertainment, and paid no mind that he stammered or fell silent in the face of her confident enthusiasm.

Vincent had never met anyone who could match his enthusiasm like this, and he was awestruck.

"Where are you headed from here?" she asked.

"I'm not sure."

"How about coming with me to where I live? While you're over here. You could meet some of my friends. I'm sure they would love to meet you. Gosh, I didn't expect you to be this tall. And pale. You're as white as a chalk stick!" She seemed fascinated by this even though she wasn't all that much darker herself.

She explained that where she was from, beyond the Eastern Sea, most people were even a shade or two darker than her and that she was considered the pale one. She even listed half of her family tree to Vincent, to note where she'd inherited all of her outstanding features. It was interesting, but Vincent had nothing to offer her in return, so he wasn't sure how to respond. He'd never felt this self-conscious about his appearance or family background before, and while she didn't seem to be meaning anything bad by her remarks, he was quickly losing confidence.

Thank goodness he'd grown some height just recently or else he would've looked like one of those marble statues of naked peeing toddlers next to her. This way, he at least had something going for him when he struggled to participate in the conversation.

She seemed to like him well enough, though, despite the occasional brash comment, so Vincent was hopeful that a little time in the sun and a tiny fib here and there might take care of the rest.

V incent lost his virginity at the age of fifteen. He would have been a fair bit more pleased about it, under other circumstances. As it were, the experience left him with mixed feelings.

He was relieved to see that all of his parts functioned like they ought to. There had been no problems there. He was also relatively pleased about the partner, Rowan, who had been gracious enough to not comment on his evident inexperience during the act itself.

Sex, as it turned out, was as pleasurable as he'd pretty much guessed from his private experimentation. The problem was a bit more specific than that.

Right at the very best part, he'd come across an anomaly.

Perhaps he'd imagined it. Maybe it was nothing. He could have sworn Rowan had said something peculiar at that crucial moment, but the way she had said it hadn't sounded at all like her usual self.

He sat in the shade by his trusty vehicle, thinking back to what had happened. Rowan was off somewhere with her friends, so he had time on his own to sort his thoughts but couldn't seem to figure it out.

"Why is he so slow and clumsy? I can't believe I turned down Aidan for this," she'd said.

All the way up until that moment, she'd looked like she was enjoying herself. Vincent knew his skills were limited—it was his first time, after all—but going as far as saying something like that, right at the last minute, didn't seem entirely fair. She could have given him more feedback and some directions to follow, and he would have gladly obliged!

Then again, he couldn't be sure she'd actually said it. He'd been preoccupied and couldn't remember her lips moving other than when he'd kissed her. It seemed like it could have been the recurring symptom of his insanity, but he hadn't felt ill at all, so why now?

Could it have been the nerves? Perhaps Rowan would let him try again? He had a better understanding of what he was supposed to do, so it would probably be better the second time.

I t wasn't better at all. As far as Vincent could tell, she looked enthusiastic. It all seemed to go as well as could be hoped, but again at the best part, she said something odd.

"My God, his nostrils are huge. That is so disgusting."

Already in the middle of his orgasm, there hadn't been much Vincent could do about this unexpected critique. By the looks of it, she was having one as well... but who on earth could focus on nostrils when it felt like this? Was she faking it?

B y the third time, the level of anxiety was affecting Vincent's concentration. He'd never had any such trouble before, but the dread of hearing something nasty again led to some near to catastrophic performance issues. He barely got through it, aided by his adolescent physique.

"What is wrong with him? It's even worse than the last time."

Along with her words, Vincent lost the nerve to try again. He slipped away, too ashamed to bother with goodbyes and decided not to attempt female relations again until years later, when he'd presumably matured a little.

I t didn't get any better, no matter the number of years in between. Over the course of these years, though, Vincent became quite the seasoned traveller. Every summer, he returned to Whitskersey but left again before winter. He explored the continent of Furuyan, and even beyond, in search of something, perhaps himself or his place in the world. He hoped he'd be able to tell when he came to it, but so far he'd come across no life-altering epiphanies.

Vincent had looked baby-faced and not nearly old enough to be served at a bar before, but he'd reached a reasonable height now. Blessed with abundant and even facial hair when he forgot to shave, he resembled an actual adult man.

It was difficult not to get carried away when the girls seemed keen and the wine flowed at almost no charge. This drained a fair portion of his meagre finances, but seemed like a good investment when he found himself in bed with a beautiful girl.

Vincent's nerves were suitably calmed by the drink, so he shoved aside his previous concerns and helped himself to some carnal pleasures.

Certainly, she had seemed to like it. Even at the last minute, she hadn't voiced anything nasty or unnerving. She'd egged him on until he was spent and tired, and she was giggling tiredly next to him, twirling his hair with her fingers. It had seemed well worth it, Vincent recalled thinking.

In fact, it had been so enjoyable, he'd repeated it the next night with similar results.

Of course, he'd had to tempt fate and go for the third. It was the same girl each time, but she seemed to get more excited every time.

Just as Vincent was congratulating himself on overcoming his previous trauma, she stuck her nails into his back and shouted, "I'm going to wring your neck, gouge out your eyes and lick your eye-sockets you son of a bitch, and I'm going to ride you around town once I've chopped off and stuffed your dick to make it a toy for me!"

Naturally, this was not something Vincent had been keen to hear. He reacted accordingly.

Buzzed from the wine, he scrambled clumsily off the girl, searched frantically for his clothes and made no effort to disguise his panicked haste when he rushed to get the hell away from her.

She was too surprised to say or do anything more, and Vincent certainly did not stick around to listen to any of her explanations. It would remain forever a mystery whether she'd meant what she'd said, but 'not knowing' was not going to be the part that kept Vincent up at night.

He was deterred enough to cross the whole town off his map so as not to run into her again, and he most certainly swore to never, ever sleep with a woman he'd only just met.

T his was not the end of Vincent's poor luck with women. It reared its ugly head again a few years later when he fell in love and entered his first long-term relationship.

He abstained from almost all physical intimacy with her for as long as he could. They shared many tender moments of casual proximity and sincere, impactful conversations that deepened their bond on an emotional level.

It got to a point where Vincent wondered if he'd found what he'd been searching for, and if she was the one he was meant to spend the rest of his life with.

He'd prepared for that special night with care. He'd figured he was safe this time, because there was no way anything could ruin what he had with her. There was nothing she could say that would change his mind about her. He was sure of it.

They spent the evening on a picnic, watching the stars as they appeared on the dimming evening sky, feeding each other morsels of food she'd prepared and gazing into each other's eyes. It was textbook romance, and though Vincent did not consider himself a romantic person, he was pleased with himself for making such a decent effort.

The mood was set just right, and things were steadily moving towards that dreaded but also long anticipated moment.

They retreated back to a hotel room Vincent had arranged for privacy. It was a cheap hotel, but everything seemed better when she was there. He hardly noticed the cracks or cared about the stains. All that mattered was that she was wonderful.

It was like magic up to the very last moment, but like any magic spell, this too was unavoidably broken.

She'd uttered someone else's name.

He'd felt like he'd been stabbed in the chest. For a moment, he'd considered ignoring it, but it didn't take him long to realise his insecurities were too severe. Even if it had been a figment of his imagination, and he was filling in the blanks with his worst fears to sabotage his happiness, even if he was really just insane, he would not be able to let it go. It would continue to torture him as long as he was with her.

It would poison the relationship and hurt her in the process. She did not deserve to be needlessly hurt for loving someone else.

And so Vincent erased her from his mind and left before it got worse.

CHAPTER 22

V incent was not old enough to be the bitter old man at the pub, but he sure acted the part. He'd made a valiant effort to change the scenery, but was now running out of money and wondered if there was any point in going on. He was tired. It wasn't as if anywhere was ever going to be far enough to get over his heartbreak. He thought a few more thoughts, much to that vein, and drank some more beer along with them.

Amidst the wallowing, he was offered some pub-counter counselling from a weathered sailor, who sat down next to him and inquired how he was doing. Vincent did not answer, just stared at his pint.

"That bad, aye?" The sailor rubbed the stubble above his upper lip and made an attempt at philosophy. "Life's like that sometimes. Rough sailin'."

Vincent grunted. The sailor sat there in silence for a while and the two of them shared a manly moment of contemplation.

"Women trouble?" the sailor asked. When Vincent responded with a single nod, he grunted and nodded back. "Yes, oh yes. Ah, women." He kept on nodding as if he knew everything about women, or at least everything he deemed worth knowing about them, which probably did not extend much past that they were trouble.

Vincent opened his mouth to say something but changed his mind before he'd formed the sentence. It didn't seem worth discussing. He was out at the other end of the world. His last coins were going toward a couple of pints of beer. It didn't seem like things could get much worse than that unless he got himself mixed up in a bar fight or got mugged.

Maybe if his vehicle got stolen?

Then again, who would want that heap of metal and trash? He hadn't had the money to repair it recently, so riding it was only a hair faster than walking.

Losing it might still be an inconvenience. If it rained, he could sleep under it and parts of him would remain dry if he lay completely still. If he could find the right person to trade with, perhaps he could sell some of the parts for more beer... That seemed like an idea worth exploring, so long as he left enough to take shelter under.

"So, where yae headed?" the sailor asked.

"Nowhere," Vincent replied.

"Staying 'ere then?"

Vincent hadn't thought about it. Evidently yes, unless he was going to make a walk of it.

"You're not from around 'ere, though?" the sailor remarked.

Vincent sighed, ordered himself another beer and gave up trying to ignore the man. "No, not from around here."

"So whatcha doing 'ere, then?"

"What does it look like?"

"Pathetic, is what it looks like." The sailor burst out laughing and slapped Vincent on the back.

Vincent had just raised his pint to his lips, hoping to pour the beer toward his throat and not across the counter, over his hands or on his shirt. The latter was where most of it landed regardless, due to the unsolicited correction of course.

He gave his hands a vigorous shake and wiped them onto his sides, eyed the sailor as sharply as his condition allowed, and tried again once he was sure he wouldn't be interrupted.

"Right, yae got troubles." The sailor helped Vincent wipe the counter with a handkerchief. "But yae look a bit too green to be taking it this hard, if yae don't mind me sayin'. Youth's no time to waste pinin'. Best leave it to the veterans such as myself."

Vincent concentrated on the remaining half of his pint. He didn't feel like trying to cheer up, since he wasn't nearly done wallowing yet.

"Look, I'm sure it can't be that bad. Is she such a fine wench you'll want to win her back?"

"No," Vincent said, then corrected hastily: "Yes, she is fine, but no, I don't want her back."

"So, yae should move on. Plenty of fish in the sea."

"I can't be having fish. Fish don't seem to agree with me."

"Nonsense. What is the problem, exact? Maybe I can offer yae some fresh perspective."

"There's something wrong with me that can't be fixed."

"Yae'd be surprised by what can be mended with the right tools, lad."

"Insanity as well?"

"That's all about perspective, lad. Not one of us is all right up there, in the noggin'. But if yae look the right way, it doesn't show on the outside."

"That's not very helpful." Vincent knocked back his beer and burped while wiping his mouth onto his sleeve.

"Have yae thought about seeing a *specialist*?"

"A specialist of what?"

"Of the mind, of course. A shrink. A mind-wrangler. Them types of doctors that deal with yaer mental side of things." The sailor looked at Vincent, who looked perplexed. "Really. How d'yae know it can't be fixed, if yae haven't even been t' see the right kind of doctor fer it?"

Vincent let go of his pint and tried to use the last shred of sober reasoning to consider it.

He'd always assumed whatever was wrong was a permanent part of his identity as the so-called possessed devil's spawn. Even when he'd never managed to sustain belief in God and thus didn't believe in the devil either, he'd been equally blinded by the flawed logic that if a man of cloth couldn't help him, then no one could. It seemed silly in retrospect. With there being so many different religions and ways to view the world, life was not as black and white as he had been conditioned to think.

"It's a mental illness, yae know," the sailor said knowingly.

"What is?" Vincent felt particularly dense after the strain of formulating his previous, almost coherent thoughts.

"Insanity, yae fool. Drink yaer beer, sleep it off and go see a doctor for it, get it treated. That swill's not gonna fix yae up, but he might."

T he specialist's waiting room was well-lit and organised. There were plants. Vincent guessed they were supposed to make the space feel more calm and inviting, but someone had placed them all wrong, so that they received either too much or not enough sunlight.

They looked reasonably healthy, but their soil was so dry he knew it was only a matter of days before the leaves started to shrink and fall. If a novice were to water them now, the plants would likely drown from over-watering.

Vincent ground his teeth.

Someone had brought these poor plants here to suit their fancy, but then lacked the decency to give them even the minimal care they needed.

Spurred on by the predicament of the plants, he felt compelled to check for dust. Instead of being calmed and reassured by the presence of greenery and the organised decor, he was further agitated by the thought of someone deserving a whooping for neglecting their sweeping and wiping duties. How was this supposed to be welcoming? How was he supposed to feel at ease here?

Vincent was quite riled up by the time he was called in. Because he didn't have a proper outlet for his feelings, he sat down, mute, with one corner of an eye twitching. Adding to that the excessive drinking from the night before, and he must have appeared in dire need of some extensive treatment.

The brain-doctor could probably smell this potential money flow from a mile away, but unfortunately for him, Vincent was nearly broke, and the one session fee was all he could afford.

"Hello, nice to meet you." The doctor offered to shake Vincent's hand. Vincent was about as enthused about the handshake as an octopus with a heat-stroke. That was also an apt description of the speed and cadence with which the doctor lumbered out his words. "And how are we doing today?"

"Cut the chit-chat and fix me," Vincent requested. He hadn't the patience nor the money for a leisurely in-depth analysis.

"All right. What seems to be the problem, sir?"

"I'm broken. You need to fix me. I hear that's what you people do."

"Yes, that is true." Judging by the pace of the doctor's speech, the octopus was still slowly, carefully stroking its heat. "However, we may need a bit more to work with. Can you give me some details, some specifics? What has brought you to my office today? What is bothering you?" Several of its tentacles had been run over by a boat and the octopus was now actively dying.

"I hear voices." Vincent tried to hurry things along by being concise.

"All right. And these voices, what do they say?"

"The problem is not so much what they say, but *when* they say it," Vincent said. The doctor nodded. "Actually, the problem is also what they say. But mainly when. It's at, shall we say, *inconvenient* times."

"All right. And how does this make you feel?"

"It makes me feel angry!"

"Good. So you are in touch with your anger. That is a good start. Anything else?"

"Betrayed. Frightened. Upset. Sad."

"When is this *inconvenient* time?" The doctor did a somewhat unflattering impression of Vincent's intonation. "Are they related to a specific thing?"

"Well." Vincent hesitated. It wasn't the sort of thing he wanted to discuss with a stranger. Then again, he only had this one session, and he did not want to waste it. There was no time to be polite or coy. "Basically, I get them when I'm having sex."

"Oh." The doctor was clearly taken aback by this but recovered quickly. "And how does that make you feel?"

"It makes me feel awful, is what it makes me feel," Vincent barked. "I know how I feel. That's not the problem. I want it fixed. How do I stop hearing them?"

"Maybe that's part of the problem..."

"What?"

"You are suppressing them and refusing to listen to what your inner voice is telling you. You say you hear voices, but it's possible it is just one voice: yours. It's telling you things you don't want to hear, so you become irate. Let's perform a small exercise. Listen."

Vincent wasn't sure what he was supposed to listen to but made an attempt to comply.

The room was quiet save for some stray noise coming from somewhere outside.

"Look, I'm not su—"

The doctor shushed Vincent back to silence. He listened to the same inconsequential nothingness Vincent was hearing, as if he were making an exceptionally weighty point.

After some minutes of this silence, he cleared his throat and the octopus was revived enough to form the following sentences.

"Could be trauma, something in your past that has triggered these voices. How would you describe your relationship with… *sex*?"

Vincent tried to process this abrupt proposition. It was difficult to wrap his head around the logic of himself saying something like "I'll chop your dick off" due to childhood trauma.

"How was your childhood? Happy?" The doctor wiped his spectacles with an embroidered handkerchief, but his efforts smeared the grease all across the lenses instead of cleaning them. Vincent looked away.

"Not particularly, no."

"Is there anything there, something that might have happened that has stuck with you, that you haven't dealt with? It could be that matter resurfacing. If we have severely upsetting memories that we hold in and deny for long enough, they tend to force their way out. Perhaps that is what you are hearing."

"I don't know…" Vincent could think of a number of unpleasant memories, but he hadn't ever felt like he'd consciously had to hold them in. He hardly even thought about them these days.

"Maybe it's something so far deep down that you don't even know it's there anymore?" The doctor looked a bit smug. This annoyed Vincent, but since this was his only chance to try to get this fixed, he ignored it. "How is your relationship with your mother? How about your father?" the doctor asked.

Vincent cringed. There was an issue there if ever there was one. He definitely did not enjoy thinking about it.

"I don't—" Vincent cleared his throat. "So you think this might have something to do with them?"

"What do you think?"

"They haven't been in my life for some time now."

"Yes, but is it of consequence?"

"Pardon me?"

"You have an issue with them, correct? How big is this issue? Their physical presence is not necessarily relevant if they are an important part of your life. Do they still matter to you, even when they're not there?"

"Of course they do."

"Any unresolved issues?"

"Probably."

"Well then, perhaps therein lies the key to your unhappiness. You must listen to your inner voice and find out what's really bothering you. It's probably childhood trauma. You should look into that." The doctor tapped the top of his watch. "Now, I fear our time is up."

"Already?" Vincent frowned. That was quick. "But I'm still broken."

"Yes, well, we can schedule another session for you."

"But I don't have, um... the time. I have to be going... ah, elsewhere."

"Well, the rest is up to you, then." The doctor shrugged. "Good luck to you." The man ushered Vincent out of his office, not much better off than when he'd entered.

CHAPTER 23

With nothing worthwhile where he was, and tired of the unfamiliar scenery, Vincent turned his speeder around to head back home. He was sorely in need of money to cover his travel expenses, so he decided to look for another job—something he could do while on the road so as not to slow him down. That was when he stumbled upon writing stories about his travels for the small local newspapers.

Vincent had to do some extensive grovelling and pleading before he was published, but he did get paid a tiny sum for it. His first paycheck went toward fuel, and although he spent a few days without eating much, he covered the distance all the way to the nearest border, across it, and to a larger town with better opportunities.

He wouldn't have been so shamelessly persistent had his travel-speed not depended on it. He could have found a better-paying stationery job had the situation demanded it, but he was so inspired by his initial success with the newspapers, he became obsessed and could only focus on writing and getting his stories sold. It wasn't as if he needed to eat absolutely every day, anyway.

Vincent put to good use the host of useful skills he'd acquired during his years of letter-writing. Once he gained momentum and a decent reputation, selling his stories became much easier.

However, the editors continued to do their best to make his life difficult, even when he'd gained some celebrity. They were hoping and expecting him to fail, but they were reluctant to have him do it on the page of their newspaper. In being picky and harsh, they forced Vincent to hone his skills, and he also gained a healthy confidence and became more thick-skinned about the feedback.

Once he had an audience and could deliver the goods, he could bring in the money just about wherever he went. It was a good feeling, and it made his journey a lot smoother.

F or someone supposedly in a hurry to go home, Vincent sure was taking a lot of detours. There were some additional delays when he stopped to meet fans or indulged in beverages, although he remained adamant to abstain from entertaining women.

He took a scenic route through a jungle. Strictly for educational purposes, of course. It had nearly, almost, practically nothing to do with wanting to have something more interesting to write about. Might as well, he thought, while he was already out in these parts of the world, anyway.

He certainly learned a lot about himself when he was bitten by a venomous amphibian—the venom of which caused paralysis and hallucinations—with the closest civilization with antivenom about a two-day hike away.

It was especially enlightening because he happened to hallucinate that his transport was a giant, fire-breathing parakeet that he could no longer bear riding and had to leave behind to brave the rest of the jungle on foot.

These were the moments that really revealed what he was made of.

That is to say, made of a whimpering mess of potato mash: clumpy and stupid, wetting himself at any sign of anything he perceived unusual—which included absolutely *everything*—and crawling on his hands and knees, since, even when he could move his legs again, he was too distressed to stand up for feeling that his head was too high up and the ground way too far down. There was probably an exotic disease or two in the mix, making sure that attaining any personal growth from these experiences was a decent challenge.

The estimate of 'a two-day hike' was only accurate provided that you weren't writhing in pain and stumbling into every stick and puddle along the way. It ended up taking Vincent two weeks to get out of that jungle. It only took him a day and a half to retrieve his vehicle once he was healthy and sober-headed enough to ride an elephant to get back to it.

There was also the episode with the mistaken taste test of a fungus that was objectively not suited for consumption. It had been a lesson Vincent had learned well enough not to repeat again, no matter how hungry he got.

He steered clear of any mushrooms for a while, and was wary of and unnerved by cauliflowers for quite some time after, but it had made some rather juicy fodder for his writing: A cauliflower could be surprisingly eerie when it was staring at you right in the face, with its beady eyes ablaze, and its long beak and antlers ready to pierce your gut repeatedly, without mercy. Since he'd survived the altercation with barely any visible scars, he considered himself richer for it.

No longer quite as excited by the detours, though, Vincent heaved a sigh of relief the magnitude of a corked-up hippopotamus passing gas when he crossed another border to a more familiar climate and more familiar dangers.

V incent took shelter from the light drizzle under an overhang on the deck of the ferry. He sat down on a bench and breathed in the sea air. Ah, finally some peace and quiet.

People had recognised him as soon as he'd reached the docks. A child had pointed him out to his mother and waved enthusiastically. A group of people had greeted him as if an old friend. This caused everyone to turn their attention to him, even though some of them didn't know why they were looking.

The fame was flattering, but it also made him feel like he was being watched all the time. It felt unfair that strangers recognised him, but he hadn't the faintest of clues who they were. Perhaps he should have forgone publishing a picture of his face next to the articles, but he couldn't have guessed his popularity, and it was too late to regret it now.

It was his first time back since he'd been published. He'd written letters home about it but hadn't expected the local newspapers to pick up his articles from the newspapers on the mainland and reprint them in his absence. Not many remained who hadn't read at least one of them. Most had read them all.

Now, at the age of twenty-four, he'd become a wealthy man, collecting paychecks for the reprinted articles alongside selling the new ones. The papers were eager to pay him extra to smooth over the issue of publishing without consent, and to butter him up so they could get their hands on some more, preferably exclusive, articles.

There weren't very many other passengers on the ferry, so Vincent relaxed and enjoyed this rare moment of privacy. He closed his eyes, lulled by the gentle sway of the waves, and didn't open them until the ferry arrived at its destination.

The town looked much the same. It couldn't have been more than four years since his last brief visit, but so much had happened it felt much longer. He wondered how everyone was doing and if they would be surprised by his return. He'd mentioned his locations in his letters, so, though he hadn't explicitly stated he was coming home, anyone with half a mind could probably tell where he was headed.

He stepped onto the dock and, because he wasn't in a hurry, moved aside so others could pass. Deep in his thoughts, he didn't notice anything until he was being squeezed with some gusto by a woman he recalled having been much bigger and taller.

"Vincent!" Celandine's voice cracked, and as Vincent pushed her back gently by the arms, she looked about to cry.

"Celandine." Having made sure it was indeed her, Vincent hugged her back and even lifted her briefly off the ground as emotion overtook him. He hadn't realised it until now, but he'd really missed her. "Where's Aster? She's not here, is she?"

"She's at home with Arthur, but she's anxious to see you. We should hurry up and not keep her waiting. Her husband is there too."

"How did you know...?"

"Oh, don't be daft, luv. We've been expecting you. I've been checking the docks since last Tuesday. You took your bloody time!" Celandine grinned and gave him a wink. Vincent felt bad about not giving them a proper warning. A part of him hadn't wanted them to feel obliged to come, and another had been afraid they wouldn't want to.

"I had some business to take care of..." Vincent picked his bags and followed Celandine, who started walking up the street and into town.

"Are you hungry? Tired? Need something?" She turned around every time she asked, but kept on walking all the while.

"I'm fine. How's everyone?"

"Mostly the same. No need to look so worried." Celandine chuckled.

"Ah, good." Vincent smiled. With that out of the way, he wondered how to bring up the extra bundle of cash burning a hole in his pocket. He was keen to dispense it, but the Brambles weren't the money-hungry sort. He'd have to present it the right way so as not to insult them.

"Vincent?" Aster squealed even before Vincent had stepped into the house. She was somewhere in the kitchen and her voice well preceded her slight frame, which moments later arrived at the door with some speed, bumping into Vincent and sending him a few steps backwards.

"Oh, Vincent!" She looked happy, then stern in reprimand, and finally relieved. The sisters pushed Vincent inside while George walked down the stairs. The man shook Vincent's hand formally. He didn't care much for hugs, but it was clear from the firmness of the handshake he was happy to see Vincent.

"You seem to have become a real man since I last saw you," George said.

"Perhaps you'd like to wash up while we prepare lunch?" Celandine suggested before any lengthier conversation had the chance to start. George looked a little disappointed but said nothing. Vincent didn't dare to object, agreeing that he'd probably passed the smell of no return long since, although his nose had endured it until he was immune.

He was escorted into the bathroom as if he'd had time to forget where it was. At least Celandine did not follow him in but merely handed a washcloth, some soap and a towel from the door. Once she was gone,

Vincent could hear excited chattering coming from the kitchen. Though the walls obscured the words, he could guess what the topic was.

He took his time in the bath. It was one more thing he'd remembered being bigger. When he dried himself up, the towel did not even reach around him, despite the fact that he wasn't a particularly wide man.

Vincent had had the foresight to bring his bag but couldn't recall when he'd last had the chance to do any laundry, so the contents smelled ripe enough for even him to tell they were past their prime.

"Um, excuse me, Celandine?" he called from the door, trying to hold the miniscule towel so that it at least covered most of the relevant bits.

"Yes, luv?" Celandine's head popped from the kitchen into the corridor. She looked to be busy with something, holding her hands up. They were covered in what appeared to be flour. Evidently, the occasion called for fresh baked bread.

"You wouldn't happen to have... uh, nevermind."

"What is it, luv? Need something?"

"I was just—"

"You're out of fresh clothes, aren't you?" She laughed. Aster swooped past her and headed upstairs.

"Just one moment," she said as she passed Vincent. Vincent retreated back into the bathroom.

Well, that was embarrassing. He hadn't expected how difficult these things could become once he'd grown up beyond a certain point and perhaps also a little apart. The sisters seemed unfazed. In fact, they seemed curiously amused by the situation.

There was a knock on the door and Aster peeked in. Struggling not to blush in a manner too obvious, Vincent took the bundle of clothes and thanked her. She stayed at the door for an uncomfortable while, made a poor attempt at disguising her amusement, laughed and left Vincent alone to dress.

The shirt was much too small. It wasn't any of his old shirts, but probably George's. The width was fine, but the sleeves only came halfway past his elbows.

The trousers weren't much better, but the socks at least were loose and generous. The ensemble reminded Vincent of some of the mountaineers he'd met a few years ago; only the characteristic hat with a feathery brush and a corded colourful hatband was missing.

The clothes were clean and comfortable, and, though they caused some hilarity when he walked into the kitchen, at least the embarrassment wasn't as bad as when he'd been bungling with the towel.

Aster came into the kitchen at Vincent's heels. She'd acquired Vincent's bag and was now rummaging through it to assess his laundry needs. This wouldn't have been a problem had he foreseen it, but it didn't take Aster long to run into some of Vincent's bundled finances. She yelped at the sight of them.

"What did you do, rob a bank on your way here?"

"No, of course not!" Vincent hurried to take the bag out of her hands, but she retreated with it, out of reach. "That's just some of my pay."

He'd deposited some into a bank inland for later use to avoid having to carry it along with him. He'd also left standing agreements with a few of the newspapers so that they owed him until he could come collect his share later. The island bank had been unclear about its agreements with the mainland banks, so a transfer between accounts would have potentially taken too long to arrange. Thus, bringing some cash had been the quick and reliable option.

"*Some* of it?!" Celandine hurried to look in the bag. Her hands were still in dough, so she poked at the bag with her elbows.

"It's dangerous to walk around with a lot of money, but I—" Vincent swallowed. They were looking at him like he'd done something wrong. It was his money. He'd worked for it. It did seem a bit unethical to receive that much money for such little work, especially compared to the hours of a hall boy working for nothing but his measly keep... But he'd earned it by working. It was his money.

"What do you plan to do with it all?" Celandine asked, suspicious. Vincent was painfully aware that, as she held up a swath of bills, she held the equal of two years' pay for a local fisherman.

"I thought I'd, um... give some... to you..." Vincent's voice trailed off, though he'd tried to remain firm. This wasn't quite how he'd wanted to bring it up.

"What? Give it away? To us? Nonsense!" Celandine spat air, insulted by the preposterous idea.

"But—"

"Don't be silly, luv. You don't owe us anything, and this is *much* too much money to just *give* away. You should spend it to buy something. Something lasting." As Celandine spoke, her voice became a bit softer, and her initial anger died down. She did still peer at Vincent, expecting some sort of reasonable solution from him.

Vincent shrugged. He hadn't really thought about it. He had more than enough for his travelling needs, and he could always write more. That was all he cared about. His carefree attitude would not please either of the sisters, so he knew he had to come up with an acceptable compromise.

"How about I buy the cottage?" It had crossed his mind before, though he'd only ever entertained the thought half-heartedly.

The Brambles had purchased the cottage at the brink of abandonment back when Vincent had moved into it with Celandine. They didn't have much use for it now that Vincent was all grown up, so it made sense for them to part with it. It hadn't cost much, but it had required some repairs and it was still in great condition, so surely they would accept at least a decent price for it?

Celandine looked ready to protest. Aster said nothing, but her expression was similar to her sister's. They exchanged glances amidst what seemed like wordless negotiations. George stayed out of any conversation where the women had raised their voices, but also when they were suspiciously silent like this. Vincent held his breath.

"Fine." Celandine squinted. She looked displeased but grabbed some of the money from the bag and gave it to George for safekeeping. "The cottage is yours. At least you won't be spending it on anything untoward."

Celandine resumed her baking, Aster smiled at Vincent reassuringly, and Vincent finally remembered to breathe again.

It had gone better than expected!

Come to think of it, owning his own home seemed especially convenient after today's less than ideal bathing experience. She'd taken more than he'd dared to hope, but he still had plenty left for whatever renovations he fancied. The thought of having a spacious garage for his projects intrigued him greatly.

CHAPTER 24

The new garage was splendid. Vincent used the word splendid for a lot of things, but it fit this occasion exceptionally well.

It was quite a large extension to the house, but it still managed not to be too imposing. From the outside, it blended seamlessly with the old cottage.

There was plenty of space for just about any project he wanted to start, and boy, did he have a project in mind! The old vehicle paled in comparison. Then again, it had been a mere mouse-step faster than walking in its run-down condition. He'd sold it to a farmer on the mainland for parts, so at least some of it had gone into good use.

Vincent had already made some preliminary drawings and acquired most of the key parts he needed to get started. Now that he had a place to put it all together with no disturbances, he began work, and no one saw him for weeks.

M s Buttercup had been worried enough to enlist the help of Vincent's closest neighbours to see if his lights were on in the evenings and make sure nothing had exploded in the vicinity. They wouldn't pry further than that, but the neighbours, who lived close enough to see Vincent's cottage as a dot far off, sent regular reports that he was doing fine. Sometimes, if they were away or too busy, it was up to Edward Steadfast to pass by on behalf of Ms Buttercup to confirm nothing was amiss.

It wasn't until sometime in early September when Vincent emerged from his cottage with a prototype. He came into town for more supplies and to let everyone know he was still alive. When he turned up at Edward's newly established parts shop asking for advice, Edward was more than delighted to get reacquainted and participate in developing the new speeder.

The prototype was, in itself, already a massive improvement from Vincent's previous contraptions. It wasn't a matter of skills, but rather because he'd gained so much practical experience on the road, and he now had the finances to afford the things he wanted to try.

Vincent didn't talk about his finances, but there had to be large sums going towards all the parts and equipment he needed. Edward, though aware of Vincent's growing reputation and wealth, was more impressed by how little Vincent seemed to care about them, so long as he could afford what he wanted.

With a steady stream of parts funnelled through Edward's shop, he had a valid reason to check up on Vincent on delivery days. Vincent didn't seem to mind taking short breaks on occasion. In fact, he was usually beaming as he explained what he'd done since Edward had been there last.

This lasted up until the disaster with the fuel valve. It was a minor miscalculation and nothing important got destroyed, but it sent Vincent into a hyper-obsessive hunt where he examined every detail that could have played a part in causing the failure. Once he was done with his investigation, he put protocols in place to prevent it from ever happening again. It was meticulous and redundant, considering how simple a flaw it had been, and typically like Vincent to go so overboard with it.

The incident, in its entirety, wreaked havoc on the schedule of Vincent's project, but he was too intensely midway in it to care. He'd said he was going to leave the island before the winter, but didn't even notice there was snow until Edward gently pointed it out to him. In November.

That was around the time when Vincent ran out of parts.

Edward had to take great care explaining to him that parts were like mail this time of year: they did not arrive from the mainland. Because no one here had use for such advanced things as Vincent needed, they were all something Edward ordered specifically for him. When something was out of stock this time of year, the only option was to make it locally, but neither Vincent, Edward or the local blacksmith had the skills or machinery to produce the kind of quality Vincent's projects required.

Vincent looked indifferent when informed about the weather and the ferries. He said it had been a while since he'd seen that much snow, but then he shrugged and turned his attention back to the drawings for the speeder.

"Do you need anything?" Edward thought to ask.

"Huh?" Vincent seemed preoccupied, but it was already unlike him to notice someone speaking when he was doing something else. He must have been distracted by something other than his usual intense focus.

"The weather is pretty bad and that thing won't run, so I was wondering if you needed something. I could bring it by next time I'm in the neighbourhood. I picked up Mr Mason's snow ploughing rounds. His arthritis is getting worse and I have the time."

"Oh, right."

"So, do you need anything?" Edward repeated his question.

"Huh?" Vincent was frowning.

Edward helped himself and checked the pantry. There was a fair amount there, but it wouldn't last more than a week. "I'll bring you some food, right? Anything else? Lamp oil?" He made a list.

"What did you say?" Vincent was roused from his thoughts and finally made an effort to join the conversation. "I guess..." He looked around himself, confused, evidently still working out that something out of the ordinary was required of him. "Food, right. Lamp oil. Some paper would be nice." He started adding up the costs.

"I'll put it on your tab," Edward said.

"Thank you."

"Ms Buttercup was asking if you needed a knit sweater or mittens or something such."

"It's been a bit cold recently," Vincent admitted. Then he seemed to turn back to his previous thoughts. "I could make the whole of the steering system smaller. That way I could fit a bigger pump on the side."

"It doesn't have to be the bigger model pump," Edward pointed out kindly.

"But you don't have the smaller ones in stock."

"Are you going to redesign the whole thing instead of waiting until you can get a smaller pump? What's the hurry? You're not going anywhere any sooner. Besides, I still don't have the eight-mil, half-width brackets, so you'd be just as stuck, with a loose pump lying around."

"But—"

"Face it, man, you've done all you can do for now besides polished the thing. Do you have letters?"

Vincent always had letters. The postman no longer made rounds except in town, but Edward didn't mind delivering Vincent's while he was making the trip here, anyway. Vincent handed him a set of five out of a stack of ten.

They were not as many and not as thick as what he'd written as a child, but the names and addresses were written inhumanely neatly on top. Perhaps he'd switched from quantity to quality? Edward wondered what else had changed.

"Anything else?" Edward asked one more time. Vincent shook his head, too busy with something to even voice a reply. "All right. I'll be going now before it gets dark. Annoying to drive in the dark." He knew he was talking to no one but himself, but he still said goodbye before leaving. Vincent would probably notice he'd left, eventually.

CHAPTER 25

Something mysterious had happened during the following week. Busy with other things, Edward had postponed taking Vincent his supplies by a few days, so before he had time to go, he received word from Ms Buttercup. Ms Buttercup, in turn, had received word from Vincent's neighbour about there not having been a light at his cottage the day before.

This seemed a little peculiar, but Edward didn't think too much of it. Perhaps Vincent's rhythm had changed as it sometimes did on the cusp and during polar night, and he'd just slept at abnormal hours? According to Ms Buttercup, the man had the tendency of falling ill in the winter, and recalling back, Edward could remember there being times when he hadn't seen Vincent at school much between November and February. Since she was so worried about him, Edward promised to go take a look right away.

Ms Buttercup packed a whole bundle of things to take to Vincent, which amused Edward, since, despite his quirks, Vincent was a grown man, presumably fully capable of taking care of himself. He didn't dare to say anything, though, just smiled and packed the things to the back of the snowplough.

Even as he drove there, Edward wasn't particularly worried. The uneasy mood only reached him when he parked the plough at Vincent's house, where no lamp was lit despite it being a cloudy, dark day. Perhaps he'd run out of lamp oil?

Edward knocked. There was no reply, and no one came to the door. He helped himself in, now a little more concerned.

"Vincent?" He was met with silence. Everything looked fine. Nothing had exploded in the garage. The fire had died, but the bricks were warm to the touch, and the temperature inside was reasonable.

Judging by the kitchen, Vincent had eaten something recently. Edward wasn't sure what it was, but it had been prepared that day. It looked and smelled suspicious but seemed edible. Probably a stew of some sort.

"Vincent?" Edward called again. He didn't enjoy the eerily quiet and dark atmosphere, so he lit a few lamps and built a fire in the fireplace. Then he checked the other rooms. Nothing.

"Vincent?" No response. He checked the front yard, and as he'd suspected, the only footprints in the snow were his own. The back door was snowed in and frozen shut. Vincent had to be in the house. Edward checked the garage again.

"Vincent? I brought your supplies. Ms Buttercup... she's a bit worried. Vincent?"

There weren't that many places in the house to hide in. Vincent was not in the bedroom, nor his study. The guest room was empty. Where else could he be?

Edward sighed and sat down in the kitchen. He was at a loss. A man could not just vanish into thin air. It hadn't snowed for a couple of days, so the timeline made no sense. If Vincent had left around the time when it had last snowed, the cottage would have been much colder and the food he'd prepared would have likely gone off somewhat despite the cold. But if he'd left later, then there would be tracks. The speeder did not fly when it was this cold, besides it was safely tucked under a tarpaulin in the garage.

He still wasn't sure if he was really supposed to start worrying or if Vincent was going to appear from somewhere and be as if nothing had happened.

"If it's a trick, you got me. You can come out now!" he tried. Still nothing. He was a calm man, but this did irritate him a little. Vincent had better have a good excuse for making people worry. "Vincent?!"

Edward sat there for five more minutes. He'd brought the supplies; he'd searched the house. What else was there left to do? Wait for a body to turn up? What?

He listened. Maybe if he listened carefully enough, he would hear something. The crackling fire was about all he could hear. He should have prioritised this and come here sooner.

Damn it. Maybe there was a secret room somewhere? There was no attic. The roof and the ceiling were the same except for one of the bedrooms. There was a small compartment there for storage, but Vincent kept it pretty full. Edward had checked.

A cellar, then? Where would the access be? Outside? Probably not outside. Again, there would have been footprints. So beneath his feet? Edward looked at the floor. He started to check the rooms again, one by one. It took a while, but he eventually found the hatch in Vincent's office.

"All right, you'd better be in there," he said, and pulled it open.

A staircase led down into darkness, deeper than he'd expected. It wasn't just the usual metre or so that lifted the house a reasonable distance from the ground. There was a proper room down there.

Edward lifted his lantern to shine some light on the steps to avoid slipping and breaking his neck. He didn't have to look much further to find Vincent. He sat at the bottom end of the steps and turned to look up, shielding his eyes.

It was a creepy sight. He was a gaunt man with the sort of sickly pale face one did not want to see in scarce lighting, and he looked like death itself. Had it caught Edward completely off guard, he might have jolted, perhaps even let out a tiny scream. Instead, he rolled his eyes, annoyed.

"Well, at least you're alive. What the hell are you doing down here?"

"I... Dhe..." As expected, he sounded stuffed to the brim with snot. "Id was... I..." Vincent shrugged and gave up.

Edward sighed and helped him up and into the office. He stumbled a bit but did a better job than expected from the looks of him.

"I brought you the supplies. Ms Buttercup was worried. She sent you a sweater. Hell, I'm no longer surprised she worries. Look at you. Are you even fit to be on your own?"

"How did—? Righd, dhe subblies..." Vincent seemed to assume it was merely a scheduled visit. The stupid man probably hadn't a clue he was being watched, and how much Ms Buttercup and the rest of his family worried about him.

"Sorry do hab worried you," Vincent said. He walked into the kitchen and sat down at the table.

"That's all right, but it would have helped to know you have a cellar."

"Yeah, I dug it oud a few days ago. I needed de space. Bery conbenient."

"I see. Will you manage? You look a bit... dreadful," Edward noted.

Vincent reminded him of a dimwitted little brother that he needed to keep an eye on, so he wouldn't swallow a marble or burn his fingers on an oven handle. He wasn't sure if it was safe to leave him unsupervised like this. "Maybe I could bring Ms Buttercup here for a while. Until you feel better?"

"No," Vincent rejected the idea. "I can dake care ob myself. It'd jusd worry her more. I'm fine..." As he was saying this, he seemed to pass out on the table.

"Right." Edward exhaled his mounting frustration. He left Vincent to lie there while he put the supplies away, some of them into the pantry and some into the kitchen cupboards.

A while later, Vincent woke up again, but if possible, he was even less coherent.

"I feel like I'm being watched," he mumbled.

"Oh?" Edward was surprised by the astute observation. "Right now?"

"Yes, and id's making me uncombardable."

Ah, so not so much an astute observation as a case of paranoia brought on by his illness? But it wasn't very often that Vincent expressed his feelings openly like this, Edward realised. Not unless he backed them up with a carefully worded reasoning.

Even as a child, Vincent hadn't done much complaining unless he was defending somebody else. When he did talk about how he felt, it was usually much later after the fact, and even then, he spoke of himself as if he were a character in one of his stories. While Vincent's lug-headedness frustrated Edward, he was actually quite glad that the man was opening up a little.

"Even de snake wasn't dis bad," Vincent grumbled. "I'm drapped in dis bubble, and someding beyond dere, in de dargness, is watching me."

"The snake? Oh yes, I think I read something about that." Again with the stories. Edward wondered if they were actually true and not made up to sell more papers. He'd received a few letters and read the articles, and while they'd mentioned a lot of the same things, he had his doubts.

As far as he could tell, Vincent had never lied to him, but then again, these articles were aimed at others. "So the snake part was true," he said to himself. He didn't expect Vincent to be listening, but evidently the man's undivided attention was now fixed on Edward, and he responded.

"Id's all drue. Maybe a bit, um, coloured in here and dere, but drue."

"Coloured in?"

"Id was boring."

"Really, even the snake?"

"Had to edit a lod of it oud for being doo repedidive. Boring. Who wands do read about days of differend dypes of dorture. De editor said id was depressing. He wanted someding exciding, but nod so dark it would scare de younger readers." Vincent sat up in what could graciously be called a more upright angle. "Well, not dorture. Dat's an oversdatemend. Jusd... a lot of writhing and padedic moaning. Who wants to read something like dat?"

"The visions?" He'd mentioned some in his articles.

"Oh yeah, dose." Vincent seemed reluctant to elaborate on the details, but presumably those had been real then. "I'd radder dake de bisions than dis bloody bubble."

"Are you hungry? I could fix you something while I'm here. I can't stay for very long because of the weather, but a couple of hours should be fine."

"I guess." Vincent slumped down again. He haphazardly reached for a handkerchief at the other end of the table and blew his nose in a manner that made Edward wonder if a part of his brain had become expelled through his nose in the process. Then he turned his head so that he was watching Edward with his ear still pressed against the table. "Sorry about this," he reiterated. "I didn't mean to worry anyone. There's no one on the road to worry, so..."

"I get it."

"This probably looks worse than it is. I always catch everything in de winter."

"Yeah, that explains some things." Edward started to prepare the dinner. He wasn't much of a cook, but anything was better than the unidentifiable stew Vincent had made.

"So long as dere's no feber," Vincent said and blew his nose again. It must have dislodged what was left of his brain because his forehead consequently came down on the table with a thunk. "Ouch."

"Heh, have a care. You might still need that."

"Right," Vincent mumbled sourly. "Feels useless and heavy now."

Edward felt bad for him, feeling so under the weather, but what did he expect when he ate this unhealthily and spent time in a cold cellar without being properly dressed?

"Here's the sweater, by the way." Edward lifted the package with the knitted sweater onto the table. Vincent poked at it. "Put it on. Maybe you'll feel better," Edward suggested.

"Yeah, bud de feber…"

Edward helped unwrap the package and threw the contents over Vincent's head. The man seemed to snap out of this whiny lethargy for long enough to dive into the garment. Ms Buttercup had made it a generous size, even for Vincent.

"Looks warm," Edward commented.

"Mm." Vincent made an effort to snort and swallow some of the mucus before slumping back into his previous position. "Just so you know, once the fever starts rising, I will probably say stupid stuff so… if dat happens, you should jusd leave."

"Oh?"

"I don't want to make you uncomfortable."

"Don't worry about it," Edward replied, preoccupied by his cooking. Then, as he slowly put two and two together, he burst out laughing at the ridiculousness of the notion. "Is that why you were in the cellar?"

Yes, fevers could sometimes rise high enough to cause shivers, aches and hallucinations. They could be unpleasant for sure. But to go as far as freezing yourself solid, sitting in a bloody cellar to avoid a fever was just the sort of idiocy one could expect from Vincent! Edward had to wipe his eyes from laughing so hard.

"Id's cooler dere." Vincent didn't even sound offended. "Dat's not id dough. Dere was anoder reason." Too tired to reach for the handkerchief, he retried the snorting tactic but ended up sniffling and wiping his nose to his sleeve instead.

"Oh?" Edward handed him the handkerchief. This could be interesting. To think of it, this was probably the longest discussion he'd had with Vincent outside of a project, perhaps ever.

It wasn't as if Vincent were bad at small-talk. He could sometimes talk your ear off about a subject he was passionate about. But an actual back and forth conversation? Especially one where he was saying things about himself? Edward felt guilty for wanting to exploit that further.

There was a lengthy silence and an even lengthier nose-trumpet solo before Vincent continued, but Edward was certainly listening.

"I know." Vincent raised his head to look at Edward. "It's illogical to find comfort in a memory that wasn't very pleasant to begin with. It was just familiar there."

"Familiar? In a dark, cold staircase?"

"Yes." There was another lengthy silence with no telling whether Vincent would even continue, but Edward did not want to spoil it by saying something wrong.

There was probably nothing all that intriguing or mysterious in Vincent's past, but the less he talked about it, the more it bothered Edward. After all, what the hell could have happened during those first eight or nine years to make a man grow up this strange? Certainly, it wasn't the influence of the island. Vincent had been different right from the start.

Maybe Ms Buttercup knew something about Vincent's background? It probably wouldn't hurt to ask.

"Hmm, warm," Vincent mumbled dreamily. "So you want to know? Why does it bother you so much?"

"What?"

"You're right. It's not that interesting, and it wasn't nine years. It was just one. Maybe a little over one."

"Uh?"

"Well, you asked."

"Oh? Right... I guess I did." Edward frowned. Had he? Well, it didn't matter. Vincent's fever was likely on the rise now that his body temperature was improving, and these were probably the weird things he'd say that he'd warned about.

"Yes. No wait. You didn't say that. Never mind."

"What? What do you mean?" Edward tried to get Vincent to respond a couple more times, but the man no longer seemed willing to continue the conversation. His silence persisted for close to half an hour, despite Edward periodically commenting on something about the food or the weather as he tried to change the subject to something a little less loaded.

"Could you hand me something cold to drink?" Vincent finally opened his mouth to ask. He looked distinctly unwell now, sweating and breathing heavily. It was good to sweat it out, so long as it was bearable. Edward checked Vincent's forehead and inquired after a thermometer.

"It's in de dop drawer over dere." Vincent sneezed.

"What's the red notch for?" Edward asked, trying to ignore the violent explosion of snot. There was a red dot at seventy-four.

"Oh, that's the record," Vincent replied, wiping the carnage.

"What degrees are these?"

"That's the Basenyett System." Vincent took the thermometer and wiggled it into place under his arm. Then he gulped down the cold water Edward offered him and proceeded to collapse on the table, though sideways this time, so as not to break the thermometer.

"How does that compare?"

"Sixty-five is considered a fever. I can only remember that seventy-four smelled of strawberries." Vincent shrugged. He checked the thermometer. "It's about seventy. Not bad." He wiped it negligently on the shirt sleeve and dropped it to the table. Edward glanced at it to confirm the number.

"Right, so that's a fever, then."

"Yes." Vincent sighed and tried to make himself comfortable lying across the table. This seemed futile considering the shapes of the two forms trying to merge.

"Are you sure you'll manage?" Edward asked. The dinner was almost done, and he was getting ready to leave.

"Yes, id's fine." Vincent cleared his throat and swallowed. "Thanks."

"I could ask the neighbour to come over to look after you."

"Nah, de fewer widnesses de bedder. Are you going?" Vincent moved to get up. He looked so unsteady on his feet, Edward hastily told him not to bother. Perhaps it was best to stay a while longer? At least until Vincent had eaten and gone to bed, since there seemed a fair chance he would do neither if he was left to his own devices.

"Hah, dat's true. Dat might be good." Vincent chuckled, but the sound was muffled by the table he was facing and the sweater between them.

"Do you want me to feed you as well?" Edward wasn't about to run out of patience yet, but he was edging much closer to it.

"Dat's all right." This time, Vincent was halfway up to get some food for himself before Edward stopped him.

"Sit. I'll get it for you."

"I'm not a cripple."

"Just sit. I'm here, so I might as well look after you a bit. Ms Buttercup will have my head if something were to happen to you."

"Hah, right." Vincent seemed to think it was a joke. He ate frustratingly slowly, but Edward waited without commenting on it. While he ate, Edward made sure that the fire was lit in the bedroom and the fireplace was tended to so that he could leave with his mind at ease that Vincent was not going to freeze to death, or die of carbon monoxide poisoning, or that the house would not burn down.

"Thank you," Vincent said when he was finally done with the meal. "I'll go rest now."

"Good. In the bedroom and not the cellar, I trust."

"I don't like it but yes."

"It's just a fever. It'll pass."

"No, I'm quite insane. It's bringing it out more than usual."

"That might be true," Edward agreed jokingly. Vincent didn't seem amused. "Look, if it bothers you, you could go see the doctor for it. We have one of those mind doctors in town." It was an off-handed suggestion, but Vincent seemed to be considering it in earnest. "Well, I'll be going now. Try to get yourself sorted out. And for the love of Maury, do not disappear into the cellar again. It's disturbing." Edward patted Vincent on the shoulder, and once he'd confirmed that the man headed for the right room, he left the house.

CHAPTER 26

At his rightful place in his nest of blankets at the foot of Vincent's bed, Mr Swifty had only just settled in for the night.

They had returned to the cottage after Midwinter day tea at the Poppycocks'. Vincent had seemed eager to leave, but they had talked him into staying for a while longer for the sake of the little human, Vincent's weak spot. Mr Swifty had enjoyed the ample snacks, but his tummy was glad to be home.

Mr Swifty was roused by the sound of a creaky door. Sometimes a draught would move a door if it had been left ajar, so this sound alone was not peculiar. However, he could have sworn he could hear footsteps.

He wasn't too happy about leaving the warmth of the bed, but the sooner he checked that nothing was wrong, the sooner he would be able to relax again, so he jumped down from the bed to investigate.

The cottage was dark. Mr Swifty peeked into the kitchen. Everything seemed as it should. He sniffed the floors for something unfamiliar, but nothing stood out. He heard another sound, this time from somewhere below.

Ah, yes. There was space under the house. Perhaps a mouse or a rat, then? He snuck into Vincent's study, hoping to engage in a bit of a chase to be rid of the nervous energy.

The hatch was open. Didn't Vincent usually keep it closed? It was heavy, but Mr Swifty knew how to pull it aside by the piece of string attached to it, so he could usually crack it open enough to check on Vincent if the man was having one of his sits in the staircase. The hatch being open did explain the draught, though.

Mr Swifty peeked down. As he stretched his neck lower to locate the whereabouts of the rodent, he was thoroughly scared by something big and dark coming right at him. The cellar shouldn't have been lit, but both light and warmth flooded Mr Swifty's senses. He panicked. He hadn't time to determine the source of the light nor assess what was charging at him. All four of his paws were doing their best to take him away from the scene.

Holy hell, that was one big rat!

Damn it, this wasn't how it was supposed to go. He'd thought the timing was convenient with Vincent away celebrating the Midwinter in town with Dr Poppycock and his relatives, but why had he decided to come back already on the evening of the following night? Most people spent the whole week together with their families!

There had been a decent chance of still pulling this off because Vincent had gone to bed almost as soon as he'd come home. It probably would have worked out all right if he hadn't been daft and forgotten to bring his own matches. He'd been dumb enough to borrow Vincent's lighter, despite guessing it was not going to be an ordinary lighter.

The papers had certainly caught fire in an instant, but the same could also be said for the wooden trunk behind the stack, as well as half of the shelf behind it, with boxes upon boxes of letters and postcards.

Once all of that had joined the party, there hadn't been a way to call it off. All he could do was drop everything and retreat up the stairs in horror.

With Vincent asleep in his bedroom, but not wanting to get caught red-handed, he banked on the cat to rescue the situation. He peeked into the bedroom and saw the creature's eyes gleam somewhere under the bed. Uh, how unsettling! But it was there. Good.

He slammed the door shut and ran as fast as he could through the thickening smoke, into the garage and out the back. Busy backtracking over existing footsteps, he couldn't stay to wait for Vincent to emerge. He could only hope the man would get out safely.

M r Swifty was beside himself. It wasn't often he had to face this type of fear and worry. The door had slammed shut, with the monster on the other side. Unequipped to handle something that big, Mr Swifty tried to enlist Vincent's help. He pranced a few rounds on top of Vincent's stomach to no avail.

Mr Swifty leapt to the door and pressed his nose to the crack at the bottom. He could smell the smoke and feel the heat on his whiskers, and it caused him to sneeze repeatedly. He darted back to the bed, meowing and howling and pouncing on top of Vincent in a desperate attempt to wake him up.

By the time Vincent finally woke up, the fire was blocking the escape route through the garage. Something flammable had combusted in there with a loud bang. It was an inferno.

Vincent scooped Mr Swifty up, for which the cat was eternally grateful, because he was at the end of his wits. There was no sign of the monster, but the flames and smoke were far more frightening in Mr Swifty's mind than any large, dark creature.

For several minutes, Mr Swifty was too much in shock and panic to understand exactly what was happening, but amidst all that, he could tell Vincent was trying to break through the front door, which had been jammed by snow for most of the winter.

Because it wouldn't budge, the man broke the adjacent window with a heavy pail, ripped off the glazing bars with his bare hands, and climbed through, holding Mr Swifty securely against his chest as he did so.

Vincent supposed it wasn't an altogether illogical chain of events that had led to the towering flames roaring through the windows and the ceiling now caving in before his eyes, but this did leave him dumbstruck. Was it a stupid prank? Revenge? Was someone out there trying to get him killed? What had he done to deserve such an enemy?

He held Mr Swifty in his arms. The poor creature was in shock.

Vincent wasn't sure whether to let the cat go or not but was holding on for now. If released, he was afraid Mr Swifty might run away to who knows where, and since the house was currently burning to a heap of bricks and soot, there would be nothing left to come back to. With all of his worldly possessions thus being reduced to dust, Vincent was reluctant to be separated from the one thing he'd managed to save.

He'd been so close to a breakthrough that could have allowed him to leave the island with Ren. He'd come back early to work on the details, excited and hopeful that he was finally on to something.

He'd also meant to take another look at some of his old letters and notes to track down that vague feeling of something he'd forgotten.

Maybe the answer had been hidden somewhere in Mr Benton's correspondence with the matron of the floor? If it had, the letters Vincent had received from both parties, along with all of the other records and documents they had sent—everything he had obsessed over at Ren's expense—were now gone.

When his health had finally improved in the spring, and he could have theoretically got back to it, Jones had turned up to edit the stupid book. Some of it, the part that Jones hadn't yet collected and taken with him, was also being used as fuel for this magnificent bonfire.

It was difficult to comprehend that none of it was there anymore. The fact that he was standing here in his pyjamas, warmed by the intense heat of the fire, at Midwinter no less, only made the situation feel more unreal.

T he blaze had no doubt been visible from afar, but it was the middle of the night, so the nearest neighbours were probably in bed.

Vincent had sat down where he'd stood. The grass was still damp, but the snow had melted around him. He'd let go of Mr Swifty, who had taken some precautionary steps back, but now that the flames were only knee-high and at a distance, he was calm enough to stay close by.

Vincent stared into the fire. He felt drained and unsure of what to do. The neighbour's house was half a kilometre away, but he was barefoot and in his pyjamas. He'd waited here because he wanted to see how it ended, even if the end result was no surprise.

Maybe something would survive the heat despite the odds?

The few pots he hadn't sold, he'd placed on the windowsills. Their distorted shapes remained where the windows and their sills hadn't yet collapsed. The charred husk of his speeder was now visible with its plates buckled and frame mangled. He could tell from a distance that it was wrecked beyond repair.

There had been that brief moment when Vincent had weighed whether there was a chance to save something by running to the neighbours' houses to gather hands to throw buckets of snow at the fire, but a quick calculation of the size of the fire, time and distance, and the available manpower had deemed it a wasted effort.

Perhaps it would have helped to do *something* for the sake of trying, but Vincent didn't want to waste time or energy believing in miracles. He would have jumped at it had there been a reasonable chance, but as hopeless as things stood, he could only stay and witness the sad end of it.

Realising there was something left unscathed, Vincent got up and walked to the postbox. He didn't expect there to be anything in it, but contrary to expectations, he found the newest issue of a knitting magazine from a local press. He had completely forgotten he'd subscribed to it, and busy with other things, he'd had no time to shovel the snow for the exercise. Even though it had probably lain in the postbox for quite some time, it was still in perfect shape.

Vincent took the magazine and sat down to browse through it. In some perverse way, the soft and flickering lights from the flames still licking his house lit the pages just enough for him to read and look at the pictures of knitted sweaters, hoodies, slippers, stockings and teapot warmers.

This issue gave instructions on how to dye your own threads. Vincent found himself thinking that he might give it a try, maybe use the large basin he had in his garage, only to realise it was probably now cracked and useless.

He noticed the pages were getting smeared by the half-dried blood from the cuts on his hands, from when he'd busted through the window. It was a pity to ruin the smooth and freshly pressed paper with his fingerprints, so he made a few futile attempts to wipe it off before setting it aside.

Vincent fell back to look up at the starry night sky. A hint of green flashed across his field of vision, but the aurora was gone as soon as he'd seen it.

It was all gone, just like that, even that solitary hopeful sweep of the fox's tail. For a moment, he'd tasted happiness and the next? She was gone. Everything was gone. His house, the speeder, everything he'd owned.

Was this really happening? What should he do? What could he do? This had to be a dream, but there was no bubble around him, no voices or unsettling hands to keep him company. He was alone.

Was he supposed to do something? What difference did it make what he did. What sense was there in anything anymore. It was all gone.

As the flames died down to glowing embers, and darkness surrounded Vincent, he sat up to look for Mr Swifty. Mr Swifty stood behind a tree some ways back, licking his paw as if nothing had happened. He did seem a little scruffy and skittish, but at least he was still around.

"Come boy. We need to... go..." Vincent said. He'd started off trying to sound encouraging, but hearing his own voice, he swallowed, and the rest was a mere whisper. Mr Swifty looked hesitant but followed Vincent toward the cluster of houses barely visible in the distance.

Vincent wasn't in a particular hurry, despite walking barefoot. It hurt, of course, but not enough for him to try to fix it somehow. He walked in a numb haze.

It wasn't until right at the door of his neighbour's house that Vincent could hear the muffled voice of Mr Swifty asking him: "Are you all right? Are you all right, Vincent? Are you—?" He didn't turn to look at the cat but waved at him absentmindedly.

"I'm fine," he said. Then he knocked on the door.

CHAPTER 27

V incent sat at the kitchen table in the Tweeds' house when Mrs Tweed came in with the cavalry. He breathed a sigh of relief that it was Aster and not Celandine. Celandine was probably still cross with him for the stunt he'd pulled, using Ren as leverage to help mend the rift between Aster and George.

"Good heavens, Vincent. We heard what happened!" Aster exclaimed from the door. She was talkative, but rarely was she this boisterous. She gave Vincent a tight hug. "Whatever you need, luv, just ask!"

"That's what I've been telling him," Mrs Tweed said. "How's the throat? Still giving you trouble?"

Vincent nodded. "It's a little troublesome. Hurts."

"I'll put the kettle on. Some tea with lemon and honey will take care of that." Mrs Tweed showed Aster where to put the enormous basket of things she'd brought with her and turned her attention to the tea.

"You weren't in the house for long, were you? Inhaling all that smoke, luv, it ain't healthy." Aster sat down at the table opposite from Vincent. "What with you being a reasonably tall man as well! You crouched down, right?" She offered him a biscuit from a tin she'd brought.

With her inclination to offer food as a cure-all remedy for sadness, and Mrs Tweed being more of the tea-offering variety, the two of them seemed to complement each other nicely.

Mrs Tweed put down some cups and served her tea. Vincent watched her add a dash of brandy, some lemon and a generous spoonful of honey into his cup.

"How are you holding up?" she asked. Vincent had a feeling she'd asked it a few times before.

"I'm fine," Vincent whispered. "It's just the throat."

"You shouldn't whisper with a sore throat. It's worse than talking, luv," Aster advised.

"You're not fine. We can well see you aren't. And you shouldn't be! No need to act poised and brave for our sake." Mrs Tweed served Aster, filled her own cup and set aside the teapot.

"Thank you." Vincent sipped his tea. He wasn't even half done with it when Mrs Tweed interrupted him.

"Oh dear, you're getting that pesky fever again, aren't you?" She took his temperature with the back of her hand. *Do they always run this high? Poor thing, no wonder he doesn't enjoy the winter.*

"I brought some medicine with me. You should take some of that. Always clears me right up." Aster jumped to her basket and started to dig. *Oh dear, I hope I can fix this so he doesn't say anything odd in front of Violet.*

"Don't worry, I'm—" Vincent sought Aster's eyes, meaning to give her a reassuring smile. He was too tired to disguise how lousy he was feeling, so he quickly realised it probably had the opposite effect.

"Lie down for a bit and rest, luv." Aster guided him from the kitchen into the living room and onto the sofa. She and Mrs Tweed fussed over the dosage until the two of them agreed it was enough for someone Vincent's size, and he was spoon-fed the concoction. "This should help to bring it down a notch. Oh dear, Violet, you were right, he is burning up!" It was Aster's turn to test Vincent's forehead. *Oh, no. How do I make this go down? It's already so high. I hope the medicine works.*

"He is, isn't he!" Mrs Tweed agreed. "Let me find my thermometer, and we'll see how much!"

There was measuring, prodding and even a little bit of poking as the two women tried to make sure Vincent didn't need a doctor or a hospital and that he was comfortable.

"Thirty-eight? My dear. Look at this, Aster. It says thirty-eight! Have you seen such a fever since the children all fell ill last year?"

"How much was thirty-eight again...?" Vincent tried to ask, but he was ignored.

"Oh my! I didn't know grown men could get such high fevers," Aster lied.

"Neither did I, Aster! Neither did I," Mrs Tweed said.

The two of them were inspecting the thermometer as if it was also capable of lying. Vincent was too tired to repeat his question. It didn't really matter. A fever was a fever.

Mr Swifty jumped on top of Vincent to massage his tummy and purr. Vincent looked at him but decided not to push him away even though he was a little heavy.

"Is the cat bothering you?" Aster asked him. Mr Swifty gave her an angry look.

"No," Vincent said.

"Oh, thank you, thank you, thank you!" Mr Swifty said and resumed the pawing.

"You're welcome," Vincent said.

"What did you say, luv?" Aster spun around. *Is he already doing it? Oh Maury, if he finds out...*

"Nothing," Vincent replied. Maybe it was time to stop talking for the day so that Aster didn't have to worry about him blurting out something embarrassing.

"So, you're talking to me again?" Mr Swifty asked. Vincent glanced at the women to be sure their attention was now firmly on their own conversation.

"Yes," he replied. "I'm sorry if you felt ignored before." He gestured at his throat, hoping the cat would understand.

Mr Swifty made a nest for himself from the loose folds of Vincent's shirt and purred contentedly. He didn't seem to be holding a grudge.

"I've had a talk with George. He wasn't opposed to it. Arthur is not interested in moving out there. He's got his own house and his own family.

The place is a little run down, but Vincent is handy when he's his healthy self," Aster was saying to Mrs Tweed. *It's the least we can do.*

"We have a lot of wood left over from fixing the barn last summer. Might have other supplies too, as well as everyday items and clothes. I could ask around for more." Mrs Tweed led Aster back into the kitchen and out of sight to resume their tea. "Has the fire-chief had time to visit yet to give his opinion?"

"No. He said he'd do it first thing on Monday, though." *I'm glad it all burned down. Maybe there's nothing left to investigate.*

Vincent frowned. He must have misheard that last part. With Mr Swifty now fast asleep on his stomach, he couldn't sit up to see whether their lips were moving or if it was his fever supplying the more sinister but fictional narrative.

"That's good. I don't see how anyone could have done it intentionally, but it's good to know what started it in case it's something that can be avoided by being a bit more careful." *It was probably one of those experiments of his.*

"Yes, we shouldn't leave candles or lamps unattended. You never know when a cat might knock something over." *We've come this far, and we will see it through. It's for the best, even if it hurts him now.*

"Did she just blame me for burning down your house?" Mr Swifty cracked an eye, not as fast asleep as Vincent had assumed. "There was someone in the house with us."

Vincent yawned. This should have probably made him more outraged, but he felt lethargic and uninterested. How curious that he'd felt like absolute death only a moment ago, but now, even his throat felt fine.

Ah, it must have been that medicine Aster had given him. He yawned again.

"Vincent? You don't think it was me, do you? There was someone in the cellar. I didn't see who it was, but I didn't smell anything unfamiliar." Mr Swifty lifted his head to look at Vincent. Vincent nodded. His throat didn't feel as bad, but he felt groggy and had a growing suspicion his mouth was not going to cooperate. He also didn't want to draw the women's attention.

"There was a dark monster in the cellar, and it slammed the bedroom door shut." Mr Swifty's words admittedly sounded a little ridiculous. What kind of a monster would have wanted to burn him to death? And if that was the case, then shouldn't they have propped the bedroom door with something to lock him in?

"Vincent, luv?" This time it was Aster. "How are you feeling? Will you manage if I go upstairs with Violet for a moment? She has some old clothes in the attic that might fit you." *Looks like it's working. Oh, thank goodness.*

"I'm," Vincent paused. There was a really very unusual lag from the moment he thought he was going to speak to where he actually heard his own voice. "Fff... fine, but—"

"Just rest, luv. You'll feel better tomorrow." Aster smiled. *Maybe it was a touch too much, but he looks comfortable.*

"I trust you, but—" It was sometimes hard with the paranoia and the voices. Aster would never hurt him. She was only ever looking after him, and after all she'd done for Vincent, it was rude to even entertain the thought that she might have been scheming something behind his back. "Did you, uhh, have to give this much? It seems excessive."

"How is he?" Mrs Tweed looked over Aster's shoulder.

"You were right. The smaller dose might have sufficed." Aster let out a light giggle. The ladies both seemed amused. *The main thing is he gets some rest.*

"Well, let's leave him to it, Aster. We best be heading up so we can get this done before supper." Mrs Tweed's words sounded distant and distorted somehow. *He looks completely out of it. Holy Maury, Aster, that stuff was potent.*

"Yes, let's get to it," Aster agreed. *I wouldn't have had to do this if you weren't so bloody persistent, luv.* She was looking right at him, but she seemed preoccupied. *Damn that woman to hell for causing so much trouble! Mr Benton was right. Some people are just not fit to have children.*

CHAPTER 28

Vincent heard Dr Poppycock breathe a heavy sigh. He tried to concentrate on where he was, but his mind was mulling over some disturbing thoughts, as well as a persistent echo of his previous loop of panic and depression.

"I would like to help you. Is there anything you would like to talk about? Anything at all?" The doctor was still trying to engage him in the conversation.

"Uh? Not really," Vincent replied. He hadn't felt like coming, but as soon as his symptoms had eased, Aster had insisted on it. The doctor had had to postpone some of his other appointments to prioritise Vincent, so it was poor form to waste his time like this.

It had only been three days, no, four? Four days since the fire. It was all a blur, what with the shock, the fever and Aster's medicine. He was still sorting it in his head.

"Can you try to describe how you feel? Do you feel sad? Do you feel depressed?"

"No, not really." Vincent shrugged.

"Angered, enraged, desperate, inconsolable, upset, anything?"

"No."

"Happy? Delighted? Joyful?"

"What?" Vincent frowned at this.

"I asked you, do you feel happy, delighted or joyful."

"About what? No. No, I don't feel... I don't know."

"You must feel something."

"Confused." Vincent bit his lip. "I don't understand how, why... it doesn't make sense."

He looked up at the doctor. He'd hoped to have a voice of reason in Dr Poppycock, but the man seemed strangely stand-offish about the situation. Was it because of what had happened on Midwinter's eve, after the festivities? Had he made things awkward by referring to the man by his first name?

"Should it?" the doctor asked.

"Yes." The questions were grating on Vincent's nerves more than usual, but he reasoned it was because he was annoyed at the situation rather than at James. "It should make sense. I... I think I'm entitled to as much."

"I see. I'm sure it wasn't your fault. These things happen all the time."

Were they all assuming he'd burned down the house himself? Even the doctor? Granted, there had been times when it could have happened, but this was not one of them.

"No, I mean, I was careful. It shouldn't have happened."

"But it did. The sooner you accept that, the sooner you will be able to move on."

"I don't care about moving on!" Vincent snapped, frustrated. The doctor cocked a brow as if he'd witnessed something incredibly telling and was now drawing his conclusions. Vincent had to take a moment to calm down before he continued. "I just want to know why, how... how it could have happened."

"Did you speak with the fire chief?"

"Yes. He says it started from the kitchen. The problem is, I didn't have anything burning in the kitchen. I distinctly remember putting logs into the fireplace for the next day, but I had no reason to light it because I had the stove on in the bedroom. I'm quite sure I didn't.... I'm... quite sure..." The way the doctor was eyeing him, seemingly weighing his every word, made Vincent lose his confidence. Maybe he had dreamt that part?

"If you didn't light the fire, then who did?" Dr Poppycock asked.

"I don't know. It wasn't me. Mr Swifty said…" Vincent hesitated. It was a mistake to mention Mr Swifty, but he'd blurted it out without thinking. It probably wouldn't help to try to correct it, but he still gave it a go. "I think there might have been someone in the house with us."

"Did you see someone?" The doctor had that look to him of someone who was only humouring you to be nice, but who did not believe a word coming out of your mouth. Then again, Vincent wasn't sure he could blame the man. A cat was not a particularly reliable source.

"No, not personally," Vincent replied.

"Who would want to hurt you like that? And why? Don't we all love and care about you?"

The doctor's words made Vincent feel uncomfortable. His chest felt heavy. Why mention love in this context? How could people throw that around so easily? None of them knew the real him, so how could they love him? As for wanting to hurt him, surely there must have been people he had unwittingly upset.

"I'm not sure, but maybe Jones? He seems to hold a grudge against me."

The young man's actions had seemed baffling, but Vincent supposed they'd had something to do with unmet expectations. Why he would go as far as burning down the house, Vincent wasn't sure. But this theory made him less uncomfortable than the alternative.

"And I overheard Aster say some things that were a little worrisome." It felt awful to say it out loud, but he needed to get this out before it festered and took root in his mind. Perhaps the doctor could talk some sense into him.

"Oh, Vincent, my dear friend. You don't seriously think Mrs Bramble would have something to do with this? She took you in and helped to raise you as one of her own. What has she ever done that would merit this distrust?" The doctor's apparent disappointment made Vincent feel even worse.

"I know. This whole thing must be messing with my head. She mentioned they might let me use the cabin at the cape until I'm back on my feet. I thought I might renovate it a little."

The voices in his head often seemed to indicate that she was lying, but she'd never done anything to hurt him. It was usually one of the things that made Vincent distrust the voices the most.

Why would she say those things and then be nothing but kind to Vincent? Not that she'd ever said anything as vicious as what Vincent had heard others say, but something about her often triggered Vincent's paranoia.

"That sounds good. Will keep you busy," the doctor commented. He spent a while stroking the squirrel's butt under his nose and then continued with his assessment: "You don't suppose you might be distrustful toward her because she's such an important person in your life? It could be a manifestation of your fear of intimacy and vulnerability. Your mind is searching for reasons to push her away because she's so important to you. Does that make sense to you?"

"Yes." Vincent was glad of anything that would alleviate the cognitive dissonance he felt for not trusting Aster. "That's probably it. I wonder if Jones—"

"Are you sure it's not possible that you did light it and then forgot about it? There were no footprints there other than yours. And why would anyone want to burn your house? That seems extreme, even if Jones were holding a grudge."

"I-I— I'm not sure." Mr Swifty had seemed sure that there had been someone else in the house, but Vincent himself hadn't heard or seen anything unusual. Maybe it was just his mind creating a diversion, trying to shelter him from something?

"You don't remember lighting the fireplace?"

"No."

"Do you remember what you had for breakfast that day?"

"I... don't."

"How well do you remember in general what you did that day?"

"Not... very well."

"Isn't it possible that you were tired from the trip back and did it without really paying attention to it? It can be difficult to admit to one's own shortcomings."

"I don't understand how I could have been so careless."

"It may take a while for you to be able to accept it. The main thing is to not let yourself fall through the rabbit-hole of paranoia. We've worked hard to fish you out before, and I'm not about to let you fall in there again. It's a dark and lonely place, and trust me, it doesn't lead to anywhere good." The doctor gave Vincent a gentle but somewhat condescending smile.

"I want to trust you." But it would take a while to shake off the unpleasant feeling that everyone was out to get him.

Who else could it have been? Maybe he had lit the fireplace himself without realising. Maybe the conversations with the cat were his coping mechanism.

It was funny how some aspects of his life could be so logical and predictable—like mechanics, chemistry and working out how to prevent accidents from happening—but as soon as it had anything to do with his feelings, he would fumble like this.

"You shouldn't be too hard on yourself. These things happen. You can rebuild. I'm sure everyone will support and help you. You're not alone," Dr Poppycock assured him. "You'll get through this. Just let us help you."

It was a relief to have people around him who were so patient and willing to guide him back when he was about to lose sight of where he was heading.

S hortly after Vincent had left Dr Poppycock's office, Mr Jones marched in without an appointment. Since it was at the end of the day, and Dr Poppycock had no other patients waiting, he agreed to entertain the young man for a moment to hear his concerns.

This time, Mr Jones made no pretence of being there to discuss his own issues but hurried instead to pry about Vincent's. Dr Poppycock was forced to remind him that he would not discuss other patients' issues. Mr Jones refused to hear it.

"Are you sure you are asking out of concern for him?" the doctor asked.

He was not going to entertain Vincent's delusions about grudges or conspiracies, but he had to admit Mr Jones did seem to be acting like he was up to no good. It made sense that Vincent might have picked up on some form of animosity from the young man.

"Yes! As I've told you before, I need to know. I should know."

Now that Mr Jones no longer lived with Vincent, and whatever working relationship they had did not require divulging such intimate details, Mr Jones's words sounded especially hollow.

"But why?" Dr Poppycock asked. It was his turn to feel impatient. "Have you been to see Vincent yourself since the fire?"

"What does that have to do with anything? I would have, but he is living with... whoever he is living with now. I don't know where he is."

"If the two of you are as close as you suggest, he would have contacted you by now, and you could have asked your questions directly."

"I haven't heard from him at all. That's precisely why I'm so worried. Are you sure you can't tell me anything?"

"I really don't know what it is you are looking for. He is shaken and upset, as is expected. I can tell you that much, but if you want to know more, you'll have to ask the man himself."

"But he won't talk to me!"

"If it is important, he will eventually," Dr Poppycock said. It was clear the relationship was nowhere near as close as Mr Jones had tried to imply, but it might be interesting to see how far the young man was going to take this.

There was a moment of silence as Mr Jones thought of what to say.

"Well, do you know if he's still talking to his cat, then?" he asked, changing his angle all around.

"Uh, you'll have to excuse me. What cat?" The doctor pretended to shuffle his notes. Since Mr Jones seemed incapable of understanding doctor–patient confidentiality, the easier route was to play dumb.

"What good are you if you don't even know that? His cat. The one he talks to. Has he been doing it as of late?"

"Why does this interest you?"

"Has he been saying something else that's odd? Has he been replying to you without you actually talking to him?"

"Without talking? I assure you, Mr Jones, I am in possession of all my mental faculties." Ah, so that's what this was about. Vincent's neat party-trick. He'd played it on Mr Jones, and now the poor young man was confused and wanted answers. With Vincent uninterested in keeping in touch, this issue would no doubt resolve itself with time. "My advice is to let it go."

"No!" Mr Jones lost his composure. He vented his frustration on poor Mr Goose, the ink blotter, who was sent flying across the room. "You must have seen it happen. You've known him for ages! I need proof that he can do it, or they'll laugh at my face!"

Ah, the lack of respect and decorum. Dr Poppycock walked over to the goose and dusted it off.

"Do you know what the goose signifies?"

"I don't care!"

"Well, I hope you don't mind me educating you, regardless. Communication and teamwork are two of my personal favourites, but perhaps even more importantly, it signifies family, loyalty and the readiness to protect one's own."

"What does that have to do with anything?"

"I guess you're a little too young to understand the meaning and weight those concepts carry."

"Spare me your sanctimonious bullshit about loyalty! He's going to get away with it, and the world deserves to know!"

"Get away with what? You'll have to excuse me; I don't quite follow."

"He's duped us into believing he's been all around the world, when he's been reading people's minds all this while!" Mr Jones looked at the doctor as if he was the one that was being an idiot. "I bet he gets all his stories and information like that. He hears it from other people, even when they don't tell him. And then he writes about it as if he'd done these things himself. He is a fraud, and I will expose him!"

"Oh." Dr Poppycock was dumbfounded by this notion. The lengths to which people's imaginations could stretch, to justify a sensational narrative...

It did make sense in its backward way, but even had Vincent possessed such a fantastical skill, he would have never used it for deception. The man would perform a party-trick or stoop to a prank, but he didn't have such an egotistical bone in his body that he would knowingly lead people on for the sake of fame.

"I think our conversation has ended. And I will instruct my secretary to not reserve any further sessions in your name until you have apologised to Mr Goose. I hope you understand. We do aim for a certain level of etiquette here to maintain civility."

CHAPTER 29

M r Jones had been exiled to a cramped hole of an apartment at the edge of town. For a while, he'd worked on his edits, even though it felt like he was polishing a basket of turds. He wasn't even sure whether Vincent was ever going to send him the last few chapters, because he hadn't heard a peep since moving out.

It would have made sense had Vincent thrown him out on the spot back in October, but since the man had kept him around almost all the way up until Midwinter, it felt immensely unfair to be kicked out right before the festivities when he was still in the middle of gathering his evidence.

Dr Poppycock had proven useless. The supposed doctor was a hack and an imbecile for being so blind to something right in front of him. It seemed these backward islanders were hell-bent on covering up for Vincent, as if it made no difference that the man was clearly an unscrupulous liar. Why did Vincent have to be this dagnabbit charismatic and successfully manipulative that no one here was willing to help with the exposé?

The story Mr Jones had written for the local newspaper about the house fire had been received well, although they'd wanted him to tone down some of the—in his mind the best and juiciest—details of the incident.

He had received a fair compensation for it, and seeing his story on the cover of a paper, albeit a small local one, did feel like an accomplishment. None of it would hold a candle to the exposé he had in mind, though, and he'd lost none of his determination to write it.

Unfortunately, the house burning down meant that any damning evidence Vincent might have had in there, had burned along with it. But Mr Jones was not the type to give up so easily, oh no, he would persist until he'd exhausted all of his means. If nothing else, perhaps he could squeeze another tragic news story out of Vincent by pushing the man's buttons a wee bit.

That was why he was sitting at the back of the snowtrain as it carved its path through the snow and out of town. It was no small feat that he was sitting here right now.

In his desperation, he had ventured to the door of the Brambles to wring what he needed out of the missus, but the blasted woman hadn't been home. To his horror, her tight-lipped husband had begrudgingly informed him she'd gone to visit her sister, and Mr Jones had had no choice but to face the frightful Ms Buttercup again.

After that ordeal, he'd managed to learn that Vincent was moving out to the cape. Ms Buttercup hadn't volunteered this information herself, but she'd received a revealing phone call that Mr Jones had had the self-appointed privilege to listen in on, with his ear pressed to the front door, after he'd been kicked out.

As per this useful tip, Vincent and his creepy feline companion had boarded the train from its last stop before it headed out to the sparse side of the island.

The man looked gaunt and flustered, and with a single dainty handkerchief, he was combatting the sort of flood of bodily fluids you rarely saw come out of just one person.

People dispensing this amount were usually confined to their homes, forced to stay somewhere near an abundant source of handkerchiefs, yet here was Vincent, making his way out there for what seemed like extensive renovations based on the amount of supplies he'd hauled in.

He stuffed everything into the adjacent compartment from where Mr Jones was now ducking to avoid being seen. The cat planted itself onto Vincent's lap.

Mr Jones had several shaky fledglings of plans, but he figured that even if most of them failed, one still might work.

One of them was to offer his help as compensation for his earlier transgression and tag along to force himself back into the man's good graces. This would give him more time and opportunities to dig up evidence, but he wasn't holding his breath for it to succeed.

Another possibility was to feed all of Vincent's insecurities and paranoia until the man slipped up and made people worried with his erratic behaviour. Perhaps even Dr Poppycock would come to his senses and change his mind if Vincent seemed to truly be losing his marbles. Others might also be more forthcoming with the relevant information.

Mr Jones would have even confessed to the arson to achieve this, if not for the fact that he could not be entirely sure that people would believe his word over Vincent's. The risk of getting into serious trouble was much too great. But if he could first make Vincent ruin his own credibility, then perhaps later, it might be an extra card to slap on the table to rile him up.

After plenty of practice, it wasn't difficult to silence his guilty conscience. He didn't think of himself as a completely heartless, bad person; he just preferred not to delve on the consequences of his actions. It had all become a lot easier when he'd admitted to himself that he did not like Vincent very much, anymore. Perhaps he never truly had?

From where Mr Jones sat, he could see Vincent dozing off. The cat's presence was inconvenient, but it, too, seemed deep asleep. This seemed as good a time as any, so he took a careful, deep breath, exited his compartment and snuck over to Vincent's. In the ambient noise of the train pushing through snow amidst what seemed like a building snowstorm, neither Vincent nor his cat woke up when Mr Jones sat across from them.

There was something infuriating about Vincent and Vincent's stupidly handsome face, strange proportions, messy head of hair and calmly courteous attitude. The man looked faulty, as if there had been drunkards on his assembly line, and yet when his pieces were put together, he wasn't half as ugly as he should have been.

It was an insult to men everywhere that women seemed to like this silly caricature of a man. He had mild manners and could give subtle or garish compliments—whichever suited the situation—with no shame. He also looked incredibly stupid and apologetic at just about every turn, so one couldn't stay mad at him for very long.

And worst of all, no matter how idiotic Vincent seemed, he would sometimes say things that made Mr Jones feel intellectually inferior. Mr Jones could stand that some people were smarter than him, but to have this manipulative dunce be smarter did not sit well with him.

Vincent's relaxed and non-threatening sociable front was what fooled people into liking him. It was why he seemed to get along with everybody. Mr Jones, however, knew better. It was nothing but a mask. It was built on a constant, outrageous habit of lying. A sham. It made Mr Jones want to kick Vincent in the calf.

"Ah, Jones. Did you say someding?" Vincent opened his eyes—that is, if the thin crack could be called open. This caused the dreadful creature on his lap to also open one of its eyes.

"What? No?" Mr Jones suddenly felt chills. This wasn't going to be one of those moments when it felt like Vincent was probing all of his secrets inside of his head, was it? Now would be the worst time for that.

"That's odd. I dink I had a dream that you were talking about my face, and I was agreeing wid you." Vincent frowned. He blew his nose on the already thoroughly soaked handkerchief.

Mr Jones did a quick review of his inner dialogue and realised he'd thought some rather damning thoughts only a moment ago. Like that part about confessing to the arson. Surely the man hadn't heard all that?

"All what? What arson?" Vincent asked.

"What?" Mr Jones backed against the seat and tried to look away.

"Just now, you said it, didn't you?"

If Vincent had been asleep a moment earlier, he was awake now, and he seemed to be in a worse mood than usual. The cat was sensing the mood and seemed ready to attack.

"I said no such thing. You must have been dreaming." Mr Jones peered around to see if there were other passengers in the same car with them, but could only see an elderly woman fast asleep at the other end. She wouldn't be much of a witness if Vincent decided to go berserk over the whole house-burning thing. Ah shit, thought Mr Jones, I have got to stop mentioning that...

"You were mumbling about it again. Was it you? Did you burn down my house?" Vincent was surprisingly quick to step forward and grab Mr Jones by the collar. It even took his cat by surprise, and the thing hissed and rounded its back on the floor at their feet.

Mr Jones wasn't sure which was worse, getting beaten up by Vincent or shredded to strips by the cat.

"No! I wouldn't, I'd never!" Shit, he's not going to believe me, no matter how much I try to deny it. I'm screwed, thought Mr Jones.

"I knew it." Vincent's reasonably calm exterior was betrayed by the strength of his grip, the tightness of his jaw and the slight wrinkles on his brow. It was enough to create the impression that he was livid, simply by contrast. "You should have stayed out of my sight. Do you know why I let you get away with all of this shit you pull? I wanted to give you a chance to grow up, show some spine and redeem yourself! And this was how you repaid me for that lenience? All I needed from you was to leave me the hell alone."

"I'm telling you, it wasn't me..." It was true he'd taken the opportunity to scour Vincent's cottage for clues on the night of the fire because he'd thought the man was away for the Midwinter fest, but he'd left in haste when he'd heard someone else turn up. "You've got to believe me."

"I don't know what you're after, but is it really worth trying to murder me in my sleep?" Vincent glared at Mr Jones straight in the eye.

"I wouldn't!" Mr Jones had never considered Vincent very threatening, but he found himself feeling like he might soon wet himself from the fright. The man was too skinny, despite his height, to be a real threat, but his eyes looked sharp like he was about to snap, and people teetering right on that edge between sanity and madness had the tendency to be the most frightening by default.

"Killing me might make the book sell better, is that it?" Vincent leaned closer. From this close proximity, if he survived this confrontation, Mr Jones was sure to catch whatever unearthly bug had Vincent in its grip. His nose was leaking like a faucet, which only made the mad gleam in his eyes look a hundred or so times worse. "I opened my home to you. I respected you for your skills and literacy. I know I'm not much of a writer, and you certainly worked hard to make my writing presentable. Why wasn't that enough? Did you absolutely have to ruin me for it?" Vincent had raised his voice now, though with his illness, he sounded like a hissing kettle. Consequently, that made his words even more eerie.

Mr Jones glanced again at the little old lady, but she was fast asleep. There was no one to witness Vincent's outburst, save for the cat, and even if the cat could have testified, it would have done it in Vincent's favour.

In this state, Vincent would not listen to reason nor believe anything Mr Jones tried to say. There was no other way to escape the situation than to push Vincent off and make a run for it.

He'd intended to jump to the next car, but with Vincent and the cat at his heels, he'd picked the wrong direction. At the end of the train, there was nowhere to jump to. The cat launched at him, and in a panicked frenzy, Mr Jones struck at it sideways, sending it skidding across one of the compartments. Vincent was right behind him, breathing heavily.

"Wait!" the man yelled after Mr Jones.

"Like hell I will!" Mr Jones yelled back and without thinking it through, jumped right out of the train.

"No, you idiot—!" were the last words he heard before hitting the fluffy bank of snow.

CHAPTER 30

To say Vincent was feeling like a heap of faecal matter thrown at a wall would have been a grave understatement. He'd rolled in the snow like a rag doll until he ran out of momentum and came to a stop, face down.

Ah, the snow felt pleasantly cool against his face, but it did make breathing a bit cumbersome. He propped himself up to sit and tried to catch his breath.

Oh my God, oh my God, what do I do? What the hell do I do?

Jones was dangerously ignorant and thoughtless, and Vincent was furious with him, but even so, he couldn't sit back and let a person die.

He didn't feel particularly smart himself, having jumped after the insufferable oaf, but Jones would never survive out here for long enough for a rescue team to find him. It would have taken more than an hour for the snowtrain to reach anywhere near a telephone, and another hour or two for a rescue team to be deployed and reach the scene.

Who knew how far off course Jones would have wandered by then? The likelihood of finding the young man before sunrise was close to zero, and with the gear he'd been wearing, he would have been as good as permafrost by then.

At least Vincent had had the foresight to grab a suitcase before he'd jumped, although it took him a while to find it amidst the snow.

Shit, where the hell am I? Oh God, I'm going to die out here. I'm going to freeze to death!

Vincent waded through the snow, pulling the suitcase in his wake, feeling like his lungs were about to burst and his head turn to mush from the already rampant fever. It wasn't difficult to know which way Jones was, what with him shouting continuously, but it was slow going through all of the snow.

When Vincent reached him, Jones still tried to get away.

"Oh, shut up, and stop being an idiot!" Vincent grabbed him by the wrist. "You're going to die out here unless you do exactly what I tell you."

"I said nothing." Jones sounded defiant but did not struggle.

"We're almost at the cape, but I don't think we can make it before the blizzard is on us. It's better to find shelter somewhere close by for now."

"Well, I don't see anything," Jones pointed out. The view was conclusively snowy.

"There's a bridge if we follow these tracks. That's where the train crosses the river. We may have a chance of lighting a fire under it if there's enough shelter from the wind." Vincent shoved the suitcase into Jones's hand before pulling the man in the right direction. "I'm sure as hell not going to carry this. Don't lose it. Your life depends on it."

Mr Jones was confused, but what choice did he have but to follow Vincent? The weather was getting atrocious, and he had no idea how to get out of this mess. Getting off the train did seem like lunacy, no matter how he looked at it.

Vincent appeared determined, but he also looked like a man who hadn't slept well, who was stuffed with snot and feverish, and about to collapse from having to wade through the snow. Thankfully, the snowtrain tracks were still visible, and the weight of the train had packed the snow, making it easier to walk on.

Once they reached the bridge, Vincent took the suitcase and started making a fire. The fortunate part was that there was some surprisingly dry, old timber underneath the bridge from when it had been mended some time back. The old bits and pieces had been left there to be picked up in the spring. Had there been none, they would have had to burn the contents of the suitcase, but for now, Vincent used them to make a seat next to the fire.

"Whose suitcase is this?" Mr Jones asked, looking at the clothes and items. Vincent looked back at him and rolled his eyes.

"What does id m-matter?"

"It's not the poor old lady's suitcase, is it?"

"I will m-make sure Mrs Beansbury geds her dings back and I'll p-pay for whad's ruined. Be grateful. Have some c-cake."

"Cake?"

"She was k-kind enough to bake it. Now, eat it. It's all de s-supper we're getting." Vincent nibbled on a piece but didn't seem to be enjoying it. This made Mr Jones suspicious, but upon tasting the cake, he realised it tasted just fine.

"Stop m-making so much noise, I can't hear m-myselb dink." Vincent slouched over his knees tiredly.

"I didn't say anything," Mr Jones repeated like a broken record. It was true he'd gone on a mental tirade to berate Vincent on the train, but he did find himself a little worried for the man. "Are you all right?"

"Ob course I'm not all right! I feel like I'm d-dying. Can you do me a fabour and s-shut up? I'd like to rest." Vincent tightened his grip on his knees, presumably to reduce the shaking. Mr Jones bowed down to see the man's face. He didn't look too good.

"You probably need a doctor."

"One ain't g-going to appear f-from dhin air now, r-right? So, s-s-shud up." Vincent tried to hold his hands closer to the fire, but his arms shook quite violently, so he stopped. "Id's so d-d-damn c-cold," he mumbled.

It was cold, but the few layers Mr Jones was wearing were keeping him warm enough to not complain. He was far from comfortable, but, if the fire lasted and if he kept his hands and feet moving, he supposed he would weather rather well until morning.

In retrospect, Mr Jones was grateful that Vincent had jumped after him, but it now seemed it might cost the man his life. For the first time, Mr Jones felt bad. It was much more difficult to ignore his guilty conscience when he'd gone and caused a situation where Vincent, who had actually come to his rescue despite having every reason not to, was now suffering at the brink of death on his account.

Then again, Mr Jones told himself, how was he to know that Vincent would do something like that? He hadn't asked him to. It would still count as a suicide in the karmic sense, right?

"S-stop b-babbling..." Vincent was at it again.

"I can't shut my thoughts off just like that. I'm sorry," Mr Jones said. If only Vincent could have picked up on when he was being serious and truthful, then none of this would have happened. "I wish you would stop listening in on me."

"W-what are you t-t-talking about?" Vincent coughed. Mr Jones offered him a handkerchief.

"You're hearing my thoughts, not my voice."

"N-n-nonsense."

"I may have lied to you about some things, but I'm not lying now. You must have noticed it."

"I have m-m-my issues, bud I'm still in t-t-touch with realidy. There's no s-such ding as—" He stopped to cough again, then blew his nose. "T-t-t-telepathy."

Sure there is, Mr Jones thought.

"Shhh, there isn't."

But clearly there is, Mr Jones thought again.

"S-s-s-stop it. I'm d-d-delirious from the f-fever. T-t-that's all."

"I'm not judging you. It's so blatantly obvious I'm surprised it's not public knowledge. I think I could prove it if you let me." He'd put a few things together as he'd been investigating Vincent's past, and there had been some leads he'd meant to follow up on as soon as the ferries ran again.

"D-d-don't be stupid. You just w-w-ant your s-s-sc-scoop." Vincent seemed to sulk, though it was difficult to tell amidst his shaking and coughing.

"Well, yes, I'd like it. Do you think you could cooperate by any chance?"

"And d-do w-w-what? T-tell the w-world I'm a raving m-m-m-madman? A f-fraud? I'd rather n-n-n-not."

"Yes, but don't you see? I never told you that. The only reason you know is because I thought about it in your presence."

"I'm p-p-paranoid enough to f-f-figure out as much. That-t-t's all t-t-this is. I have a f-fever, and it-t-t m-m-messes me up."

"I don't think you're insane or messed up. I think you can actually do it. And I think I know a few people who might know why. They're just refusing to talk to me, but they'd probably be willing to talk to you."

"N-no," Vincent insisted. "Even if it w-were true, I wouldn't w-want t-to l-l-live my life having to p-p-prove m-myself to everyone. I get enough p-people telling me I'm a f-f-fraud as it is. S-s-sure, there are a lot of p-p-places I haven't v-visited, and I only t-t-tell s-stories about t-t-the t-things t-that w-were most impressive. Usually, it's m-m-much less g-glamorous. B-but-t-t I'm t-tired of having to d-d-d-defend m-myself. It's why I come b-b-back here every year. The p-p-people are kind, and t-t-they d-don't c-c-care about m-m-m-my reputation or m-m-my p-past." Vincent bit his lip to stop his teeth from clattering, but it didn't help much. He closed his eyes.

Mr Jones watched him and wondered why he'd been so agitated by his mere face before. The man didn't seem all that irritating now. He felt no miraculous affinity towards him, but he'd lost that burning hate he'd been fostering. Vincent looked like any other person.

Mr Jones sighed. This did not feel good. There was no nagging remorse, but he'd lost his driving force mid-push, and it felt too tiresome to continue up the hill. At the same time, there wasn't much waiting for him down below. He sat there watching the fire, adding wood carefully—enough to provide sufficient warmth, not so much that it might run out.

Tomorrow someone was bound to pass here. The plough maybe? Mr Jones tried to recall its schedule but couldn't.

"Vincent." He poked Vincent gently on the shoulder.

"W-what?" Vincent responded with a lag.

"How are we getting out of this mess, exactly? Is there a train or a plough coming tomorrow?" It did not look like Vincent would last a whole day and another night here.

"S-s-should be something b-before noon," Vincent replied without bothering to open his eyes. "If n-not, we'll try to get to the c-cape."

"Could you explain to me where that is?" Mr Jones asked. If Vincent wasn't coherent enough tomorrow, then at least he'd have something to work with.

"S-s-south, there's a h-h-hill, not f-f-far from there. If it's c-c-clear, you can p-probably see it."

"If we survive this, you're not going to have me convicted, are you?" Maybe he could somewhat redeem himself by making sure they both got home safely. Surely, Vincent would appreciate that?

Vincent opened his eyes to glare at Mr Jones. Even in his miserable state, he didn't seem willing to let it go.

"Is there no way I could convince you that it wasn't me?" Mr Jones was fairly sure he'd been careful enough to not leave behind any evidence of his visit, but even if he had, with the house burnt down to the ground, they probably wouldn't find anything incriminating.

Even so, these islanders lapped up Vincent's words like cream. There was no way they wouldn't believe him, no matter what anyone else said or how many times Mr Jones swore his innocence. If Vincent was determined to have his head for this, he would have to pay.

"I l-l-let you g-g-get away with f-f-fooling m-me once and l-l-l-look where t-t-t-that got m-me." Vincent looked like he might have jumped at Mr Jones's throat one more time had he not been too busy shivering and trying to survive the cold.

"Fair enough."

It was snowing rather heavily now, but at least the bridge was doing its part. The fire merely crackled a little but remained firmly lit. There was a breeze, but it wasn't too bad. With more than twelve hours until morning, it would be a long night. Plenty of time for Mr Jones to think of his next move.

T he first winter back on the island after his travels seemed endless.

Vincent spent most of it sitting on the stairs in his new cellar to keep cool. He'd dug it out only recently to get more storage space, but having the staircase was an added bonus. He felt less insane there and no one or nothing was talking to him or around him. It was the only place he could sleep without seeing the strange, vague border that had started to form around him, and he kept on returning there, even if his bed would have been more comfortable.

When Vincent felt well enough, he headed into town to see the town psychiatrist Dr. Poppycock. The doctor was a bit peculiar, but it helped to have someone to talk to, even though Vincent had a hard time opening up.

Because he was now living alone in his own house, he also tried to go out and visit people as often as he could, but he couldn't help feeling like he was sinking into something deeper and deeper every passing day. No matter how he tried to grab a hold of the world around him by meeting people, engaging himself with projects or reaching out to a professional, he felt separated from everything.

He started to wonder why and how he had become this way. Had he always been flawed like this, or was it because of his twisted workhouse upbringing? The words of his first doctor sprung to mind, and he wondered if the issue indeed had something to do with his parents. He couldn't remember much about them and didn't really care to, so he failed to see the relevance.

He did mention this to Dr Poppycock, though, who seemed delighted by the notion.

The problem was that Vincent couldn't really ask his parents any of the burning questions because he didn't know who or where they were. The earliest he could recall with any degree of certainty was Benton House, and that he'd been at a workhouse before it.

Dr Poppycock encouraged him to get in touch with someone who might know more, but because it was winter and there were no telegraph cables from the island to the mainland, there was nothing Vincent could do but sit in his cellar and wait for spring to follow that advice.

S pring came, though as if to spite Vincent, it came later than usual. The increased daylight woke him from his depressed slumber, and he began to set things in motion. He finished the new and improved speeder. He made all the necessary preparations.

The Brambles and Celandine weren't happy to see him go, but it was only a matter of days after the ferry had started running again that Vincent rode his speeder on to it, only barely avoiding a hefty bill to pay for damages.

A few of the other passengers made sure to stay at an unnecessary distance, even when Vincent had turned off the engine and the ferry was out to sea and on its way.

Theoretically, the speeder could have flown across the water, but the weather was a little unpredictable this time of year, and experiencing a fuel failure mid-flight did not sound appealing.

Vincent didn't mind the slight delay. Everything was much better now that he was no longer cooped up and had room to breathe. It felt like a massive relief to be on the road again.

He was even a bit hopeful that he might find what he was looking for.

I t had been years since Vincent had last been to these parts of the world. The last he'd been here, he hadn't even understood where 'here' was in relation to the rest of the world.

He'd written ahead to the lady of the house, who apparently was his fan. She had gladly invited him over and was eager to arrange a 'small gathering' in his honour. He was an invited guest of honour in this house whose shits he'd cleaned up almost two decades ago.

The rooms were unfamiliar from this side of the walls, but he could tell he had been here before. As per custom, there was a cleanly clad servant to guide him to the reception room. He did not know her, but it had been a while and this was Benton House: Staff here were a fluid and ever-changing commodity, save for the topmost few.

"Ah, Mr Vincent." The current head of Benton House, Richard Foxwick-Benton the sixth of the Eastside Foxwick-Bentons, entered the room with the sort of absent-mindedness that people of considerable status liked to maintain, as really no other person besides royalty could command their full attention.

Benton House was not as powerful and glorious as it once had been, but it remained prestigious and refused to lower its standards of nonchalance for anything or anyone.

Richard Foxwick-Benton the sixth of the Eastside Foxwick-Bentons had taken over for his grandfather Richard Hartford-Benton of the Hartford Heights' Bentons, who was, though still alive and in reasonable health, no longer as interested and eager to act the part as his grandson. He rather liked having his gentlemen's club friends call him Dickie in his old age, and it was difficult to keep a distinguished and strict image that contradicted your favourite nickname.

Vincent was about to address Mr Foxwick-Benton out of an earlier habit but bit his lip unsure what custom dictated now that he was no longer a member of staff. He could remember most of the advice from his guidebooks, but they were directed toward servants, not guests.

As it turned out, there seemed to be no set guidelines for proper guest behaviour, aside from whatever was trending as gentlemanly behaviour.

Apparently, Vincent's silence in the face of bafflement was thus received as the sort of refined nonchalance that Mr Foxwick-Benton himself was fond of showing.

"Please make yourself at home. Her Ladyship has requested me to extend our courtesy for as long as you prefer, but I must confess, I would be equally honoured to do so on my personal behalf. I am a devoted fan. I hope you will grace us with your company until such time as you are required elsewhere." His words seemed genuine, and he appeared almost excited as he shook Vincent's hand.

Vincent stared at their hands shaking. It made little difference that this was not Mr Hartford-Benton. As head of the Benton House, it still felt as if the master was eagerly shaking the hand of the lowest of his servants, not even realising it, thinking they were equals.

Knowing that, in this world of strict hierarchy, you did not climb up the ranks to such a position, Vincent marvelled at the thought that the hand being so vigorously shaken had once washed the young master's parents' and grandparents' chamber pots. Mr Foxwick-Benton was blessed to be so ignorant.

"Her Ladyship is arranging a dinner party in your honour this Saturday. With such a short notice, we did not receive a response from you confirming that you are available to attend, so I am hoping the timing is suitable for your schedule." Mr Foxwick-Benton proceeded to clean his round lenses with a corner of his handkerchief.

He seemed nervous, no doubt because he feared Vincent might refuse to attend at the last minute, thus foiling the plans for the grand party with distinguished guests, who—along with the rest of the area—would come to know of Vincent's presence at Benton House. The man was trying to act casual, but there was no mistaking it. Vincent was tempted to decline just to see his reaction.

"Certainly." It took a bit of lip-biting and breath-holding to refrain from adding "sir" to his reply, but Vincent experienced some perverse pleasure making this effort. Knowingly omitting it was much more fun than never having learnt to add it in the first place. It was *satisfying* not to have to.

"Marvellous!" Mr Foxwick-Benton rang the bell almost as vigorously as he'd shaken Vincent's hand. The butler rushed in to hear his instructions for making the necessary preparations. "Pass it on to Mrs Sivens, my good

man, and have her send someone to take care of Mr Vincent." He turned
back to Vincent. "It would please me tremendously to give you a tour of
the house."

"All right." Vincent knew the house, but it probably wouldn't hurt to
see it from this side of the enormous gulf between the classes.

"I have to attend to urgent business right now, though." Mr
Foxwick-Benton glanced at his pocket-watch as theatrically as only someone born to money and status possibly could. "You do not mind, do
you? I am terribly sorry... I have this footman—" He glanced at the butler
pleadingly. "What was his name now again?"

"Marcus, sir."

"Yes, that one. He has been with us for... well, I don't know. Longer than
most. He knows this house as well as... As well as whatever one might expect
to know well from having known it for so long. He will show you around,
and if there is anything you need, you can ask him. He's a dependable lad,
if a little dim." Mr Foxwick-Benton made some obscure, hasty gestures at
the butler, who, probably from years of experience dealing with upper class
gentlemen, could interpret what it was the man wanted done.

"Sir," the butler addressed Vincent. "If you could wait here for a moment, sir. I shall send Marcus to you momentarily."

Both the head of Benton House and the butler left the room, heading
in opposite directions.

Vincent heaved a sigh and tried to relax. Maybe Marcus would not
recognize him. Maybe it wasn't the same Marcus at all.

CHAPTER 32

Vincent traced the line of carved clovers that ran across the edge of the mantelpiece. This must have been what they'd referred to as the clover room.

While the rooms on this side were richly decorated in distinctive styles, the servants had to use markers to navigate the bland and dark staff passages. None of the concealed doors led straight into this room, but Vincent could recall passing the clover marker on his way to that staircase. It must have been somewhere nearby. If he could locate the nearest concealed door, the markers on the other side might refresh his memory.

Then again, he wasn't here to reminisce. It seemed silly to want to revisit the darkness when he could finally enjoy the brighter side.

It was a beautiful house, certainly, on this side. It had been difficult to appreciate its beauty when the only times he'd seen it were when he'd dived into the bedrooms to retrieve someone's smellies.

Vincent peeked out into the hallway and to the grand staircase. There was a huge, ornate chandelier hanging from the ceiling. He'd certainly seen it before, but it hadn't been at all as impressive and enjoyable to look at when he'd had to polish the crystals one by one.

And there were a lot of crystals in that chandelier. Six-hundred and fifty-two, if memory served. He hadn't been the only one counting, so errors were likely. Nevertheless, it had taken much too many days to polish, and he'd had sores on his fingers for days after. It was difficult to enjoy any of the grandeur without being reminded of the pain behind it. He retreated back into the reception room.

"My most sincere apologies for making you wait, sir." Marcus entered in Vincent's wake. His voice was much more mature now, but it had the same tone and cadence.

"Don't worry about it..." Vincent found himself trailing off and swallowing nervously. Marcus was dressed much more neatly than before, as a footman should, but there was no mistaking who he was.

Vincent wasn't sure how much he himself had changed. He didn't feel different, but at the same time, the surroundings seemed far removed from where he'd come from.

"If you would follow me, please, sir," Marcus said, eyes downcast and avoiding looking at Vincent. Even his hand gestures were as well-honed and graceful as one might expect from an experienced footman.

"Marcus," Vincent said, to create a deliberate pause. He hoped that this break from the expected was enough to get Marcus to look and for his cogwheels to start turning.

Marcus frowned. Then, before reacting to what Vincent was saying or doing, he leaned back to look into the hallway. Once he'd looked both ways twice, he turned back to Vincent, and his expression lit up with the sort of excitement one might expect from a fox jumping into a pile of snow.

"You're *that* Vincent! Oh, I don't believe it!" He seemed unable to decide whether to charge forth or keep his composure. This made him look like a tilting doll, swaying back and forth. "Oh, sorry! My manners, they're atrocious... but hell, it's you!"

"Yes," Vincent said. His hands felt about to cramp, so he stretched, wiggled and massaged his fingers to release the tension. Marcus didn't seem to be holding on to any resentment. That was promising. Maybe it was safe to relax a little.

"Holy hell, I know Vincent the Traveller!" The man took a couple of steps forward this time but backed away similarly. He looked like he wanted to hug Vincent, but it would have been an outrage to even touch a guest, much less show affection. This wobbling back and forth was amusing, but also a little sad.

"There was no one out there, was there? Stop prancing back and forth and do it," Vincent suggested. These conventions were despicable, but around here, he had to abide by them for the sake of his career and image. So long as no one was there to witness to give either of them grief, Vincent had no qualms with ignoring the conventions. "You know I'm of as piss-poor birth as you are," Vincent added when Marcus was still hesitating.

This made the man smile, and he dared a very awkward, brief hug with a tentative pat on the back before pulling back to resume his role as a footman.

"You seem to be doing well." Marcus measured Vincent's travel attire from head to toe. Vincent had tried to choose his cleanest and least embarrassing clothes for the occasion, and while they weren't as obnoxiously opulent as his current peers', he looked respectable.

"As do you." Vincent was glad to see that Marcus had defied expectations by moving up in rank.

"Do you still want that tour of the house?"

"I suppose I have to keep up appearances so as not to disappoint the fans. Besides, I don't believe I've seen much of this side."

"Say no more. We won't say a peep. There's just me, and Mrs Sivens you remember, and Bryony is the new head housemaid for Mrs Sivens. Only a few of the others remain. You know how it is. Well, we best get going or she'll have my hide for keeping you." Marcus guided Vincent out of the room.

Almost as soon as they'd entered the hallway, Marcus faced the wall as the third daughter of Mr Hartford-Benton passed them. She greeted Vincent, but, because they were yet to be formally introduced, she merely curtsied, bobbed her head and carried on walking.

Surely, at her own home, her Ladyship should have commanded more respect than a mere guest? Yet she appeared tight-lipped and meek and would not engage in conversation before a male member of her household gave her permission by introduction.

Having been away from these customs, they felt bizarre to Vincent. Watching Marcus pretend he wasn't there was equally strange. Once the man emerged from trying to camouflage himself as the tapestry, they continued walking.

Marcus diligently showed Vincent the main rooms in two of the wings, but by the time they'd reached the second wing, the tour had become somewhat repetitive, and it was getting late.

"Are you hungry? I could have them cater for you in one of the dining rooms," Marcus offered. It wasn't a regular custom, but since Vincent had arrived from afar, it would have been severely impolite to make him wait until dinnertime.

"Hmm," Vincent hummed, "it seems like a whole lot of trouble over me."

Digging through the recesses of his memory, he was fairly certain there was a servants' passage right around the corner, and it conveniently led to the kitchens. It was probably why Marcus had been reminded of food just then.

Marcus hadn't the time to don an appalled expression when, without making a sound, Vincent opened the barely visible door into the passage.

"You always were better at that than me," Marcus noted sourly as he followed Vincent into the passage and closed the door just as quietly. "The butler will have my head if he finds out I let you in here," he mumbled. Vincent assured him it would be fine.

The passage smelled as awful as Vincent remembered. The passages at this part of the house were slightly better because of the proximity of the kitchens, but the stuffy stench of work-clothed, sweaty people with all the different—often unsavoury—things they had to carry was unavoidable. There were few things worse than this.

"Ah, the sluice room."

"You're thinking about the sluice room on the way to the kitchens?" Marcus exhaled and rolled his eyes, failing to disguise his exasperation.

"I know, I know. We're at the other end of the house... but it's been a long time since I've smelled this." Vincent heard Marcus taking a couple of sniffs behind him to check. "Maybe when you become the butler, you can have them clean up the passages more often," Vincent suggested.

"That would come right out of my pay," Marcus objected.

"They would thank you for it," Vincent assured.

Marcus grumbled, but he seemed to be considering it.

What Vincent was proposing was ludicrous. Not so much for the idea of cleaning the passages more often, but because Benton House would never hire any of their footmen as the butler. The likelihood of Marcus becoming the housekeeper by changing his name and gender was higher.

Vincent and Marcus popped out of the passage and into the kitchens, where everything looked the same as how Vincent remembered it. Only the cook had changed.

"Bryony is very nice to me," Marcus said as they passed the scullery.

"Didn't think she'd ever give you the time of day."

"I can be spineless, but I can also be persistent."

Bryony had certainly grown, and the way Marcus eyed her, she had grown in all the places he preferred. Compared to Marcus, it took Bryony slightly less time to recognise Vincent but more time to believe her eyes.

"Slop boy!" she exclaimed at the sight of him. She received some angry looks from the cook.

The cook, noticing the stranger in her kitchen, hurried to inquire what was going on. The way Bryony had unwittingly introduced Vincent, the cook was understandably suspicious of the visitor.

"Slop boy?" She questioned Bryony, Vincent and Marcus, and her gaze would've been acerbic had she not been short and tubby, face round and jolly by default.

"It's an old nickname," Vincent explained.

"And what are you doing in my kitchen?"

It struck Vincent that his familiar mingling with the help had probably ruined his credibility beyond repair, and she might not believe him if he tried to claim his status as guest.

"This is Vincent!" Marcus butted in. Vincent rather hoped the cook hadn't heard of him: Neither him the insane slop boy, nor him the mildly famous traveller. She continued to ogle Vincent, and her ogling was only interrupted when Mrs Sivens entered the kitchens.

Mrs Sivens suited her role as the housekeeper like milk and lemon to tea. She'd been apt at her job as the head maid, but she appeared to have made a point of being more than apt as the housekeeper. The post required a certain amount of severity and distancing from the rest of the staff, and she fulfilled these requirements masterfully.

When she appeared, the cook's meagre ogles were nothing in comparison. Mrs Sivens eyed her staff first, to remind them of their place, and then turned to Vincent.

Vincent was glad of his height to not have to face her downward gaze. He was painfully aware that he was too lean to not look awkward in his fancier set of clothes, but at least she seemed to deem him manly enough to command some respect.

"Marcus. Why have you brought our guest into the filthy kitchens?" Mrs Sivens frowned. She had identified Vincent as the visitor from having met him briefly when he'd arrived, but evidently she had yet to realise anything else.

Marcus cowered instinctively behind Bryony. Vincent waited, unsure if he should point out who he was. It wouldn't be right if Marcus had to bear the brunt for this spontaneous excursion after Vincent had so negligently assured it would be fine. It was this guilt that finally drove him to open his mouth.

"Technically, I wasn't brought," Vincent began and coughed, "old habits, you see." He couldn't resist scratching the back of his head, abashed. He hadn't felt like this for a while, like he'd been caught red-handed trying to steal treats from the treat tray.

It was the third such time a face lit up from recognition, and it was quite the relief because, instead of deepening her frown, it seemed to ease Mrs Sivens's demeanour. There was always the fear that bad blood lingered between Vincent and the people he'd known in the past, but this did not seem to be the case for a lucky third time in a row.

"Well, you've certainly stretched upwards in more ways than one," she said briskly. "Neat clothes, good to cover those gangly knees of yours. Tell me, did you really go all the way to Cumbering?" Cumbering was not very far compared to some of the places Vincent had seen, but he nodded. If that was enough to merit awe, then it seemed improper to brag further.

"Are you hungry, is that why you're here? For heaven's sake, you're a guest here. You needn't come down for a snack. You could have asked to be served." She sighed and motioned for Bryony to bring a plate and some freshly baked apple pie.

"Just wanted to see the place one more time." Vincent tried to refuse the pie in vain.

"Don't go prying my mind now, lad. You may have moved up, but my mind is still mine!" She shooed Marcus and Bryony out of the kitchen as if the place were too crowded for all of them.

The cook was allowed to stay because she was the cook, but she took some distance and returned to her duties. Mrs Sivens sat down on a stool and inspected Vincent, who wasn't sure where to stand. He laughed nervously.

"Don't worry, I'm no longer insane. I grew out of it."

"Oh no, dear, you were never insane! But the devil's got a part of you, and she ain't letting go what she's acquired. Just keep away from my mind and the two of us will be fine." She smiled. Vincent wondered if he'd ever seen her smile before.

"I don't do any of that anymore, trust me." It had caused a stir back in the day, and it hadn't been the sort of stir one wanted to stir.

"Ah, lad. I'm glad you got out of this house. It was not a good fit for you." She looked genuinely pleased. "How's the pie?"

Vincent was reminded of it and took a bite to be polite. It was fine, and he commended it.

Most people recalled cakes from their childhood fondly, as something perhaps their mothers or grandmothers had baked. For Vincent, they reminded him of the sneaky exchanges and guilt, perhaps the occasional well-deserved reward, but above all, getting to observe and smell, but be denied the taste. They were tasty but not as tasty as he'd imagined them to be.

"You shouldn't be skulking around in the servants' passages. If the master sees you, he may raise an eyebrow and be tempted to look closer. You have a life now and a reputation. You shouldn't risk it," she advised him kindly.

Vincent knew of the risks, but his travels had never been about the reputation. Remembering that he needed to maintain his was usually an afterthought.

But it was sound advice. He needed his readership for his stories to sell, and he needed to be able to sell his stories to afford his travels.

"Well, they won't be coming down here, and if I hear someone whisper one word of it, I'll have their head on a platter, rest assured." Mrs Sivens laughed, but her expression quickly turned grave again, and she added, "I'm glad to see you're doing all right." She shook Vincent's hand with both of hers. "I really am."

CHAPTER 33

T he house was silent save for its creaks and pops of wood and the clattering of branches against the window panes. Some of the staff were no doubt still awake doing the last of their chores somewhere below, but no one was up and about anymore at this hour.

Vincent had a mild fever.

It was to be expected after the excitement of the journey. He wasn't ill, but he often felt a bit warm before bedtime, so he'd requested somewhere peaceful, knowing that his ailment might return.

He'd received a room on the second floor of a less used wing, away from the rest of the current guests and the family bedrooms. There were plenty of guest rooms, but they lay vacant because it was the oldest of the wings, its furniture out of date and the rooms draughtier than the rest.

One floor up, there were the rooms of the butler, the housekeeper, the first footman and the head maid. Vincent could hear a few faint stray thoughts, but nothing clear enough to keep him awake.

There were two reception rooms and a drawing room downstairs, and one of these was the one by which Vincent had spent a lot of time those years ago. The whole first floor was empty of people now.

Underneath the reception room, there were still a few rooms, such as one of the cellars and some passages leading out of the house. These weren't much used as there were similar spaces beneath the rest of the building. The whole of this wing was quiet and familiar.

On the other side, the servants' hall and their bedrooms were all underground, where the air was musty and there were no windows to let in any natural light. Vincent felt guilty about having a whole room to himself. It was upsetting to think that so many wonderful guest rooms remained empty when the servants were forced to bunk in the cramped and confined spaces beneath his feet.

Vincent sat up, got out of bed and sneaked into the hall. He thought about using the staff passages, but opted not to, as no one was about and the floors more used were also more loud. The soft carpeting beneath his bare feet muffled the rest of the little sound he made. Regardless of this, he made sure to walk light-footed, though no one was under him now. Sounds could travel through the passages, and he did not want to disturb anyone trying to get rest after a hard, long day of work.

There was somewhere he wanted to visit on his own, somewhere without having to hurry or worry that someone might appear behind his back.

The reception room and its globe.

As expected, the room was dark and empty. Vincent lit the gaslight, marvelling how nostalgic it felt to do so when you'd cleaned, trimmed and filled these for months as a child. He hadn't been here very long, but some things weren't as quickly forgotten.

He walked to the globe and turned it. It had probably never been oiled; the sound it made was unpleasant to the ear. This suggested it also hadn't been used much and that the face facing the wall was likely the same that had faced it before. Vincent located the right corner and confirmed what he'd expected.

The name was partially torn off by a scuff mark, but he could tell by its relation to the mainland: indeed, the island he'd seen on this globe as a child was Whitskersey. He'd suspected as much, but he'd always wanted to make sure. The young Vincent had unbeknownst fulfilled one of his dreams. He chuckled.

It looked so tiny!

Vincent's moment of reminiscence was interrupted by the clearing of a throat. As much as he'd wanted to avoid this, his luck had failed him. He turned around to look, hoping to think of a good excuse on the spot, but such seemed to elude him.

"You could not sleep either?" the man asked. He was old, white in beard and hair, wrinkly and pale, but a solid man for his age. His eyebrows were bushy and overshadowed his slightly beady eyes, but he did not look unkind or upset and sounded much like Vincent remembered.

"Sir," Vincent said, forgetting to suppress the habit.

"It was you; I knew it!" The man seemed to congratulate himself for noticing despite having to squint. "Don't worry, boy. I have no reason to tell."

He waved at Vincent to get him to sit down. This time, Vincent sat in a chair and not on the floor. The chair no longer looked too clean and expensive to sit on. In fact, it even looked a bit scruffy. It was just a chair, and it had seen a lot of use.

Mr Benton sat down as well, although he did so behind his desk. He looked smaller than Vincent remembered. Then again, everyone here looked smaller now that Vincent was at his full height, almost a head taller than most everyone else.

"I trust you have been well?" Mr Benton asked. Vincent nodded, lapsing into silence. Mr Benton chuckled. "I wouldn't have thought you'd ever stayed here, under the floors, had you not that skulking look about you like our servants. Of course, that is how my brother likes them. He believes servants are a commodity, nothing more, and that you shouldn't have them believing they are anything other, or you're inviting trouble. I hear you've established yourself as quite the traveller these past few years. Did the island not suit you like you thought?" He seemed amused by Vincent's hesitation. "You can knock if that is easier for you."

"The island was fine. I just needed to see the world... sir." One did not have to be a servant to show courtesy to someone senior, Vincent told himself. He did not want to appear rude.

"I see. I never did know your name. Vincent, is it? Fancy that. To have read about you and not known I knew you." He seemed much more relaxed and less gruff than Vincent remembered him. Perhaps it was the age?

"I apologise for having been a nuisance," Vincent said.

"Indeed. It's rare for a servant to cause enough chatter for it to reach our ears, but there was certainly chatter back then. Talk about a devil's child, silly things like that. It amused me to think that you were right there, on the other side of the wall, and what harm did you do? Nothing. You were helpful even. I don't think I received a letter back once complaining about my words being too unclear. Saved me a lot of stamps and time."

"Thank you."

"No, thank you," Mr Benton said. "I realise this might seem a strange scene to an outsider, me thanking you, but I did impose on you! You were such a tiny, timid thing. Sometimes I wondered if your fists would break if I told you to knock harder. Did they even feed you? Such a frail sack of bones."

"They fed me. I just tend to get poorly during the winter."

"So, it wasn't a ploy to get out of the house?"

"Uh?" Vincent frowned. More rumours must have circulated than he'd known about.

"I certainly would not have blamed you!" Mr Benton added quickly. "This is a wretched house, especially during the cold season." At this, Vincent did chuckle. As he recalled it, the house was balmy compared to the cottage on the island. You had to keep the fire going or else you'd wake up with frost over your face. Here, the water never even froze solid.

"Tell me then, why did you come back? I hear you were invited, but I would've thought, seeing as you are who you are, that you would have declined the invitation."

"I invited myself," Vincent confessed. "There is something I'm searching for, and I thought I might find it if I came here."

"Is that so?" Mr Benton raised his brow.

"I couldn't write it in a letter, as it is a delicate matter. I have been losing some of my post. Pilfered. Possibly fans."

"Sounds troublesome."

"It's difficult to imagine why someone would want to, but it happens, and I couldn't risk it. Too many people wanting and waiting to bring me down."

"Oh yes. Success brings along one's share of enemies. So, what is this matter, then? Anything I can help you with?"

"Perhaps. I'm hoping to find out the name of the workhouse I came from." Vincent hadn't intended to bother Mr Benton with something like this, but since he hadn't managed to bring it up while chatting with Mrs Sivens, the man now seemed like the right person to ask. If Mr Benton didn't know, he probably had the means to find out, and he didn't seem to have an urge to tell anyone.

"Ah." Mr Benton's face twisted into an awkward frown. "I was hoping this wouldn't be what you're here for. I suppose you can't be persuaded to let it go?" He heaved a heavy sigh.

"I will keep on searching until I find it," Vincent said.

"Why is it so important to you?"

"It may be a little late for this, but I'm looking for my parents." Vincent had been hopeful just moments earlier, but Mr Benton did not seem forthcoming. The man rubbed the creases on his forehead and massaged his temples for a while, as if considering it was almost unreasonably strenuous.

"As much as it pleases me to see you and know you're doing well, you shouldn't have come." He rummaged through the desk drawers for a piece of paper and a pen. "Seeing as you are an adult now, I will give you the address, but I urge you to be careful." He wrote it on the piece of paper. "It will take a while to gather everything. If you give me your address, I will have my personal courier deliver it to you. I think you should go through it all before you make up your mind about whether you want to pursue this. You're likely better off not getting yourself involved now that you're clear of it."

"I can wait here if that's all right, so you need not send it."

"I don't think you understand. This is the type of stuff I want to steer clear of. I want you far away from here when you read it. For everyone's sake. I'd rather not even discuss this with you, because you never know when someone might be listening. That wretched woman has already caused enough trouble for me to last for a lifetime." Mr Benton handed over the address. "If you go there, try not to draw attention to yourself. Whatever they give you, you'll do well to pay attention to what's missing."

"What wretched woman?"

"Your mother."

CHAPTER 34

It was no surprise that the workhouse was no longer in business after so many years. It had served the needs of several towns in the area, but some of them had dwindled into villages as the result of people moving into bigger cities. The town it was in, Dritsby, had retained its size as some of its neighbours had added to its population, and it was doing reasonably well taking care of its poor without the need for such an archaic, heartless institution.

The building was still there, but it was used as office space. Vincent knocked on the door.

"Good day, sir. What can I do for you?" A peppy young receptionist opened the door for him. She seemed young to be working as a receptionist, as she couldn't have been much older than fifteen.

"I was wondering if you could help me with something," Vincent said. The receptionist stepped aside and let him in. He took off his hat and looked around. The interior had changed considerably, and there was no signage that would immediately give away whose office it was and what it was for. "Do you know what was here before? Would you happen to know how I could get in touch with anyone who worked here at the time?"

"You'd have to be more specific than that. The owner has changed many times in the past few years." She returned to her desk at the back of the room.

"I'm interested in getting in touch with someone that might have worked here about twenty years ago, if it's at all possible." It did not seem very promising. The receptionist looked at Vincent a little troubled, but then turned to her archives and seemed to be looking into it. She then dialled the telephone and made an inquiry.

"Yes? It's Ms Wakefield from Mr Farthistle's office. Please excuse my intrusion, but there's a gentleman here who wishes to know about the history of the building. I have the deeds here, yes— yes... Excuse me, sir," she turned to Vincent. "Could you please elaborate as to why you need this information?"

"It's a private matter."

"Oh." She thought about it for a moment and got back to her phone conversation. "Sir, it seems very urgent and much too complicated for me to relay accurately, but it sounds awfully important, sir! Yes, all right. I'll tell him that. Thank you." She hung up. "You're looking for information about the workhouse, right?" She was nodding as she spoke and seemed empathetic.

"Yes," Vincent said. "Can you help me?"

"It might take a day or two, but I'll see what I can do. Will you be staying? You're from out of town, aren't you?"

"Ah, yes. Would you happen to know a good place to stay nearby?"

"You're in luck! I know just the place." She checked the time from her desk clock and looked displeased. "Oh dear, I'm on the clock for another twenty minutes. Would you mind having to wait?" Evidently, she intended to show him to the place personally.

Vincent nodded. He was not in a particular hurry. It had taken its sweet time to get here, so waiting a couple more minutes made no difference.

T he receptionist checked her desk clock and stood up promptly.

"Sir, I believe I am now officially off duty. Thank you for waiting," she announced, grabbed her coat and headed for the door. She checked to see that Vincent was following before she proceeded to chat his ear off about the weather and local news.

Vincent was too distracted by her dangling earrings to listen. They were light and wispy and reached quite low down, almost touching her shoulders when she moved. These did not look like the sort of earrings one might wear to work, but she also did not look like a typical receptionist. Her attire was mature and plain save for the subtle, laced frills on her collar. On the surface, she looked delicate and feminine, but something about her mannerisms did not match the exterior. She wasn't precisely uncouth or clumsy; she just seemed like someone had decorated a birch tree for Midwinter.

"It's my father's inn. This is shameless advertising, but it is irrefutably lovely! I'm sure you'll like it. It's not far. Just a short walk, really." Everything was probably only a short walk away. It wasn't as if the town was massive. "You are Vincent, aren't you?" she asked to confirm.

"Yes," Vincent admitted. It still felt queer to have people recognise him.

"I thought you looked familiar. I've been reading your articles. They're wonderful."

"Thank you."

"My mother is also a fan. Father... not so much. But don't mind him!" Something about her talkativeness was oddly familiar and made Vincent uncomfortable, even though she herself seemed affable.

"Am I making you uncomfortable? I'm sorry. I'm a bit excited. We don't get celebrities around here often."

"It's all right. I must be a little tired from my trip."

"Well, we've come to the right place. I'll arrange a room for you in no time. My name is Iris, by the way." She opened the door to the irrefutably lovely inn and guided Vincent toward the reception area with a counter and some seats. "Father, I brought a customer!"

"Oh? That's nice, dear." Iris's father's voice rumbled from the back room. He appeared at the counter shortly, and as soon as he did, it became clear why she had said Vincent looked familiar.

Vincent lost his usual bland, sociable smile. Standing in front of him on the opposite side of the counter was a man as tall and as strangely off-proportioned as him. The man seemed to take notice of this as well.

Iris was a little put off by the silence and asked what was wrong. It was an odd moment to pick to be oblivious of the resemblance.

"Nothing," Vincent said. "I'd like a bed for the night." He kept his eyes on the innkeeper while something inside him was boiling, wanting to burst out. He wasn't sure what this feeling was, but he had to concentrate to not do anything peculiar.

"Iris, could you go prepare room twelve, please?" Iris's father asked. Iris looked confused by the chilly tone but obeyed.

Soon the front room was empty except for Vincent and the innkeeper.

"Iris did mention you weren't very fond of me. I think I can see why," Vincent said after a while.

"What do you want?" the innkeeper asked.

"There are some things perhaps you could help me with."

"Not here."

"Obviously." The innkeeper clearly didn't want his daughter to find out.

"In an hour. There's a pub down the street. You can say your piece then and be done with it."

I t was a pub of the more seedy variety, and Vincent had seen a broad enough selection to be able to tell. He ordered a drink and went to sit in a suitably shady corner to wait for his father to show up. The man was late, despite being the one to specify the time.

"What do you want?" The innkeeper asked upon showing up. He made no effort to disguise his distaste.

Vincent had had the past hour or so to sort his thoughts and get past his initial shock. He wasn't sure how to get the answer he was looking for, but he'd ruled out some of the more rash and hazardous options. He did have a strong urge to say a few things though, even against his better judgement.

"I hope she never has to choose," Vincent began.

"She won't. And even if she had to, I trust she'd make the right choice."

"Well, thankfully, she'll have the benefit of over a decade more years to avoid making an ill-informed decision."

"I know I must seem like a bad person to you, but I refuse to regret what happened. You made your choice."

"That wasn't the decision I made, though, was it?" Vincent bit the inside of his lip to remind himself to keep calm. Drinking more beer seemed to help as a distraction.

"What do you mean?" The innkeeper frowned, agitated. "Why wouldn't it be?"

"Don't play dumb. You knew I didn't understand the question well enough to give a valid answer."

"I did not raise a son so devoid of comprehension," the man dared to defend himself.

"You did not raise a son at all, though, did you?" Vincent hissed. The man did not appear apologetic in the slightest; he was eyeing Vincent just as angrily.

"That's true. A son of mine would take responsibility for their own actions."

"I was four!"

"Is that what you came to tell me?"

"No. Although, I think this already explains a lot."

"What more do you want from me? I've moved on. Don't ever think I'll let you march here and screw it up for me again. You've done enough," the innkeeper growled.

"What is that supposed to mean?"

"It was your fault in the first place. You know this."

"Let me remind you again, I was *four*."

"You were thoroughly wicked, like your mother! You were sick, evil, and you would not keep your mouth shut. Do you know how relieved I was when you said you didn't want to come? Do you know how happy it made me that she left it up to you and didn't insist we take you with us?"

"Aren't you exaggerating a tad? What could I have done to deserve this much hate? I was a child."

"Don't tell me you don't remember?" The innkeeper let out a curt, dry laugh. "If not for the hell you put me through, I would probably be thanking you for exposing the madness in your blood."

"What the hell are you talking about?"

"Your mother, of course. How is the insane harpy?"

"Why do you ask me?" After so many years, Vincent couldn't even remember his mother's face.

"You're no longer in contact? I would have thought with you being such a sneaky momma's boy..." The innkeeper frowned. "Well, I suppose you couldn't be pleased about her putting you into a workhouse. I must admit, I did laugh when I heard she did that. Daft bugger."

Vincent fell quiet to process this, but he figured he was missing a vital piece because he couldn't make it make sense. Hadn't his parents left together? They'd seemed like a reasonably happy couple, but from the way he addressed her now, their relationship must have since fallen apart. Did his father resent him because his mother had decided to return and they'd had a fight over it?

Had his mother come back? When? When he'd been sick? Why couldn't he remember seeing her?

"How did you escape, anyway?" The innkeeper asked before Vincent could decide which of his questions were worth asking out loud.

"Escape?"

"Yes, did you run away from the workhouse, or was it after they'd placed you? Did they throw you out once they realised you were damaged? I hear you're a storytelling drifter these days. Probably can't stay anywhere for long before they discover your true nature."

"Like father, like son, I guess," Vincent noted acridly.

"So, you *are* here to rat me out to my family after all? Do you intend to make them hate me for what I did to you? You want revenge? Whatever it is, you'd better leave Iris out of it."

"I'm not a sociopath. I have nothing against Iris. Why would I want to hurt her?"

"Well, if you're here for money, you can forget it."

"I don't care about your money."

"Then what do you want? You must want something." He looked oddly insistent. For all his arrogant confidence, he was probably looking for some assurance that Vincent would keep quiet and leave him alone.

"No, I think this was enough. I really don't want anything from you." Vincent emptied his glass.

"Why did you bother coming, then?"

A good question. There were plenty of shady hints being thrown around about his parents and his past, and he would have preferred not to be kept in the dark. But having to deal with this sorry excuse of a man made being kept in the dark seem like the better option.

"Maybe to see your sorry face. Maybe to make sure that what I'm looking for is not here, and I'm better off without." This, at least, seemed obvious to him now. There was no way there would be enough pay dirt under this steaming pile of horse manure to justify digging. "It really doesn't matter. I'm leaving." Vincent stood up.

"Stop! What are you going to do? It was your mother's idea to come here to rattle me up, wasn't it? Does it bring you some twisted pleasure to torture me like this? You want to ruin my life, is that it? I knew there was something wrong with you the minute I laid my eyes on you, you sick son of a bitch. Fine," he seemed to change his mind. "Go ahead and leave! You vile, crooked, demon child, I wish you had never been born!"

Vincent felt cold inside. He could've tried to interject, but it seemed meaningless to try. Walking out without saying anything felt worse, though. He stood there for a moment and sat back down. Why should he have to leave? If his father wanted to be rid of him, he'd have to make that decision on his own this time. None of this "you made your choice"–bullshit.

"I didn't ask for this!" The innkeeper was still fuming.

"Neither did I."

"How long does she intend to make me suffer—?"

"Not everything is about the two of you," Vincent interrupted. "I'm not something that happened to you, I'm something that happened to me. I've had to live with myself my whole life, while you only had to be around for a fraction of the mess. And you know what? This is all in *your* name. *You made* me. You're responsible for *all* of this. You and her. It doesn't really matter what I said or did. You only have yourself to blame."

"I should have just killed you when I had the chance," the innkeeper snarled. His face was twisted from the anger. Vincent wondered if that was what he looked like himself when he was angry. It wasn't very attractive. He'd have to remember that.

"Well, I appreciate that lapse in your judgement, I guess," Vincent said, now feeling oddly calm. "I hear your current wife's a fan of mine. Iris too, evidently. I guess there is some poetic justice in that. I hope it eats you inside and keeps you up at night."

"You are a twisted being." The innkeeper eyed Vincent, still as sharply, but it no longer seemed very menacing. Something inside Vincent had changed. It didn't really matter whose fault any of it was, not anymore.

If this man could be a decent father for Iris, Vincent didn't see a reason to ruin that. It was enough of a revenge to know that the man was forced to see him do well for himself in spite of everything. He was doing fine, wasn't he?

"You can go now," Vincent said, with an urge to shoo the innkeeper away with a flick of the wrist. He didn't have to, though, because the effect was sufficient even without. The man looked appalled, nay, mortified. If nothing else, Vincent could take away from this the satisfying memory of that face. "Really, I believe this was all. You can go," Vincent reiterated. The temptation to shoo him was immeasurable.

The innkeeper stared at him, his hands milling and grinding, probably fantasising about wrapping his fingers around Vincent's throat to strangle him. But what could he do? He couldn't even raise his voice without someone at the pub giving them dirty looks. Most of these people probably knew him personally and were already wondering what this conversation was about.

"Don't ever come close to my family again," the innkeeper said.

"What about my reservation?" Vincent asked innocently.

"We don't cater to your kind."

"Blood relatives? That's peculiar. Won't your wife and daughter wonder why you drove away the celebrity customer?"

"That is none of your concern."

"All right." It wasn't worth arguing about. He'd have to find somewhere else to sleep tonight. Maybe take a nap at the speeder and ride off later? It didn't matter. There was no reason to stay here for any longer than necessary.

Well, except for maybe one more drink to calm his nerves, since his hands seemed to be shaking. The innkeeper paid no attention to it, though. He was out of things to say. He grunted, turned around and stomped toward the door. Because of his height and build, his departure looked about as threatening as a petulant camel pushing through a sandstorm. Vincent snorted, failing to suppress his amusement.

Well, now he knew what stock he was from. It wasn't impressive, but he mused it wasn't so much a case of what you had, but what you made of it. Maybe he'd make a man out of himself yet; someone better than that, at least.

One thing he knew for sure: He was never bringing a child into this world. If the insanity was hereditary, it had caused enough trouble.

CHAPTER 35

V incent felt unsteady. He'd stayed to have a couple more beverages since he hadn't a place to sleep. He was roughly aiming for the speeder. He was admittedly not at his smartest, but thankfully did not feel stupid enough to try to ride it.

The speeder itself wasn't built for sleeping, but at least he had some blankets in the baggage compartment. If it got too cold or rainy, the baggage compartment was big enough to house him, though it would not be comfortable having to fold many times over.

He wondered about building a sidecar of some sort to sleep in if he needed to. He'd make plans as soon as he could see straight. Oh, but he would probably need some paper for that. And a pen. Well, he was fairly sure he had a pen somewhere. But he was definitely out of paper.

The speeder hadn't been stolen. That was nice. It was always a nice surprise that no one had stolen it, considering how crappy his countermeasures for theft were.

There was a lock of sorts. And then of course, the thing itself looked strange enough to deter the less adventurous types. But the lock could have been picked with a twig and the steering system wasn't all *that* complicated. At least not usually.

Vincent looked at it and his brain fumbled a bit. Then he recalled he wasn't supposed to try in his current condition and thanked himself for remembering. It could have made for a dire situation had that not crossed his mind! Haha, disaster averted.

He rummaged through the baggage compartment. Yes, definitely no paper here. But there was a blanket. Hmmm, the blanket was soft and comfy. He almost fell asleep on the spot.

Of course, it would have been difficult to sleep with his bum hanging halfway down from a hovercraft. It was not the most restful of positions. He realised this most concretely when said bum hit the ground as he fell out of the compartment.

At least he'd grabbed the blanket with him on the way down, so he had no need to climb again to get it. The first three times had already been enough exercise for the evening.

Vincent leaned against the side of the speeder and looked up at the stars. That was nice. A bit of stars, some moonlight, an owl somewhere. The sound of other drunkards making their way home somewhere far enough away to not be a bother. Very atmospheric.

Vincent no longer felt sleepy. It had been a long journey, but he'd been on long journeys before. On this one he'd reunited with some reasonably all right people like Marcus, Bryony, Mrs Sivens and Mr Benton, whom he wouldn't even have met had it not been for the two assholes who had given him life.

He'd had a chance to say a few choice words, so he would probably be able to find closure now, even if he'd thought of several juicier, more fun insults after the innkeeper had left. Because it seemed likely that his parents had been the gigantic, smelly poo-poo heads, and he'd just had the misfortune of being their child, he could finally focus on something other than looking back at the past to try to figure out what went wrong.

He wished he could've met his mother too, just to be sure that she was equally poo-poo, but since his dad did not seem to know or want to know where she was, it would still take a while to find out for sure.

It occurred to Vincent that he should have at least asked for her name, but it would probably be mentioned somewhere at some point in the workhouse's records or in some of the stuff Mr Benton had promised, so he wasn't too bothered about it.

Just about everyone who had mentioned her had had something unpleasant to say about her, anyway. It wasn't a great thing to hear nasty things
about one's mother, but the thought of having been abandoned by a jerk
rather than someone nice was comforting.

All things considered, it hadn't been a bad day. He'd gained new appreciation for the people who were a positive influence in his life. This was well
worth the last celebratory drink.

Vincent pulled the blanket closer and watched the sky sway a bit as he
breathed in deeply. All right, maybe the last drink had been a bit much,
but he was bloody well entitled to a mistake or two every once in a while.
A mistake or two didn't make him an insane demon child, yet.

He could do better—that was to say worse—if he wanted to. He just
didn't want to. That probably meant he wasn't as bad as they'd thought he
was. Possibly. This made perfect sense in his addled mind.

"Um, Mr Vincent?"

Vincent had to do a double-take to determine whether he'd actually
heard an actual real voice and not one of his usual stupid inner fake voices.
When he looked up, he saw Iris looking at him worriedly.

"Oh, hi."

"You're a bit drunk, aren't you?" She also sounded worried, but it didn't
seem accusatory.

"Yes, I suppose. It's not, I don't usually..." Vincent hurried to explain.
He didn't venture to get up but sat up a bit straighter, checked the grass
next to him, determined that it was pretty dry and possibly not too dirty
and gestured for Iris to take a seat. It took him a while to make this assessment, but he wanted to be thorough. It paid off as Iris sat down next to
him.

Ah, yes. She was his half-sister then. He hadn't really thought of it that
way before just then. Well, that was... interesting.

"It's all right. Did something happen? Did my father say something
awful to you? He can be pretty rude sometimes."

"No, don't worry about... it... that... uh," It would have been so much
easier to be reassuring if sober, but it was what it was. Sometimes making a
bit of an ass of yourself by slurring and messing up the words couldn't be
avoided. Especially in front of your half-sister, who you'd met for the first
time that same day. It couldn't be helped. Shit like that happened.

"I didn't know he disliked you that much. He's stubborn. You don't have to sleep out here because of him. I can get you in through the back."

"Thanks, but maybe it's best if I don't." Vincent felt fine where he was. It wasn't ideal, but he didn't want to get Iris into any trouble.

"Well, I'll keep you company for a while then, if it's all right with you?" Iris offered. She was a strange girl, but it was probably something that ran in the family.

"Won't you be missed? This is not exactly the time to be out and about," Vincent said. Or at least he thought he said that. He came close enough for Iris to get the gist, at least, because she answered the intended question.

"It's all right. They think I'm asleep. And it's not far from here. You don't mind?"

"Why would I mind?"

"You probably get pushy fans trying to talk to you all the time, so I thought maybe you wanted some time to yourself."

"Is that what this is?"

"Well, not exactly," she said, then backed up a bit and added sheepishly: "Maybe a little. But you're Vincent. And I was worried. The locals can be a bit rough with newcomers."

"They were generous." Vincent chuckled. Since his fame had spread, he'd certainly had less of a need to pay for his drinks.

It seemed people were very keen on giving him things as if he didn't already get paid for the work he did. It was silly. They gave no pay to a hall boy, but as soon as you fed them some cat's scat about some stupid crap that happened to you when you were being an idiot foreigner abroad, they couldn't wait to shower you with money and gifts.

Luck was such a fickle thing sometimes. That was why he intended to make the best of it while it lasted.

"So, if I find out about the workhouse thing tomorrow, where can I get in touch with you?" she asked.

"Oh, that. Right. I don't know if I need that anymore." Mr Benton had suggested he read that other stuff first anyway, so as not to open a can of worms, presumably. He'd figure out the rest later if it still felt worth the effort.

"Really? Why not? I can get you the information, it's no trouble."

"It's all right. I'll be leaving tomorrow, anyway. I think I got what I came for."

"That's a shame."

"How so?"

"I was looking forward to seeing you again. You seem nice. In person too." She smiled at him. It was infectious. Vincent smiled back.

It was a nice evening. The stars, the moon, a pretty smile. A family member that didn't shout obscenities at him and wanted to keep in touch...

"Maybe I'll come back sometime," he said.

"That would be nice," she replied. She let him sit in silence for a while and then asked if she could ask another question. Such a kind and polite girl.

"S-sure, why not." Vincent hoped it was something easy because he wasn't in the mood for anything difficult.

"People probably ask you all the time, but could you tell me a story?"

"A story?"

"Yeah, something you haven't told anyone else before."

"Like a secret story?"

"Yes. Something like that."

"Can I trust you?"

"No, I might tell my mother."

"Anyone else?"

"No, I don't think so. No one else."

"All right, fair enough." Vincent chuckled and tried to think of something secret enough but not too private. "What sort of a story would you like?"

"Well, you never talk about your family," Iris said. Her eyes were fixed to Vincent, and when Vincent looked, they were like two sparkling blobs of intense interest spilling all over. Or maybe that was just him. Yeah, it was probably just his drunken head again. Her eyes were not blobs. They were properly eye-shaped.

"Hmm, well, I have a mother and a father, an aunt, and a little sister," Vincent said without having to lie.

"Oh! What's she like? The little sister. Are you close?"

"She's a bit excitable, like a puppy, I suppose." Vincent laughed. "And she's happy and kind."

"I'd like to meet her."

"I bet you'd like her. She's a bit like you."

"Really? In what way?"

"Well, she wears ridiculously large earrings that don't necessarily suit her, for one."

"How rude!" She glared at him for a moment. "But I'm going to forgive you for that because you are drunk, and you don't know what you're talking about. They're a family heirloom. I happen to like them."

"All right. Thank you for your kind understanding." Vincent laughed again. Laughing felt nice. He wondered if this was the first time he'd realised that.

"Anything else you could tell me? Does she travel with you? Do you have pets?"

"No, she stays at home. And no, we don't have pets, but there are a lot of cats in the neighbourhood. Cats are nice. They're independent-like."

"Stray cats? A bit like you?"

"Maybe, yes. I like that. Thanks for bringing that to my attention."

"Well, I'm certainly glad to have met you, Vincent. You are a very nice man, although you seem to have poor judgement when it comes to alcohol. But nevertheless, I will continue to read and wait in anticipation for your articles," she said matter-of-factly, though once she'd said it, she smiled brightly again.

"I'm glad to have met you too, Iris. If you give me your address, I could maybe write to you some time and send you another story?" Vincent suggested.

"You would do that?" Iris's voice rose and she grabbed Vincent's hand to shake it excitedly. "I'll do that, that's wonderful! Can I write to you? Is that troublesome? I could send you anything I find about the workhouse, too, in case you change your mind and want to know."

"No, no, I mean, yes, by all means, write to me. That's fine. I have a summer cottage on an island. It may take a while until I receive them, but if you send a letter there, I'll get it eventually," Vincent said.

"Great. Thank you." Iris turned to look at the stars and her face was now all a smile.

Actually, perhaps the best part of this trip was right now, thought Vincent.

"I'm sorry this wasn't a proper conversation. I'm a bit, muddled."

"No, you're fine. Don't worry about it."

"All right. I won't then." Vincent let himself smile as broadly as he felt like. There was always something holding him back, like he wasn't allowed to be genuinely happy, ever, or something bad might happen. All of the times he did smile, chuckle and laugh, they were meant for other people. It felt good to be able to smile just for himself.

He tried to convey this to Iris, but it was even less successful than any of the sentences before, or at least it made Iris straight up giggle at him, but that was fine. For once, he felt like he was in on the joke.

CHAPTER 36

M arcus had his eyes on Bryony. He'd had them for quite some time. There wasn't a lot of time or opportunity to do something about it, but Marcus was determined to make time even if it earned him a beating.

Bryony was quite fair. She had blonde, fair hair, light grey eyes and a small mouth and a nose. Her nose was also small. Marcus quite liked small noses, but any nose would do.

Bryony didn't look like the kind of girl who was supposed to be working in the scullery all day. She was pretty enough to be a guest here. If she had dressed the part, she would have easily passed as a noble woman. At least, if you did not look at her hands.

Mr Benton, the sixth Foxwick-Benton, ordered for a photograph to be taken of the staff. It had been a while since one had been taken last. It had been before Marcus's time, but some of the staff in the picture were familiar, though much younger looking.

Marcus wasn't sure what the fascination was with taking pictures of the staff but voiced no complaints when he was handed a prop and told to stand still for the longest of times so that the photographer could take the picture.

In the group shot, he got to stand right next to Bryony, and so, spurred by this sign from God, he took Bryony by the hand that evening and pulled her into the linen closet across the hall.

The linen closet was dark. Marcus lit a lantern, but it wasn't very bright, and he could barely see Bryony's face as she blushed.

"Marcus! We'll get caught," she whispered firmly. She peeked through the crack of the door, but there was no one out there and no one cared.

If caught in the closet, the sight of the two of them would raise eyebrows, but Bryony was a strong girl; all she had to do was deny she'd ever lower herself to Marcus's level, and no one would doubt her. After all, Marcus had the reputation of a goat needing to be kicked to stay out of the garden, and Bryony was no ordinary garden flower. She was a tulip.

Marcus made sure to tell her this, grabbed her closer and shut the door. She shushed him.

"You idiot. Someone will hear."

She could have easily hit him in the head with a mallet, or anything at hand that was heavy and hard. She wouldn't have thought twice about it, had she seen the need. Instead, she eyed him, looking a little bothered, frowning, waiting for him to say something.

"They won't hear if we're quiet."

"The walls are paper-thin, stupid. They'll hear." She rolled her eyes.

Marcus's heart sank. He would have risked getting caught and flogged, but he couldn't ask this of Bryony. He did not want to hurt her. She huffed a sigh.

"Tonight, after ten thirty. If you can get away from the hall, I'll be waiting for you under the west wing, the last exit. Wait here a while before you come out." She pushed him back, took a pile of linens from a shelf and backed away from the closet.

Marcus's heart was pounding; his palms were sweaty. In this condition, he had no confidence to come out until he'd calmed down enough to not raise suspicions. Once he'd caught his breath and deemed it safe, he leapt out of the closet and ran to the servants' hall to tend to his duties.

I t was closer to eleven when Marcus got away. The butler had gone to sleep upstairs, but the footman keeping an eye on the rest of the male staff had taken his time to fall asleep.

The door of the servants' quarters was always locked for the night, but this posed no problem for Marcus. He hurried through the wine cellar and past all the storage rooms, to the very last exit in the cellar of the west wing, hoping against hope that Bryony would still be there. When he saw her, he was so happy and relieved his steps quickened, and he nearly bumped into her before he could stop himself.

Bryony deserved to be treated like a lady. He took her hand and kissed it. She looked at him a little bemused but said nothing. Walls had ears.

She gestured toward the exit, and they slipped through it. The door was old, and its lock had long since broken off. The hinges made a sound, but it was no louder than whatever clunks and rattles the old house itself made during the night. It also happened to be a windy night, so had anyone heard, they would have attributed it to the weather.

At first Bryony led Marcus, but as they came closer to the gardener's cottage, Marcus took over. The head gardener and his underlings were not in. He knew as much from having heard it the day before. It surprised him that Bryony had also heard and taken notice. She was squeezing his hand now and once they were inside, she turned around abruptly.

"You are not much to look at," she said, "but I like your spunk." Her eyes glistened in the dark. Marcus would have said something poetic about the heaving of her bosom, but it was too dark and he could only imagine it.

She did breathe loud enough to be heard, but that could have been caused by the brisk walk. He didn't want to make assumptions. He also did not want to chicken out when everything finally seemed so promising.

"What on earth are you waiting for?" Bryony's voice was anything but timid.

"Bryony!" Marcus fumbled, unsure whether it was all right to do what he wanted. Then again, he wasn't even sure what he wanted. He wanted to touch Bryony, that much he knew. He wanted to touch her soft body all over in places no one else could touch her.

Bryony grew anxious and tired of waiting. Marcus was startled almost to death by her lips pressing against his.

"This is what you want, right? Right?" she sought to confirm.

"Yes," he said. It was not like him to hesitate, but her forwardness made him nervous.

"All right then." Her hands slipped inside Marcus's shirt and to his waist. This made Marcus's ears buzz. To hell with hesitations. He pressed Bryony against the wall and pushed his tongue into her cleavage.

"Oh—?" She sounded surprised.

This time he could be sure her bosom was heaving. She breathed heatedly into his ear. "Do it then, why don't you." She ruffled his hair and kissed him.

That was when items of clothing started to fall on the battlefield. The corset was the trickiest as it was tight and tied at the back, and Bryony whined impatiently as Marcus tried to pry it loose. He could have left it on, but frankly, when it came off and he could rub her freely flowing breasts, he knew it had been worth it. The underpants were easier.

"Oh dear," she whispered as Marcus made sure there was absolutely nothing in between him and her. "That's unexpected," she noted.

"What is?"

"It's... it's... *bigger.*" Her breath was louder than her whisper. Well, of course it was big now.

But he could appreciate the surprise. He'd known Bryony for quite a while, and they had been fairly young when they'd met. It was no wonder she had an inaccurate impression of his physique. Marcus had no problem showing Bryony just how much he'd grown.

He shoved himself in.

All right, he didn't shove himself in. He *eased* himself in. It would have been rude to barge, and he did have some manners, contrary to expectations.

So, he eased himself in, and then nudged a little to get a bit deeper still. She was mostly quiet. She hadn't made much sound before then either, out of necessity; she didn't want anyone to hear. But she was especially quiet then, holding her breath.

"Breathe," Marcus advised. "Does it hurt?"

"N-no..." Bryony said bravely.

"It must hurt a bit?"

"Well, just a little."

"I'll just take it out then. Slow...ly..." It really felt quite nice. He'd expected as much, but it was not worth it if Bryony couldn't enjoy it. She was squeezing Marcus's hand.

"Look, if you're nervous, we can stop." He tried to be chivalrous. It would be disappointing beyond measure, but this was Bryony. He adored her.

"No," she said and breathed in deliberately. "Do it... slowly," she said.

Oh, the blessed girl! Marcus kissed her eagerly, overjoyed to hear those words. He did as told, though it pained him to restrain himself. He only prayed his body would not fail him now. He thought of the scullery. Fresh-baked apple pie. The housekeeper's face was effective, but perhaps too effective, so he shook it out of his mind.

"Does it still hurt?" he asked. It was cruel that it could hurt her when it felt so good for him.

"N... no," Bryony whispered.

"You don't have to lie," Marcus told her. "We can just be like this," he suggested.

"No, no. You should move— a... bit... please," she did not sound like her usual self.

At first, Marcus suspected there was something wrong with her, but then her grip became painful, and she lifted her legs up to wrap them around him.

"A... ah..." She breathed very shallowly. "Mar... cus..."

Surprised, Marcus pushed himself in once more. She yelped. He'd heard her yelp from pain before when she'd stubbed her toe or scalded herself, but this was different. Out of curiosity, he tried it again. Out came another strange yelp. She seemed unable to help herself. Another. And another.

"How does it feel?"

"S-soft, uh, b-but... hard..." She clung to him. This pleased his ears, but he had to make sure.

"Tell me right away if it hurts, all right?"

"It doesn't hurt," she said quickly. "It d— ahhhh!"

Marcus dared to be a touch more forceful about it. He'd never felt such a high in his entire life. Even when he'd got away with stealing a whole pie...! He'd been starving, but still. He would have starved any day in exchange for this. For once in his wretched life, he was happy to be himself right here and now. Too happy.

"Ahh!" He'd had something like this happen to him before, and it was to be expected, but this was his first time with company. He was somewhat unprepared. She looked at him surprised.

"Did you just—?" She blinked. "Well, never mind. Go on, just a bit more. Please, Marcus!" She pushed him up, and he was so surprised that it took him a while to find the rhythm.

She appreciated his efforts, he was sure. At least, he assumed she did based on the way she bit his shoulder with no small force and made noises he'd never heard before.

Then, when she seemed done to satisfaction, she lay there out of breath. He lay down next to her, unable to think straight, but also unable to move, he was so tired.

"Well then," Bryony said once she'd managed to catch her breath. "If it turns out to be a girl. I'll call her Ren," she said.

"What?" Marcus breathed out in horror.

CHAPTER 37

M r Swifty had tried to draw the snowtrain driver's attention to the things Vincent had left behind in hopes the man would understand that something was amiss. Alas, the driver had not caught the drift.

Instead, he'd mumbled something about having to drop that stuff off the next time he was out there, as if Vincent had just casually forgotten to take his belongings with him when he'd climbed off. What kind of person did they mistake him as? Mr Swifty was furious.

As soon as they'd arrived in town, he had done a full tour of the people who knew Vincent. None of them had grasped the gravity of the situation, regardless of how clearly he'd tried to convey it by vocalising or biting at their ankles. It had taken him two full days to realise that no matter how much of a ruckus he tried to cause, the people he sought help from did not understand that it was an emergency. It was no use.

Mr Swifty gave up after the third time trying to grab Dr Poppycock's attention. The doctor seemed sympathetic to Mr Swifty's predicament, but he'd mistaken it as intentional, and that Vincent had left Mr Swifty behind on purpose.

This was probably because of that one year when Mr Swifty had indeed been left behind for the winter, and he'd made sure to let people know how displeased he was about it. It had never occurred to him that it might come back to bite him in the tail.

What other options did he have left? He could have tried to sneak back on board a snowtrain and hop off somewhere to try to find Vincent, but it had already been two days and he was only one cat. It would take ages for him to find anyone out there, and even if he did, what else could he even do?

What Mr Swifty would have needed was for these people to understand they needed to go out there en masse and bring Vincent back. Who would fix the house situation if there was no Vincent? Who would give him strips of bacon, listen to his bountiful wisdom and let him curl up on their lap? Even Ms Sylvia couldn't provide him with all three. She struggled with the first one, even on a good day!

Mr Swifty trudged across the market square, eyes sweeping over the snow-encrusted cobblestones, uninterested in the few passers-by still out this late in the evening. The town's rodents were also safe for the day. He had no appetite for the hunt, though his stomach had started singing its own lament long ago.

It started to snow. The large clusters of snowflakes stuck to his fur like wads of cotton. He sat down to lick his paw, unsure what else to do but try to comfort himself with something repetitive and familiar.

He ran through his list of people one more time. Maybe he'd forgotten someone? He'd tried the Poppycocks, the Steadfasts, Dr Jacobs, the doctor's wife and even the governor. Old-man Mason had been no use, the Brambles... Hmm, there was the little human. He'd dismissed her before but was desperate enough now to reconsider.

Would someone so small be of use somehow? The girl was larger than himself, at least, and knew how to talk to humans. She wasn't as understanding as Vincent, but she'd seemed more inclined to keep trying if she didn't understand. Other than that, she didn't seem particularly capable or resourceful, but under these circumstances, Mr Swifty would be glad to have his expectations proven wrong.

He shook the snowflakes out of his fur and made a brisk run for it.

It was past Ren's bedtime, though Celandine would not complain so long as Ren stayed in her room and was making an effort to prepare herself for bed.

Celandine would sometimes peek in to remind her not to read or write for too long, as those were the two activities that most often made her lose track of time, but she hadn't peeked in yet today.

She had probably already fallen asleep after a long day of visiting friends to collect donations. There were boxes upon boxes of stuff at the bottom of the stairs, near the front door.

Ren had been told about the house fire, but it wasn't until she saw the amount of replacement things that she grasped to some extent the severity of the situation.

It must have been awful for Vincent, but as far as Ren was concerned, the only thing that mattered was that Vincent was still alive and well—at least as well as Vincent could be.

She could remember her parents and that they'd loved her, but the place she'd come from was nothing she missed. She was old enough to understand why sending her away to live on Whitskersey had been the better choice.

She didn't mind the thought of going back to Benton House someday to see them, but after living on the island for over five years now, Vincent felt like both her home and her family. It would have been devastating to lose him.

"Eep?" Ren did a bit of a hop on her seat when she saw the black shadow appear at her window. Her bedroom was on the second floor and birds very rarely frequented her windowsill, so it wasn't often that something popped up to block her view. "Mr Swifty?" she whispered and confirmed it was who she thought it was.

Her window was frozen shut, so she tried to point the cat toward the window at the other end of the hall. It was tricky to reach because it was higher up, but she'd opened it before and wasn't afraid to do some pre-bedtime gymnastics to get to it.

She tiptoed out of her room, made sure Celandine wasn't around to tell her off, and climbed up to the sill to open the other window.

There was no sign of Mr Swifty. She couldn't very well call him at this hour, so she leaned out through the window to take a look. It was a wee bit chilly out here in her pyjamas.

Ah, there he was. She waved at the silly cat.

Mr Swifty eyed her admittedly slightly precarious dangling for a moment but didn't take too long to jump across and enter the house. Ren pulled herself back in and closed the window.

"What on earth are you doing, girl?" Celandine's voice sounded more alarmed than angry, but she would only call her girl if she'd messed up somehow.

"I just wanted some fresh air."

"Did you let that cat in on purpose? You know he will clean the whole pantry if he manages to sneak in there!"

"Oh, no, he happened to be there right as I opened the window."

"What have I told you about fibbing, young lady?"

"Well, I didn't want to leave him out in the cold when the weather is like this! Moreover, can't you see how distressed he is?" The cat was now circling both of their feet and meowing so loudly it was difficult to talk over his clearly extremely important news.

"He was here earlier today, and yesterday, making that horrendous noise. Who knows what's gone into him this time. We did check that he's uninjured, but I fear he may have hit his head or eaten something disagreeable. I will have him sleep outside if he doesn't pipe down this instant!" As soon as Celandine had said it, Mr Swifty stopped meowing. She turned to look and frowned.

"You see, he's quiet now. Can he stay for the night, please?" Ren lifted Mr Swifty up and gave Celandine her most beseeching look.

Celandine rolled her eyes with enough theatrics for Ren to assume the woman might actually keel over, or at least she might have assumed so, had she not seen Celandine roll her eyes before.

"You know you'd have to be a good girl first for that look to work on me," Celandine said.

"But I am a good girl..." Ren furrowed her brow and let the corners of her mouth fall ever so slightly. Mr Swifty let out a single tiny, miserable meow.

"Fine." The corner of Celandine's eye started to twitch. "But if I hear one peep out of the two of you, he's out! Now go to sleep."

"Yes, madam!"

"And Ren."

"Yes?"

"Please don't lean out through the window like that. I almost had a heart attack."

R en carried Mr Swifty into her bedroom, closed the door and set him down on the bed.

"What's the matter? Did Vincent send you over?" Ren knew Mr Swifty was an exceptionally smart cat, and even if he wasn't very fond of cuddles and could get bitey if provoked, she held him in high regard for keeping Vincent such good company.

Mr Swifty looked like he might start meowing again, but with Celandine just a few thin walls away, he seemed to know not to make noise. With no common language, it might be impossible to grasp the details, but Ren figured it wouldn't be too difficult to suss the gist of it. She sat on her bed next to him.

"Do you need me to try to guess what it is?" she suggested. The cat had seemed to respond to yes or no questions before.

He would not be here unless it was something important. What else could be important but Vincent? Ren felt more chilled than outside in her pyjamas a moment ago. "Did something happen to Vincent?"

Mr Swifty pushed against Ren's hands, pawed at her with his claws withdrawn, and milled around on the bed in a manner best described as frantic.

"Oh, dear." Ren felt a burst of panic and a lump in her throat. "Celandine!" She yelled and ran back out of her room. She got all the way to banging Celandine's door before she responded.

"What is it, dear? What's wrong?" Celandine took Ren by the hands to steady her.

"I-I-I think something must have happened to Vincent!"

"What do you mean? How do you know?"

"It's Mr Swifty. That's why he's here. Something must have happened! Look at him." Ren pointed at the cat, who had followed her and was cooperating by meowing in agreement.

"He's sometimes like this when Vincent heads out after the summer. It's probably nothing to worry about."

"Where is he now? When did you last hear from him?"

"Your Aunt Aster and Uncle George gave him the cabin at the cape. I told you about this, didn't I? He left out there two days ago—"

"When is he coming back? Can you ring him to check that he's all right?"

"There is no phone out there, dear. He said he might come pick you up once he's done with the cabin."

"But why would he leave Mr Swifty here? We need to go!"

"Calm down, dear. You know how he is. He sometimes needs some time by himself." Celandine pulled Ren into her arms and stroked her hair. "There, there. I'm sure he's fine."

"But—" Being held like this was comforting, but Ren could not shake the feeling that something was wrong, and she needed to act right away.

"Don't worry, my child. He may seem peculiar at times, but he's a capable man. He can take care of himself," Celandine assured her. This seemed a little thick coming from a woman who frequently orchestrated neighbourhood surveillance missions together with her sister, and who had mere minutes ago chastised Ren for fibbing. "I will send someone to check on him tomorrow," she added, more in line with her usual agenda.

"What if he's been out there in need of help for two days already? You said you saw Mr Swifty here yesterday."

"There's not much we can do in the dark, dear. No one is heading that way at this hour. I'll send someone at first daylight." Celandine gave Ren a hug and a squeeze. "Do you think you could go back to sleep in your room, or do you want to sleep with me in mine?"

Ren didn't feel like sleeping at all with Vincent potentially dying out there, but Celandine probably would not relent, and it was already a significant victory that she was willing to humour her by sending someone over later.

"I'll go sleep in mine, thanks," Ren mumbled. At least she had calmed down somewhat from the initial shock. "Come, Mr Swifty. We'll fix this first thing in the morning."

Mr Swifty didn't seem happy but followed her.

CHAPTER 38

The following morning, Mr Jones had loaded Vincent on top of Mrs Beansbury's suitcase, tied the man's belt to the handle and dragged the load through nearly waist-deep banks of snow to reach the cabin at the cape. He'd been incredibly tempted to leave Vincent out there to die simply because the man was heavy. Clinging on to his last shreds of optimism, Mr Jones was hoping for a less gruesome solution to all of this, so he'd pushed on and reached the cabin sometime in the afternoon.

There had been no sign of a snowtrain that day, but because Mr Jones couldn't recall the schedule, he wasn't sure whether any were due in the morning or in the evening. Staying in the cabin for the night—with a wood stove, a warm bed and actual food—seemed like such a step up that Mr Jones wouldn't even be mad if no train passed by.

It was another evening to weigh his options and maybe talk it over with Vincent if the man started to feel any better once he'd warmed up and had something to eat.

With his arms roughly the consistency of marmalade from pulling the suitcase, Mr Jones made no attempt at lifting Vincent into a bed. He spread a reindeer pelt and a couple of blankets near the stove where it would soon be warm and dragged Vincent onto them. He pulled off the man's snow-filled boots and socks and set them aside to dry. Whatever else seemed like it would be soaked after thawing, he removed and tried to replace with an item of clothing from the closet or another blanket.

Vincent was not unconscious, but his grunts and mumbles were mostly unintelligible, and he was in no shape to cooperate much. On the plus side, the noise he was making meant that he hadn't yet died from hypothermia and likely wasn't about to drop dead within the next few minutes.

Once Mr Jones had wrapped Vincent up, he tended to his own needs, changed into dry clothes and rummaged through the house for food.

There were some dry goods still in the pantry. He'd suspected as much, but he was glad to see the selection was better than he'd hoped. He put the kettle on for something hot to drink and started preparing supper.

Vincent stared at the ceiling. Where was he? He pushed aside whatever was covering him, sat up and tried to look around, but his limbs didn't seem to be working right. He wasn't cold or shivering, so why?

"Hey! Don't take that off, I only just got you in there!"

"Huh?"

Why was he being wrapped up again? Where was he? Who?

"Since you're sitting up, try to drink some of this. It'll warm you up." Jones offered him a mug.

Oh, it was Jones. Why was Jones here? Where was this?

What an ass, why is— such a stupid piece of sh— I need to fig— maybe— killing him, but then— Sinewy bastard.

"You burned down my house," Vincent thought out loud. Was he supposed to forgive and forget because he was offered a mug of... tea? "Is this tea?"

"Tastes like it is. It didn't say on the label."

These idiot islanders and their stupid aversion to labels.

"Are you trying to poison me again?" Why was he feeling so lethargic? Was there something in this drink? Aster had drugged him. Why did they all want to hurt him?

Vincent threw the mug at a wall. It took him a while to realise he'd just thrown the mug at a wall. The mug had broken. He'd broken Aster's mug. She'd be angry.

"Stop that!" *Why d— have to be like this? St— It's j— tea for crying out l—.*

Vincent turned to look at Jones. Why did it seem like he was tuning in and out of the conversation? Had Jones drugged him? He stared at the wet spot on the wall where he'd thrown the mug. He hadn't drunk any of that, though, had he?

Jones was picking up the shards from the floor. That was Aster's mug! Who broke Aster's favourite mug? She would be so upset.

"You didn't have to throw it if you didn't want to drink it. You could have just handed it back to me. Sheesh." Jones set the shards aside and wiped the wall and floor with a rag. *This is so— Why do I have t— I guess I need t— for the time being. How am I sup— when he doesn't ev— trust the tea. Maybe his— because of the fever or— Could it be hypothermia?*

"I'm supposed to trust you? That's a bit thick, don't you think?"

So is your skull, you— I can't believe I have to p— with this. Jones sighed. "At least keep the damn blanket around you." He draped one of the blankets over Vincent's shoulders and added some more wood into the stove.

"You burned down my house."

"You can repeat that all you want, but it's not going to make it true."

"You drugged me."

"I gave you the wrong medicine once, but that was not on purpose."

"No, you did. It was in the biscuits. Mr Swifty told me."

"Oh, that..." Jones offered him a different cup of tea, this time holding it to Vincent's lips himself. "Well, this is just tea. You don't have to believe me, but I'm still going to make you drink it. You need to warm up. Your skin is ice-cold." Jones barred Vincent's hands from interrupting.

Not that Vincent was resisting this time. Bad things always happened when he defended himself. He'd broken Aster's cup, hadn't he? There was still a stain on the wall, so he must have. But why was there a bubble around him? Didn't that usually mean he was dreaming?

The tea felt close to scalding as it hit his mouth and throat. He struggled to swallow, and his stomach felt like it was burning. He wanted to vomit but thankfully didn't.

Jones placed the half-empty cup into Vincent's hands to warm them up. What an unpleasant, distinct feeling, for being a dream.

"For what it's worth, I'm sorry," Jones said.

"Which crime are you apologising for?"

"Only the few I'm guilty of." He was interrupted by a knock on the door. *Oh, shit. Who is th—?*

Jones hurried to the door. He didn't open it right away but peeked through a crack after the second knock.

"Hello?" *How should I play this? This c— be bad.*

"I believe you left your things on my train yesterday. I came to drop them off. Is everything all right?"

"Oh, everything is fine. It must have just slipped my mind. How kind of you to bring them by. Saves me a trip into town."

"It was no trouble. I was out here anyway. And it looks like the weather might be a bit rough for the next few weeks, so I thought I'd make sure these got to you. You don't want to run out of supplies during a storm, right?"

"That is so thoughtful of you."

"I'd best be going now, so I don't fall behind on my schedule."

"Right, I was about to offer you a cup of tea, but I'll offer it some other time then. Thanks again." Jones closed the door and smiled. "Well, that was convenient."

"Who was it?"

"The train driver."

"What? Wait. Aren't we getting on it?"

"So you can turn me in as soon as we get back? I think not."

"You—!" Vincent tried to get up.

"Don't worry about it. We're all set here for a while. It's fine."

"What part of this looks fine to you?" Vincent pushed himself up but had to lean to a wall to not lose his balance.

"You just need some rest."

"I'm dying here!" At least that's what it felt like when his body started to warm up, and his skin was being pricked by thousands of needles. He felt like he was about to pass out from the exhaustion, he couldn't seem to breathe normally, and he was shaking uncontrollably again.

"Calm down. If you keep breathing like that, of course you're going to feel like—"

"Shut up! This is the only way I," he gasped for air, "can breathe right now!" He drew in more air, but it caused a coughing fit. That, in turn, made him feel like he was about to choke, so he gasped for more air.

"I'm telling you, it's worse if you get into these hysterics—" Jones tried to wrap another blanket over Vincent's shoulders.

"I'm not bloody hysterical!" Vincent was trying to suppress the anger burning in the pit of his stomach. He threw off the blankets and tried to steady his breathing. Don't, he reminded himself. It would only lead to something worse. He needed to keep his mouth shut.

He felt out of breath and light-headed. There must have been something in that tea! Jones was up to no good and clearly mocking him. The anger flared up again.

"I'm going to fucking kill you!"

"Whoa, please don't." Jones backed away. *Holy shit, he looks furious.*

"Am I not supposed to be?! Am I not allowed?" Vincent growled between his clattering teeth. Soon, he would pass out from this, leaving Jones free to do whatever the hell he wanted. He needed to do something before that happened.

"Calm down. You can be angry, it's fine. Whatever you want. Just don't—" Jones tried to stall.

Vincent charged at him. If he was already done for, he might as well try. He swung at Jones. He hit something with a loud smack, but he was too disoriented to know what.

Jones tried to back away, but Vincent grabbed him by the front of his shirt and tried to offset his balance to get another chance to land a punch. What good was it to stay quiet and let everyone walk all over him if this was the sort of crap he always landed himself in, anyway?

"Vincent, stop!" Jones tried to fool him with a concerned look. There was no way he was going to fall for his shit again. Vincent shoved him with all his strength. Jones stumbled to the table and chair behind him.

"I'm done talking to you!" Vincent screamed at the top of his lungs and doubled over to cough said lungs out.

M r Jones tried to duck Vincent's frantic punches, but the man managed to land a few with sheer determination.

"Listen to me, you're not yourself. Calm down, and we'll talk about it when you feel better." Mr Jones had been trying to reason with the man for several minutes now, but it only seemed to rile him up further. "I don't want to hurt you."

What else was there to do but fight back? Mr Jones had assumed Vincent would pass out or fall asleep at any moment once he was warm and comfortable, but the man was still standing and showing no signs of stopping his frankly quite ferocious attacks. Was he possessed by an evil spirit?

"I'm n-not!" Vincent was reading minds again, the creepy bastard. Maybe that was why he could predict Mr Jones's moves so well? This should have been an easy fight, yet Mr Jones had his hands full trying to keep out of Vincent's range. The man was truly frightening.

"We can sort this out!" Jones was hit in the gut. It wasn't much of a punch, but it did hurt enough to be irritating. "Look, I'm sure I deserved that. Can we call it even now?" He hadn't much time to recover when Vincent was at it again.

"For the love of—" Mr Jones slapped him across the face. "Stop!"

Vincent fell over but scrambled back up and grabbed a chair to swing with. This was getting serious now. What next? The hot kettle?

As soon as Mr Jones had thought of it, Vincent threw the chair at him and grabbed the kettle.

"No, no, no! Don't do it," Mr Jones squealed and ran. He was barely fast enough to dodge the hot water flying from the kettle.

Vincent continued to swing the kettle around like an enraged drunkard. While he hadn't yet managed to hit Mr Jones with it, some of the items on the tables and counters, as well as the furniture itself, were getting banged around, causing a tumult of clinks, clatter and crashes.

"For the last time, I didn't burn down your house! I was only there to poke around for evidence. If you give me a chance, I'll find a way to prove it!"

"I d-d-don't b-b-believe you!"

"You have bigger problems than messing around with me. I'm not the enemy!"

"I d-don't c-care!"

Mr Jones sighed. He was at the end of his patience.

"You leave me no other choice." He grabbed a frying pan, took a few steps to gain speed and swung it at Vincent's leg. Vincent lost his balance, dropped the kettle and fell sideways like dead weight. "There! Are you happy now?"

To vent his annoyance, Mr Jones kicked Vincent a couple of times until he realised the lunatic wasn't trying to get back up again. Had he hit his head?

"Get up! You're the one who wanted to fight." Mr Jones poked him with his foot. He wasn't moving. "What the hell. I only hit you once. Are you faking it, so I'll lower my guard? We'll see about that..." He kicked Vincent in the backside. The man made a noise but no effort to get up.

"Was that all? Really?" Why was Vincent not getting up? It hadn't been that hard a hit.

Still wary that the man might bounce back at any moment, Mr Jones knelt closer to check. "Why aren't you saying anything? Weren't you going to kill me?"

Vincent was alive. He was breathing, and his eyes were open, but he did not respond.

"What the hell is wrong with you?" Mr Jones frowned. Vincent's jaw was tight. Was he in that much pain? Why? The leg looked odd. Ah, shit. It wasn't supposed to look like that, was it?

Mr Jones bit his lip. He'd meant to rough Vincent up so the man would relent a little, but were people really this brittle?

"I didn't—" Mr Jones swallowed. "You've got to believe me..."

What was he supposed to do about this? There was really no talking himself out of this one, was there? Mr Jones felt out of breath. He tried to straighten the leg, but it was not going to mend itself with willpower.

"Why couldn't you listen to me? All you had to do was hear me out for a bit." Mr Jones stood up and tried to think. He'd never be forgiven for any of this. Why had he even thought that could be possible?

"All you had to do was fucking listen to me for once!" There was no going back now, so Mr Jones gave Vincent another kick. It only made him angrier, since Vincent merely grunted. "I didn't want to hurt you, but you're so damn aggravating! I tried to help you. Why do you have to be such a daft boot?" He kicked Vincent again, this time a little harder. "You're an idiot, a ramhead, a dimwit and a jerk, and I hate you!"

A couple more kicks made him feel better, but also worse. He continued kicking and raised his voice until he was screaming. "You're so stupid! Why couldn't you give me a chance? I did everything you asked me to. I did more than you asked me to. I wasn't asking for much, was I? Get up, you ass! Say something! All I ever wanted was to be your friend!"

Mr Jones stopped and wiped his face. He'd never wanted it to end this way.

"Why didn't you want to be my friend? Was I not good enough for you?"

C elandine had headed out after breakfast and was back home before
lunch.

"I spoke with the snowtrain operator, and he said Vincent had forgotten
his things on the train, but that he'd seemed fine the next day. He must have
been tired when he got off the train and forgotten Mr Swifty too," she said.

Ren wanted to object, but Celandine seemed convinced that this explanation made sense, and when she was convinced about something, it was
no use trying to talk her out of it.

Why would Vincent leave his things, much less Mr Swifty, on the train
like that? No matter how ill and negligent Vincent could sometimes be, he
wouldn't have made that big of a blunder unless something was seriously
wrong.

Ren could believe that the train driver had gone out there and even that
he might have seen Vincent, but would he have been able to tell if he was
gravely ill? Maybe poor Vincent was out there alone, so ill he was delirious
and in danger?

"We have no school until the start of February. Couldn't I go there to
check?" Ren suggested. Celandine took Ren by the shoulders and sat on
her haunches.

"I know you're eager to be with him, but he will be busy with the renovations, and you might get in the way. He'll come pick you up when he's ready. All right?"

"I wouldn't get in the way." Ren knew how to cook a few simple meals and do a lot of the chores.

"I'm sorry, dear. As soon as we hear from Vincent, or he comes to pick you up, you can go, but he wanted to head out there alone. It's probably also so he can clear his head after what happened. Don't worry. I'm sure he'll get in touch with us soon."

There was always some excuse as to why it wasn't practical. Even when Vincent had specifically requested for Ren to come up to the cabin for a fishing trip with him and George earlier this year, Celandine had blown a fuse over it because it would have interfered with Ren's school work. She'd even marched over to Vincent to give him a lecture over it, as if a fishing trip couldn't have been as educational as a few days of school.

Celandine and Aster had both been in a right state for several weeks afterwards, though Ren had tried to convince them she would be extra cautious and look after Vincent and George while they were out there.

Ren was almost eleven years old. Surely they could have trusted her just a tiny bit more than this? Unfortunately, with not a penny to her name, she could not take matters into her own hands and pay for her own train ticket. She was at Celandine's mercy, so there was nothing she could do but try to soften Celandine with her appeals and wait patiently.

V incent sat in a pool of his own excrement.

It seemed only fitting that this was where he'd ended up.

He'd had some time to reflect, and, while clearly a low point in his less than glorious existence, this wasn't the worst thing he'd experienced. However, it did sit firmly in the bottom five favourite things he'd done so far. Perhaps even bottom three.

He'd guessed he would have the debatable privilege of dealing with issues with his plumbing later in life, but having to sit through this in his thirties was wholly unexpected.

With no memory of his nappy years, this seemed like a novel experience, and as such, something he rarely came across anymore at his age. It wasn't worth bragging to his friends about but valuable, perhaps, as something to learn from? After all, he could henceforth fully appreciate how wonderful it was to not sit in his own excrement, and veering to the side of hysterical optimism, he was confident he would never mistakenly make a career out of it.

The days were mostly dim and dark this time of year, but somewhere above him Vincent would sometimes see a spot of light, presumably through a ventilation hole. While his eyes had long since adjusted to the darkness, there wasn't much else to see, so he usually kept them closed. Because of this, he'd lost all sense of time, and could only assume he'd been stuck in here for days.

Eyes closed, Vincent could hear nothing but the sound of his breathing and the steady drip of water trickling down from the ceiling. If he turned his head and leaned forward a little, he discovered the water was just at his reach. This seemed more of a cruel joke to prolong his suffering, but he was too thirsty to ignore it. He waited in an awkward position with his mouth open until his jaw was aching but he'd had his fill.

One could adapt to a lot when they hadn't much choice, and this was no exception. The stench was horrid in such a small confined space, but Vincent had got used to what little he could smell through his stuffed-up nose.

The pain was more difficult to bear, though. It occasionally worsened until it was searing enough to demand his full attention. Thankfully there were gaps where he'd slept, or at least momentarily lost consciousness, to give him some relief from the agony. But not knowing when all of this would end made it that much worse.

Vincent was fairly sure it was not going to end well, but he would've liked to know, nevertheless.

He'd heard people could survive for days with nothing but water, and water was the only luxury he had, even if it tasted like rust and soil. Other sustenance was an issue but, so long as it was scarce, at least there was less cause for further disgust.

When he'd read stories about people facing captivity, they'd seldom mentioned the gross but unavoidable result of not being able to move while retaining basic bodily functions. A person with a vivid imagination would imagine a bucket or a pot where prisoners did their business, but something like that required premeditation and a captor who cared enough to bring a bucket and haul it away when it needed to be emptied.

Also, it required being able to stand up, which was something Vincent had considered but hadn't yet felt compelled to try. Having a broken leg had something to do with it, but even with a broken leg, he could have pushed through the pain, crawled a bit and propped himself upright somehow.

It was more so a combination of several of these discouraging factors that kept Vincent's ass disappointingly firmly on the ground. Chief among which were the pain and discomfort, the unrelenting exhaustion and the near-to-complete loss of morale. The best he could do was to scratch himself by nudging his booty a bit back and forth.

How disheartening to think that this was the best he could do with his time: alleviating the horrible itch of having his faeces glued between his butt cheeks. He wasn't keen to die, but if this was what he was reduced to for the rest of what remained, he rather wished he wouldn't have to wait for too long.

He wasn't entirely clear on how or why he'd ended up where he was, so he couldn't make a proper estimate of what his chances were, but since no one had come to check up on him so far, and he'd seemingly been left here to die, his odds of survival were probably close to zero.

Where was this even? A hole in the ground? It was only barely warm enough to be tolerable, but at least because it was so chilly, Vincent didn't have to be plagued by his usual feverish hallucinations. Some degree of delirium could have distracted him from the ordure he was sitting in, but it was difficult to decide which was worse.

Vincent had a hazy recollection of falling off the snowtrain, which might explain the leg, but everything after that was a blur. Had he hit his head, or had it been the fever or the cold? He felt battered and bruised, possibly from the fall, but also, he had an inkling that he'd fought someone.

Which of these fragmented memories were real and which had been a dream? He couldn't say. He hoped most of it had been a figment of his imagination because the thought of being engulfed by such anger and aggression made him extremely uncomfortable and ashamed of himself.

After giving it some thought, Vincent was fairly sure he wanted to die. It wasn't the melodramatic wish someone made when they were hoping for sympathy or attention. It wasn't a figure of speech, either. It was the simple, calculated realisation that he was better off dead than pointlessly suffering.

He'd probably lose the leg even if he did survive. It was so bad that, despite there not being much light, when he lifted the front of his trousers he could tell it was discoloured, the shape of it looked all wrong, and it was probably a matter of time until it rotted off. What else had he mangled that he couldn't feel or see?

Then again, his gangly legs had never been his most attractive feature.

Fine, he could've made do without a leg, but if his life wasn't particularly meaningful or productive with both of his legs, it sure as hell was not going to improve by there being only one. How was he supposed to be of any use to anyone with only one leg? He'd barely been functional with two.

It was upsetting that he could not for the life of him remember if he had specified that he wanted to leave everything to Ren. His possessions were gone, but according to his calculations, he would still have some savings left on his account after all his debts were settled. Ren could have used that as a nest egg.

Vincent regretted having wasted so much money on the improvements on the stupid speeder. It was funny how pointless that project seemed now that he'd cemented his butt-cheeks together with his bowel products.

At least he could take solace in the thought that, with the speeder now beyond repair, no one would get themselves killed trying to ride it when he wasn't looking.

None of that mattered, though, if Ren wasn't included in the will. He felt like an absolute idiot for not taking care of these things when he should have.

Why couldn't there be a piece of paper in this ratty, dank shit-hole? He could have written it down so that when they finally found his stinky grave, they'd know who his last few pennies belonged to.

That left him with no choice but to try to get through this so that he, and his shitty pants, could amend the will if it needed amending.

The pain was bad, but the continuously itchy bum was starting to get on Vincent's nerves. He could get used to the smell, but knowing how bad it was made him feel filthy and ashamed to the core. He felt as if he should have done something to prevent it. He should have held it in indefinitely or at least until he died. It seemed his fate was to be a disgusting slop boy, all the way to the end.

He tried to squiggle and shake something loose as if that would make a difference. There was no way he could get out of his trousers to clean anything up. He could barely move his hands enough to wipe his eyes.

There was nothing wrong with his hands, but he was tired from being cold, ill and without food. He recalled making an effort to free himself from his prison some days ago. Some pointless flailing and exertion had been involved, and even thinking back to it now was exhausting.

Coughing, however, seemed like a reasonable pastime. He'd also tried weeping for a moment. Though he'd felt a touch self-conscious about it at first, he'd given it his best effort. However, one could only cry for so long before it got tiresome and stopped making sense.

O n the fifth day, which could have also been the fourth or the sixth, a tray of food was slid into the space where Vincent lay.

"Excuse me?" Vincent tried to get the attention of whoever was there. His current best guess was that it was Jones because Jones was most prominently featured in the dreams he'd been having. His grasp of reality was even worse than usual, so really it could have been anyone. Being sick and trapped in a dark hole didn't help. "Excuse me, can you help me?"

If any of his memory could be trusted, he'd jumped off the train after Jones, and they'd spent the night under a bridge. Whatever had happened after that was a jumbled mess, but he could recall having been angry and possibly losing his temper.

"I can't reach whatever the bloody hell you pushed in here. I'm assuming it's food by the smell of it." The smell was better than the general odour he'd had the privilege of enjoying for the past few days. "It's not going to be of any use to me if you leave it there... asshole." It was probably safe to assume that whoever had bothered with the food was, in fact, an asshole, if for no other reason than for doing such a half-assed job at helping out.

"Look, I'm dying here. My leg's about to explode with maggots, and I've shat myself. The least you could do is push the tray close enough for me to reach it."

It wasn't going to happen. Whoever had been there was probably already gone. Talking to the air that had a moment ago been occupied by someone was in a sense better than talking to absolutely no one at all, but only by a slim margin. Vincent tried to see if there was any way to reach the food but came to the conclusion he would have popped or cracked something trying to bend unnaturally, and it didn't seem worth the effort.

"The least you could've done was to do something about the damn leg. Saw it off or something. Make an ornament out of it, I don't care."

Vincent swung one of his functioning limbs at the tray and, with a stroke of luck, found the edge under his fingers.

Why, how considerate to make sure I get some exercise before dinner!

It took him a while to prod at the thing to get it close enough to see what was on it, but at least it passed the time.

A cup of... milk possibly? And a piece of bread.

He'd hoped to see something more festive, but it would have to do as his last meal. Perhaps he could imagine himself eating something tastier while he ate it.

He was past hunger, so he took his time chewing and swallowing. By the time he was finished, he was glad to be done but enjoyed a lengthy yawn as dessert. He wanted to sleep most urgently.

Oh no.

He had barely finished the thought when he keeled over and hit the floor.

CHAPTER 40

"Well, Mr Swifty. I guess it's up to the two of us to make sure Vincent is all right." Ren sat on her bed with Mr Swifty curled up next to her. "It's been two weeks with no word from Vincent. There's no way it would have taken him more than two weeks to make the cabin livable. Right? He'd do that in less than one, even with a fever."

Mr Swifty watched her intently. He'd seemed more subdued than usual lately, and Ren could relate. It was no fun being a child or a cat, unable to buy a snowtrain ticket and having someone keeping an eye on you throughout the day.

"We need to find a way to get to the cape." It was too far on foot. Ren knew roughly where it was, but she'd never gone out there alone. She wasn't sure she would find it without a map.

She did know where Vincent's cottage was. It was a long walk from here, but not at all impossible to achieve within an afternoon if she hurried. It was a long shot, but perhaps if she could prove someone had burned it down on purpose, Celandine would have to admit Vincent could be in danger. Then she'd have to let her go check it for herself.

Ren started packing. She packed plenty to be on the safe side, but also because she wondered if, when she got there, she might find the train tracks and even venture a little further. That would mean she wouldn't be back in time for Celandine to not miss her, but if she felt confident she could do it, she wanted to have the option open to her.

Layers of warm clothes, emergency supplies, a pocket knife, a lantern, kindling and a lighter... Ren got dressed and tossed things into her backpack.

"I suppose something for you as well?" She snuck out of her room and into the kitchen to ransack the pantry for something to eat and drink.

This was the first time Celandine was out of the house for long enough for Ren to attempt her rescue mission. Two weeks was a long time, and, if Ren's gut feeling was correct and Vincent was in trouble, she might not only be too late to help but also making a mistake, putting her life in danger for no good reason.

She wasn't worried about how she would handle the winter weather, but if, and likely when, Celandine found out about this, Ren would have to use all her wits and skill to avoid a swift death sentence.

"Come," she told Mr Swifty and let him out the front door.

T he charred ruins of the cottage were a sadder sight than Ren had realised. She was glad to arrive, but she felt as if the air had been punched out of her as she walked around what was left.

A lot of it was buried under snow, but it had also been windy, so some bald spots here and there revealed the state of the ground beneath. There was a gigantic hole where the cellar had been. A layer of snow filled some of it, but she could still see where to step to avoid falling into it.

With not a lot of daylight left, Ren started digging. After a few minutes of mucking about aimlessly, she found a bucket to turn around and sit on.

This had been a stupid idea. She'd had a feeling it was, but after two weeks of not doing anything, she'd needed to do something.

"What do you suggest I do, Mr Swifty?" Ren bit her lip to not pout.

Mr Swifty watched her, and she watched him back. If only he could have spoken to Ren as he did to Vincent. "There's nothing here to find. Mr Hartley—that's the Fire Chief—would have said something if there was."

Ren sighed. It started to snow. A few tiny flakes fluttered in the wind, but sitting still made her feel cold and more exposed to the elements.

Approximately ten metres behind her stood what was left of Vincent's speeder. Ren stood up and walked to the side with the sidecar.

The chassis was black from soot and bent from here and there, but there were no holes that she could see. The hinges screeched and wailed when she opened the hatch into the luggage compartment. A cloud of soot puffed up from within.

Ren wiped the floor with a finger, but it wasn't as black as she'd expected. She felt the floor with her palm. It was sound. She hopped and reached farther inside the compartment.

A blanket.

"That's curious." She pulled the blanket out. "Look, Mr Swifty." It wasn't even singed. Ren would have been inclined to believe someone had put it there after the fact, but the inside of the luggage compartment was clean. The cloud of soot had been blown loose from the outside surfaces.

"Oh my."

This got Ren's brain fired up and running top speed. She circled around the speeder, going through the details one by one. A flap was missing. That could be replaced with anything. The skis were ruined. Mostly a cosmetic issue.

She knocked on the chassis, and there wasn't a spot on it where her hand went through. There was some structural damage on the struts of the sidecar, but even that was laughably minor.

"You don't suppose, Mr Swifty, that it's still intact on the inside?"

Ren took off her backpack and rummaged for her pocket knife. It was tiresome to open screws with it, but it was easier than trying to find a screwdriver amidst the snow and rubble.

Two of the screws had fused to the surrounding metal, but with the other two off, Ren was able to peek inside.

She lit her lantern to try to see better, but she could not be entirely sure whether everything looked as it ought. There was another way to find out, but if the thing was badly damaged inside, there was no telling what it would do.

Ren had never been against trying risky things, and this wasn't even all that risky. There was a list of safety precautions Vincent had taught her before he'd let her into the garage. She couldn't follow each of them under the circumstances, but she was fairly confident the remainder would suffice.

"Vincent is not going to be happy with me, though," she told Mr Swifty. "There was a reason he never let me drive this thing, and I don't disagree with it, but this is an emergency. You should go to a safe distance first. There's no reason why we should both take the risk." With that acknowledged and out of the way, Ren climbed up to what could loosely be described as a cockpit. It wasn't much of a pit, but it did provide some cover from the elements during flight.

She had watched Vincent do this thousands of times, so there was no way she didn't know the sequence by heart.

"This might also completely fizzle," she reminded herself.

Vincent had shown her the drawings for the new filtering system before Midwinter tea. He'd also planned to make some changes to the fuel-intake system, and they'd spent the few hours before tea putting it together in the Poppycocks' living room.

The engine turned on as expected. It did make a few concerning superfluous creaks, but once it was running, it sounded normal. Ren tried the controls. Everything seemed to move what they were supposed to move, except for the missing flap.

Now all that were missing were the new fuel-intake system and the filter. The filter didn't exist yet, but the fuel-intake system...

Ren jumped down from the cockpit and started to comb through the snow-covered rubble. At the approximate five-minute mark, she turned off the engine as per Vincent's cool-down protocol. Then she continued the search.

"Mr Swifty!" Ren called the cat back. He sauntered over to the open-air garage and waited for further instructions. "I need to find the fuel-intake system. I don't think it's installed yet because the power output was close to zero when I turned on the engine. It's about this size." She spread her hands apart, about the length of Mr Swifty's tail. "It's the thing Vincent must have been carrying when you returned here after Midwinter tea. Do you remember where he might have put it?"

Mr Swifty stared at her.

"Is it too complicated? Don't you understand?"

Usually, he seemed to understand everything just fine. Why was he hesitating now? Ren continued to dig through the snow. It would be dark soon, and the lantern would not be bright enough for a proper search in the dark.

Mr Swifty meowed. Ren turned to look. He did a few circles around himself, sniffed the ground, looked around and jumped over to what had been the kitchen.

"Watch out for the cellar," Ren reminded him. He leapt over to Vincent's bedroom and pawed at one of the corners. Why would it be there? That seemed a little silly.

Ren walked around the whole cottage to avoid the treacherous middle. The spot where Mr Swifty was pawing had been at the foot of Vincent's bed. Some of the bed frame was still up, but everything around it had burned.

Everything but a leather sack. Ren hurried to open it. The sack itself was toasted to crisp, as were the clothes Vincent had stuffed into the sack last. The fuel-intake system was merely scuffed underneath.

"Yes!" Ren grabbed the thing and took some joyous polka steps around Mr Swifty. "Now we're in business!"

She rushed back to the speeder and opened the second service hatch to access the fuel tank and the backside of the engine. It was still warm in there, so she had to be careful not to touch anything while she took some rough finger measurements and tried to make sense of where everything went.

When she was satisfied that she'd grasped the gist of it, she closed the hatch and stashed the fuel-intake system into the luggage compartment.

"I need parts," she said to Mr Swifty. "But it's getting late. It's too late to get back without Celandine noticing I've been gone all day. I have to find a place to stay for the night, get the parts and come back to finish the speeder without getting caught. They're probably already looking for me."

The temperature dropped as darkness descended. Ren considered starting a fire, but she knew that might have alerted Mrs Tweed, and Mrs Tweed was a tattletale.

"Where do you think we should go?" she asked Mr Swifty. Mr Swifty sat down to lick his paw. "I thought you wanted to find Vincent. Aren't you going to help me?"

The cat glanced at her but continued to lick his paw.

"I'll give you all the cheese, bacon, roast and ham you can eat if you help me."

Mr Swifty's ears shifted and perked up. He seemed to disapprove of something but started walking back towards town. Ren wasn't sure if he'd decided to leave or help, but she didn't want to stay here alone, so she followed him.

F ollowing the little human had been a mistake. She was much too young and inexperienced to be of use.

Mr Swifty stomped in the track they'd made coming here. He hadn't had any better ideas. Not after he'd been kicked off when he'd tried to get on the snowtrain to go look for Vincent himself. And now he was wasting his time guiding the little human on this fruitless excursion instead of making rounds, trying to get one of the adults to come to their senses.

"Are you upset?" Ren was trailing after him.

What a silly question. Of course he was upset. He'd thought the girl had had a plan. Instead, she'd come here to dig through stuff and to play with Vincent's noise machine.

As far as Mr Swifty was concerned, that thing should have burnt to cinder in the fire. He'd been forced to ride in the sidecar a handful of times, and he hadn't enjoyed it one bit. That thing was the reason Vincent usually disappeared for the winter. It was a menace!

Mr Swifty was smart enough to tell that the piece she'd been looking for was the thing that would have enabled Vincent to come and go as he pleased, and that the man would have done a lot more going than coming.

"I'll get it moving so we can take it to the cape. I just need some more parts and time. And your help."

That didn't seem like it would work, but Ren had promised treats, so Mr Swifty was cooperating, for now. He'd take her to a warm place to sleep, but the rest would be all up to her.

CHAPTER 41

Vincent woke up elsewhere than where he'd fallen asleep. The floor was different: it did not stink of a horse's arse, and it was smooth and surprisingly warm. There was a blanket draped over his legs. The place was almost as dark as before, though.

In this light, it was difficult to see the details, but the blanket seemed like one of Aster's. That meant that Jones, presumably, had dragged him all the way to the cabin at the cape. His previous prison must have been the earth cellar behind the cabin, and he was probably now upstairs in the cabin's attic space.

Curious, Vincent patted his legs to check whether they were there. Wow. It seemed they were both still attached to him. Even the one that had fared worse. Jones was such a wimp.

The drawback of not being in pain was that he couldn't move his legs. He wasn't completely paralysed since he could feel a faint twinge when he pinched himself, but everything below his waist was useless.

His arms felt heavy, but he could move them, so he dared to hope this condition was temporary due to whatever Jones had drugged him with, and not because his whole lower body was now out of commission for good.

The milk and bread had reawakened Vincent's appetite, so he checked his surroundings for something more to eat. There was a possible cockroach, but he decided to save it for later, for when he was feeling a bit more desperate.

"Hello?" he tried calling. Perhaps Jones was still somewhere close by. "I'm awake and mostly sane right now. I'd appreciate an explanation."

The silence wasn't promising. If this was the level of involvement Jones aimed for, it was only a matter of time until Vincent soiled himself again, and things became as miserable as before, garnished by the lovely smell of poop.

Thankfully, he didn't need to defecate yet, so he had some time left to try to enjoy the dry and the... well, not exactly clean, but less rancid state of being.

"Any chance you could let me go after this?" Vincent had gone through several bouts of anger and despair this past week, and it was starting to feel old. If he'd attacked Jones, like he was now assuming he had, it didn't really matter why he'd done it or whether it was justified, he felt embarrassed about it.

He knocked on the floorboards. "Look, can you hear me? I'm sorry about losing my shit earlier. I'm ready to have a chat with you. Maybe we can talk this through?"

"Stop wasting your breath. I'm not letting you go."

At least it was a reply.

"Let me down from here and leave, and we can pretend nothing ever happened. How does that sound?"

"It sounds like you're lying. Do you really think I'm stupid enough to fall for that?"

"I won't bother you, I promise. You're free to go. All I'm asking for is a fair chance of dragging myself to a train and back into town."

"No."

"What? You won't even consider it?"

"You'll have to sit up there for a while. I'm working on finding some proof it wasn't me who burnt down your house. The rest was for self-defence, and you can't prove otherwise!"

"I can't prove you burned down the house, either. It was just my madness accusing you of it. And who's going to believe me even if I did try to implicate you? I'm not exactly mentally stable. Everybody knows that."

"They'll still believe you over me. But if I can prove someone else did it, the rest will seem like you're accusing me out of some personal vendetta. That way, I'll stand a decent chance. Now, pipe it down up there, I'm trying to think."

Jones sounded serious. Was he innocent, after all? Or merely determined to find someone else to pin it on? Either way, this seemed like it would take days, if not weeks, to resolve.

"Could I at least get a bucket up here?" Vincent sighed and massaged his thighs. He was uncomfortable sitting on the hard floor, but it was a promising sign his butt and legs were regaining some feeling.

"I left one in the corner."

"Oh?" Vincent squinted and tried to spot it. Light trickled through the cracks between the floorboards, but it wasn't enough to aid his poor eyesight. "It's too dark, I can't see it."

Not that it mattered if he couldn't get up.

He pulled the blanket aside to take a better look.

Oh, thank Guardian! Jones had switched the soiled trousers to a pair of George's old loose breeches. They made the inspection much easier but didn't provide a whole lot of warmth, so Vincent was glad to have the blanket.

The more rotten leg was wrapped up in a manner that suggested Jones had taken a look at it and decided that what it most needed was wrapping up. Hah. Vincent untied the makeshift bandages to see what shape it was in.

It didn't seem as maggot-ridden as he'd feared. The sides of his thigh and calf were covered by gruesome, yellowish-black bruising, and his knee was still swollen, but now that the leg wasn't twisted in such an unnatural position, it looked much better. He wasn't even sure he'd broken any bones like he'd assumed based on the pain.

Vincent tried to move his legs. They responded despite feeling stiff as timber. He shook and rubbed them to encourage blood flow. It seemed to help. Really? Could they really still be functional?

He dared to stand up.

He wasn't adventurous enough to put weight on the more misshapen of his two tree trunks, but leaning on the wall, he managed to stay upright. It made him feel a bit less like he had one foot in the grave, even if his better leg was in no shape to be carrying all of the weight, and his success was short-lived. He would have tumbled back on the floor had he not been close enough to use the wall to slide down against.

"Can't you at least spare me a lantern up here?" Vincent banged the floor a few times.

"You'll get used to it."

"Water?"

"Later."

Vincent pulled the blanket back over himself and tried to find a more comfortable position. There was no comfortable position available to him. His legs were starting to ache. The throbbing of the swollen knee was getting worse.

"Something for the pain?" Vincent clenched his teeth. The leg looked better, but it had been in its abnormal position for what must have already been a week.

Whatever Jones had done to move it back into position had introduced the worst kind of nerve pain Vincent had experienced, even considering he'd blown himself up with and crashed the speeder a time or two in the past. It felt like someone had thrust a hot iron rod through his leg. Not just through his knee, but from the sole of his foot all the way to his lower back.

Jones did not respond. Vincent was in no mood to beg, but what was the sense in upholding his pride after all the humiliation he'd already endured? The only reason he wasn't already repeating a series of pleas was because he'd tensed his jaw so tight it was difficult to form the words. He tried to massage his leg gently, but it only made it worse.

"Please, Jones. Knock me out," Vincent forced himself to say between involuntary grunts and groans. Suddenly, the paralysed numbness didn't seem like such a bad option. "P-please."

Time dawdled on as if it enjoyed every second of pain it could inflict on Vincent. Jones was also not in a hurry to respond.

"Fine. I need to head into town anyway," Vincent heard him mumble. The hatch at the opposite end of the attic opened up just enough to slip through a glass of milk and a loaf of bread before it was drawn shut again.

This time Vincent did not bother mocking Jones's lack of imagination. The distance wasn't more than perhaps three metres, but crawling in pain, it seemed to increase at least tenfold. Vincent grabbed the glass and gulped down the milk.

He wasn't sure what the function of the bread was, but he ate it, if only because chewing momentarily distracted him from the pain.

Lying there, sprawled on his stomach and whining, he recalled it having kicked in much sooner before. He was at the verge of tears when he finally felt the pain ease somewhat and his thoughts slow down as if his mind were submerged to a barrel of treacle. Shortly after, he lost consciousness.

Ren shut the nagging voice of her insecurities out of her mind and focused on each of the tasks, one at a time. She'd never had to rely on herself so heavily before, and, had she stopped to think about it, the weight of the worry and responsibility would have crushed her. Thankfully, she was oblivious of all of it once she'd set her mind to doing what needed to be done.

Obtain the parts. Make sure no one caught her pilfering or paid enough attention to report her whereabouts. Get back to Vincent's speeder. Construct a flap. It didn't have to be pretty. It just needed to work. Install the new fuel-intake system. Go through Vincent's safety checklists. Run the hydraulics maintenance cycle. Prepare the engine. Complete the pre-flight checklists. Pack the speeder. Strap in. And in theory, fly the thing.

Ren was glad to have an innate interest in Vincent's hobbies to have paid attention to the details. She didn't have the checklists on paper, but she'd been there when Vincent had revised them. Together they'd gone through them enough times for her to remember most of them by heart. There were a few aspects she was a little hazy on because he'd drawn a line on letting her try some of the more hazardous tasks, but even then, he'd let her observe.

She'd hauled several giant sacks of stuff on a runnerless sledge from Edward's backyard and storage shed without the man noticing. Because she lacked the proper tools and wasn't sure what exactly she needed, she'd had to improvise. All of this had taken her several days of running back and forth, but somehow she'd made do.

Because she'd found nothing to repair the undercarriage of the sidecar with, she'd had to detach it completely. This meant that the balance adjustments Vincent had made to the speeder to accommodate for the sidecar might potentially cause some problems.

Ren did not know how to do any of the necessary calculations to fix that, but she did bolt the sledge to where the sidecar had been and added some weight on it, as well as space for Mr Swifty. It was lighter than the sidecar, so it didn't need its own undercarriage. While it wouldn't be a perfect counterbalance, it was better than nothing.

Ren strapped the horrified cat into the sledge and did some of the pre-flight checks while the engine warmed up. The cat wouldn't necessarily need to be subjected to the test flight, but in case the test flight was going to be the only flight, Ren wanted to be ready to go all the way to the cape.

As she tested the flight controls, it did cross her mind that she might have reached the cape on foot by now, had she tried. However, at least this way she would have the means to bring Vincent back quickly if he needed medical attention.

She wished she had a better rescue plan, but she was committed to making this one as good as she could make it.

As she pressed the throttle lever, she closed her eyes and hoped against hope all the effort wouldn't be for nothing. The sound of the engine grew exhilaratingly deafening. The seat under her juddered. Ren affirmed her grip on the handlebars and took deep breaths. This was her favourite feeling in the whole world.

The engine purred and rumbled. The gauges showed familiar readings. Ren glanced at Mr Swifty, who shook and trembled in his sledge seat, looking like he would soon run out of either courage or patience.

On a bright summer day, the speeder would have moved by now, but then again, on a normal, bright summer day, it would have been Vincent at the helm.

What else was there? Ren pressed the lever almost all the way down. Was it not going to work? Was it too cold? It had been minus twelve this morning, but it seemed a little warmer now.

The speeder nudged forward. Ren flashed Mr Swifty an excited smile.

It was moving? It was moving! And it picked up speed as it rolled down the hill from the ruins of Vincent's cottage. The freezing wind blasted Ren's cheeks and forehead, and the only thing keeping her hat on were the pompom-ended straps tied neatly under her chin. She calibrated the secondary steering system and set the flaps. As the downhill ended, the speeder glided a few dozen metres on the snow before lifting off the ground.

The sheer joy of seeing the ground draw away from under her made Ren let out an excited shriek. It had been so long since she'd last got to experience this. She wanted to cry; she missed Vincent so much.

CHAPTER 42

"Vincent, are you up?" By the sounds of it, Jones used something longer and harder than an arm to knock on the floor under Vincent. "Wake up!"

The accuracy was uncanny. Vincent was roused from a vague state of semi-coherency by the banging noise and vibration right by his ear.

"I'm up..." Startled by the onslaught after hours of peaceful, numb existence, Vincent rushed to push himself upright to avoid having to listen to the banging where it felt like it might split his eardrums.

The hatch at the other end of the attic opened and Jones raised a lantern to see better.

Vincent felt woozy, and the light seemed much too bright for his eyes, so he turned to face the wall.

"I've got something for you." Jones tossed something at Vincent's feet. "Come on. Pick it up!"

"That light is too bright," Vincent complained, shielded his eyes and tried to grope at whatever Jones had thrown in. Jones blocked some of the light with his hand.

It was a small stack of paper? Vincent had trouble focusing.

"What is this?" He turned it around. A cheque book? "What do you want me to do with this?"

Jones exhaled audibly. He pushed the hatch open, climbed up to the attic and knelt down next to Vincent.

"Here." He flicked through some of the stubs and stopped at one of the newer ones. "Read the date." It was dated the day after the fire. Next, Jones pointed at the sum. Vincent stared at it for a moment, struggling to follow.

"That's a large number," he said, since Jones seemed to be waiting for a reaction.

"Why are you this addlepated?" Jones groaned, as if he didn't know the cause of Vincent's longer than usual processing time. "Here. This is the beneficiary. Does that ring any bells, or do I need to spell this out for you?"

The letters 'W' and 'H' had been scribbled on the line Jones was so impatiently pointing at. Vincent wasn't sure that would have made much more sense had he felt more clear-headed.

"You're going to have to spell it out or wait 'til I sober up." He felt about as muddled as if he'd had six pints of beer.

"Can you at least tell whose handwriting this is?"

It did indeed look familiar, but without context, Vincent struggled to place it, so he shook his head.

"Can you explain why we're looking at this? Someone wrote a large cheque to a person with the initials W.H. and... then what?"

Despite his confusion, something about this was triggering Vincent's curiosity. He sincerely wanted to understand what Jones was getting at, but his brain was seriously misfiring. However, this was much better than writhing in pain, so the mild inconvenience seemed worth it.

"Look at the other stubs." Jones flicked through them slowly. "G.Q. Parts Incorporated. Johnson Shipment Company. Mr Andrew Bennett," he read out loud. "The names are all written out, except for this one. And do you happen to know the name of the esteemed fire chief, who inspected your cottage after the fire?"

"No." But Vincent wasn't far enough gone to not realise what Jones was getting at.

"William Hartley. This is hush money, Vincent. And the person who paid this didn't want anyone to know what really started the fire." Jones grabbed the cheque book, turned it around and held it in front of Vincent's face.

An awkward silence ensued as Jones again waited for a reaction out of Vincent. Vincent cleared his throat.

"I'm far-sighted," he said. There was no way he could have read anything from that distance without his reading glasses. Jones seemed like he was about to have an aneurysm but pulled the cheque book back some ways.

"Where did you get this?" Vincent felt his insides curdle. He grabbed the cheque book and held it where he could see it best. Yes, he definitely knew whose handwriting this was.

"It was on his shop counter. Do you believe me now? There was someone else there." Jones beamed with pride. "And you can bet your ass the fire didn't start in the kitchen. I'll eat my hat if it doesn't have something to do with those stacks of paper in your cellar. What the hell did you have in there? I wish I'd known you had that cellar earlier, so I could have busted this whole thing wide open ages ago."

A small grace then that Jones had been interrupted when he'd found it, Vincent thought. He was still staring at the text at the back of the cheque book.

It would have been an incredible feat if it was a forgery. Jones had the skills and the attention to detail, but he wouldn't know to write this. It was the heat distribution calculation for the different materials for the speeder's secondary cooler, with some markings Edward had made while checking it through. Vincent hadn't even realised this was what he'd grabbed when he'd needed a quick surface to write on.

"Why would he do something like that."

"About that." Jones grabbed the cheque book and thrust it into his pocket. Then he fished out a crumpled envelope from another pocket, looking especially smug. "I have something else that might interest you."

Whatever it was, Vincent wasn't sure he was ready for another heartbreak. Why the hell would Edward burn his house down. What had he done to deserve it. Weren't they supposed to be friends.

Jones pulled out the letter and shoved it into Vincent's hands. It seemed to be a page from somewhere in the middle. Vincent read it reluctantly.

"—in circumstances too dangerous to keep housing him. I would like to bestow him into your care if this does not put you off. As you're well aware of the gravity of the threat the boy's mother poses, I understand should you decline this proposition. Naturally, I will compensate for any inconvenience and reward you for your courage should you accept..."

Something about this letter felt strangely familiar. The message itself was foreign, but a few of the sentences prompted distinct memories of having to knock on a wall. Vincent shuddered. The year on the date matched. The signature at the bottom confirmed his suspicion.

"Can I see the envelope?" Vincent requested. Jones handed it over to him. There was no stamp or address, merely the initials A.B. It had been sensitive enough to require a personal courier.

Vincent closed his eyes and tried to focus, but he was overwhelmed by the flood of thoughts and questions.

"There's more," Jones interrupted him. "I haven't had the chance to read them all yet, but they're from this Mr Benton, and the recipient, as you must have guessed, is Aster Bramble. You're the boy they're referring to, right? Silly me, I thought Aster might be your mother, but it turns out she's been hiding you from her. What did your mother do that was so bad? Or does Aster just want to keep you to herself because you're rich and famous?"

"Shut up!" Vincent ground his teeth. His busted knee had started to throb again, and the pain was shooting through his leg, feeling nearly as bad as before.

At a glance, Jones looked more startled than someone in his position should have been. He clearly had the upper hand, being in possession of his full wits and functioning limbs. Using the pain to give more weight to his words, Vincent took the opportunity to scream at the man. "Give me something for this pain right now or I'll rip you to shreds!"

Jones dropped the letter, retreated to the hatch and disappeared from the attic. The hatch closed with a bam. Vincent rubbed his legs frantically, even though massaging them really, *really* did not help.

Why would they do this to him. He was stuck here with that imbecile, and no one had cared enough to come rescue him. Surely someone should have realised something was wrong by now. The pain was excruciating.

The hatch opened and a glass of milk was deposited into the attic. Unfortunately, it would take a while before he had relief.

S till out of his mind, Vincent lay down on the wood floor and listened
   to Jones's disgusting yammering somewhere below.

Even if he could have somehow opened the hatch, in this condition, he
was no match for Jones. How was he supposed to get out of this one?

Now that Jones was busy going over Aster's private letters, he would
likely not be leaving the cabin for a while. Even if he did, he would probably
time it so that Vincent would be begging for pain-relief and rendered
unconscious for however long Jones decided to dose him.

The man still didn't seem to be willing to let Vincent go, despite un-
earthing what seemed like fairly convincing proof he hadn't burnt Vincent's house. The letters had derailed him right back into his exposé obses-
sion, and it seemed he preferred to have Vincent trapped in the attic, either
to keep him out of the way or to probe for additional information.

Vincent listened to him recite one of the letters for the second time.
It was not from Mr Benton but an anonymous entity who Aster had
seemingly hired to tail someone whose name was never mentioned in their
correspondence. Vincent speculated it was either his mother or someone
close to her.

It made no sense that they referred to her as if she were a monster.
Vincent had no other unpleasant memories of her except that she had left
him without saying so much as a goodbye. Shouldn't he have felt some
animosity lingering if she'd ever treated him poorly?

Jones stopped reading. Vincent wasn't at his sharpest, but he thought
he'd heard something. He held his breath to listen.

He figured he was now losing his mind completely because he could have
sworn he knew this sound. He didn't have time to analyse his sanity nor the
sound because Jones exited the cabin, slamming the door behind him.

Vincent crawled to the hatch and tried to pry it open. Jones had had the
foresight to remove the handle, but all Vincent needed was the bent, rusty
nail he'd found while staring mindlessly at the floorboards, to push into a
screw hole and turn to make a crack to fit his finger in. He lifted the hatch
and looked down for any sign of Jones.

The coast was clear.

Even if the man was busy with whatever he was doing, it might not take him long to notice Vincent gone. With the leg this banged up, Vincent would need a considerable lead if he wanted to stand a chance. He needed to be smart about this, but his head still felt like it had been stuffed with cotton, and he wasn't particularly confident about his choices.

At least it didn't hurt much when he lowered himself down and dropped the remaining half a metre to the floor.

Vincent waddled to the table where Jones had been reading the letters. There was a bottle of medicine and a cup of tea conveniently left on the table next to them. This was an easy enough puzzle even for Vincent to solve.

He didn't have time to read up on the dosage, but considering the bottle was roughly half-empty, he probably wouldn't have to use much. He added about a generous spoonful into the teacup and swayed his way into the separate bedroom to lie down for a moment. It was too soon for him to be up feeling this dizzy, but this might be the only chance he got.

A volubly cursing Jones returned into the cabin. Vincent could hear him pace around the room until the slew of curse words died down to but a few. The chair made a creaking sound when he sat down. Jones resumed with the letters.

Vincent could tell his plan was working when Jones started to stumble over every other word. The two consecutive thumps were Vincent's cue to move.

As expected, Jones had rolled all the way to the floor. Vincent was decent enough to make sure he was breathing and wouldn't choke on his tongue but was also tempted to give him the parting gift of a proper kick. The only reason he didn't was because he would have likely ended up hurting himself more than the recipient.

He would have felt much better if he'd had rope to tie Jones with, but the closest thing he had was the bandage keeping his knee stable, and he was not about to relinquish that. It probably wouldn't even have held Jones for very long.

Vincent tried to find something warm to wear, but every moment wasted looking was a moment shaved off of the time he had to get away. With no coat in sight, he grabbed an extra shirt and pair of wellies from the front door and put them on. As an afterthought, he shoved the letters into his boots, both to fill them up for warmth but also to rob Jones of his evidence. He even nabbed the cheque book from Jones's pocket.

It was dark when Vincent exited the cabin, but whether it was evening or morning, he couldn't tell. The sky was clear. There was just enough light to see where he was going.

There was a snapped broomstick on the porch. It would serve as support to avoid having to strain the knee as much, but also as something to hit Jones with if the man caught up with him. Vincent hobbled across the yard and made a proverbial run for it.

CHAPTER 43

Ren steered the speeder above the tracks of the snowtrain. It was burning through fuel much faster than she'd expected—perhaps due to the cold—but there was half a tank left when she finally saw the cape ahead. If she could land safely, there would be enough to get back to town if she picked her route carefully.

She couldn't afford any detours or accidents after the one she'd had. It had been a tiny, *miniscule* really, steering mishap. She was ruffled by it, but the speeder had survived without much damage.

The ride had been thrilling, but her enthusiasm had died down after the *slight* accident, and in part also because the icy wind made her face hurt worse than running face first into a bush of nettles. At least the mittens Vincent had knitted for her were warm and comfortable, and the woolly hat did its job adequately.

Ren glanced at Mr Swifty, who had turned into a furry rug, claws fastened to the pelt in the sledge. Ren reminded herself to try to cover the poor cat with something on the way back.

The cabin came into view behind a sparse, low-grown cluster of trees. There was a lot of empty space to use for the landing, but Ren decided to aim for a spot that left some of the trees between her and the cabin. This decision was made partly because steering the speeder was tiring, and she wanted to avoid having to make any sharp turns. The snow also seemed much thicker and the terrain less rocky on this side of the trees.

The reverse-thrust made an awful screeching noise as it engaged. The effect was abrupt, and Ren clutched to the steering instruments with all her might to not be thrown overboard. She knew she wasn't supposed to close her eyes as the person solely responsible for steering, but a gust of ice particles puffed at her face at the critical moment, and she couldn't help herself.

The speeder crashed deep into a snowbank. As far as Ren could tell when she calmed down enough to look, the shock of it was worse than the damage.

Nearly half of the speeder was submerged in the snow, leaving the sledge, and the cat in it, unscathed.

Mr Swifty jumped out and ran off. Ren could not blame him. She dusted herself off and tried to figure out how to pull the thing back out from the bank.

The engine was still on, and she set it to cool-down mode. The tasks she was familiar with were easy, but troubleshooting the situation was much less so. She rubbed her forehead and tried to recall if the speeder had a reverse gear and how that might be used. Nothing came to mind.

Her thoughts were interrupted by the sound of a door slamming. She turned to see who had exited the cabin, but she didn't recognise him. He seemed younger, shorter, sturdier, as well as much angrier than Vincent.

Alarmed by the stranger's foul mood inspecting the yard, Ren turned off the engine and hid behind the speeder. The speeder itself was probably not visible from the cabin if you didn't know what to look for.

Once the stranger had circled the yard for a while and determined there was nothing of interest out here, he returned into the cabin. Ren could breathe a sigh of relief, even if her mind was now filled with questions.

Who was that? Where was Vincent? If that angry man had done something to Vincent, and this situation required a swift getaway, how would she get the speeder out? She wanted to run over to see whether Vincent was there, but she had a strong hunch she was supposed to do something about the speeder first.

Battling against her urge to go check, Ren focused on the problem at hand. She climbed back onto the speeder and stared at the control panel in hopes something would spark an idea, but she couldn't seem to get herself to concentrate. She didn't want to make any hasty mistakes, so she took her time.

Feeling a smidge of panic building when several minutes of staring didn't provide her with an answer, she went through all of the buttons and levers, trying to remember what each of them did. She wasn't sure if the sound of the engine alone would be enough to alert that man, but there was absolutely no way for her to dig or push the speeder out, so using the engine was her only option.

'Reverse-thrust' sounded like something that would do more than just reduce speed and act as brakes. Vincent had gone into detail about a lot of the minutiae, but this hadn't come up during their conversations. If it was reversing the thrust, Ren reasoned, she would have to add thrust and then reverse it, even if it seemed counterintuitive to drive the speeder forward and deeper into the snow. It had also made a lot of noise when she'd deployed it earlier, so she hesitated to use it again. But what else was there?

Thankfully, the cold weather slowed the acceleration so much, the speeder moved only a few dozen centimetres before Ren could apply the reverser. The noise was loud, but not as loud as the first time.

As soon as the speeder had reversed out, Ren slapped the cool down mode back on and shot several furtive glances towards the front porch. She snapped the engine off the second it had cooled down enough. Had she done it? Was she in the clear?

No sign of anyone.

She looked for Mr Swifty. He appeared from behind a pile of snow, walked to Ren and sat next to her.

"Who was that?" She could have sworn Mr Swifty looked disapproving, but that could have been a lingering opinion about the speeder ride. "Should we go take a look? Will it be dangerous?" She waited for the cat to give any indication of anything, but alas, he merely looked back at her. She was alone, having to make all the decisions. The responsibility felt crushingly heavy and her insides hollow.

Ren shook it off and crept toward the side of the cabin, with Mr Swifty in tow, to look through the windows to see what was going on inside. Maybe it would spark an idea of what she was supposed to do.

She reached up to peek into the dark and empty bedroom. No sign of Vincent. She circled around the house to the next window where she could see into the main room, but the angle was poor. There was one more window on that side, but it was high up with no footholds for climbing, and the curtains were drawn.

Ren recalled there being a small spyhole next to the front door, so she headed there next. The view was unobstructed and toward the table in the middle of the room.

The angry man was sprawled, seemingly asleep on the floor next to the table. What a strange place to sleep, Ren thought. Wouldn't a bed have been more comfortable?

Then again, Vincent also sometimes slept in peculiar places when he was ill, so perhaps it was one of those nonsensical things adults liked to do.

There was no sign of Vincent. Celandine had specifically said he'd come to the cape. This was the cape, wasn't it? There were no other cabins close by and she'd been here before. There was no way she could have made a mistake.

With the man asleep and not moving, Ren dared to open the door and peer in through the crack. No signs or sounds of movement. She wanted to be absolutely sure Vincent was not in the cabin—not in the bedroom under the bed, up in the attic, or stuffed into a closet out of sight—so she snuck inside. Something about this situation seemed very wrong to her.

Mr Jones opened his left eye. The right side of his face felt odd. He watched the view ahead, but it made no sense to him. Everything was sideways. Where was he? What the hell was going on? His head felt sluggish and heavy.

There was someone in the room with him.

"Vincent?" Had Vincent escaped from the attic somehow? Jones tried to summon a sense of urgency, but he felt slow as if trapped underwater. "Damn it, Vincent, what did you do?"

He pulled himself up using the table as support and ignored his head spinning to scan his surroundings.

Where was that blasted scat-sack? There was someone there, but it wasn't Vincent. This was someone smaller... A child? Why was there a child here?

"Who are you?"

"What did you do to Vincent? Where is he?"

"How should I know?!" Mr Jones checked the bottle of medicine on the table. There was no way to tell if there was less of it, but that bastard must have drugged him. His legs felt numb, and they weren't moving like they were supposed to. He held on to the table to not fall over.

"This is not your house! Are you a burglar? Where's Vincent?"

What an irritating child. Mr Jones was already feeling irate, but the whinging little girl was making it worse.

"Vincent, Vincent, Vincent... Shut up, you annoying brat! I'm trying to think." He raved at the girl for a moment more to shut her up. She took some steps backwards. Good.

Just as he was about to gain a rudimentary grasp of the situation, Mr Jones noticed the cat. Something within him snapped. That damn creature was here? Now? Why? He roared and threw his teacup at the thing.

"You piece of shit! I wouldn't be in this mess if it weren't for you!" That cat was the reason he'd panicked and run the wrong way on the train. Who knew what might have happened had he reached a car with other people where Vincent wouldn't have dared to touch him.

He looked for something else to throw and grabbed anything at his reach. The cat dodged and ran to cower behind the little girl. Mad from the drug and the rage, Jones threw a pot at the both of them with only a sliver of sanity guiding the trajectory. It hit the wall behind the girl. She screamed and looked at him in horror.

Yes, he'd meant to scare her, but he had no intention of adding homicide to his list of crimes. His head reeled and he wanted to vomit. Where the hell was Vincent? Did he get away?

R en shook from the fright. The strange man had woken up and was now attacking Mr Swifty and even her. He must have been drunk by the way he was acting. She backed away toward the door.

If she went back now, would they believe her and hurry up and do something? She had no idea where Vincent was, she was alone, and if this madman didn't kill her, Celandine probably would.

She bit her lip to brace herself, but the tears welled up in her eyes. She hoped she would be able to retreat from the cabin at least, while the stranger seemed momentarily distracted by something on the table.

"Where are they?" He turned to look at her. "Did you take them? Where the hell are they?!" He banged his fists on the table and lurched towards Ren.

Ren panicked. She scrabbled to open the door behind her.

"Stop right there! Did you fucking take the letters?!" He charged at her just as she managed to slip out the door with Mr Swifty. As she pulled the door shut in front of her, she could feel it be thrust shut by the man on the other side.

There was a peculiar noise. Ren held on to the door handle for a moment, confused. No one was tugging at it to open it from the opposite side. There was a faint thump of something hitting the porch.

Ren glanced at Mr Swifty. Mr Swifty looked at her and sniffed the thing that had fallen at the hinge-side of the door. It looked like a tiny sausage.

Ren frowned.

In any case, she was at the very last edge of her courage and not interested in tiny sausages, so she ran off without looking back.

M r Swifty saw Ren run off towards the speeder and decided firmly against following. There was no way in hell he would get on that thing again. Besides, he was fairly intrigued by the piece of fresh meat that had fallen through the door crack. He nabbed it into his mouth and took a few tentative steps across the yard.

The cabin door opened behind him and freeloader-Jones crawled out onto the porch. He was holding his bleeding hand while frantically searching for something. Mr Swifty chuckled inwardly.

Their eyes met and the nominal genius seemed to realise that what he was looking for currently resided between Mr Swifty's teeth.

Jones let out a mewl.

"Give it back!" He started running unsteadily towards Mr Swifty.

He was slow even for himself, stumbling and staggering, so Mr Swifty had no trouble evading his attempts at capture.

"Please, you stupid thing, give it back!"

Once Mr Swifty was bored of the humorous play-chase, he headed north, following a faint but familiar smell. He glanced back to see that Jones grabbed his coat and a lantern to come after him. That was fine. If he was following this way, he wouldn't bother Ren.

"Stop! Don't eat that! Please..."

Hah, like he would ever stoop as low as to eat any part of the idiot moocher. Mr Swifty glared at Jones and bit down decisively. Then he leapt agilely over some boulders and down the hill, with the man stumbling at his tail.

CHAPTER 44

Afer dragging himself through the craggy, snowy wasteland for the better part of an hour, there wasn't much adrenaline left to keep Vincent going. His escape felt much less promising now than when he'd first left the house, but then, he'd still been stewed from the spiked milk and befuddled enough to head the wrong way in a supposedly genius ploy to throw Jones off.

In hindsight, he couldn't say what the best course of action would have been, but forsooth, he should have given it some more thought before committing.

The direction he'd chosen had led him down the windswept northern side of the cape and back up on the far side of the forest, away from the route of the snowtrain. Jones would definitely not think to follow him here first, so even if Vincent moved slowly, he'd have a fair head start.

The wind had carried most of the snow off from this side of the cape, so he'd left practically no footprints for Jones to follow. With less snow, the trek had been easier than if he'd had to wade.

The downside was that he was far off-course if he aimed to find a safe place or be rescued. He didn't know these parts of the island very well and couldn't remember anyone living here. His only consolation was that he likely wouldn't have been much better off heading the other way. He couldn't be sure of the day of the week, but if it was one of the many when the snowtrain did not run, or he turned up at the wrong time, Jones would have easily recaptured him.

Vincent clutched his extra shirt and broomstick and climbed clumsily over a cluster of boulders. The further he went, the stupider he, and this venture, felt. He was still in George's bloody breeches, and his calves were only barely covered by the damn wellies.

The positive side to this annoyance and self-loathing was that it propelled Vincent forward for another half an hour. The pain, the cold and the added scrapes and scratches as he limped forward were enough to keep him going for yet another.

Despite these efforts, he hadn't got very far.

If not for a hill and some trees in the way, he probably could have seen the cabin in the distance. Looking back, he hadn't left an obvious trail, but it would only be a matter of time before Jones caught up. Even if Jones had searched in all the other directions first, a healthy pair of legs moved much faster than Vincent's lame and injured pair. His only hope was to find a place to hide before Jones woke up, started his search and reached him.

Not that Vincent was using his legs much. He was dragging himself along and swinging forward between rocks whenever he could. He'd had to put a lot of weight on his arms across uneven, often slippery or scratchy surfaces, so his palms and forearms were sore and bruised despite the two shirts. His left wrist throbbed from having twisted it after losing his balance one too many times, and he had to wonder how long he could go on in his atrocious condition.

Vincent crawled under some short, bushy evergreen trees to rest for a moment. A cave or a rock formation of some sort—something that could have sheltered him from the snow and the wind—would have been better, but at least the leaves provided some privacy.

Already freezing and shivering, taking a break reminded him of how cold he felt and how stiff his joints could get the moment he stopped moving. He was exhausted from having never fully recovered from his cold, so he was forced to take a moment to gather himself and to catch his breath. After resting only for as long as he absolutely had to, he pressed on before the chill made his muscles too taut.

Cold and miserable, Vincent was warmed by a solitary thought: At least he was not sitting in his own excrement.

Anything was better than smelling like a log and developing a devilishly itchy butt-crack rash.

He knew life began and ended with having to soil himself from time to time, but he'd taken solace in not having all his wits about him when that happened. The chances of him losing his marbles before he became incontinent were absolutely in his favour: After all, half of them had been missing throughout his life. He'd figured he'd be too far gone to know what was going on by the time old age did its final cruelties, or that he would die young and not have to deal with any of it.

It made him positively *seethe* to have to experience this prematurely. Feeding his anger helped him drive himself forward for another couple of minutes. After that, he used every bit of the inane shit he'd had to endure as fodder to fuel his discontent—and there was a lot of it. The discontent, in turn, proved an effective distraction from the budding hypothermia.

Imagining the various deliciously vengeful things he would do to the people who had ever wronged him, Vincent found himself nearing an actual house well before he ran out of steam and just as the sun, still resting well below the horizon, painted the sky a rich shade of blue.

The house was empty. As with most houses around these parts, the door was unlocked and, since this was an emergency, Vincent let himself in.

The house was cool, so the owner had been away for more than a day. That indicated a reasonable likelihood they were not coming back today. Though the island community was small enough for almost everyone to know everyone else, this house fell into that rare category outside the "almost".

Vincent didn't dare to light a fire, or even a lantern, for the fear that Jones might see it through a window and decide to come knocking. He washed up with some cold water, even if he was too stiff to reach everywhere or see what he was doing.

There wasn't much he could do about his injuries, but he figured he ought to at least try to check what state he was in. Funny how nervous he was about what he'd find when it hadn't been long since he'd resigned to his death.

The knee desperately needed a splint or a cast, or anything at all, to keep it in place. It had been left untreated for such a while, who knew whether it could be saved, but at least the swelling had gone down some, and the bruising was turning a healthier shade of yellow. He could still not be entirely sure whether he'd fractured one or several of his bones. But judging by the amount of pain slowly returning as Jones's knock-out medicine wore off, it wouldn't come as a surprise if he had.

In truth, if all of this could be solved without surgery somehow, Vincent reckoned he would be satisfied and grateful. He was not a big fan of what, in his mind, seemed more like witchcraft and irresponsible play with sharp knives and other cutting implements. No matter how much he appreciated most things to do with science, the thought of cutting into living flesh unnerved him to no end.

Of course, there was always the chance he would not need surgery on account of being too dead to reach a surgeon, but frankly, he wasn't entirely sure which was worse: Surgery or blundering this escape when he was so invested in it.

Perhaps best not to think that far ahead and focus instead on his more immediate needs, such as pain-relief, rest and perhaps even sleep, if he was lucky.

Vincent searched for a medicine cabinet and helped himself to some of its more familiar contents. There was a pouch of the local pharmacist's special all-purpose pain-relieving herbal mixture, which Vincent had tested on occasion and knew to be effective without any exceedingly risky side-effects.

He took the maximum dosage and looked for a suitable place to hide to get some sleep. He dismissed the most obvious but made do with a sizeable linen closet at the back of a storage room. His long and bruised legs fit in—if he took off the wellies and folded them just right—and he could still close the door. It was far from comfortable, but even if he couldn't fall asleep in such a confined space, being able to relax and feel some semblance of security was an improvement.

There was no sign of Jones when Vincent decided it was time to get up. The house was quiet save for the soft hum of the wind. He hadn't dared to rest for long but felt well enough to scramble out of the closet to resume his escape.

It was light outside.

After picking his brain for a plan, all he could come up with was to continue along the coast in hopes he would run into another house or one of the sturdy fishing vessels that the local fishermen used along the north coast, where the ice cover was at its thinnest or the sea did not freeze at all.

Vincent discarded the moist extra shirt and 'borrowed' a pair of trousers and a thick winter coat from the storage room. The coat was heavy but seemed a necessary addition to surviving out in the cold. He pulled his wellies back on and stuffed them with the now considerably more battered letters.

It was too risky to leave a note. Vincent's conscience nagged about it, so to silence it, he made a firm mental note to find out who the owner was, so he could send his thanks and an apology once he was out of harm's way. He also needed to remember to compensate Mrs Beansbury for her cake and suitcase. More reason to try to survive this stupid ordeal.

The beach wasn't far, but Vincent's hobble-wobble crawl was even slower than before. It had taken another dose of the all-purpose pain-reliever just to get upright, much less to move without screaming. He had to bite his lip to avoid drawing attention to himself, but at least he was mobile.

The wind was brisk and biting, but it blew from behind him—a small but welcome blessing. He felt compelled to glance back every few minutes to make sure no one was following. No matter how deceptively safe his lead felt, one of these times there would be someone there.

"Heavy fucking coat," were the only words Vincent snarled from between his clenched teeth as the coat hem got stuck and dragged against the rocks he was struggling to climb over. He couldn't remember when he'd last had a situation that had called for swearing as much as this did. "Coat. Fucking heavy!" The only words but spiced up by intonation and varying word order. "Fuckingheavycoat." He yanked it along and rolled his eyes dramatically.

At least he still had the energy to roll his eyes dramatically.

It would have been smarter to conserve that energy and use it to get down the steep, icy, rocky bastard of a hill with no path to speak of, but he was low on morale and had no interest in optimisation.

Vincent considered sliding down on his ass, but the terrain was much too unfriendly for this method of descent. By the time he reached the bottom, his ass would have shone through his loan-trousers with a side dish of blood, artistic engravings across his bony buttocks, and tiny rocks embedded nicely into his flesh. While it still would have felt less embarrassing than spending time in his own excrement, it did not sound tempting.

"Fucking coat." Had it served as viable ass protection, there would have been more sense dragging it along, but even if he could have fastened it to his butt to slide down the hill, the friction of the coarse wool would have stopped him in his tracks.

It had sucked in moisture like a sponge, and snow now held onto it for dear life until it wasn't even all that warm anymore. The sleeves provided some protection from the sharper edges of the rocks, but Vincent was already too bruised for it to make a difference. Instead, the rough fabric rubbed against his raw skin and stung like little needle pricks where his shirt wasn't thick enough to shield him.

Frankly, at this point, the colder he was, the better: Numb skin seemed more tolerant of the abuse. He abandoned the coat with a few more repetitive curse words, and because he was now close to the beach and fed up with everything, he did not bother hiding it.

"Fucking Jones. Go ahead and follow me," he mumbled as he tossed it aside.

The yielding layer of loose, soft snow near the frozen waterline was despicable. That it dared to make walking even more difficult was as if the universe was slowly lifting up its middle finger. After all that, the least it could have done was to cooperate, but what would an escape be without some miniature hardships to go along with the larger hurdles, to maximise his suffering?

Vincent tried to estimate the time. Judging by the position of the sun, which was barely visible somewhere behind him, he'd made it here around noon. The estimate was rough because he couldn't be sure how accurately this part of the coast faced north, but if anyone had planned to head out to fish today, the few hours after sunrise was one of the best times to do so. Perhaps there would be someone out there now?

Vincent missed the coat but didn't bother retrieving it. It was only twenty metres from where he stood, but he'd fought hard for those metres.

He sat down where some of the surrounding rocks had formed a bald spot on the snow cover and the rock-hard sand underneath was visible.

Sand. The excrement of the sea. At least it smelled better. Frozen solid, it didn't smell much of anything. Vincent tried to keep himself entertained with his thoughts, so as not to fall into a stupor while looking out for any sign of a boat or a ship.

He couldn't believe he'd made it here in one piece, but 'here' was disappointingly far from home and safety.

Then again, he didn't really have a home to go to. The place he'd fled from was the closest he had, but he didn't think he could stomach going back there again. He imagined having to store his preserves in the space where he'd lounged in his butt-juices for however many days. The smell would probably linger there forever. No, he'd rather find an apartment somewhere in town.

Looking back at his recent and not so recent experiences, Vincent had to wonder if it wasn't somehow deliberate that he was being tortured with this seemingly endless series of misfortunes. Was there an entity out there figuratively shredding his arse with a rusty kitchen grater just to see if he twitched? Was that why he almost always felt like he was being watched?

What, still alive? Still wanting to live? Well, here's some more shit for you, my friend. Enjoy.

This message became louder and clearer as time lumbered on with no sign of a boat.

Well, thank you again, life, for this kind gift of consideration. It had to be a holiday of some sort, today of all days.

Vincent tried to think of what holidays there were this time of year but couldn't quite recall. There was a boat or two going out almost every day of the week, usually several. The whole island lived off of fish, for heaven's sake. There should have been at least one going past here by now. Should have, but wasn't.

A fter a few hours of daylight, it was already getting dark. There was no sign of Jones, but also, no sign of a boat, either. Vincent was more than fed up with his predicament, and the persistent irritation was the only thing keeping him semi-alert.

Had Jones turned up right now, Vincent would've made his best effort to bite the man's head off. It was rare for him to sustain anger for this long, but he was hardly tortured and made to sit where he'd rather not sit every day.

The stabbing pain in his leg was a constant reminder of the injustice, but now he was also losing light. At this rate, he might be able to see the boat, but no one on the boat would see him. A thin, frosty haze had developed, and though it wasn't pitch black dark yet, visibility was poor.

Vincent succumbed to the horrible truth that he was going to have to venture out onto the treacherous ice if he wanted to stand a chance of being rescued. If he waited here until he saw a boat, he would not make it in time to be where they could see him. He didn't have a light source, and all he could do was try to flail and perhaps dare a shout to get their attention. If he did that and Jones decided to join him just then... well, his game would be over if he wasn't out of striking distance.

The further out he trudged through the calf-deep snow, the grippier the wind became. The fast ice, stretching from the beach to somewhere in the distance, was mostly thick and clear this time of year, but sometimes a thinner second layer formed on top, sandwiching icy sea water between the layers.

Vincent's makeshift walking stick sank through the first layer of ice from time to time, and while it helped him choose where to step, sometimes there was no avoiding the riskier areas.

He'd never been as grateful for a pair of wellies as now. They were so tightly packed with the letters, his feet felt toasty compared to the rest of his body, even when he fell through the first layer of ice and his feet were submerged a little past his ankles.

He was almost at the edge of the fast ice when he noticed something on the beach. He was too far to be sure, but it seemed like it could have been Mr Swifty. What the hell was he doing out here? Had he been at the cabin all the while?

Vincent was about to yell and see whether the cat would come if called, but thankfully hadn't the time to do so when he realised that another figure followed.

No, it wasn't help like he'd hoped. It was Jones.

Vincent wasn't far enough to be out of sight, so he threw himself onto the slush-covered ice and crawled toward where the snow cover seemed thicker. Unfortunately, once in it, it didn't seem thick enough to shield him from Jones's eyes.

With his lantern held up high above his head, Jones was too busy combing through the crevices between the rocks and boulders to look out to sea. The bastard probably hadn't yet thought it worth checking, since no one in their right mind would head out here.

Perhaps it would eventually occur to him that Vincent was not in his right mind? If Jones did decide to look, it wouldn't take much for him to notice Vincent against the mostly white backdrop.

Quickly assessing his options, Vincent realised he would rather have drowned than gone back. He rolled over the snow and slush, towards the start of the drift ice some metres away. This was suicide, and not a pleasant one at that. But anything was better than sitting in shit.

Vincent rolled over the ice and was enveloped by the piercing cold sea. His muscles constricted with all the force left in them, and he felt as if his breath was violently sucked out of him.

He grasped at the edge of the ice, only barely managing to keep his head above the water. Lacking all control over his breathing, gasping quick and frantic, shallow breaths, his only goal besides keeping quiet was to avoid breathing in any of the water.

Ideally, once Jones had moved further away, Vincent would have wanted to climb back up onto the ice, but considering his abysmal condition and the added cold shock, he'd guessed it was not going to be possible even before he'd rolled in.

Jones had stopped to inspect something—probably the coat Vincent had abandoned.

After surviving the first two minutes, Vincent fought to steady his breathing to calm himself down. His body was refusing most of his commands, but at least he was still holding on to the edge of the ice.

He reminded himself that now that he was soaked, it wouldn't have made a difference even had he managed to climb out of the water. With his body rendered this immobile, there was no way he could have reached anywhere warm before his heart gave up.

Upsides, he prompted himself. He could usually put a laughable positive spin on most of his torturous predicaments.

No cauliflowers were about to attack him here, no one was shouting insults at him, and there was nobody around to critique his pathetic performance in bed.

No one was going to betray his trust again. He wouldn't have to see the faces of the people he'd mistakenly considered his friends and family. He wouldn't have to rein in his temper or hide his insanity from anyone anymore.

He was relieved.

He could no longer feel his legs. There was pain, but it was so all-encompassing, his brain was no longer processing it properly. His chest felt like it was experiencing a massive cramp, but at least he did not smell of shit anymore. He bobbed slowly in beat with his soundless, jagged laugh.

Vincent watched the shiny dot of Jones's lantern disappear behind a ridge. The sky had turned from solid grey to a gradient between clear black and a milky, dark shade of bluish green near the horizon. The haze had cleared, so he could see the stars.

This seemed like such a soothing and beautiful moment to die, if not for his body gasping for short breaths, nearly triggering his long-suppressed coughs. If only it could have hurt just a little bit less... Well, it wouldn't hurt for much longer.

CHAPTER 45

George Bramble hadn't been out fishing in the winter for several years now. His arthritis acted up more or less constantly nowadays and his eyesight could have been better, so to placate his wife's nerves, he usually asked someone younger to come along with him.

This year, he'd most often gone with Vincent, but the man had been busy with other things recently. When the weather had cleared up and his son, Arthur, had offered to come, George had jumped at the chance.

They were at the docks, ready to head out, when he saw Aster run towards the boat.

"You need to go to the cape!" she shouted as she ran. "Ren is back. She says Vincent is not at the cape. Something terrible must have happened!"

George was relieved to hear Ren was back. They had looked for her continuously for two days after her disappearance, and most of the town was still keeping an eye out for her a week later. Part of the reason George had wanted to go fishing was to relieve some of the stress and to see if maybe he could see a sign of her somewhere along the coast.

"Calm down, dear. Is Ren all right? What did she say?"

"She's safe, but she's been at the cape. She was frightened out of her mind by a stranger at the cabin. She said she saw no sign of Vincent. You'd better go take a look!" Aster was breathing hard. She must have run all the way from the house.

Sometimes children came up with the wildest tales, but Ren wasn't the type to lie. To not waste time, George forwent setting up the fishing trawl. If nothing was amiss at the cape, he would have plenty of time to fish on the way back, but getting there quickly took priority.

"I'm going over to Celandine's to tend to Ren, so I may not be home when you get back. Be careful. Maury keep you safe." Aster reached over the side to give George a kiss to send him off.

"We'll let you know if we find him, Mum," Arthur said and detached the boat.

George started the custom engine Vincent and Edward had built for his twenty-metre steel-enforced trawler. She could do twelve knots if there was a thin layer or no ice, and even in rougher conditions, they would reach the cape in no time.

T he first sign of trouble was when Arthur spotted Mr Swifty trotting at the beach, some ways from the cape. Arthur yelled to catch the cat's attention, and the cat strode and leapt across the ice to a spot where they could pick him up.

As if the cat's presence wasn't peculiar enough, he dropped a severed pinky finger onto the deck. It was much too dainty to be Vincent's, but it did raise both of the men's eyebrows.

V incent's skin felt as if it was peeled right off of his body when something yanked him up by the back of his shirt. He imagined he made a noise, but he was preoccupied by the queer combination of intense agony and fascination over still being capable of feeling something worse. He could tell there was an overwhelming amount of pain, but he was separated from it, as if it were happening to someone else.

Somewhere above him, the green serpentine tail-sweeps of the fox's fires flared across the sky. Aurora. This could have been such a magnificent send-off if he could have drifted off, undisturbed. There was always something ruining things, wasn't there?

Vincent's back hit the deck, and his view was obstructed by the people coming to his rescue. He was vaguely aware that his soaked clothes chafed against his skin, and he felt uncomfortably warm. He would have removed some of them had his hands been functioning.

In a moment, someone did that for him, but then wrapped him up in a blanket.

The faces were familiar, but he couldn't produce the names. His ears were as if stuffed with wads of cotton, so all he could hear were muffled voices and a steady buzz.

They moved him over like a piece of meat. He tried to help, but his limbs were not obeying. He pushed the blanket away, and it was forcefully re-wrapped around him.

"George." That was the name. Vincent wanted to tell the man off for fussing with the blanket when he was already feeling hot.

The other one stepped in to hold Vincent still so he wouldn't discard the blanket again, and after a brief struggle, Vincent gave up.

Ooh, boy, this looks bad.

"Arthur." The name popped back into his mind when he heard the voice. "You should have left me."

Being rescued meant he would have to put in more effort. Where else could he pull from at this point? He had nothing to give.

He could feel his heartbeat at his throat, slow, harsh and occasionally thumping a few beats faster, but at least it was trying. He coughed.

Did he do it on purpose? Was he trying to kill himself?

Vincent was too tired to correct the assumption. He sat hunched over, with Arthur guarding the blanket, and watched a single severed digit rolling ever so slightly back and forth on the deck.

G eorge's boat reached the docks, and Arthur jumped over the side to tie the ropes.

"Watch him. I'll go get Edward." He ran off before Vincent could object.

Vincent was not in the mood for more audience—especially not the kind that had had something to do with the burning of his house.

"Don't..." He'd even bothered to raise his hand for this, albeit a minute or two late. He let it fall down and reminded himself to breathe.

While his heartbeat had now improved somewhat, his body was making some pathetic attempts to shiver, and it was messing up his breathing. Like an engine trying to start with no fuel left in the tank, he trembled a few times before stopping and closed his eyes.

"Oh, try to keep awake, son, until we get you warmed up and looked at." George shook his shoulder gently.

"I don't know if I can," Vincent heard himself slur. His lips and tongue felt stiff and slow. Most every part of his body felt stiff and slow.

"Here I am. What do you need me to do?" Edward climbed onto the deck. *Oh, holy shit, Vincent! What the hell happened to you?*

"Grab him by the legs," Arthur said. "Dad, can you take care of the rest here? We'll take him to the doctor." *Hold on a little longer, brother. We've got you.*

"Of course I can!" George huffed. "Now hurry up with it."

Arthur lifted Vincent up under his armpits, and Edward took a hold of his legs. George adjusted the blanket before they hauled Vincent off the boat and towards the doctor's office, which, as luck had it, was near the docks.

V incent was barely conscious when they reached Dr Jacobs' office, and he was glad of it. Once they'd made him drink something warm, fed the fireplace until the room was blazing hot and Vincent's body temperature was improving, the doctor insisted on treating the knee, as well as the other injuries Vincent was less aware of.

This included going under the dreaded knife, for which Vincent insisted to be medicated, mustering surprising fervour.

It was not complex surgery; the doctor just wanted to drain an abscess near a wound on his calf. However, as Vincent's body temperature improved and he started to regain some of his senses, everything was sore and ached. Dealing with the pain while exhausted left him unable to suppress his whines, and the doctor took pity on him.

Once Vincent was medicated, the rest of it was much more tolerable.

"I'm going to pull now. Are you ready?" the doctor asked.

Edward and Arthur were holding Vincent still by his arms. They were trying to set the knee back into its proper place before splinting it. It had travelled a bit during the escape and would have been hellishly painful had Vincent not been high as a kite on the best stuff the doctor had to offer.

"Yeah, sure," Vincent said. When they pulled, it did make him howl from the pain, but the pain seemed amusing rather than distressing. "Can I request something before you pack me up?"

"What is it?" Edward asked.

"Oh, not you. You burned down my house." Vincent tried to wave Edward away. "Arthur, would a bath be too much to ask?"

They'd spent close to an hour going through his injuries, so surely they must have been aware that Vincent was in need of a good scrub.

"I don't have a tub." Dr Jacobs looked apologetic.

Ah, they probably would have warmed Vincent up in one had they had it.

"Anything else I could use...?" It would be more of an inconvenience in his condition, but he desperately wanted to feel clean. Jones had presumably given him a wipe with a washcloth, he'd tried to wash himself at the empty house, and the sea had given him a bit of a rinse, but some of this uncleanliness was mental and it was *sticky*.

"I have a stool and some pails in the washroom. I could ask my wife to boil some water for you." The doctor frowned for a moment and turned to Arthur. "Can you help him out with it?"

"Sure. That's no problem."

Vincent glanced at Edward. Edward was staring at him with his mouth half-open. Oh, right.

"You did burn down my house, didn't you?" Funny how it didn't aggravate him half as much when the perpetrator was Edward.

No, wait. Vincent realised he was heavily medicated and snorted at his own stupidity. Well, this was certainly helpful. He didn't really want to fly off the handle over this thing again, and now he didn't feel the need to do so.

"It wasn't on purpose." Edward looked weepy.

"You left me in there."

"I slammed the door so you'd wake up. I definitely didn't mean to hurt you." He hung his head, absolutely deflated. "Afterwards, I wished I'd had the guts to face you and make sure you got out safely, but I panicked."

"Why did you do it?"

"I'm sorry. I can't get into it right now. Let's get you on the mend first, and we'll talk about it later. I promise."

Vincent sighed. Well, he was too tired to concentrate now, anyway.

"You'd better build me a new house," he said and almost dozed off where he lay. "With a bigger garage!" he perked up to request.

"All right, but let's get you cleaned up first," Edward said.

CHAPTER 46

Vincent found himself in a familiar room. It was the guest room he'd stayed in when he'd lived with the Brambles for a while as a child.

He couldn't tell how long he'd been out, but he felt significantly better. The knee still hurt, and his wrist was sore, but most of the other stuff was unnoticeable so long as he was careful and didn't agitate anything.

He sat up breathing in and out for a while. He'd expected to have a worse cough and a fever, but he felt fine. Maybe it would hit him later, but he would enjoy this while it lasted. It gave him the rare opportunity to think and digest everything he'd been through.

Sometime in the not so distant future, he would have to confront Aster about the letters and the lying. He was also currently sober enough to be disappointed and upset with Edward, although that had eased considerably with how miserable and sad the man had looked when Vincent had brought it up.

Although Edward had yet to explain why he'd done it, at least it hadn't been intentional, and he'd seemed to regret it. While Vincent wondered if things could ever return to how they'd been, he was glad no one seemed to hate him enough to have burnt down the house intentionally.

Now all that remained was to somehow sort all of this out without losing his temper and making more enemies so that no one decided to burn his house down again when it was rebuilt.

The door opened without a knock. This was, of course, impolite, but not reason enough to throw a fit. However, Vincent was a little on edge after everything, so he jumped, startled, on the bed.

"Sweet son of a perch, Celandine! Knock!" he exclaimed, covered his bare chest with the covers and tried to calm his strained heart.

Celandine entered and eyed him with mild disdain.

Was she still refusing to let go of her grudge from before? Or was this to reprimand him for scolding her now?

Ren came in at her heels and made one of those squealing female noises, possibly indicative of being happy.

"Vincent!" she shrieked, loud enough for him to fear his hearing was the next victim in this seemingly endless series of ghastly incidents. She jumped on the bed to hug him, then sat next to him with her legs dangling over the side.

Aster also entered the room, but instead of acknowledging Vincent, she watered the houseplants on the windowsill.

"I'm glad you're all right." Celandine's face was as stiff as a board.

Aster said nothing but put down the watering pot and leaned over to give him a hug. Then she glanced at Ren, looked back at Vincent, and slapped him.

"The hug would have sufficed." He rubbed his jaw. It hadn't been a hard slap, but it was hard enough to sting a bit. Aster hadn't the habit of resorting to physical violence, so the emotional shock was worse than the blow.

"Why would you do something like that?!" The strength in her voice exceeded her slight frame.

"That seems more like something I might ask," Vincent stammered, confused.

Celandine moved over to cover Ren's ears.

"We heard from George that you tried to," she lowered her voice to a whisper, "kill yourself."

Was that why they were so upset with him? They thought he'd deliberately gone out there to off himself?

"It was an accident," Vincent defended himself hastily.

With Ren there, despite Celandine trying to shield her from hearing, he didn't want to go into much detail. In fact, he didn't particularly fancy going into any amount of detail with any of the people present.

"An accident?" Celandine squinted the way stern women did when they did not believe a word of what they were hearing.

"I'm fine now. I hope I didn't cause you worry?" That usually calmed her down.

Aster slapped him again. Not as hard this time, but still with some force.

"I—" she started, then glanced again at Ren, then back at Vincent, "*she* was so worried, she went looking for you!"

"Oh? Where? When?"

"She was away for a week and only got back the day before yesterday," Celandine explained in her sister's stead.

"Oh."

"You could at least pretend to care. You can't just tell her all these wonderful lies about wanting to live together or go out on an adventure to see the world, or even promise a fishing trip with her when you're this depressed and undependable!"

Celandine's words didn't sound right to Vincent, but he hadn't the time to comment when Aster continued:

"She ran away, stole things, destroyed property and put her life in grave danger. She could have been killed!"

"I'll pay for them when I can, so it's not technically stealing," Ren corrected.

"With what money?" Aster eyed Vincent with some desperation, as if Vincent was supposed to do something about it on the spot. "You are her guardian, despite what you might think. Say something."

"I'll pay for it, of course. What did she steal that was so important? What did she destroy?" Vincent was so confounded by the unexpected topic of this conversation all he could do was aim for some damage control.

Ren avoided looking at him, but both Aster and Celandine were glaring more than enough to make up for her share.

"What is it?" Vincent asked. "Do I have something in my beard?"

He hadn't had the chance to shave, and it was long overdue. The beard itself couldn't have been too much of a surprise; he'd had a beard before.

It wasn't as if he'd grown a pair of horns or a humongous tumour onto his forehead in what he assumed was less than two weeks. What was so bad that it required this much staring and indecisiveness?

"I stole parts for the speeder," Ren whispered. Vincent frowned.

"What do you mean, 'the speeder'?" Not the speeder, his husk of a speeder, certainly—?

"I fixed the speeder, so I could come and find you, but then I ran into a tiny bit of trouble on the way." Ren hesitated.

Vincent was still stuck trying to get over the hump that there had been enough of the speeder left to fix, and that she'd managed to fix it, presumably all by herself.

"Go ahead. Tell him what you told me," Aster coaxed her. Ren looked forlorn but started recounting.

Ren had fixed the flap, but she hadn't taken into account how big a difference a small detail could make. Because of the unconventional design and material she'd used, the steering had been unstable. Nothing completely unmanageable, but for someone Ren's size, it was a handful and tired her out.

The combination of keeping an eye on all the gauges while wrestling with the controls spelled, if not 'disaster', at least 'near-death experience' and 'unwanted and excessive excitement'.

First there was a whizz. It was gentle and sounded benign. Ren thought very little of it. The consequent rapid acceleration and change in direction caused more alarm, especially since said direction was toward some rather solid-looking trees and a collection of buildings below.

Shortly after, the whizz was followed by a sharp, continuous cat-shriek from Mr Swifty, who had reached the peak of his tolerance for speed and excitement. He was holding on for dear life with his claws digging into the pelt but looked about ready to abandon sledge.

Ren tried to steer. It proved impossible with her arms now tired and about as tough as aspic. She made a noise that blended seamlessly with the cat's screaming. Collision seemed imminent, but at least the people down below had ample warning to run out of the way or take cover.

The descent took longer than Ren first supposed, but when it ended, it did so with no delay. The front of the speeder took the brunt of the blow as it somehow slid miraculously through a large open window on the upper floor—albeit taking a chunk of the frame and the walls along with it—and through the whole house and out the other end, coming to a stop in a tree in the backyard.

Ren discovered, much to her joy, that she was still alive. Mr Swifty had stopped screaming and stared at Ren, wide-eyed and trembling. The speeder looked structurally sound; it was surprisingly sturdy. The tree had seen better days, but at least some of it was still standing.

"What happened?" someone asked behind them.

From the hole in the wall of the house that had once looked respectable peeked a confused lady with her hair tucked into a shower cap and her body draped in a towel. She hid behind the remnants of a wall, and her bathtub was leaking foamy water into the downstairs living room.

A man emerged from the shed bellowing, red-faced and angry. His shed was fine, but he was probably steamed about the house and his half-naked wife.

A full row of children's faces Ren recognised from school stared out through one of the downstairs windows at her and Mr Swifty with equal interest.

"What is the meaning of this?! What have you done!" were the two sentences Ren could make out amidst the curses.

Recovering from the shock, she tried to think of a way to settle this, but she was fairly sure she could never afford to pay for such extensive damages. She hoped she would be able to reach an agreement to do chores or pay it back in small increments... It did not take long to realise that no agreement was to be reached, and if she did not get the speeder moving again this instant, she would soon meet her demise.

The man from the shed was flailing an axe. The lady draped in a towel screamed and tried to stop her husband from doing anything rash. This reaction did not build confidence. Ren tried to restart the engine.

The children in the window were giggling. The axe flew and there was a heavy clank when it hit the hull of the speeder, barely missing the sledge.

Other things started to fly: Sharp things, large things, heavy things and hard things. Some of them had better aim than others, and the aim improved as the man came closer.

"Oh, poop!" Ren yelped. It wouldn't have taken her all that many more minutes to wet herself from the fear had she not managed to get the speeder going.

"Stop throwing things at the poor child!" the lady screamed, but her husband was not hearing any of it.

"She hit my heirloom tree!"

A piece of firewood flew by Ren's ear as she forced the speeder upwards at an unnatural angle that would have resulted in a stall had the speeder relied on conventional aerodynamics and lift alone.

The ride was bumpy as the speeder was not in the best of shapes, but it moved fast enough to leave the crazed man behind.

"I'm so sorry!" Ren thought to yell when they'd reached a safe distance.

A ster and Celandine looked at Vincent expectantly.

"What?"

"Well, the way we see it, it was your negligence leaving the speeder unattended like that, which ultimately caused her to crash. So, in effect, you owe the Mossgraves compensation for the damage inflicted on their house." Celandine's expression was level. After a while, Vincent couldn't help but ask.

"How big a house are we talking about?"

"It's the Mossgraves, so a two-storey, large country house," Celandine estimated.

"You could call it a small manor," Aster added speculatively.

"And you went through—?" Vincent turned to Ren.

"Just the walls at either end," Ren noted. "And there was some damage to the floor."

"And ceiling," Aster added.

"And ceiling, yes," Ren agreed. The three of them looked at Vincent, still just as expectantly.

"And the tree?"

"It was an old fruit tree. I suppose you may want to add a little on top of what you think is appropriate. Old fruit trees don't usually produce very tasty fruit, but it had sentimental value for Mr Mossgrave," Celandine said.

"I see." Vincent was still in two minds whether he was actually expected to calculate a suitable sum, or if all this was an elaborate joke. People sometimes had such a strange sense of humour.

"And," Celandine continued, "you should consider writing a letter of apology. Mr Mossgrave is a fan of your columns. I feel that might go a long way to appease him."

"Ahha." Vincent looked down at his hands. Well, that would deplete what was left of his savings. He'd have to work hard to pay for everything, but the main thing was that Ren was all right.

"You didn't hurt yourself, did you?" he confirmed.

"No, I'm perfectly fine."

"That's a relief." Vincent gave Ren a reassuring smile and tried to do the same to Celandine and Aster, but the two women seemed even more peeved.

Couldn't they just be glad everything was reasonably all right? Vincent wasn't exactly in the mood to deal with this with his knee starting to throb and him feeling like he could have used something to eat and a long nap.

"You say it was an accident, but we can't have more accidents like this, you understand?" Aster sought to look Vincent in the eye. That she hadn't referred to him as 'luv' once during this conversation made him feel a strange lump building in his stomach.

"I would prefer that myself," he said, subdued. Even had she not slapped him, Vincent could easily tell how upset she was with him. Her disappointment and anger were overriding the difficult emotions Vincent was harbouring, and he was grateful that, because of her, he was fixated on regulating someone else's emotional state besides his own. "I'm sorry. I'll try to do better and not cause more trouble for you."

In the end, it didn't really matter that she hadn't told him about the things mentioned in the letters. She could hardly be getting much out of this relationship worth the trouble of keeping him from his mother, so maybe she was indeed protecting him from the goodness of her heart?

Then again, perhaps she was this upset because she'd gone through all the trouble just to be disappointed by the outcome and Vincent? He'd even gone and caused all this extra mess and worry with Ren because he couldn't take care of her like he was supposed to.

"It's good that you understand, but—" Aster sounded different. Her voice had been tight from anger before, but it was now a little softer and more worried. Maybe she was about to let him off the hook?

George had come to the door, holding a pair of wellies in his hands. He hadn't said anything, but he had a few of the letters in one hand, and it was that which had caught Aster's attention. She frowned.

The letters were moist, and the ink had smeared the fronts of the envelopes, but a clearer spot here and there revealed them for what they were. She could definitely tell. She turned back to Vincent, the softness gone in an instant.

"Where did you get these? Did you steal them?" She took a few steps forward to the foot of Vincent's bed. "Did you read them?"

What use was it to try to deny any of those statements? She probably wouldn't take his word for it. Vincent was beginning to feel just a tiny, *tiny* bit irate.

"No, I did not steal them, and no, I haven't had the chance to read more than the one that Jones sho—"

"Jones?" As expected, Aster looked at him as if he'd told an outrageous lie. "Who is Jones? The editor? I thought you ended your business with him over a month ago. You're not still using the poor boy as your personal footman to run your errands for you, are you?"

"Jones does whatever the hell he pleases and takes no orders from me, trust m—"

"Why are you bringing him into this, then? As the scapegoat?"

"Why do you bother asking me if you're not willing to hear a word I say?"

The other outrageous accusations aside, those weren't originally even his wellies, yet she'd drawn the conclusion he was to blame. Vincent strained to not let his exasperation get the better of him.

"Don't take me for a fool, Vincent! These were taken from my drawer a few days ago!"

"Yes, and I was clearly not here a few days ago, was I?"

Why was the bloody knee acting up right now, too? There was, indeed, always something.

"You might have been!"

George took Aster by the hand to calm her down. She glanced at him and looked confused. He shook his head. Vincent was infinitely grateful that the man had stepped up this time because he wasn't sure how much longer he could keep all of this frustration in.

"What do you mean?" Aster whispered to George. George whispered something back. Aster looked horrified.

This exchange prompted her to march over to the opposite side from where Ren was sitting to pull up the cover. A small grace that Ren could not see what Aster had made so obvious to everyone else in the room.

"Bloody hell, Aster!" Vincent snatched the cover to pull it back down.

Yes, he was wearing breeches, so it wasn't *all* brought to view, but he did not appreciate her gawking at what was left of his lower limbs. They were discoloured from the cold, not to mention badly bruised. Thankfully, the splint was hiding most of the knee.

"Holy Maury, Mother of the Sea and Weaver of the Waves!" Aster swore with conviction. Based on her reaction, George had been discreet about the extent of Vincent's injuries when he'd mentioned his suspicions about their cause.

"What is it?" Ren looked startled.

Vincent tried to assure her as calmly as he could that it was nothing she needed to worry about, while both Aster and Celandine were overreacting, holding their chests and hyperventilating in unison.

Celandine was the one to berate Vincent next. She exhausted her traditional selection, touching on important points such as 'how could you', 'you should take more care', and 'what is wrong with you', as if he'd done this deliberately to cause them grief.

With Ren in the room, Vincent could hardly divulge the full gruesome details of what had happened, even if he were to change his mind about sharing them with the two now hysterically yodelling cows. What the hell was wrong with them, anyway?

Vincent's stomach was cramping from hunger, and his knee felt like it was being stabbed repeatedly with a barbed skewer. He was tired and no longer feeling at all as fine as he had when he'd first come to. He couldn't even hear himself think in this noise.

"Shut the bloody fuck up!" he clutched the covers as he roared, unable to contain it any longer. "Can I not be assaulted for one whole day? Is that too much to ask? Can you not see I need some fucking space to breathe?!" He tried to restrain himself, but once he'd started, the words were begging to come out. "I've tried to do everything you ask of me, but nothing is ever good enough for the two of you! I know I'm not perfect, not even close.

I'm a raving, embarrassing lunatic demon making your lives miserable. Is that what you wanted to hear?"

Vincent screamed a wordless scream to vent his frustration and drown out the pain.

"And you deceitful, conniving *sow*!" He aimed his words at Aster. "You've been lying to me for years, and you have the gall to accuse me of theft with no proof? When did I do anything despicable enough to merit such distrust? I'm the one who should refuse to believe a word you say!" He turned to Celandine and snarled the rest of what he had to say. "Don't you *ever* dare to question my feelings or my intentions toward Ren, you *old hag!* I've done nothing but try to play by your rules and accept your judgement, above my own, so that I would do right by her and this family. Your worthless deities help me, if I hear so much as an errant thought from you, I will ram it so deep into your digestive system it's not coming out even if you eat a bucket of prunes every day for the following fortnight. Go ahead and *try me*!"

Vincent realised he'd propped himself up regardless of the knee, and the people he was yelling at were looking at him with the same sort of fear he'd seen on Jones's face when he'd lost his temper last.

His insides froze, and he glanced at Ren. She was looking at him, eyes large and tears streaming down her cheeks, petrified.

The anger still roiled and churned within him, but it was mixed with icy waves of terror and nausea. Much like when he'd fallen into the sea, he had difficulty breathing.

His mind was filled with the image of his father's distorted face.

CHAPTER 47

W ell, that was it then, Vincent thought. He'd gone and done the thing he'd never wanted to do but always feared he would. His body trembled.

Even if he couldn't have trusted any of them ever again, they had been better than not having anyone at all. Ren seemed frightened enough to possibly be traumatised. Aster and Celandine would never forgive him for what he'd just said. He'd been ostracised for much milder words and deeds before.

Celandine stormed out of the room without saying a word.

Vincent wondered if any amount of smiling, grovelling or apologising would smooth this over, but truth be told, he was too angry and hurt to even try. The only thing he was truly sorry for was forgetting Ren was there and scaring her.

"One thing I will not tolerate is abuse," Aster broke the silence.

"Go ahead and leave, then!" Vincent had a childish urge to throw something at her. Then he realised this was her house, and she meant he was no longer welcome. "Right. I'll go, I'll leave." He wrapped his covers around his waist and leaned on the bedside furniture to pull himself up to stand.

"If you want to leave, I won't stop you, but I will have you hear my piece first." Aster looked him straight in the eye, unwavering. She'd never had a physically commanding presence, yet she'd always had the enviable confidence to act as if she did. But even she sounded strained. "Yes, I kept things from you and yes, I also lied to you. You have a full right to be upset with me. But you also need to know that I never meant to hurt you. I kept it from you because no one should have to know something like that about their parent. Least of all you, after what you've been through. I don't mind being the villain if you need someone to blame." She took a hold of his hand as if to confirm something before she spoke again.

"I realise you're old enough to know the truth, and I will tell you everything I know if you want me to. All I ask is that you think it over carefully, because sometimes the truth is not something worth knowing."

The fact that she was even talking to him confused Vincent enough to almost miss the words she was saying. What was she doing? Was she acting nice to make him feel guilty? When was she going to strike?

"I don't trust you," Vincent said.

"I can see why you wouldn't. I'm sorry. I'll work on regaining your trust."

"What are you playing at? What is this?"

"I realise I may have been too hard on you." She seemed apologetic. "Have you calmed down a little? You were scaring Ren."

Ah, so that was the angle. She wanted him to calm down so she could rescue Ren from the raging monster. They were always scheming, aiming to take her away from him!

"I know I was bloody scaring Ren! Did you bring her here on purpose? To poke at me until I lost it, so you could prove me as unfit and take her—!"

This time Aster did take some steps back to retreat out of Vincent's range. She looked at him, worried, but for whatever reason, she no longer seemed angry.

"I'm fine!" Ren interrupted. She sounded nasal, and she was wiping her eyes, but she had reached over from the bed and taken Vincent by the hand without him realising.

Vincent floundered. What was this? Where was the rest of the abuse? The tremble had become more of a shake, and he realised he was frightened rather than enraged.

"Please don't be mad," Ren asked. Why was she asking? Was it because she was terrified he would do something to Aster?

"I'm not going to hurt her," Vincent said.

"I know." Ren looked like she was going to cry again.

"I'm really not— why are you crying? Is it because I scared you? I'm sorry..." Vincent glanced at Aster, now thoroughly confused.

"Do you feel any better?" Aster asked him.

"Why are you asking? Aren't you supposed to—?" He wasn't even sure what he was expecting any of them to do.

George was standing at the door, looking worried. Even Arthur was watching them behind his father. Was he here to help them throw Vincent out? What were they waiting for?

"Please sit down before you fall over." Aster helped him take a seat on the edge of the bed. "Do you still need to vent? Do you think you could try to calm down a little?"

What the hell was going on? Why was she so nice to him?

"Why...?" Vincent frowned.

"As I was about to say, I won't take abuse from you, and I can't pretend to be happy about some of your recent word choices, but I'm glad and relieved you made your feelings clear." Aster sat down next to him. "I truly am sorry. You're usually so calm and detached we assumed you didn't care or that we weren't getting through to you."

The irony that all the effort he'd put into not being a nuisance, complying without question and trying to put them at ease by belittling and hiding his issues had been misinterpreted as him not caring.

"You're sorry? You're not going to throw me out?" In what world did anyone ever bother to sort things out with him? Vincent felt like he'd entered a whole other dimension where things were operating backwards.

"I see this discussion was long overdue. You don't seriously think we would throw you out for expressing your anger and frustration, do you?" She made it sound like a silly rhetorical question. Vincent had a feeling he wasn't supposed to respond with a yes. "That's not why I haven't heard a peep out of you all this time, is it?"

When he still struggled to respond, Aster looked about as sad as Ren, who, by the sounds of it, was now sobbing behind their backs.

"Oh, luv." She leaned over to give him a tight hug. "I really shouldn't have slapped you. That was all my misunderstanding. I'm so sorry." She squeezed him and stroked his hair like she had when he had been little.

"What about Celandine?" Vincent swallowed. He'd called her an old hag. Surely that was inexcusable...

As if called, Celandine appeared at the door. George and Arthur stepped aside to give her way.

"Has he calmed down?" She set the tray she was carrying down on the bed. "You'd better not call me an old hag again. Is that clear?" She gave Vincent a stern look but then relented. "I figured rage like that could only be brought on by having too much to drink or not enough to eat, and because you've had neither food nor drink, I brought you some breakfast. It's best you eat before we discuss anything more."

"Really?" Where was the bubble? This had to be a dream. He'd died in the icy sea, and he'd been transported into this odd alternate universe where people were nice to him, even when he was behaving like an ass.

"Did you already tell him about the house, or what was that second outburst about?" Celandine asked Aster.

"No, not yet." Aster sighed. She looked tortured when she turned to Vincent. "We'll rebuild it for you in the spring. The cape seems a tad far for you and Ren..."

They were going to let him live with Ren? Would Ren still want that? Vincent turned around to see how Ren was faring. Not only had she stopped sobbing, she was smiling so brightly he felt compelled to shield his eyes.

"I can still move in? When?" She started doing frog-hops on the bed. The shaking was hurting Vincent's knee, but he couldn't bear to tell her to stop. Aster started feeding him the soup that Celandine had brought.

"We'll discuss it when the house is finished," Celandine replied in her usual manner.

"Will you be all right here? We had some unfinished business down-stairs." George nudged at Arthur and handed Aster the wellies he'd been holding all the while.

"Yes, go ahead, we've got this." Celandine ushered them away.

"I have to say, you do look surprisingly vicious when you're angry," Aster told Vincent and fed him a lightly buttered piece off of a steaming bread roll. "I didn't think you had something like that in you."

They were all treating him much the same way as before, if not better. What was this strange feeling? Relief? Something else? He'd seriously thought he'd lost them. That's what was supposed to happen, right?

"Are you feeling at all better, luv? Does the leg hurt?" Aster asked him, worried.

"Yes, but—" Never mind the leg. For some reason, his chest hurt.

"What is it? Do you need something?"

"I don't quite understand what just happened."

Aster fed him another spoonful of soup.

"We had a slightly heated family discussion, I suppose?" She looked at Celandine, who nodded.

"A what now?" Vincent tried to wrap his head around it, but his head was not the shape to wrap around anything, much less this combination of words. He'd been at the receiving end of plenty of Celandine's outbursts, but he hadn't realised he was allowed to take part.

"A family discussion. And we should resume this when you're feeling better because it seems like we have some important things to discuss. I heard you wanted a bigger garage for the new house." Aster stuffed his mouth with more bread.

"Should we really be encouraging that if Ren moves in?" Celandine shook her head, disapproving. "And do we even have the money?"

"We will find the money." Aster sounded determined. "We really didn't mean to burn the whole house. I asked Edward to destroy the files, so even if it was an accident, I feel just as responsible. I hope the bigger garage makes it a little easier for you to forgive me."

Vincent was busy chewing on the bread, which was good, because he had an urge to say something not particularly nice to Aster about her involvement. By the time he was done with the bread, he'd given up on the anger.

"Which files? The ones from Mr Benton or the matron...?" he asked, instead.

"Both. You were obsessing over them last year, and it seemed like you might relapse. I felt bad for both you and Ren. James suggested we steal them, but I had the stupid idea of burning them instead, so you'd see they were destroyed. I thought if we did that, you might not go senseless looking for them, thinking you'd misplaced them. It's so hard for me to see you in that state but that is no excuse. I'm sorry." Aster sounded pained. "We were thinking of pinning it on one of Arthur's boys if you started a manhunt for the culprit. They were surprisingly eager to help, but we couldn't blame them for burning down the entire house." She sighed and shook her head, visibly ashamed.

"Why didn't you just talk to me about it? Am I really that unreliable?"

"I'm so sorry. The truth is, I keep thinking you're my little boy, my tiny, sweet Vincent. It's difficult to remember you're all grown up sometimes." Aster raised her hand the way she did when she would pinch his cheek but hesitated and patted his shoulder instead.

"I still don't think we should enlarge the garage," Celandine muttered. "That speeder breeds nothing but trouble."

"No, it doesn't!" It was Ren's turn to interject.

"Shush, child. It's not right for a girl—"

"What's not right for a girl? Why's it so bad if she's genuinely interested?" Vincent wasn't sure how far he could push Celandine, but he'd called her an old hag, and she was still there. Perhaps it was time to be brave and test the waters. "Have you seen her at it?"

"No, but—"

"I'm her guardian, am I not?"

She nodded.

"Then please shut up." Vincent maintained a level tone. Celandine looked about to protest, but Aster raised her hand to stop her.

"Let it go. We'll build the size of a garage they need, and that's that."

"Thank you!" Ren jumped to hug Aster and then even Celandine.

Vincent hadn't realised it would mean that much to her. Something about this was making that strange feeling in his chest worse. Was he having a heart attack, or had he sprained some obscure muscle?

When it was Vincent's turn to be hugged, Ren stopped short and hesitated.

"Can I hug you?" She sounded unexpectedly tense and wary. Vincent frowned.

She'd already hugged him when they'd arrived, so why was she asking for permission now? Was she afraid of him even when he was no longer actively erupting?

"Of course you can," he tried to put her mind at ease.

"Does it hurt?" She knelt next to him on the bed.

She'd not seen the injuries but must have inferred a few things from the sisters' colourful reactions. Could this, then, be worried curiosity rather than fear?

"Can I see?" Ren asked.

"Most certainly not!" Celandine forbade her.

Vincent gave Celandine a brief glare. He was never going to learn to trust his instincts if she kept butting in.

"It looks pretty bad. And yes, it does hurt, a lot. I'll let you look if you think it will make you feel better. I know your imagination, and I have a feeling you might be thinking it's worse than it is," he told Ren. She nodded.

"Are you ready?" Vincent confirmed before lifting the covers.

Ren took a moment to prepare herself and gave a signal that she was ready. She let out a gasp at the sight, but gave Vincent a smug grin only a moment later.

"They're both still there," she pointed out.

"Yes, the other one might not work very well, and I may need some help for a while, but you saw me stand up. I'm sure it'll improve with time."

"You were right. I thought it was worse." She eyed the ladies, who had raised such a ludicrous hullabaloo over it. Then she gave Vincent the gentlest of hugs and whispered in his ear, "Just so you know, I didn't cry because I was scared. I cried because you looked like you were in so much pain when you were screaming. I wanted to help but didn't know how. I'm sorry. I'm really very happy you're home safe, and I hope you feel better soon."

That was about as much as Vincent's heart could handle, so he squeezed her back and started to sob.

CHAPTER 48

Vincent had considered letting Jones off the hook again simply because he felt partially responsible for how things had escalated. The injuries were too grave to dismiss, and ultimately the risk that the young man would end up doing something equally stupid to someone else if no one intervened weighed more than any mercy Vincent decided to show.

The Brambles reported the matter to the police the day after Vincent was fished out of the sea. As expected, the town constable called Vincent and Ren in for questioning and put out posters and an arrest warrant for Jones.

It seemed the earth had swallowed the man.

Vincent had thought recounting his experience was hard, but having to listen to Ren's side of it was in some ways much harder. He didn't care so much about his own injuries. Those would heal with time, or not, but he'd deal with them the way he always did. It was much more difficult to grapple with his failure to protect Ren, and to guide her through the aftermath.

"I would like to see this cabin for myself, if that's possible," the constable said.

"I'll show it to you!" Ren offered. "I can come, right?" she asked Vincent.

"I don't know..." The thought of leading the constable to inspect the cabin from top to bottom made Vincent uneasy. Taking Ren along when it sounded like Jones might have trashed the place sounded at least equally disturbing. Who knew what they might find?

"I want them to catch the man that did this to you. I'll make sure they don't miss anything!"

"The good Constable Winkley is not incompetent, Ren. I'm sure, having heard your excellent testimony, he and his assistant will find everything there is to find," Vincent tried to remind her.

"I want to make sure." Ren stood her ground.

Vincent was tempted to call on Celandine to forbid her, but he couldn't keep relying on her authority every time Ren was being stubborn. After thinking it over, Vincent decided to let Ren come on the condition that she was to enter last, if at all, after they had checked that nothing too disturbing had been left behind.

V incent, Ren, the constable and his assistant headed out to the cape the following day. When they arrived, on the outside everything appeared normal.

Vincent felt ill.

Whatever proof they found once they entered was no doubt going to be something he would have preferred to bury somewhere deep below the earth's crust. He especially avoided drawing any attention to the cellar at the back.

Ren waited across the yard while Vincent, the constable and his assistant entered the cabin.

The door had been left open, so the wind had come in for a rambunctious visit through the main room and out a kitchen window. Not counting a few pieces of debris here and there, nothing major seemed amiss. There were no signs of struggle or suspicious stains waiting to be discovered and examined. Either Jones had cleaned everything up, or none of it had happened.

Vincent watched the constable climb into the attic. Considering how little there was to see on the main floor, Vincent didn't think there was going to be much up there.

He could have, of course, directed the men to the cellar at the back, but either Jones had cleaned that up, or it was still soiled and disgusting. Either way, Vincent was not keen to revisit, and excrement alone would not make for compelling evidence.

Ren was called in, and she explained what she'd seen and where. Vincent sat down on the bed in the bedroom.

This seemed like a wasted effort. There wasn't much of a case without the evidence.

"I don't understand how it can be like this. He was throwing stuff at me. There was a vase... At least a vase and a teacup." Ren sounded upset. Jones must have spent a great deal of time getting the place this spotless. Unless this was a dream. Vincent leaned back and watched the ceiling become curved and obscure. Was it getting worse because he was tired? But how could he be tired? Hadn't he slept through most of yesterday?

"Vincent, I swear I saw something fall through the crack in the door when I was leaving. Maybe if we can find it, we can prove that man was here," Ren spoke from the door.

"All right, I hope you find it." The ceiling turned back to normal. Vincent had a vague memory of a finger rolling back and forth on the deck of George's boat, but whether that had been real or not, he couldn't say.

"You look tired. Maybe you should take a nap while they're still looking?" Ren suggested.

It was probably a good idea, but now that the ceiling was back to normal, Vincent didn't feel like risking it.

A week later, the newspaper reported that an unidentified body had washed ashore near the docks. It had been beaten beyond recognition between the waves and the rocks, but some effort was made to check the list of missing persons to determine who the deceased might have been.

The constable invited Vincent to see whether he could identify the body as Jones's. It was a gruesome sight, with not much left of the face, but it did seem to belong to a man of similar build and stature as the missing editor.

Perhaps most telling was the familiar pinky finger dangling from the side of his hand by a piece of frayed thread.

CHAPTER 49

I ris saw her father come in, face dark as a tar pit. He said not a word but rushed past her, ignoring her efforts to inquire about his mood. He was difficult to deal with, even on a good day, but she loved him regardless. If he was left to simmer by himself for a while, he'd be back to normal the following day.

Iris had a few guesses on what had happened, but she wanted to know more. She took care of her chores downstairs, let everyone know she was 'going to bed' and left her bedroom shortly after.

Vincent had not checked in to the small bed-and-breakfast at the other end of town and there weren't many other options. Perhaps her father had already chased him away? She hoped not.

She couldn't understand why he disliked Vincent so much, but whatever the reason, he was a stubborn man and would not admit to any errors in his judgement. It seemed likely he'd once made a misinformed decision about Vincent and stuck to it blindly.

Iris was not a stranger to late night escapades around town. She knew where to look, but she couldn't for the life of her locate Vincent. After searching for a few hours, she was making her way back home when she saw Vincent exit the seedy pub.

The poor man was so juiced he could barely stay upright. Damn those ruffian bastards with their overindulgent ways, Iris thought. They'd probably sucked him into their antics without leaving him much choice in the matter.

Iris knew of this because she'd once made the mistake of going there herself, despite being much too young to have any business going. It had landed her in some frightful trouble with her father, and she wouldn't dare to ever do it again.

She trailed after Vincent to see where he was going. He seemed to be heading towards a mechanical contraption at the edge of the town.

She'd read about the speeder, but she'd never seen a picture of it published anywhere.

It looked quite... interesting. A bit like what might come out of a person's bottom. Yes, the design could have been more attractive, but the size was commendable. For a moment, she tried to imagine the size of the giant trying to pass that thing.

She'd heard it was capable of flight, but it most certainly did not look the part. Whatever its method of propelling itself forward, Iris was happy to see that Vincent did not intend to ride it now that he could scarcely differentiate his left foot from the right. He'd fallen flat on his behind with a bit of a groan and some laughter and lay there in a drunken daze.

Um, oh dear, Mr Vincent, I wonder if you need help, she thought.

"Oh, hi," Vincent said, when he noticed her there.

He sounded and smelled like he'd emptied a barrel of the worst whiskey Dritsby could offer, but at least he was looking in the right direction. Iris was surprised and impressed to be caught red-handed but waved at him.

He looked silly. If she ignored the silliness, he also looked distinctly familiar.

She hadn't thought it more than a curious coincidence until the two of them had stood right next to one another. Vincent looked exactly like her father. A bit more gaunt around the cheeks and slightly taller, but other than that, very much alike. If he was not directly related, Iris doubted whether she was either.

She held her hand up to compare with his and they were similar, though not identical. His was much bigger and more calloused.

"You're soused to the gills, aren't you?" she commented on the state of him. He'd sat there in silence and watched her do her comparison, as if it were an everyday occurrence. She couldn't help but be amused.

"Yesss... I s-suppose. It's—" A gulp or a hiccup interrupted him there. "Not... I don't—"

The following word was probably 'usually', but it was difficult to discern because he tried to speak quickly when he had zero capacity to do so, and he abruptly gave up as if satisfied with his output.

It took Iris a while to interpret what his bumbling might mean, but she eventually figured out he wanted her to sit down next to him.

When she hadn't immediately understood him, he'd briefly tensed up like an animal ready to jump. Not that he was in a condition to do any jumping, but Iris made a point to put him back at ease, so he wouldn't be daft enough to try.

"It's all right. Don't worry about it." She smiled and sat down. "Did something happen? Did my father say something awful to you? He can be pretty rude sometimes." Iris hoped Vincent wasn't too upset over it.

Because the two of them did not know each other very well, Vincent wouldn't be able to read her father like she could. It wasn't difficult to imagine this leading to some severe misunderstandings.

"No, don' worry 'bout t'hat. I'm fine." He waved his hand dismissively. He was precious, trying to spare her feelings, all the while looking about as convincing as a thrashing tit in a rum barrel.

"I didn't know he disliked you that much. I suspected, but I didn't expect anything this bad. He's stubborn." She'd seen how her father had looked at the newspaper articles. It hadn't made sense to her then, and it made about as little sense now. Vincent was currently way past tiddled, and understandably not at his best, but he'd only ever been kind and polite to her. "You don't have to sleep out here because of him. I can get you in through the back."

"Thanks." He straightened himself and took a deep breath in an evident effort to clear his head. It wasn't happening. "But m-haybe it'sh besht I don't." He leaned back.

Well, it was probably indeed for the best. It would have taken a miracle to get Vincent all the way over to the inn, with her not being of much use to him.

"Well, I'll keep you company for a while then, if it's all right with you?" She didn't think she would get such an opportunity again.

"Won't you be miss'd? Tis not exactly t' rhight time to be out hhere abouts."

"It's all right. They think I'm asleep. And it's not far from here. You don't mind?"

"Why whould I—?"

"You probably get pushy fans trying to talk to you all the time, so I thought maybe you wanted some time to yourself."

"Ish that wh-hathish is?" His reply was a bit lagged, but Iris could tell what he was aiming for.

"Well, not exactly." She could hardly blurt out that she wanted to get to know him because she suspected they were related, could she? The thought of having Vincent as her big brother was like expecting the best Midwinter gift imaginable. She just wasn't sure she'd been nice enough to deserve it yet.

Obviously, he wasn't much of a drinker. She thought she probably could have drunk him under the table with no trouble. But she had no other siblings, and she'd always dreamt of having at least an older brother to teach her things.

"Maybe a little, but you're Vincent," she said, hoping it sufficed. "And I was a bit worried. The locals can be a bit rough with newcomers."

"They were cert'nly very generoush." Vincent chuckled. His laughter was pleasantly low. It reminded Iris of her father.

"So, if I find out about the workhouse thing tomorrow, where can I get in touch with you?"

"Ohhh, that... rhm, I dun need thhat ne'more."

"Really? Why not? I can get you the information, it's no trouble. It won't take more than a day or two!" Iris would have loved for him to stay for at least a day or two. She hated the thought of never seeing him again.

"No thanks, t's ahlright. I'll be leaving t'morrow. Th—ink I got what I came for."

"That's a shame."

"How so?" Vincent frowned. Then he slapped himself while stretching an arm.

"I was looking forward to seeing you again." Iris hoped her smile did not look too crooked as she fought not to laugh. When Vincent smiled back, she thought she would burst.

"Meh-be I'll come back smtime," Vincent said, now looking up at the sky, eyes droopy and yawning wide.

"That would be nice." She watched him stretch again—this time with less violence—and lean back drowsily to watch the stars.

Hmm, she wondered. Would it be prudent to ask him something more before he passed out? To keep him chatting.

She patted him on the shoulder to gain his attention.

"Sshure, whynt," he mumbled.

"People probably ask you all the time, but could you tell me a story?"

She watched him consider it. He seemed weighing his options. He looked confused.

"A shtory?"

"Yeah, like something... something you haven't told anyone else." Something a big brother would tell his little sister in confidence, something like that, she thought.

"Like a shecret shtory?"

"Yes, something like that."

"Can I trusht you?" He gave her what was probably supposed to be a stern look. It was more like his thick eyebrows having a squirmy fit.

"No, I might tell my mother." Iris laughed. She would probably tell her mother everything. She always did.

"Anyone else?" Vincent asked.

Iris thought about it. No. She had no reason to.

"'L'right. Fhair enough." Vincent looked to be in a good mood despite having difficulty pronouncing most of his consonants. "What short of a shtory 'd you like?"

There was so much to ask, so much she wanted to know. But first and foremost...

"Well, you never talk about your family in your articles," she tried. It seemed worth a shot.

"Hmmmwell, I h-have a mother, who ish kind, but can shumtimes be a bit overbearin' and she lies to me."

"Oh? That's not nice."

"She's jus' tryin' to protect me, I think. I'm ah little unshtable. Is pro'ly a good thing." He didn't seem too bothered by it. "And I have a father who doesn't talk very m—uch, though smtimes I think he sh'd, and he fishes—c, a lot, to get out of the house."

"I'm sorry..."

"No, no, he takesh me with him, to eshcape my mom and aunt." Vincent laughed, evidently not bothered by it. "Hmm, and they have a rheal son they replaced me with, buth tha's fiiineeee, and an aunt—"

"They replaced you with another son?" That sounded horrible.

"I saysh is fiiiine. He's much better than me, anyway. Wh—c, where was I? Oh, rhight! My aunt. She's pushy but usuawly she's fair, but she keepsh buttin' into my business, an' she's reeeallly haaard to please! And then I have... a little, uhm, brother, I s'pose."

"Besides the real son they replaced you with?"

"Yeah, he's a hhalf-brother."

"Ooh, what's he like?" She had a feeling she'd hit the jackpot. "Are you close?"

"He's a bit small, like a lil dog baby..." Vincent laughed again. That he was describing what he saw in front of his face would have been obvious to the blind. Substituting the word 'sister' with 'brother' was not going to fool anyone. "And he's, mmm, very hap-py, conshiderate an' kind," he said. She blushed.

"I'd like to meet him," she said.

"I bet you'd like him. He's—c, uh, like you."

"Really? In what way?"

"Well, I'd say, as far as— tell, the difference is that he's a he, and you're presew-mably a girl, with silly earrings."

His response made Iris snort.

"How rude!" Presumably? The nerve! "But I'm going to forgive you for that because you are drunk, and you don't know what you're talking about."

"All right, thank you." Vincent was slurring a little less when he made an effort, but his laughter was bubbly, and his eyes were wandering aimlessly. He seemed to be thinking about something.

"Anything else you could tell me? Does he travel with you? Do you have pets?"

What she wouldn't have given to travel with Vincent. Her father would never let her, but it didn't hurt to dream.

"No, he shtays at home. And no, we don't have pets. But, uh, there 're a many, lots, of cats in the neighbourhood. Cats, seemmm nice and fluffy. They're ah, you know, independent-like."

"Oh, like you? The stray cats, I mean."

"Hmmmmaybe yes. I like—c it! Um, thanks for tellin' me." Vincent seemed pleased by this comparison. Pleased enough to launch into a sluggish, sporadic belly laugh. Iris couldn't help but smile at him for being such a dense yet lovable idiot.

"Well, I'm certainly glad to have met you, Vincent. You are a very nice man, although you can't seem to hold your liquor any better than a piss-ant would in a vodka bottle. But I'll still read your stories as soon as they come out, don't worry." She grinned.

"Twas nice to meet you too, Rhis. D'you like me to write you sometime? Or send you something—"

"What, really? You'd do that? That would be wonderful!" It would've been sad to lose touch. "Can you give me an address so I can write to you? Or would that be too troublesome? I could send you anything I find about the workhouse too, in case you change your mind and want to know. Do you have an address?"

"No, no, thas fine. I have a summer home, is on an islan'. It'll probably take a bit, but I'll get them if you send them there." As he was putting together this sentence, he lost his trail of thought a couple of times, but Iris was getting used to the pattern and had less trouble deciphering. "Have you—c a pen and paper, maybe?" he asked.

"Ah, no. But if you whisper it to me, I'll definitely remember."

Vincent leaned closer to whisper it to her and by a stroke of luck didn't do a half-bad job of it. As soon as he was done, he bobbed with such an intense hiccup, he swayed for a moment trying to recover.

"Great. Thanks!" Iris had to hurry to look away so as not to laugh at him.

"Sorry this washn't a proper... conversh—ation. I'm a bit, mud-dled." At a side glance Iris could tell he was looking at his fingers, embarrassed. She had to give him points for gallantly trying.

"No, you're fine. Don't worry about it," she tried to dispel his fears. This was already more than she could've asked for. Possibly even better since he was much less guarded and relaxed than had he been sober.

"All rhight. I won't then." He looked up again and he couldn't have smiled any wider. "I'm allowed t' be h-happy, right?"

"Yes, of course you are."

"Thas what I thought! An— An, and—" He seemed to be struggling with the words, not just because he was slurring, but because of the subject matter. "And I can be myself, and do it for myself, and it doesn't mean sumthin bad is gonna hap'n jus' 'cause."

The effort he was putting in was *tangible.* He was flailing his hands every which way as he tried to explain it. Iris found herself relating to him somewhat, but it was difficult to take him seriously when he looked so comical.

"Shouldn't waste time trying to be who I'm not, right? Ahm sorry, thish doesn't make much sense to you, doesh it?" Vincent had probably meant to look at Iris, but this time he missed the mark by about a half a metre. He made a correction and stared at her for a moment. "You look different," he said.

"What? How so?" Iris looked at herself. She thought she looked the same as she always did.

"Never mind, I thought... Ah, it doesn't matter. I'm happy, so I'll bloody well be—c, happy." He heaved a significantly elongated sigh, and his face was redder than a red turnip, but he definitely looked happy.

Iris couldn't hold it in anymore. She let out a giggle and couldn't stop until her tummy hurt.

A s soon as most of the snow had melted in early March, some of the islanders including the Steadfasts, the Brambles and the Tweeds re-erected Vincent's cottage in one big push of bustle. They finished the frame, the roof, the cladding, and the windows and doors in less than two weeks and furnished it with whatever extra furniture everyone had available to donate.

The garage had no walls yet, but it had a roof on top of its support pillars, so it would provide shelter from the spring rains when they were working on the speeder. Ren stood there scrubbing the last of the soot off of the speeder's fuselage. She took notice of Vincent out in the backyard, thanking everyone as they were leaving on the last day of work. There were some individual tasks left people had offered to help him with, but the cottage was now livable.

After one last round of inspections, Aunt Celandine came out of the house through what would be the door to the garage. She, Aunt Aster, Uncle George, and Arthur and his wife and kids were the last ones still here. It was them and, of course, Vincent and Ren herself.

"It is satisfactory, but how do you feel? Are you tired?" Aunt Celandine asked Vincent.

"I'm fine," Vincent replied as per his usual habit. She waited patiently for a moment until he added, "Yes, I'm tired and the knee hurts, but it's manageable."

She nodded.

"I don't mind taking Ren with me if you need some rest," she said. Ren turned to glare at her.

"Thanks for the offer, but we're fine." Vincent flashed Ren a smile and ushered Aunt Celandine out of the garage. That was a relief.

They'd already promised Ren she could stay as soon as the cottage was livable, and she wasn't about to sit back and accept another excuse to not let her. Thankfully, Vincent had been a lot more assertive lately, so Aunt Celandine hadn't managed to have her way more than maybe once or twice, and even then after lengthy negotiations.

Vincent went to see everyone off at the front of the house. They'd said their parting words to Ren, but she was busy washing the speeder and didn't pay much attention. By the time she was finished, they had all left, except of course Vincent, who limped out of the house sometime after four to tell her it was time to eat.

"What's for dinner?"

"Meatballs, sauce, mashed potatoes with cream, and lingonberry preserve."

"Really?" Ren dropped the wash rag and rushed inside to wash her hands. Mr Swifty turned up from one of his excursions and followed her to the table in the main room.

"Oh, I found this yesterday when we were fixing the postbox with Edward." Ren remembered the postcard they'd fished from the back of the postbox. She showed it to Vincent, who was setting up a plate in front of her.

"Who's it from?"

"I don't know. I think it's written in some sort of secret code." She showed him the back. Vincent took a look at it and chuckled.

"No, I think that's just his handwriting."

"Wow, it's worse than mine..." Ren had to stare at this miracle for a moment.

"He can write neatly when he wants to." Vincent gave her a meaningful look. "Maybe he's learning to write with his left hand." He looked odd for a moment.

"What is it?"

Vincent turned aside and sneezed into the crook of his arm. His expression was miserable when he turned around.

"You've been working hard…" Ren said gently.

Vincent had been doing remarkably well with his recovery since he'd been back from the cape, but perhaps he was now well enough for a bit of a spring cold? He grabbed his own plate from the counter and hobbled back to the table.

"Where did we put the basket we got from Mrs Beansbury?" he asked.

Mrs Beansbury had given them a basket of fruit and berry preserves, cake and home-made juice when they'd gone over to her house to reimburse her for a suitcase. She'd played it down and said she was more than happy to help to be included in Vincent's next exciting adventure story. Ren could have sworn he'd cringed, even if he'd smiled and told her to look forward to it. He hadn't even shared the details with Ren yet, so it didn't seem likely he'd want to share it with the world.

The basket was under the table next to Ren. It was a little heavy, but she lifted it onto the table, and Vincent picked out the lingonberry preserve.

"If I do get sick, are you sure you don't want to head back to Aunt Celandine's tomorrow?" Vincent asked.

"Oh, hell no!" Ren exclaimed and dropped her fork to cover her mouth. "I mean, she's nice and all…"

"I might not be able to cook for you properly." Vincent scooped a generous heap of the preserve onto her plate.

"I can cook. Leave it to me." Ren mixed some of the preserve with the creamy sauce, gathered up a huge forkful of everything and shoved it into her mouth.

"Is it any good?" Vincent asked. Mouth full, Ren nodded to him vigorously, but he still looked worried. "What if you catch the same bug?"

"Don't worry. It's not as bad for me as it is for you."

"I might start—"

"I've seen you ill before. I'm telling you not to worry." Ren gulfed down another load. "Besides, I want us to work on the speeder as soon as you feel better." She was more interested than ever to understand how it worked and how to make it even better.

"Sometimes I wonder if you're real at all." Vincent chuckled.

"What do you mean? I'm real, I'm here. Are you already getting a fever?" Ren reached over the table to test his forehead.

"Not yet, right?" Vincent confirmed. "I just didn't think I'd be this lucky."

"Oh." Ren blushed. "I didn't think I'd be this lucky either."

Done with her dinner, Ren offered to do the dishes, so Vincent wouldn't have to stand on his busted knee. Aunt Aster had said he wasn't supposed to be up and about when it was still healing, but he'd had a lot to do. He'd be forced to rest now if he was coming down with a cold. Maybe this was his body telling him to slow down.

Ren sorted the dishes, added some more logs into the fire in the fireplace and made Vincent some tea. She was tired from scrubbing the speeder all day, so that was the extent of helpfulness she was willing to offer today. It was already getting dark outside.

While Ren had been busy with the dishes and the tea, Vincent had changed into his pyjamas and made himself more comfortable at the table. There were thick woolly socks and slippers on his feet and a puffy scarf around his neck. He'd brought a blanket with him from the bedroom, and he was holding onto a corner of it, tightly, pulling it closer.

The fingers of the other hand were only barely visible as he flicked the pages of the newspaper he was reading, and they disappeared back under the blanket after each flick. His cheeks and nose were red, and he looked like the very image of someone about to sport the common cold.

That was quick, Ren thought. He must have been keeping it in somehow while everyone else was here. She'd also expected him to make more of a fuss and try to keep himself cool, like he'd done before. His outfit seemed like a marked improvement from the usual flimsy things he would wear for the occasion.

She set the cup of tea, steaming hot, next to him. He breathed over it and started to roll the spoon to mix in some honey. A sweet lemony scent wafted from the tea.

Vincent sneezed into the blanket. Then he lifted his heavy gaze from the paper to look at the postcard Ren had left on the table.

"This seems to be almost a year old." His voice was already about a pitch lower than usual. "He must think I'm a jerk for not responding."

He waved the card in the air, and it moved considerably more than the fingers that held it. It dropped onto the table when Vincent's hand retreated into the folds of the blanket, like the head of a turtle into its shell—that is to say, it didn't go all the way in, though he was trying.

Eventually, Vincent crouched down and jiggled the covers so that he was all in. He seemed to want to draw his feet in, also, to perch on his seat, but his knee was braced so he couldn't.

Ren reached for the stack of blankets that Aunt Celandine had left, no doubt knowing they would be handy for this exact situation. An extra blanket over the legs seemed to do the trick, and Vincent relaxed.

"Was it something important? The card, I mean," Ren asked, feigning nonchalance.

"It is and it isn't." Vincent flipped it around clumsily by poking it with a corner of his blanket.

"How are you feeling? Do you need something?"

He wasn't talking to the cat yet, but it seemed like only a matter of time. Not that she minded. She wished she could have known what Mr Swifty was saying, too.

"I'm not talking to the cat, yet, but the cat is talking to me."

"**G**reat. Now, hand me some of that meat you have in store for tomorrow. I like how it makes a satisfying popping sound when I chew on it. Nice and raw. And tasty." Mr Swifty pawed at him.

Vincent had set aside a dash of cream when he'd been cooking, so he pushed the saucer closer to the cat. Mr Swifty sniffed at it, gave Vincent a dramatic look and meowed, "Fine. I guess I'll make do with this for now."

"What did he say?" Ren asked.

"He wants the beef shanks for tomorrow's stew, but I'm not sure I'm up for preparing that right now."

Vincent was not quite used to Ren being so calm and accepting of his moments of lunacy. He'd been slowly testing the waters with the people around him, learning to trust them more, but he recognised it would take a while before he was ready to open up.

"I'm a little tired, but maybe we can do it together," Ren suggested. She was growing up to be such a kind helper, Vincent felt a little bad. Hopefully she'd also find her courage to be more challenging once things settled down.

"I'll cut the vegetables and prepare the meat if you bring them to me. We can cook it overnight on the fire."

"I can cut the carrots."

"As you wish, but watch your fingers. I'd rather not have any unnecessary excitement for tonight."

"Me neither." Ren handed him a knife and the cutting board and fetched the pot, meat and vegetables.

Vincent prepared the meat for the pot under Mr Swifty's unfaltering gaze. When he was done, he gathered a few choice offcuts onto Mr Swifty's saucer. The cat's eyes seemed about to plop out of their sockets as he chewed on his treats blissfully.

Before Vincent turned his attention to the onions, he remembered his tea and took a sip. It had passed 'tepid' and moved on to 'dead cold and ready for burial'. He resuscitated it with more honey and watched the spoon roll around in the cool liquid as he mixed it in.

Something didn't seem right, but he still couldn't put his finger on it even after so many years.

"I wonder why I'm like this." An edge of something loomed overhead, even though he was supposed to be awake.

"Like this?"

"Broken. Not in my right mind. Insane."

"Not insane."

"I am," Vincent said to himself. "I know I say it a lot, but I say it so no one else can say it first. Maybe it's time I admit it. I'm insane, and I can't be fixed."

"Maybe we can do it together."

"No, there is no cure for this." Vincent drew a deep breath and slumped on the table. "And besides, how would you fix it? You're not really here."

It was so difficult to tell what was real sometimes. Who was he even speaking to? Was there anyone there at all besides the bubble and the hands?

The cat looked at him in silence. It then leapt off the table and disappeared out the door.

Maybe if he'd had the courage to trust somebody, things would be different. He'd be different. Maybe if he had tried harder and not shielded himself from the pain of rejection, he wouldn't have ended up so alone.

He'd never be able to fix himself, no matter how hard he tried. It was never going to get any better. No one would care to check up on him, no one would rescue him when he was in trouble. He'd only ever run away or scared people off.

He stared at the postcard on the table. The return addresses always matched the sender. All he had was what was inside of him, and it would never be enough to fill the void. He could pick himself up for a while, but he'd still be broken and alone in the end.

He drank his cold tea and stared at the curve of the wall in front of him. Maybe if he stayed this way, it would eventually all go away.

Vincent got tired looking at the wall, so he looked down instead. In the picture of the postcard lying on the table, he noticed a drawn squiggly figure of a familiar-looking boy standing on a hill. He was smiling.

Vincent frowned. He turned the card around to read it.

> Sometimes the best things come to me in my dreams. Sometimes I have to go to them. I'll be busy for a while, because I'm moving to Schadesborough. You should take that turd of a speeder of yours and come see me sometime. Here's the address.

Vincent was startled by someone shaking his shoulder.

"Don't fall asleep there. I've cut the carrots. Should I cut the onions, too?"

"Huh?" Vincent raised his head. He felt awful. His face was all covered in goo, maybe tears? And snot, definitely snot.

"Eww, that's gross." Ren offered him a handkerchief. "Look, I can finish this off if you'd like to go to bed."

"No, I'll do it." He tried to pull himself together.

"Good, because I don't really want to cut the onions," Ren said briskly. "Don't you just hate how it stings?"

"It's not that bad." Vincent started cutting. "It's not as awful as the dream I had just now. I was asleep, wasn't I?"

He'd had a few of these strange nightmares before, but since the ordeal, they seemed to have become almost impossible to tell apart from reality. Maybe he was just more tired than usual and it would get better after a while?

"Yes, you seemed to be out for a bit before I noticed."

"Next time, wake me up right away."

"Will do," Ren promised.

"Oh, it does sting a bit..."

At least something was making his eyes water like a pair of faucets. He opted for larger cubes to be done with it quicker. Ren offered him a fresh handkerchief.

"Are you all right?" Mr Swifty had finished cleaning himself and poked Vincent with his wet nose.

"Yes." Vincent realised his teacup had been refilled with hot tea during his nap. "Couldn't be better."

"Thanks for the meat, brother."

"Brother? What, did I get a promotion?"

"Sure. I don't really need a henchman and you've been pulling your weight."

"What's he saying?" Ren asked.

"He's promoted me from a henchman to a brother."

What a strange but hopefully auspicious turn of events. Vincent smiled.

"Well, if he's Mr Swifty and you're his brother, does that make you Mr Vincent Swifty?" Ren asked with a bit of an unruly grin. Before Vincent could object, she added, "And if so, can I be Ren Swifty?"

How was he to say no when she looked so excited about it?

Swifty sounded better than taking any of their parents' surnames, but maybe the original Mr Swifty would disapprove.

"What do you think, brother?" Vincent asked the cat.

"I don't particularly care. It's just a name," Mr Swifty said, but something about his tone and expression hinted that he was pleased.

"That's a yes, right?" Ren confirmed. "We can be a real family together, with a surname and everything!"

She jumped up and down until she was struck by another one of her thoughts, and she addressed Mr Swifty with utmost urgency, "We can't keep calling you mister if you're family, right? What's your first name?" She turned to Vincent for an answer.

"Don't look at me, I don't know." Vincent shrugged. It had never occurred to him that Mr Swifty could have another name besides Mr Swifty.

Mr Swifty acted shifty for a moment, as if he was looking for an escape route. Then he seemed to accept his fate.

"If you give me a strip of bacon, I'll tell you, but you are never to tell a soul, do you understand?"

"Quickly, Ren. Give him a strip of bacon!" Vincent gestured at the pantry. Ren rushed to get it.

When the goods had been delivered, Mr Swifty taste-tested them to be sure they were worthy, before making his grand reveal.

"Not a soul," the cat repeated, "or I will disown you."

"Understood. Now, spill the beans." Vincent found himself surprisingly invested.

"Mrs Tweed calls me Seymeowr."

Glossary

May contain spoilers!

Butler, the senior male servant of the house.

Crook of the Ear, a region named after its location on the cat-shaped continent of Furuyan.

Footman, a male servant.

Forsooth, a pretentious word the author wanted to use to sound smart.

Fox's fires, a colloquial name for an aurora (aka polar lights).

Furuyan, the name of the continent where this story takes place.

Guardian, a widely worshipped deity on Furuyan, second only to the god of another monotheist religion similar to Christianity.

Hall boy, a young male servant of lowest rank.

Head maid, a maid working under the housekeeper, in charge of the other maids.

Housekeeper, the senior female servant of the house.

Inglenook, a large recess for a fireplace or a wood stove.

Làirig Áir, (Hill Pass of Hardship) a place at the southern end of the Furuyan continent.

Maury, (Holy Maury, Mother of the Sea and Weaver of the Waves) the deity most revered by the fisher communities in the Arctic regions of Furuyan.

Midwinter, a time of celebration during the winter solstice.

Reverse-thrust, the temporary reversal of an aircraft engine's thrust to provide deceleration.

Scullery maid, the female counterpart of a hall boy. An assistant to the kitchen maid.

Sluice room, a room dedicated for cleaning the chamber pots and disposing of human waste.

Whitskersey, the Island of the White Skerries, a small island in the Arctic, near the Crook of the Ear.

Workhouse, an institution to provide employment, housing and health care for the people unable to take care of themselves.

Cast of Characters

May contain spoilers!

Aidan Rowan's crush.

Beansbury, Mrs the kind old lady whose suitcase Vincent borrows.

Bramble, Arthur Aster and George's son.

Bramble, Aster George's wife, Vincent's guardian.

Bramble, George Aster's husband, Vincent's guardian.

Bramble, Ivy Arthur's wife.

Bryony a maid at Benton House. Ren's mother.

Buttercup, Celandine Aster's sister, Vincent's guardian.

Chillwell, Florentine the daughter of the head of Chillwell state.

Crumpets, the Vincent's neighbours.

Farthistle, Mr Iris's boss.

Flora Petunia Poppycock's sister.

Foxwick-Benton, Mr aka Mr Benton the brother of the head of Benton House.

Foxwick-Benton IV, Richard the grandson of Richard Hartford-Benton the sixth. New head of Benton House.

Hartford-Benton, Richard 'Dickie' the head of Benton House.

Hartley, William the fire chief.

Jacobs, Dr the primary physician on Whitskersey.

Jones, Oscar Vernon Vincent's editor.

Lampfrey, Briar a member of Dr Poppycock's extended family.

Lampfrey, Daisy a member of Dr Poppycock's extended family.

Liam a hall boy at Benton House.

Marcus a hall boy, and later a footman at Benton House. Ren's father.

Mason, Holly Dr Poppycock's cousin.

Mason, Mr the retired snow plough driver.

Mossgraves, the the family whose house gets destroyed by the speeder.

Poppycock, Dr James Vincent's therapist.

Poppycock, Marigold James's sister.

Poppycock, Petunia James's wife

Poppycock, Poppy James's sister.

Rose, Ms Mr Swifty's acquaintance.

Rowan Vincent's pen pal.

Sivens, Heather the head maid of Benton House. Later promoted to housekeeper.

Steadfast, Edward Vincent's friend.

Swifty, Mr Vincent's trusty feline companion.

Swifty, Ren Vincent's ward. Bryony and Marcus's daughter.

Swifty, Vincent the title character of the book. Ren's guardian.

Sylvia, Ms the governor's cat.

Tweed, Mrs Vincent's neighbour.

Wakefield, Iris a receptionist at the former workhouse. Presumably Vincent's sister.

ABOUT THE AUTHOR

J.B. Thwaite is the author of dozens of best-selling books that only exist in her dreams. She lives in the darkest, most inhospitable depths of Southern Finland with her spouse, scion and feline companion. She has discovered fire and re-invented the wheel in exactly the same form as before but better. With an incredibly busy schedule, she uses her scarce free time to nap, sleep and doomscroll on social media. She is also a connoisseur of the highest quality Asian homoerotic literature and a bit too neurodivergent to enjoy long walks on the beach.

Also By

The Catnap Ramblers:
Vincent and the Cat (2023)
Rhys and the Voiceless (2023)
Aurora and the Guardian (2023)

Other books in the works:
Pandion (~2024)
Fingers and Thumbs (~2024)

Printed in the USA
CPSIA information can be obtained
at www.ICGtesting.com
LVHW092127051223
765636LV00001B/20